A Distant Hero

A
Distant
Hero

EMMA DRUMMOND

SIMON & SCHUSTER

LONDON · SYDNEY · NEW YORK · TOKYO · SINGAPORE · TORONTO

First published in Great Britain by Simon & Schuster Ltd, 1994
A Paramount Communications Company

Copyright © E D Books, 1994

The right of Emma Drummond to be identified as author of this work
has been been asserted in accordance with sections 77 and 78 of the
Copyright Designs and Patents Act 1988

Simon & Schuster Ltd
West Garden Place
Kendal Street
London W2 2AQ

Simon & Schuster of Australia Pty Ltd
Sydney

A CIP catalogue record for this book is available
from the British Library.

ISBN 0–671-71791-X

This book is a work of fiction. Names, characters, places and
incidents are either the product of the author's imagination or are
used fictitiously. Any resemblance to actual events or locales or
persons, living or dead, is entirely coincidental.

Typeset in Sabon 12/14pt by
Hewer Text Composition Services, Edinburgh
Printed in Great Britain by
Butler & Tanner, Frome and London

A Distant Hero

1

GENERAL SIR GILLIARD Ashleigh sat at the head of the long polished table, in a room where the painted eyes of ancestral warriors stared down from the gilt-framed portraits on the panelled walls. He was unusually silent during this ritual of port, cigars and old soldiers' tales, contenting himself with his thoughts as he surveyed the guests who had braved the heavy snowfall to attend the Khartoum Dinner he held annually on January 22nd. This year of 1899 found no more than nine officers of the West Wiltshire Regiment at the table. Sir Gilliard's elderly sisters, their husbands and numerous offspring had been prevented by a severe blizzard from travelling to Wiltshire.

It was disappointing. The Khartoum Dinner was an occasion to which the head of the Ashleigh family looked forward with pride and pleasure. The latter was provided by the military guests who revived, for a few days, memories of a profession Sir Gilliard had served from his youth. His heart could not abandon it but, at eighty-nine, physical participation was limited to recounting past battles and glories. For most of the year his dreams had to suffice, but the Waterloo Ball, and this dinner to honour the memory of the family hero, provided an audience for Sir Gilliard's recollections, making them more vivid. The guests tonight, however, were all younger serving officers; men to whom those famous old campaigns in the Crimea, China and India were no more than history. They were more interested in the experiences of a man who had recently returned from the Sudan than in the remininscences of a past general.

Sir Gilliard sighed as he sipped his port. Was he finally succumbing to old age? This memorial dinner had not stirred him tonight. He had made his usual speech prior to proposing the toast, yet the sense of drama had been missing. Nothing was the same these days. The family was breaking up. His sisters and their husbands were ailing octogenarians. They were no longer Ashleighs, anyway. He sighed again. The inheritance was still not secure; the continuation of the line still not assured. He must remain as master of Knightshill and its many acres until his heir produced a son. Only then could he relinquish command.

His gaze rested on the young man seated at his right. Vere Ashleigh had become his heir on the death of the hero they honoured tonight. A sickly child, an invalid youth, Vere's frail constitution had denied him a place at Oxford and a commission in the West Wiltshire Regiment – the path taken by Ashleigh males. He had instead run the estate, grown orchids for Bond Street florists and *painted*. Sir Gilliard even *thought* the word with disgust. He had no time for aesthetic frippery. He also had no time for anyone with a romantic nature.

His thoughts digressed at that point to his own bride, whose face he had long ago forgotten. Caroline Ashleigh's abscondence with an Italian poet while her husband was in India had created a scandal that almost ruined the promising young officer's career. It had also taught Sir Gilliard never again to feel affection for a female. Roland, his infant son and heir left at Knightshill, had been reared by a nanny and doting servants until he followed the path of his ancestors into the West Wiltshire Regiment. Roland had dutifully sired eight children before dying of wounds inflicted in the second war against the Afghans. When his widow abandoned her five surviving offspring to marry a wealthy American, Sir Gilliard had set about moulding the three boys to his exacting standards.

Vorne Ashleigh had been handsome, dashing, gifted and immensely courageous. That last quality had led him to make a bid to deliver an urgent message from General Gordon in beleaguered Khartoum to the advancing relief force. His Sudanese companions had murdered the young officer in the desert and made away with an empty dispatch case, leaving the mortally wounded Vorne to crawl a further mile and a half with the vital communiqué cunningly strapped to his body. His valiant attempt to deliver the appeal for help failed. Khartoum had fallen; the entire garrison was massacred. Lieutenant V. E. R. Ashleigh had nevertheless been awarded a posthumous D.S.O. and his name was spoken with reverence in military circles. At Knightshill, Vorne was the supreme example held up to his brothers by their grieving grandfather.

Sir Gilliard glanced speculatively once more at the young man expected to follow that example. Vere finally wore the scarlet jacket sported by Ashleigh males, but was he even a pale shadow of the man they honoured tonight? Certainly not, for he had made his name as an artist rather than as a warrior in the campaign to regain Khartoum last year. Yet he had gone into battle several times, and survived deadly desert fevers to prove that his constitution was more robust than Dr Alderton had claimed. The old general's blue eyes narrowed as he studied Vere's sensitive face darkened by the desert sun, clear green eyes and the tall but slender build. Those gentle features were now marked by lines of experience, the eyes were sharper, missing nothing, and there was a new hint of command in his quiet voice . . . but could one feel assured of his fitness to fill Vorne's place?

The army had changed Vere. Sir Gilliard was not surprised by that, although he was hardly delighted that an Ashleigh was admired in military circles for his ability to create pictures. Nor was he pleased about his heir's firm refusal to find a bride. The young fool had melodramatically rushed off to die in the desert over the Bourneville girl. As he had consequently survived, the affair should have taught him to find a partner who would produce his sons and demand nothing more from him than the Ashleigh name and Knightshill. There were numerous healthy young women eager for an advantageous match. An early marriage and several months of determined devotion to the creature would suffice. There could be a male infant to welcome in the twentieth century if Vere would only recognize the fact and knuckle down to his duty.

The murmur of baritone voices faded as Sir Gilliard began once more to brood on the question of inheritance. When news of Vorne's death reached him it had been a double blow, for Vere was then thought likely to go to an early grave. All hopes had been pinned on Valentine, a lusty, extrovert child with a gratifying passion for things military. The child had grown to splendid youth – tall, strong, filled with Ashleigh pride – and Sir Gilliard had watched his third grandson with relief and great satisfaction. Valentine would undoubtedly sire sons and continue the military distinction for which the family was renowned. Then, at the Khartoum Dinner two years ago, the boy had declared his desire to flout tradition by shunning Oxford and the West Wiltshires to enlist in the cavalry. Determined to curb this mutinous streak in a senior schoolboy ridiculously lionized for his sporting brilliance, Sir Gilliard had crushed the short rebellion by outlining to him the folly of attempting to defy an opponent who had the military and financial power to make him toe the Ashleigh line.

Staring into the ruby depths of his port the old man asked himself yet again why the boy had become a black sheep and disgraced an honourable name. During his final term at Chartfield School he had been summarily dismissed for assaulting the wife of a member of staff. Sir

Gilliard regarded Valentine's failure to come home and take his punishment a greater crime than attempting to tear the dress off a female ten years his senior in a moment of youthful folly.

He drained his glass, and someone refilled it while he continued to brood. The boy would come to a bad end. If he had but returned to Knightshill the wild streak could have been drilled out of him. Left to develop unchecked it would bring about his ruin. After nine months of silence he had written from South Africa to tell his sister he was a corporal in the 57th Lancers – the regiment commanded by the uncle of the creature he had assaulted. *A Corporal*! Sir Gilliard's pride rejected the notion of an Ashleigh in the rank and file. Then he reminded himself that, to hide his disgrace, V.M.H. Ashleigh had given his two middle names on enlisting and was known as Martin Havelock. As such he would remain throughout his service career, thank God, so his further downfall would not touch the Ashleigh name.

These thoughts brought Sir Gilliard back to the sense of disappointment tonight. The Khartoum Dinner would never be the same again. With Vorne hacked to death in the desert, Valentine hiding behind a false identity in South Africa, and the sister to whom he had written living in sin somewhere with her lover and the two children of her marriage to a religious zealot, *nothing* would be the same again. It was a sign of the times. Old ways were being abandoned, old moral standards abused by a generation with little sense of duty or honour.

The vivid eyes that had looked out on the world and seen so many of its wonders and sorrows over eighty-nine years turned once more to Vere. The Ashleigh name and all that went with it was the legacy of the artist soldier. A bride *must* be found for him as soon as possible. If he died without male issue, Knightshill, a vast fortune, and a distinguished military history would pass to a corporal calling himself Martin Havelock. That must be prevented at all costs.

The deep snow which had obliged the regimental guests to remain at Knightshill overnight prevented Vere from venturing far from the house the next day. An urge for contemplative isolation led him to seek the path cleared as far as his bailiff's cottage half a mile beyond the formal gardens. Stopping short of the wicket gate, he turned to trudge back before turning again to head for the cottage. In an overcoat topped by a muffler, wearing warm gloves and a cap, Vere still felt unpleasantly chilled. His blood had thinned after months in the desert; he had been back less than six weeks.

A few minutes later he halted to gaze at the home he had left almost two years ago believing he would never see it again. Rising to three floors, with a large wing on each side of the central section, Knightshill had been owned by Ashleighs for thirteen generations. Its interior reflected military influence in every aspect, but women deserted for long periods while their husbands served monarch and country in far-flung parts of the world had left their gentle, yearning touch on the formal gardens. Lonely wives rearing the next generations of warriors had found solace among roses and rioting perfumed shrubs; a refuge from the home dominated by portraits of uniformed ancestors and large canvases depicting battle.

In summer, the gardens were romantic with soft colours, drifting fragrances and the calming music of small fountains. Paths wound through beds of love-in-a-mist and massed white pinks; rustic seats at every corner offered a view of the valley and distant Dorset hills. Sunny walks through ranks of rainbow lupins, delphiniums and foxgloves shut off sight of a house all Ashleigh wives must have found formidable. In summer, the shrubbery was a delight of creamy honeysuckle, dainty white jasmine and orange–blossom, pale lilacs, azaleas, and dark glossy leaves. The rose garden contained prize varieties in every hue which gladdened the senses twice over when reflected in the still water of the lily pool. It was all designed to induce tranquillity of mind and spirit.

Vere surveyed these gardens now and saw winter beauty in shrubs piled high with snow, and in bordering trees whose branches bowed low beneath a white layer, yet *he* lacked tranquillity of mind and spirit. Knightshill would be his when Sir Gilliard lost his last battle. This lovely old grey stone house with its famous Great Window dominating the front façade had once comprised all Vere's hopes and plans; as had his future with a girl whose grace and beauty had held him in thrall. When Annabel Bourneville sent back the Ashleigh rubies, ending their brief engagement, her words had driven him to the Sudan to die in the shadow of a hero he could never emulate. He had unexpectedly survived to discover the truth about the brother whose ghost Annabel had found so irresistible. He was now free from the spell she had cast, and of the burden of Vorne's supposed heroism. Yet he was no longer fulfilled by the country life he had once loved. Sir Gilliard gave him no rest from his demand to provide an heir, but Vere had no intention of marrying simply to secure a bloodline. He had made a fool of himself over Annabel, and Floria Pallini, whom he had almost loved in Cairo, remained too poignant a memory. Until he met a woman who returned his devotion unreservedly, young Val would have to remain next in line despite the old man's inflexible attitude towards a grandson as determined as himself. With that thought, Vere plodded on along the frozen pathway, still seeking the tranquillity which had grown so elusive.

Reaching John Morgan's gate, Vere turned towards Knightshill once more and stood stamping his feet for warmth. Last night, he had been offered a chance to travel to the other side of the world. He had turned it down this morning and was now wondering if he had been mad to do so. The Sudan had freed him from life beneath the shadow of Vorne. Was he now surrendering to that old captivity by refusing to join a body of men who would forever think of him as their hero's brother?

Filled with curious uncertainty, yet knowing his decision was irrevocable, Vere walked back to the house to break his news to Sir Gilliard and Charlotte. His sister would be deeply upset. He dared not guess at his grandfather's reaction. Knocking the snow from his boots, he then discarded his outer clothes and walked through to the sitting-room where the family gathered for sherry before luncheon.

Charlotte was there alone. She smiled warmly and rose to take his arm, a gesture he found increasingly irritating lately. The closeness he shared with his second sister had recently intensified on her part to stifling proportions. Self-imposed spinsterhood because of a lame foot left Charlotte with little understanding of the power of attraction between a man and a woman. Because of it she shared Sir Gilliard's unrelenting opinion of their sister Margaret, and condemned Val out of hand for an affair she knew little about. All her affection was now centered on Vere.

'Whatever have you been doing out there in the snow?' she asked in reproof. 'I was about to come and fetch you indoors. You have barely recovered from influenza, and there's no sun to counter the bitterness of the temperature.'

He released himself and went to the side table to pour sherry. 'I'm no longer the invalid we were all led to accept,' he reminded her. 'If you had seen the conditions we faced in the Sudan you would never consider a stroll in the gardens a hazard.' Handing her a glass he summoned a smile. 'Reserve your concern for our guests who are battling their way back to the barracks in Salisbury.'

'It was good of them to come in such weather,'

she said, returning to the chair she had vacated at his entry.

'They know how much it means to Grandfather.'

'To us all, Vere. You must have found the evening particularly affecting this year.'

She little knew how Sir Gilliard's eulogy to a supposed hero *had* affected him. He changed the subject. 'You were wise to breakfast in your room.'

Her nose wrinkled. 'The smell of cigar smoke penetrated everywhere on the ground floor. I instructed Winters to remove all trace of it the moment the guests left.' She regarded him speculatively. 'Perhaps it was to escape the smell of stale smoke that you tramped the path outside with such curious determination.'

Recognising her attempt to draw a confidence Vere avoided it by commenting on the excellence of the dinner she had chosen last night. During their light conversation he once more regretted her foolish belief that the unsightly boot worn on her underdeveloped left leg must exclude her from romantic attachments. There had been attention enough from young men to prove her wrong, but her consistent discouragement had led them to accept the role she cast for herself. At twenty-eight Charlotte possessed the striking Ashleigh looks, large clear eyes, and pleasing proportions, but in *her* the inbred Ashleigh determination was turning into implacability, and the well-known family charm was slowly dying beneath her increasing primness. Yet she would surely gladden many a male eye this morning in a gown of vivid green wool trimmed with ruched ribbons and beading, and with her pale hair arranged in a style emphasizing the clarity of her silvery-green eyes.

Vere knew momentary guilt. With no more than the company of a grand old soldier in this house of warriors, Charlotte would grow old prematurely without experiencing life outside these narrow confines. He then remembered that she had imposed them herself by her

9

refusal to seek love and friendship. There was no cause for his guilt.

'Have you made a decision yet, Vere?'

Her question threw him. How could she know of his night-long quandary? He sipped his sherry before asking warily, 'On what?'

'On whether or not you will sell that canvas of Winklesham Bridge to Mrs Blanchworth.'

He relaxed. 'There was never any question of my accepting her offer.'

'It's very generous.'

'Too generous.' He sat opposite her and leaned back against the mulberry-velvet chair. 'I painted it four years ago. It's quite charming and instantly recognizable to those who know Winklesham, but Mrs Blanchworth has little appreciation of art and has never set eyes on the bridge. She is simply one of the tiresome people coaxing me to sell my mediocre early work so they can boast of owning one of my canvases.'

Charlotte tut-tutted. 'You should be proud of it.'

'My dear Lottie, it was the work I did in the Sudan which made my name in élite art circles. No connoisseur would hang my early rustic daubings on his wall, I assure you. Because I am now "fashionable", every hostess must have a Vere Ashleigh in her house to impress guests.'

'As Mrs Blanchworth's guests are probably as ignorant as she on the virtue of a picture, does it really matter?'

'Of course it matters! I'll sell nothing I left here at Knightshill. It was created by an eye that saw little else but prettiness.'

'That's absurd! You thought very highly of them at the time, and your friends certainly appreciated their worth. Mrs Bourneville was delighted with the exquisite pair of orchid watercolours you presented to her.'

This reminder of a period in his life he preferred to forget sharpened his tone. 'My friends appreciated their *gifts*. I didn't sell them, Lottie. There is a vast difference between trifles given to friends and paintings created by the compulsion to show life chequered by beauty and savagery. Knightshill is a sheltered corner. Outside these acres lies an exciting, complex world of which I knew little until I was driven to leave. *That* is my stimulus now. I was no artist when I did watercolours of mice, butterflies or poppies, merely a copier of prettiness. Now I see things beyond my immediate vision.'

His sister's eyebrows rose. 'How intense you sound! There is nothing here in Wiltshire remotely similar to those desert battle scenes which brought you acclaim. So what will you do? You cannot mean to abandon your God-given talent and sit idle rather than paint the beauty of this "sheltered corner".'

Vere was spared a reply by the entry of Sir Gilliard. Tall, white-haired and erect, his features etched by years of discipline and experience, he looked none the worse for the late hour of the previous evening. The old man always drank his sherry standing, so Vere rose to pour him some before refilling his own glass.

'Saw you prowling back and forth out there,' Sir Gilliard declared in the manner of an accusation. 'Only just out of your sick-bed, man. Is it your intention to return to it and remain there, hey?'

Vere offered him the glass of sherry. 'I saw Colonel Dunwoody and his officers on their way soon after ten. They seemed confident enough of getting through to Dunstan, but if the line is blocked by snow it's there they'll be forced to stay until trains are running again.'

'*Trains!*' snorted Sir Gilliard disparagingly. 'Stage coaches simply made diversions when roads were blocked. These confounded steam engines are confined to tracks which are forever awash, blocked by a landslide or covered in snow. Where would an army be if it had to depend on a *train?*'

Vere told him. 'It would be where it was required to be far quicker than it was in your time, sir. Without the railway Kitchener determinedly laid across the sands we would, at present, be only half-way to Khartoum. Trains brought our reinforcements, ammunition and food supplies from Cairo. They were a godsend.'

Sir Gilliard grunted. 'Think you know it all after just one campaign. Common fault in young officers.'

Vere took the empty glass his grandfather held out and walked to the decanter. 'Young officers are only old enough to have served in one campaign.'

This met with a louder grunt. 'Your tongue has grown very smooth. Saw you using it to great effect on Dunwoody last night.'

It was the ideal opening for what Vere must say, yet he delayed the moment. 'He was interested in my account of the war . . . and in the sketches I did before the advance from Abu Hamed.'

'*Sketches*! Dunwoody's a military commander, not one of those namby-pamby fellahs in smocks. He don't know the first thing about pictures.'

This disparagement of something Vere loved fuelled his resolution. 'But he knows that I do. It influenced his decision to invite me to fill a vacancy in his regiment.'

Sir Gilliard's upright stance straightened further; his blue eyes grew brighter with moisture. 'Dunwoody told me the splendid news as he retired last night.' He sighed with satisfaction. 'You will be following in the footsteps of every male Ashleigh since 1542 when Sir Thomas founded the yeomanry which has become the West Wiltshire Regiment. You are finally fulfilling your destiny, my boy.' He raised his glass to Vere. 'I do not expect you to *match* the deeds of your heroic brother, but I am confident that you will do nothing to tarnish them when the regiment reaches China.'

'*China*!' It was no more than a horrified whisper from the white-faced girl who rose from her chair to confront Vere. 'The regiment is going to China? You *cannot* have agreed to cross the world to a savage land when you have barely recovered from the dangers of the Sudan. Are you mad? Soldiering has never been in *your* blood, Vere. You are an artist. You *cannot* sacrifice your talent by joining a regiment which has already taken such toll of this family.'

Sir Gilliard was lost in pursuit of his recollections. 'I was out there with the regiment during the Opium Wars, y'know. Fought the devils to the gates of Peking. Savage people; wild, exotic terrain. You will find it fascinating, Vere. I envy you. Yes, I envy you the years of campaigning ahead; the cornucopia of military experience. If I had my time again . . .' He sighed. 'Ah, well, I shall follow your career with avid interest. These damned Boxers are creating a growing threat to our trade agreements, to say nothing of our political aspirations in the Far East. Fatal to let it continue. A well-planned intensive campaign will make short work of them, I promise. What I would give to be at them again and wreak revenge! Lost some of my best men when we rushed their forts, skewered on barricades of sharpened bamboos cunningly placed around the walls.'

Charlotte's hand gripped Vere's arm in growing distress, as she cried, 'Is *that* what you want – to die in such hideous fashion? The Bourneville girl cannot still mean so much to you that you will risk your life a *second* time to please her.'

Dismayed by the way the conversation was running away from him, Vere said, 'Lottie, *please* . . .'

She paid no heed. 'Knightshill is your home. You have always loved it deeply. Stay here and run the estate as you did before. *This* is where you belong.'

'He belongs with a regiment which has been served with honour by his family since it was formed,' Sir Gilliard contradicted, his voice ringing with the authority gained by sixty-five years of military command. 'Now, my boy, it may be cutting things rather fine but there *is* time before you leave at the end of March to fix your interest with a suitable young woman. Once the Ashleigh rubies are on her finger, there will be no impropriety in her sailing to join you by the end of the year. Two of my officers married in China under similar circumstances. The brides travelled together to Peking. The regiment gave both couples a splendid party after the double ceremony.'

This speech filled Vere with the confidence in his decision which had been elusive while he had paced the snow but, on the point of speaking, he was forestalled by his grandfather, still fired by enthusiastic plans.

'Yes, yes, it is all working out splendidly! We will hold receptions, send invitations to suitable young women from whom you may make your choice. A wife will enable you to do your duty as my heir, and the West Wilts will make a real man of you.'

Never one to lose his temper, Vere came close to doing so. 'I am already a real man, sir. It *is* possible to achieve the state outside the family regiment, and I have made it perfectly plain on several occasions since my return from the Sudan that I have the right to control my own life. Despite being greatly tempted by the prospect of seeing the Orient, I declined Gerard Dunwoody's invitation.'

'*Thank God,*' breathed Charlotte, gripping his arm again. 'Why did you allow me to believe the reverse?'

Vere stepped away from her, still angry. 'Because you have both been so busy trying to run my life during the past few minutes I have had no chance to conclude the subject I started. Perhaps I may now be allowed to do so.'

When Vere turned to his grandfather he met the piercing gaze that had withered many young men, and was momentarily silenced by it.

'As you are not prone to practical jokes I must conclude that what you say is true,' said Sir Gilliard.

'Yes, sir. I'm sorry if I disappoint you.'

'You have always done that,' came the icily quelling comment, 'but I had dared to hope the Sudan had made something of you.'

'It made me realize that a man cannot be changed simply by wearing different clothes,' Vere said resolutely. 'I donned a military uniform and did the duty it demanded of me to the best of my ability, but I failed to become an instinctive, wholehearted warrior. Instead, I became a better artist. I now intend to pursue a career for which I am truly fitted.'

'You refused Dunwoody's offer to serve your queen and country merely to become an effeminate wielder of brushes?' The question was flung at Vere in tones of deepest disgust. 'You recently participated in a fierce military campaign to right a wrong and avenge the murder of your brother. You saw how men can sacrifice their own lives to save a fellow from death; how they can put aside all personal desires for the good of the regiment and the cause. You must have witnessed many instances of supreme courage in the face of the enemy, or in the bearing with fortitude of the agony of wounds. Now you can stand there and tell me you mean to resign your commission to spend your days *splashing paint on canvas*?' The voice rose to a roar. 'Have you no honour?'

Vere moved closer to impress his words upon a man nearing a stage beyond calm reason. 'I believe I have a duty to use the talent I was given. My sketches from the Sudan brought home to many the truth of that desert war. It was my manner of honouring those I watched performing all the valiant deeds you have just mentioned. Each of us has to serve in the way best suited to his ability, sir, and I shall do my utmost to bring distinction to the Ashleigh name, but with the brush rather than with the sword. There's surely no lack of honour in that.'

After several moments of contemptuous scrutiny Sir Gilliard slowly and deliberately turned his back on the young man who had shattered his glittering dreams of the morning.

Vere finally lost control of his temper as he had once

before with this inflexible man. 'You would have allowed no one to turn *you* from your youthful ambitions. You have no right to turn *me* from mine. It was because you tried to do so with Val that he behaved as he did. He was a desperate, inexperienced schoolboy, but I am twenty-seven and a great deal wiser than I was two years ago. You have ruined his future; you will not do so with mine. Membership of the West Wiltshire Regiment does not automatically make a man superior to the rest of the human race. Wearing their scarlet and blue would never have made me into the heir you require. Nothing will. You must accept me as the person I am.'

Still with his back towards Vere, Sir Gilliard said in a voice shaking with emotion, 'Be good enough to go. I do not care to eat luncheon with a dilettante.'

Although shaken, Vere stood his ground. When Annabel Bourneville had broken their engagement it had precipitated a quarrel so bitter between him and this man who could not relinquish an ideal that the rift had not closed for two years. A crack had nevertheless remained. It now widened with devastating swiftness, but Vere was stronger than he had been on that earlier occasion and determined on a course of action from which no one would turn him.

Charlotte had been forgotten until she came alongside Vere and took his arm. 'You are both tired after an evening which always heightens sad memories, and we are all still suffering the after-effects of influenza. Come to my room. We'll eat there.' Initially he resisted her attempt to draw him away but, after studying the stiff back of his grandparent who maintained standards almost impossible to meet, Vere realized the only answer was to do as his sister suggested. Anger still burned within him, however, and he unlinked their arms as they crossed the hall.

Recognizing his mood, Charlotte glanced up in appeal. 'Do try to understand, Vere. He believed his greatest dream had come true, until you disillusioned him.'

'He had to know,' he replied stiffly.

'Of course. He'll recover, in time.'

'No. He's never been prepared to accept what I am.'

His sister ignored that. 'You've made the right decision. You can run your beloved estate and paint to your heart's content here at Knightshill, a worthier heir than any other if Grandfather would only see it.' Reaching the foot of the stairs, she paused to say gently, 'One thing I must protest about. It was unjust to accuse him of being responsible for Val's disgrace.'

'He is,' Vere insisted, still in the depths of the quarrel left unresolved.

'Nonsense! Val was always wayward, and he has a history of misbehaviour with females.'

'He was once caught kissing a baker's daughter. That does not constitute a *history*, Lottie.'

'The affair at Chartfield involved the wife of his house-master, a woman ten years Val's senior,' she retaliated. 'How can you justify your claim that Grandfather is responsible for *that*?'

Vere gave a heavy sigh. 'If he had allowed Val to join the cavalry instead of the West Wilts, the lad would presently be fulfilling his true destiny and providing the old man with all the things I consistently fail to give. If you were a man, Lottie, he'd be driving *you* to despair in the same way. Be thankful he takes such little interest in you.'

She slipped her arm through his again and used tones more appropriate to soothing children. 'You're clearly in a difficult mood so there's little point in arguing with you. Walking out there in the snowy garden for so long has made you irritable.'

Anger again ignited. 'I needed to be alone and the gardens provide my only hope of solitude lately.' He disengaged himself firmly. 'My deliberations in the snow left me still uncertain of the wisdom of my decision concerning the West Wilts. When you and Grandfather began telling me what I should do with my life – two

17

opposite opinions, please note – I knew why I have chosen to leave Knightshill as soon as possible.'

'Leave Knightshill? But you just now told Grandfather . . .'

'I told him I chose not to go to China with his precious regiment, that's all. I had made plans to travel to Italy before Dunwoody gave his tempting offer. It was a case of deciding which course to pursue.'

'Italy? Whyever would you go there?' Charlotte demanded emotionally.

Conscious that their voices were echoing throughout the house, Vere drew her into a small room known as the gold salon. Winters, the butler, had probably overheard too much already this morning.

Once inside the room whose décor gave it its name, Charlotte confronted him, her expression wild. 'You have made plans to leave Knightshill and said nothing of them to me?'

'Should I have?'

She turned away to sit in a chair before the fire. 'So you intend to be cruel to *me* now.'

He was exasperated. 'Don't be melodramatic. I'm in no mood for it.' Perching on the edge of the chair beside hers, he added, 'I would have told you once everything was settled. It wasn't my intention to leave without saying goodbye, as I did when I went to the Sudan.'

'I suppose I must be glad of that, at least.'

Vere found her wounded attitude irritating, but struggled to see her point of view as he embarked on an explanation to a sister for whom their childhood bond was still very strong. 'When I read in the news of Philip's death and wrote the fact to Margaret via Nicolardi's family in Verona, I decided to deliver my letter in person in the hope of discovering her whereabouts from them. Enthusiasm for the idea led me to think of travelling on to Florence, Rome and Venice to see some of the world's greatest works of art. When influenza delayed my departure, I sent the letter by mail so that Margaret would learn the news at the earliest opportunity. By the same post I wrote booking passage on a steamer leaving for Naples next month.'

Charlotte gave a wide, relieved smile. 'I'm sorry, Vere, I misunderstood. This morning has been rather upsetting. Of course you must take a holiday in Italy. The warm climate will return you to full health.' Warming to her theme, she added, 'Why don't I accompany you? I confess to feeling a lingering weakness myself. The sunshine will do us both so much good.' She clasped her hands together eagerly. 'Yes, what a splendid plan! Can you believe we shall finally see the wonders we thought were denied us as the invalids of the family? Next month, you said? It leaves me very little time to assemble all we shall need for an extended tour abroad. I must start to make lists.'

Deeply dismayed by a development he had not foreseen, Vere knew there was no way he could avoid hurting someone who had grown too dependent on him through loneliness. It seemed to him that he was still fighting for his freedom by saying what he must.

'This is not to be a holiday, Lottie. While Grandfather remains master of Knightshill, I mean to broaden my experience in every way open to me. I plan to spend at least a year wandering the Mediterranean coast studying the works of the great masters, doing some experimental work of my own and seeking the acquaintance of those who might influence my future career. It's possible I may travel even further afield – Turkey, Russia. The rich culture of the land of white nights is said to defy description.' In the face of her dawning distress, he forced himself to continue. 'I need to be a free agent, to be able to travel anywhere, to places unsuitable for females.'

Leaning forward to impress his words upon her, he confessed to being restless. 'The desert still haunts me. Riding across it for ten days with only a Sudanese guide was an experience words cannot describe. It forces a man to put his life into perspective: it makes him supremely conscious of being unimportant to the passage of time.' As he spoke, memory took him back to that awesome, desolate, antique land, and words tumbled from him. 'The vastness is incredible. There is nothing but sand, yet it has greater power over men than the most strongly fortified city. To traverse the desert and survive is comparable to defeating a formidable enemy. Lottie, imagine waking to find a cream and lemon sky overhanging an ochre landscape, then watching that sky change to orange before it becomes a blinding, brassy heaven burning everything that lies beneath. There is no shade, no water, and one must move on for mile after mile with thoughts becoming fantasies until it's impossible to distinguish the truth.' He bent closer in his enthusiasm. 'Try to picture a moon so large it silvers everything for as far as one can see. The Nile, in daylight muddy brown and scattered with rubbish, becomes a beautiful, glittering ribbon across an enchanted landscape. The desert grows cold – a coldness one finds unbelievable after the debilitating heat – and one feels close to immortality in that argent stillness.'

Vere came from his visions to see a familiar face gazing at him with undisguised aggression. His sister's reaction was such a disappointment he heard himself murmur in flat tones, 'It's impossible to convey to anyone who has not experienced it.'

'Then why try?'

He leaned back in the chair feeling drained. 'To help you to understand why I need to get away on my own. I'm not the person I used to be.'

'No. You have become a true Ashleigh male.'

'I grew up being accused of the reverse,' he reminded her swiftly.

'Not by me. Never by me,' she cried. 'We were the different ones. We have always been close, understood each other perfectly.'

'If that were true,' he said gently, 'you would not now be confronting me because I plan to chase my destiny.'

'If it were true, you would not be walking out on your family and inheritance only four weeks after returning from your first desertion.' She rose in agitation. 'I know you acted under a foolish compulsion the first time, but if your fascinating desert made you a real man, as you claimed to Grandfather, it also made you abandon the qualities I so admired. Go on your solitary crusade; leave behind all you once loved with such passion! Learn about life, but if you ever return, Knightshill might not welcome you . . . and your loving sister might be a stranger.'

Her uneven gait was emphasized by her emotional state as she crossed to open the door, then close it very firmly behind her. Saddened though he was by this second quarrel within an hour, Vere needed no stronger confirmation of the advisability of leaving a household offering no balm to a spirit still beneath the spell of freedom. Sir Gilliard would console himself with maps, books and the reminiscences which keep alive those of his ilk. But Charlotte, poor Charlotte, would have to seek out her own freedom as painfully as had Val, Margaret and himself.

The last time Charlotte had shed tears was on realizing that Margaret had left Knightshill forever, taking her two children, because her husband had announced his intention of moving his family to an isolated mission station in the heart of undeveloped Africa. For once, Sir Gilliard had been unable to intervene. The Reverend Philip Daulton had had the right to manage his own family.

A black cloud of guilt had descended on Charlotte when her sister left. She could not forget Margaret's plea for help to escape before the dreaded sailing date – a plea Charlotte had turned aside rather than become involved in something she did not really understand. Remorse and regret had haunted those dark days. She had wept during many restless nights. When Sir Gilliard's private investigations revealed that Margaret had taken passage on a ship out of Southampton with Laurence Nicolardi, a man they had known for only a few weeks, Charlotte's feelings had undergone a violent reversal. Whilst she had been weeping with remorse, Margaret had been happily in the arms of a man who had posed as a friend of the family. Coming so soon after the scandal of Val's behaviour with a married woman, this news had turned Charlotte's remorse to disgust, intensified by anger over her misplaced sense of guilt.

The following six months had passed with leaden slowness. Sir Gilliard was invariably immersed in military studies or correspondence with other old soldiers. Charlotte's only source of occupation had been the cultivation of gardenias which had replaced Vere's orchids destroyed by a hurricane. There had been too many long, empty days during which she had counted the hours to her brother's safe return. He had arrived unannounced at Knightshill a week before Christmas. She had believed he was home to stay and her heart had grown lighter.

Sitting before a fire which did nothing to warm her, she hugged herself tightly while tears flowed. Only a year apart in age, they had grown up almost as close as twins, yet he had just now indicated that he wanted her company no longer. Did she mean nothing to him? Had he cut the bond she thought unbreakable? His words still hurt unbearably; she could not believe they had been those of the brother who had been her constant childhood companion. He claimed he needed to be alone for a year or more, but he would not experience the sense of isolation so familiar to the devoted sister he was leaving behind. He would be surrounded by interesting people, exploring picturesque countries bathed in sunshine. For a brief wonderful moment her imagination had had her sharing it with him; the most exciting experience in her life. Then he had cruelly banished her

22

dream with words which suggested that *she* was the one at fault.

After a time her weeping ceased, leaving her drained and sick with dread of the future. Dragging herself to her feet she crossed to the window. The scene outside was as bleak as her soul as she thought of the past. As a child she had worn heavy irons on a leg deformed by a difficult birth. Like Vere, she had been unable to run and play with the others. The irons had straightened her leg, but not lengthened it. From the age of sixteen she had worn a boot with a four-inch sole, which made her walk with a limp. Her one consolation had been the brother who understood what it was like to be denied the freedom enjoyed by Vorne, Margaret and Val.

Riding presented no problems so she had spent countless happy hours on the estate, sitting beside Vere while he sketched or painted watercolours of the natural beauty around them. He had been more than satisfied with what he now called 'rustic daubings' during those companiable outings. They had sat against a tree or warm stone wall to eat a picnic, talking over Vere's plans for Knightshill when Grandfather died and sharing amusement over village gossip or things Timothy and Kate had done. They both loved Margaret's children almost as their own.

All this had fulfilled Charlotte. She had believed it was the same for her dear brother until he returned from a visit to London singing the praises of a young woman he had met at the opera. Although the notion of Vere taking a bride had initially been disconcerting, Charlotte accepted that it was his duty to do so. Vowing to show warmth and friendship to Annabel Bourneville, she had been dismayed on meeting the person who had turned a gentle, laughing brother into her virtual slave. It had been apparent that the notion of being confidante and sister to this dazzling blonde beauty could be forgotten. Margaret had agreed with her suspicion that Annabel would cleverly extricate Vere from family ties to ensure that she was the only female at Knightshill when Sir Gilliard died. Both sisters had been secretly relieved when the engagement came to a sudden end, but they had not foreseen the cost to Vere. Broken in spirit and health, he had gone to London two months later without a farewell. His letter had informed them that he was to join a regiment in the Sudan, and they then realized that the loss of Annabel had made his life seem worthless.

Charlotte gripped the gold brocade curtains as she stared at the wintry scene outside. How could a man love someone so much he wanted to die rather than live without her? Yet Vere had miraculously survived, and appeared to have forgotten that love. He also appeared to have forgotten other loves. For some minutes she remained gripping the curtain telling herself *she* could not go to the desert to die of unhappiness. Being a woman, she must remain in a house full of memories and endure it.

Walking back to the hearth she sat again before the fire. Life had once been very good. Vorne had been the eldest; a man while they were all still children. After his death and Mother's departure to America, Margaret, as the eldest, had become a substitute mother to the infant Val. So they had matured in natural pairs: Margaret and Val, herself and Vere. When her sister had married Philip Daulton, Charlotte succeeded her as the lady of the house. Those years had passed so happily with first Timothy, then Kate, adding to the close family circle.

Thinking back, she realized the pattern had begun to change when Philip abandoned his work as curate at Dunstan St Mary to become a missionary. His obsessive piety had saddened Margaret and frightened the children. Then everything had gone wrong. Vere went off to die for Annabel, Val disgraced himself and ran away rather than face them all, and Margaret went off with a man she had known only eight weeks. All Charlotte's hopes had then been centred on Vere's return and the resumption of their warm bond.

The afternoon began to darken as she faced renewed loneliness ahead. Empty days, a silent house, an elderly grandfather with scant interest in her. With her brothers and sisters gone, the only visitors now were acquaintances of Sir Gilliard. Charlotte was not required to act as hostess when no other ladies were present, so she dined alone in her room as she had last night. Dear God, how she missed those days when there had been fun and laughter, warm companionship and the belief that it would go on forever.

A tap at the door heralded Sarah Clark. The ageing woman who had been Charlotte's maid for twelve years carried a tray, which she put on the table beside her mistress.

'I thought some tea and daffy cake might be welcome as you had no luncheon.' She moved about the room lighting lamps. 'On a day like this 'tis best to close the curtains on the winter. Makes a body feel colder just looking at all that snow,' she declared, suiting actions to words. 'There, that's more cheery. I've told Foster to bring a basket of logs. You'll want a nice bright blaze while you dress for dinner.'

With lamps lit and curtains drawn the room certainly took on a brighter aspect, but no children would come in to say goodnight, no sister to exchange gossip or discuss plans for tomorrow.

'Come along, Miss Charlotte, have a cup of tea and a slice of this cake,' said Sarah, pouring from the silver pot. 'Tisn't no use going hungry when winter creeps around the house.' The woman's corseted figure straightened. 'Which gown will you wear tonight?'

As Charlotte replied, a thin girl entered struggling with the weight of a basket of logs. She bobbed a curtsy before crossing to the hearth to set it down. Minnie Foster was an orphan engaged three years ago as a maid of all work. The girl looked pinched and red about the ears, an unattractive creature in most respects save for a surprisingly lovely smile. Charlotte watched as the maid added logs to the fire after raking it with the poker. This girl must know the meaning of loneliness. Her life was a great deal harder and she had none of the advantages of education and wealth enjoyed by the family she served. How did she regard *her* future?

Sarah went through to the adjoining room to lay out a rose velvet dress and accessories for the evening. Charlotte sipped tea while continuing to watch the girl Val had dubbed 'Skinny Minnie'. Red hands knobbly with chilblains swept ash into the container she would take away to empty on to the mound in the coal yard. That done, the maid rose and bobbed respectfully prior to leaving.

Charlotte delayed her. 'Foster, do you ever feel lonely?'

The question took the girl aback. Colour flooded her bony features. 'Beg pardon, madam?'

'You have no relatives, have you?'

'No, madam.'

'Then you must sometimes feel rather lonely and unhappy.'

The girl's surprising smile broke through. 'I've not been lonely since I come to Knights'ill. There's all the others y'see. It's loike a big family below stairs, and Mr Winters 'e sees to us all very well. As to bein' un'appy, that stopped when I was took on 'ere, too. It's bein' busy keeps you loively, ain't it, and there's a power o' things ter do in this place.'

'And on your day off?'

'I goes walkin', madam. Mr Winters 'e says it's all roight s'long as I keeps away from the 'ouse and gardens. This is the most wunnerful place I ever see, up 'ere on the 'ill.' Carried away with eloquence after her initial surprise, Foster smilingly confided that she enjoyed being around

26

the stables, also. 'Real beauties, them 'orses, madam. Specially Mr Valentine's two greys. I can't take my eyes off them.'

'Nor off young Alfie Griggs,' put in Sarah's voice from the dressing-room. Foster blushed from her hairline to the high neck of her brown woollen dress, and fell silent. Charlotte said she was glad the girl was happy at Knightshill and nodded dismissal, but her tea cooled in the cup as she reflected on the short exchange. There were more people below stairs than above; a feudal family to provide companionship for orphaned Minnie Foster. To keep her happy there was occupation from the moment she awoke in the chilly early hours until she crept into her freezing narrow bed after an exhausting day. And there was young Alfie Griggs to admire.

With Val in South Africa, Margaret God knew where, and Vere departing for Italy shortly there was little prospect of companionship for the lady of the house. The lame sister of beautiful, vivacious Margaret Ashleigh had never allowed herself to admire anyone the way Foster admired the stable-boy. The only hope left, then, was constant occupation from waking until sleeping. Vere had his art. Margaret had her lover and her children. Val had his precious cavalry regiment. Charlotte had always occupied her days caring for them all. She must now find an enthusiasm of her own or risk becoming one of the reclusive spinsters found between the covers of popular novels.

2

THE WATERLOO BALL held at Knightshill each June to celebrate the famous victory in which Ashleighs of three generations had fought, and of which the five-year-old Gilliard had been told by a mother in tears of thankfulness, was the second event of the year relished by a general clinging to his illustrious past. Held in a ballroom dominated by the renowned Great Window, it was always a lively, colourful occasion. As it was reported in the glossy magazines, an invitation to the Ashleighs' ball was rarely declined. The house came alive with music, laughter and lights; the guest rooms were all occupied, the stables filled to capacity. The Stag's Head Inn in Dunstan St Mary did good business for several days. In the village, preparations for the event almost equalled those at the mansion on the hill above it, and everyone was sorry when the excitement was over for another year.

Charlotte watched the last guests depart on the second morning after the ball, then lingered on the terrace feeling deeply depressed. Without Margaret to assist with arrangements this year, she had been wholly engrossed in them for several weeks prior to the event. There had been no minute to spare once family guests arrived for the prolonged visit – two of Sir Gilliard's octogenarian sisters, their husbands and various second cousins who travelled from homes in the northern half of Britain. The great-aunts were demanding; thankfully their husbands joined Sir Gilliard in his library for endless reminiscences, emerging only for meals. The other overnight guests were younger, more lively and eager to enjoy the enticements of spectacular gardens or panoramic views over the estate. Although the ball itself held little pleasure for a young woman unable to dance, Charlotte had usually enjoyed the wealth of company it attracted.

Standing alone on the terrace to gaze at the extensive, now deserted sweetly perfumed gardens, Charlotte again felt desolation overtake her. The departure of that last carriage, the waves of farewell from laughing friends, signified the return to routine in a vast echoing house shared with an old man dominated by growing bitterness. The silence around her seemed oppressive. Many of the staff had been given a day off to compensate for the extra work demanded of them over the past fortnight. Benson and his twin sons were absent from gardens where they were normally to be seen pruning, tidying or planting. The faint sound of clattering pails from the direction of the stables told Charlotte essential tasks were being done by Ned Whitely, whose personality railed against idleness. He was with his beloved horses every day of the year. Even when a fall had broken his right arm, he had carried buckets with his left and remained on duty.

Casting her gaze beyond the formal grounds, Charlotte was further depressed by the absence of movement in the meadows. For three days there had been groups of riders ranging across bridle paths leading to Leyden's Spinney, where the family used to skate on the frozen pond and where Val had repeatedly defied warnings by swimming in its dark, gloomy depths during sweltering summer days. Other guests had ridden to the downland which ran for some miles behind Knightshill, providing excellent gallops. Vorne and, much later, Val had ridden there even in the worst weather, despite Ned's warnings that they would break their necks one day.

Vorne had not broken his neck and Val had run away intact to join the army. Charlotte had crossed those downs many times with Vere, but only in good weather and at a safe canter. Vere was presently playing the bohemian in the Mediterranean, having discarded the sister who would now have to canter sedately alone.

Her mental anguish increased as she recalled her brother's departure. The rift between them had not healed. Although Vere had made several further attempts to explain why he was leaving, Charlotte's cold fear of the future would not allow her to see his decision as anything other than desertion. He had gone without her good wishes or a *bon voyage*, and there had been no word from him. She had remained cocooned by angry self-righteousness until an ageing second cousin had approached her through waltzing couples on the night of the ball to say: 'So Vere has run off again! Whatever do you do, my dear, to drive all the members of your family from home?'

It had been an intended joke, but Cousin John's words had begun to melt the ice within her to allow regret to surface and dominate every waking hour now the need to play hostess had ceased. Had her lack of sisterly understanding also prompted Margaret's clandestine escape? Should she have offered greater support in situations beyond her comprehension? And what of Val? Had he refused to come home because he knew he would face inflexible condemnation from his sister, as well as from Sir Gilliard, as Margaret had claimed at the time? Had there been damning truth in Cousin John's joking remark?

Remorse, regret, unhappiness so overwhelmed her she could no longer endure it. Hardly aware of what she was doing, yet knowing the anguish must be relieved by action, Charlotte headed for the stables where Ned was washing down the cobbled yard.

He straightened at the sight of her and leaned on his broom with a contented smile. 'Morning, Miss Charlotte, 'tis a grand day.' He nodded towards the stables. 'I've had the stalls filled up for near on a week, and 'tis good to be busy, but I prefer a bit 'o room to move about and see our own beasts is looked to properly. These past days . . .'

'Saddle Max for me, Ned', Charlotte put in swiftly.

The head groom looked surprised. 'I thought the guests had all gone. Who's still here?'

'No one. I'm going up on the downs.'

Ned wagged his head. 'Max is one of Master Valentine's fast 'uns. He's too much for you to handle.'

'I'll be the judge of that,' she snapped.

The man's monkey face adopted a stubborn look she knew well. 'I've knowed you since you first climbed up into a saddle, and I say Max is too fiery. I'll not let him out o' this stable in your charge, Miss, not over my dead body.'

Desperation precluded further argument. 'Saddle a horse – any one of them, and be quick about it!'

The little man moved towards the stable. 'Is there an emergency?'

'Yes . . . an emergency.' She followed him into the building that smelled of fresh straw and the warm hides of animals.

'In that case, I'll come along with you.'

'No!'

The sharpness of that negative made him look at her with narrowed eyes. 'You all right, Miss?'

'Perfectly. Just lead one out and help me to mount.'

Ned did so, his mouth tight with disapproval over this mysterious emergency which obliged the lady of the house to set out in an amber morning gown quite unsuitable for riding. He held the mare, Moll, steady beside the mounting-block while Charlotte settled herself with a leg over the pommel. Then he tried again to dissuade her from her intention.

'Why don't you send me or one of the lads? There's surely no cause for you to go off like this.'

Charlotte heard none of his words and was oblivious to his concern as she urged the mare forward towards

31

the path leading uphill to the east of Leyden's Spinney. Moll responded gamely to the unusual demands for speed, and they were soon on the downland stretch which gave spectacular views of Wiltshire and distant Dorset hills. The blue and gold splendour of the day went unnoticed by a young woman who was lost in recollection of Vere saying: '*Imagine waking to a cream and lemon sky overhanging an ochre landscape. Picture a moon so large it silvers everything for as far as one can see. One feels close to immortality in that argent stillness. The desert still haunts me, Lottie. I am not the person I was.*'

Racing across the turf, oblivious of the small, wiry groom following at some distance, Charlotte had no thought of possible danger from her wild gallop. The truth had suddenly confronted her. She had matured believing she could never be like other girls because of her disability. From the day she had come out into society, she had avoided the pity she dreaded by making it clear to everyone that she accepted her fate to remain a spinster. To compensate, she had created a fiercely possessive bond with her invalid brother. She now realized that she had made Vere the substitute for those male admirers she could never have.

Neat swathes of her hair edged from their pins as the breeze whipped past Charlotte's face, and her cheeks grew wet as she acknowledged the shaming fact that she had regarded her brother as her lifelong partner. Then he had defied destiny, and discovered a glittering future in which there was no place for a sister who clung to him as the only person who gave her life meaning. Humiliation washed over her as she thought of the plans outlined to him in the belief that they were bonded together forever. It had not once occurred to her that she might prove to be an embarrassing burden to a man who had experienced things beyond her own narrow comprehension. What had *he* felt on being faced with her confident proposal to accompany him to Italy?

Moll's hooves thundered across the turf as the mare sensed something of the emotions ruling a rider normally gentle and considerate. More questions bombarded Charlotte's distressed mind. How could Vere have loved Annabel so much he wanted to die when she spurned him? How could Margaret feel such passion for Laurence Nicolardi within a few weeks that she could expose herself, and the children, to social disgrace and condemnation by leaving to live in sin at a secret address? How could a schoolboy with an assured golden future become so obsessed with a woman of twenty-eight, he could throw it all away for her sake?

Charlotte could no longer hold back moans of bitter regret that burst into the glory of that summer morning, to be snatched away by the breeze which tangled her hair and whipped the skirt of her gown up above the starched petticoat. Blinded by tears she raced on, possessed by a curious sensation of terror she tried to banish with a headlong charge. She had never known such depths of feeling, had never lost control in this fashion. Part of her terror was this very revelation that she *was* capable of passion; a notion foreign to the woman she had always believed herself to be. Her sobs were still flying on the wind when she became aware of a dark shape ahead. Too late she tried to control the startled mare. Moll swerved at high speed, slipped, and fell heavily.

When daylight returned beyond Charlotte's closed lids, the thud of Moll's hooves and her own heartbeat had quietened to leave a blessed peace containing only the song of a high-flying lark. She relished it for a moment or two, then became aware of being held against some rough material by a strong arm beneath her shoulders. A hand gently pushed strands of hair from her wet cheeks, then ran over her temples with caressing strokes.

'Come on, lass, stop frightening me and open those lovely eyes.'

Charlotte felt she knew the voice but was too weary

to pursue the thought. When the tone changed to one of brisk authority, recognition came immediately. The man holding her was the bailiff, John Morgan.

'Go to the house, Ned. Tell them to summon Dr Alderton, then get back here with rugs and pillows as fast as you can. I dursn't move her lest she has broken bones. She's so white I fear the worst, so get off swiftly, man.'

Whilst this was being said Charlotte opened her eyes, but the scene spun so dizzily she closed them again. The supporting arm moved fractionally sending a wave of pain through her back forcing an involuntary moan. Physical pain banished inner anguish, and Charlotte slipped back into unconsciousness.

Dr Alderton insisted on complete rest in bed for two weeks, followed by another two of restricted activity. A kindly man who ought to have retired several years ago, George Alderton had not kept apace with medical developments. He was a great believer in 'bed and broth' cures for most ailments. Having attended the Ashleighs for many years as physician and friend, he knew Sir Gilliard's second granddaughter well and was puzzled by the incident she refused to discuss. No one could discover why she was riding on the downs in a morning gown, or why she was so obviously distressed. Ned claimed Miss Charlotte had mentioned an emergency, which was why he had decided to follow her, and John Morgan said she appeared to be in the grips of such distress she was unaware of her surroundings.

Dr Alderton continued to probe gently, without success. He had seen Margaret Ashleigh in much the same state when the death of Vorne came so soon after their mother's remarriage and departure to America. Margaret had been but fifteen, overwhelmed by the responsibility of being the eldest and the substitute mother, but Charlotte was twenty-eight and highly sensible, with few signs of the passionate trait in the rest of Roland Ashleigh's attractive brood. Alderton was mystified. Young women were the very devil to understand, he told himself, and prescribed sedative powders to the patient who had a badly bruised back, and a wrist which needed a splint to prevent movement.

Charlotte was in no hurry to resume routine. For some days she felt weary enough to enjoy the comfort of bed. Weariness merged into lethargy, which then became a curious brand of dreaminess she was reluctant to abandon. The bruising caused great discomfort when-ever she moved and this contributed to her prolonged convalescence. Sir Gilliard came once to her room to ask bluntly why she had acted in such a foolhardy manner when she was far from being a brilliant horsewoman. He left when she offered no explanation, bidding her to do as Alderton ruled because he missed her company at the dinner-table.

During the second fortnight when she was allowed to sit out, surrounded by pillows, in a chair by the window, Charlotte watched John Morgan as he went about his daily tasks. The memory of his astonishing tenderness as she lay against his arm gave her cause for speculation.

John held a unique position at Knightshill. Neither servant nor equal, he had become a respectful friend to the young men and women he had known from their childhood. Nearing fifty, the large, gentle, country-bred man with a fresh complexion and light-blue eyes had done well from humble beginnings. Joining the staff at Knightshill as a cowman on leaving school, John had undertaken additional work to pay for evening lessons from the local accountant, and he had studied manuals on farming to glean more information than he was given by the bailiff then serving the family. When the post became vacant, John applied to Sir Gilliard and became the youngest bailiff ever employed by the Ashleighs. He proved worthy of his employer's trust, and when the adolescent Vere began to devote himself to running his future inheritance, John was a generous teacher. He had never married. In fact, he rarely participated in village affairs other than those connected with his job.

Charlotte reflected that John would make a good husband. He was dependable, honest, hard-working, gentle. Why had no woman ever set out to catch him? He must be lonely in his little cottage. Lonelier than she, who had a grandfather and many servants around her? Watching the subject of her thoughts one morning as he stood talking to Benson in the morning sunshine, Charlotte guessed work left him little time for loneliness. That thought revived the problem of finding occupation to fill her own empty days. Still haunted by the suspicion that her lack of understanding had deepened the unhappiness which had driven her brothers and sister away, she remained unsettled during a convalescence she was curiously reluctant to end.

On a morning at the end of July, Charlotte was finally lured from her room by the promise of a glorious day after a rainy spell. It was already hot when she went down with the intention of taking a stroll on the terrace. John Morgan came from his office as she passed, heading for the garden door. His ruddy features broke into his usual warm smile and his eyes lit with pleasure.

'This is the best birthday present I could wish for!' he exclaimed. 'The place hasn't been the same these past weeks. We've all been very concerned.' He stopped before her, a large man in breeches and a linen jacket. 'Are you really strong enough to be on your feet again?'

He was the same John she had always known. She told herself she must have imagined his affecionate manner because of the mood she had been in that day. Yet she now felt a little constrained in his company. 'I've been lazy for too long. I should have resumed my duties several days ago.'

'Best that you didn't,' he commented swiftly. 'No sense in being hasty after a bad fall.'

Avoiding further discussion on that subject, she asked lightly, '*Is* it your birthday, John?'

He smiled. 'I've reached the age when I shall forget this particular date from now on.'

She returned his smile. 'Grandfather has never said that, and he is considerably older than you. I suppose you have received many congratulations.'

'I've no family to send them, and I don't tell others my private affairs.'

'Birthdays should not be private affairs,' she protested. '*We* all make a great fuss of them.'

'That you do. I recall days when you were all children. Little roundabouts out there on the lawns, and clowns or marionettes to entertain you. There was enough food left over to feed the village poor for weeks.' He laughed. 'Your brother was invariably sick afterwards for eating things he shouldn't, and young Mr Valentine was always in trouble with Ned for giving horses iced cake.' His eyes brimmed with mischief as he added, 'You and your sister were *very* well behaved, of course. I'll not forget how dainty you both looked in party-gowns covered in bows and frills.'

His words revived visions which were now painful. 'That was long ago, John. There were so many of us here then.'

'They'll be here again, Miss Charlotte. Mr Ashleigh loves this place. He'll return when the old general is bowing out, then he'll stay. Mr Valentine was born to follow tradition and roam the world, but he'll come home between adventures, take my word. Mrs Daulton will be returning with the young ones now she's been widowed. There'll be roundabouts and clowns again when she gets back from Africa.' He touched her elbow lightly. 'Would you like to come along and look at the gardenias? Benson's boys have been doing the packing in your absence, but I think you'll want to inspect the present

37

crop of blooms before they're sent off. It's been too damp lately. Benson thinks they may fall apart if transported as far as London.'

Charlotte walked beside him to the large glasshouses, her thoughts still on her family. Lies had been told and must be maintained. Everyone had been allowed to believe Margaret was in Africa recovering from the shock of her husband's murder, and Val's absence had been explained by a story of his decision to spend a year in South Africa with the family of a schoolfriend before going on to Oxford. That year was almost over. Charlotte had no idea what she must answer to anyone who questioned her after that time, or how she would account for her sister's failure to return from a country in which she had never resided.

Only when she began studying the flowers in the stifling glasshouses did Charlotte realize any awkwardness she had felt with John had evaporated. They were on their normal friendly footing. For about ten minutes they discussed the commercial aspects of the business she had made her own, then Benson's sons arrived to hear her verdict. The boys were identical in features, with the same hesitant grin and slow, plodding way of speaking. Simple lads willing to undertake any task which would beautify the grounds of Knightshill, they listened to Charlotte and nodded simultaneous agreement like a pair of clockwork figures.

After a while the excessive heat beneath the glass began to effect her. Simon and Sam's faces began to float free of their bodies, then the plants themselves started to move up and down in dizzying fashion. Charlotte turned instinctively, swayed and would have fallen if John had not reached out to steady her.

'You'll feel better outside in the air,' he said in tones of rough concern. 'Lean on me. I'll not let you fall.' He began leading her between the plants. 'What a fool I am to bring you here the moment you leave your sick-bed. My

wits are diminishing with age!' Over his shoulder he called
to the twins. 'Get to the house and fetch Mrs Clark for the
mistress . . . and move at twice your normal speed!'

'There's no need to bring Sarah,' Charlotte protested,
despite her continuing swimmy sensation. 'It's merely the
heat in here.'

'You came down too soon. It's easily done after
illness.'

Emerging to the comparative freshness outside Charlotte stepped away from the supporting arm. 'I've not
been ill, John. You are making a great fuss over nothing.
I felt a little dizzy, but I'm perfectly well and able to walk
back without assistance. You should not have sent for
my maid.'

'She'd have given me what for if I hadn't.'

This typical comment from him softened her enough
to say, 'You have no fear of Sarah Clark. She speaks so
often in praise of how well you manage the estate in Vere's
absence, I tire of her fulsome compliments.'

'That's as maybe,' he replied calmly, 'but she's a
termagant where you are concerned. It'll be a while
before I hear the last of blame for this.'

'Then you were foolish to have informed her of it.'

After a moment's hesitation he waved a hand towards
the path. 'I've left some papers in the office. I'll walk back
to the house with you, if that's allowed.'

She smiled. 'How absurd! Of course you may accompany me . . . especially on your birthday.' Walking beside
him she felt the time was right to say what she must.
'I believe I have to thank you for your prompt action
after my fall. I didn't see you until it was too late, I'm
afraid.'

'I know.'

They were walking alongside the east wing and the grey
stone walls threw back heat from the fierce midday sun.
Charlotte was unwilling to continue the subject, but John
made no attempt to break a silence which emphasized her

uneven footfall against the regular tread of his boots. The beauty of the rose-garden ahead, and of the surrounding estate lying beneath a haze of heat, brought an echo of the yearning she had suffered on that fateful ride. Youth cried out within her. John Morgan was fifty today and could look back with satisfaction on all he had achieved since the age of twenty-eight. What would she look back on on her fiftieth birthday? Margaret had gone forever. Val would follow his star. When Sir Gilliard called Vere back to his deathbed, her brother would settle here with a wife to raise a family. There would be no place for an ageing spinster at Knightshill.

John's deep voice broke her introspection, making her look up swiftly. 'I've known you since you were knee-high, Miss Charlotte. I've served your family with pleasure and not a little pride. If there is ever anything I can do, any help you need, I hope you'll regard me as your friend as well as your servant. I won't let you down.'

His steadfast gaze told her it was the truth, but this man could never relieve her loneliness. She was an Ashleigh and must deal with it herself.

'Thank you, John,' she murmured, then was saved from further comment by the arrival of Sarah and Winters summoned by the twins. During Charlotte's disclaimer of needing their assistance, John headed for his office leaving her to order iced tea on the terrace. Sarah protested, but was silenced and went off wearing a long-suffering expression.

When Winters came with the chilled drink in a glass in a silver holder, he also brought her mail. Charlotte left the letters on the tray while she sipped tea, lost in thought once more. It would too quickly be autumn, then winter. How could she solve the problem of her isolation and use-lessness? All manner of charity work could be undertaken, of course, but Ashleighs had always participated widely in local good causes. It might be worthy occupation, but she had found it less than totally absorbing. By the time her glass was empty she was no wiser about the solution she had been seeking since Vere left.

With a sigh she took up the pile of letters she guessed would be belated thanks from ball guests and bills from her dressmaker, milliner and Dr Alderton. Her guess was correct, yet one envelope stilled her hand holding the silver letter-opener. For several moments she gazed at the familiar handwriting while her heartbeat quickened. Her sister had left without farewells a year ago and there had been no word from her since then, not even a reply to the letter Vere had sent with a newspaper cutting reporting details of Philip's death in Africa. Why should Margaret write now, and to her rather than to Vere? As she studied the envelope, Charlotte recalled her distress followed by anger on learning the truth of Margaret's abscondence. The anger had remained until a short time ago when a joking comment had touched her too deeply. Before the Waterloo Ball she might have destroyed this letter unopened – yes, she admitted that probability – but the long white envelope now offered a chance to renew a bond she had believed irrevocably broken. Charlotte slit open the letter and unfolded a single page.

My dearest Lottie,

Are you able to forgive me for leaving without a word of gratitude for all you have meant to me over the years? We are in London to seek help for Kate, who has been ill. I suppose Grandfather would not allow me to come to Knightshill, but I long to see you and so do the children.

We met Vere in Verona as he was about to sail for Athens. How he has changed! But so happy. I am as delighted as I know you will be. He gave me a letter for you which I hope I shall not have to post.

Laurence and I were married very quietly a week after receiving Vere's news, so there will be no embarrassment over my identity. Dear Lottie, please come, Margaret

The embossed address was that of a London hotel used by those who valued peaceful, dignified surroundings. It was one of the capital's most exclusive. Margaret and her children were certainly not living in poverty even though Laurence had resigned from the Diplomatic Service.

Although she sat on for some while considering her reaction to this invitation, Charlotte knew that she was being offered a second chance to understand why Margaret had acted as she had. There was also the bonus of seeing the children she loved. This letter was surely a partial denial of the charge of driving her family away. Margaret longed to see her, so she could not have been too terrible a sister.

Leaning back in the chair, she looked over the rose-garden and distant meadows which had a moment ago created yearning and loneliness within. The scene was now warmly familiar and filled with an ambience missing since her brothers and sister left. John Morgan was right. They *would* all return because their roots lay in this grand old house. Margaret should be allowed to bring her children here. They could never be Ashleighs in name, but they were in heart and spirit. Grandfather must be persuaded to permit their visit, yet the very fact that Timothy and Kate were *not* named Ashleigh robbed them of their strongest claim to come home.

Knowing Sir Gilliard was rigid in his daily routine and had taken sherry, as usual, before eating luncheon alone in the small dining-room during her recovery, Charlotte was certain of finding him when she went downstairs after tidying herself for the light midday meal. He was standing before the empty fireplace with a glass in his hand. Charlotte had a fleeting impression of a man suffering greater loneliness than she, and she wondered afresh what kind of man he had been before his young bride had deserted him. Sir Gilliard had been her own age then. Had he suffered every day from that moment on? Perhaps not. Like 'Skinny Minnie' and John Morgan, he had filled his life with occupation to combat loneliness. Then he had had five grandchildren to mould to his design. Poor Grandfather! Only Vorne had turned out perfectly, and he had been lost at the age of twenty-four. The rest must be greatly disappointing.

Sir Gilliard walked to the decanter to fill a glass for her. 'Back on duty, I see,' he commented in military fashion. 'Damn fool thing to do, but it has doubtless taught you a lesson.'

'How are you, Grandfather?' she asked, sitting in her usual chair to sip her sherry.

'Fit. Extremely so.' He reinforced his statement by straightening his shoulders and stretching his neck. 'Don't like what's going on in the Transvaal. The Boers need to be reminded of who they'd be taking on if they persist in their outrageous practice of taxing to the hilt all but their own kind, then refusing them the rights of citizenship. Such biased legislation! We won't stand for it, I promise you. I've written to Sir Humphrey advocating a show of strength before they go too far. The government is worried about its gold investments and hopes for peaceful negotiation, but anyone can see the damn Boers are spoiling for a fight. Have been since that terrible affair at Majuba. We lost a great deal of prestige over a confrontation that should never have been forced on our troops!' He drank the remainder of his sherry. 'I wrote my thoughts on that in *The Military Journal*. Brought a flood of controversial correspondence in its wake, but a number of experienced men agreed with my opinion.'

Charlotte knew it was pointless to attempt an interruption. When Sir Gilliard rode a hobby horse he did not dismount until it was exhausted. She closed her ears and enjoyed her sherry. He would not expect comments from her; she was merely a figure at whom to throw his theories. She was aware that there was unrest in South Africa, but political affairs did not interest her. She had a theory of her own to put forward, so the complications of citizenship in the Transvaal were of less than usual interest this morning.

Sir Gilliard returned to his theme during chilled consommé, followed by galantine of duck and green salad. Only when the silver fruit bowl was placed on the table did Charlotte find her opportunity. The old general played into her hands with another familiar theme.

'The mail was late. Fourth day in succession. Must protest to the Minister again. It really is not good enough.'

Charlotte sliced an apple into neat portions, saying as calmly as she could, 'I received several notes of appreciation from guests who are habitually late in sending them.'

'Slovenly,' he grunted, then popped several black cherries into his mouth. 'Bad manners, say what you like.'

'There was also a letter from Margaret, posted in London.'

Sir Gilliard began to peel a peach in silence. It was not the kind which fell when his thoughts were elsewhere; it was a listening, resistant silence.

Charlotte summoned courage. 'She is in England with her new husband to seek medical help for Kate. Her letter did not elaborate on that subject, but it must be complex if it requires advice from a specialist.'

Her grandfather continued to eat, but she was not deterred by a weapon he used often and to good effect. 'Vere met up with them in Verona on the eve of his departure to Greece. He is apparently deriving great benefit from his travels.' She took the final plunge. 'I should very much like to see my sister and her children. May they come home for a brief visit?'

The blue eyes which retained their youthful vividness looked directly at her. 'They chose to leave in company with a man who abused my hospitality while exceeding the bounds of morality and honour. Your mother also chose to leave this house, but *she* understood the penalties and has never attempted to make contact or return. For that, at least, she earns a modicum of my respect.' He chose another peach and peeled it as if the matter was closed.

Charlotte would not abandon it, however. 'The children made no choice: they were taken by their mother. If they had not been they would have been slaughtered with Philip. Timothy and Kate love Knightshill, Grandfather. It's their home.'

'No longer.'

She began to grow angry. 'Are you saying that innocent pair, one of whom is as keen to follow Ashleigh tradition as you could possibly wish, can *never* return?'

He glowered at her beneath bushy white eyebrows. 'The sins of the father are visited upon the children.'

'Laurence Nicolardi is not their father. Philip Daulton is dead . . . and a more pious, moral man you could not encounter. He committed no sin against you.'

'He was a pompous bigot who abused my hospitality by using this house for his own ends. He preached poverty and simplicity, yet availed himself without a qualm of all Knightshill offered. It was only for the sake of those children that I refrained from kicking the fellah out. He did not deserve a place with this family.'

'But his children do,' she cried. 'Their mother is an Ashleigh.'

'She is a woman with a fancy Italian name.'

'She has Ashleigh blood.'

'*Bad* blood,' he claimed, frowning once more. 'The boy has it, too. Must be from your mother's side.'

Before she could stop herself, Charlotte said, 'Or Grandmama's.'

It was unlike her to be vindictive, and she gazed in dismay at the old man's hardening expression. It was wrong of her to remind him of someone who must have inflicted deep scars upon his pride. Charlotte regarded her grandfather with fond respect. He had been the only stable influence in their lives, setting a supreme example of morality, family loyalty and integrity. He had been generous with his wealth, and caring within his own criteria. Vere had departed without repairing the breach caused by their quarrel. Now she was making wounding remarks to a man nearing ninety, whose dreams had all melted away.

Yet there was justification for her words. Her mother had been a widow, remarrying when she left for America with her Texan; nothing in that to uphold a claim of bad blood. Grandmama, on the other hand, an officer's wife, had run off leaving her child in the care of a nurse. That her lover had also been Italian did not help Margaret's cause, but Caroline Ashleigh might be blamed for any bad blood in her descendants. Val had always been reckless and determined. Vere was simply finding his feet, and Margaret might have done *anything* to avoid sailing for Africa with a husband possessed by his zealous convictions. Bad blood was too strong an expression to use against the three, and it had been in their defence that Charlotte had hit out at the man now studying her with glacial disapproval.

'If you have finished your luncheon I will retire to the library where I shall meet with good manners, filial respect and matters of greater interest in the pages of Sir Henry Guthrie's account of the Indian Mutiny.'

He left Charlotte at the table, her neatly sliced apple uneaten. Before receipt of Margaret's letter she would have been deeply distressed by further alienation of her sole companion at Knightshill, but his refusal to allow Margaret and, especially, the children over the threshold meant she must go to them. Enthusiasm set her on her feet. Why not stay in London for several weeks; if Margaret agreed? Disability had made Charlotte reluctant to venture from the local scene, but it might be time to widen her horizon. With a married sister to accompany her, she could visit galleries and museums, stroll in the parks, maybe even go to the opera.

Hastening from the room to write a reply, she told herself she might not have been welcome on Vere's Bohemian perambulation along the Mediterranean coast, but she would make the most of this invitation from a sister who *did* want her company. As she passed a window she saw John Morgan riding from the stables on his big roan. He had been only partially right. The family would return to Knightshill only when Sir Gilliard was no longer master of it. Until that time she must re-establish contact with them all and learn greater understanding.

3

THEY WERE THERE to meet her train looking as if they had always been a complete family. Charlotte's fears of constraint were dispelled when the children rushed to greet someone they had last seen more than a year ago. In the criss-cross of passengers and general noise of one of London's busiest rail termini, she hugged close a girl and a boy she had lived with from the days they were born.

'Aunt Lottie, we have so much to tell you,' cried ten-year-old Timothy. 'We've seen camels and Legionnaires and palaces and Arab dhows and elephants and black slaves . . . and a Roman amphitheatre,' he finished breathlessly.

Charlotte laughed. 'Not all on the same day, I trust. Gracious Tim, how tall you are!'

Margaret's son was a true Ashleigh, with thick blond hair, very blue eyes, sturdy build and a restless, energetic personality. He was uncannily like Val had been as a boy. Charlotte could hardly take her gaze from him to turn to Kate, whose illness had brought them all to London. The eight-year-old appeared to have changed little. With the same light-brown hair and green eyes as her grandmother and Uncle Vere, Kate was thoughtful, slow to trust, but intensely loyal towards those who earned it. She clung to Charlotte almost desperately, tears streaking her rather prim little face. An inveterate chatterbox, emotion now prevented her from saying a word. Apart from looking pale compared with her sun-browned brother, the girl gave no signs of being ill enough to need specialist advice.

Charlotte kissed the top of the girl's head. 'How I have missed you, dear! It has been *such* a long year.'

Then Margaret was there before her, and the children were temporarily forgotten as the sisters regarded each other seeking words to express their feelings. In an amethyst silk jacket and skirt, cream organza frilled blouse, and a huge confection of a hat decked with violets and striped ribbons, Margaret looked radiant. Charlotte then realized how miserable her sister had been during those last years with Philip. How had she failed to notice beauty so dimmed? Guilt made her reach for Margaret's hands, but she could do no more than grip them.

'I hardly dared hope you would come,' Margaret confessed, her eyes sparkling with tears. 'I was awake for half the night anticipating this moment.'

'I was nervous throughout the journey. Wasn't that foolish of me?'

They embraced, crushing the children between their long skirts, then drew apart to study each other anew. 'You haven't changed, Lottie.'

'You have,' she said swiftly. 'There's no need to ask if you are happy . . . and I swear you cannot have bought that wondrous hat anywhere but in Paris.'

They both laughed and embraced again, knowing sisterhood had been re-established. Then a figure arrived beside them to say, 'There is a carriage waiting. Perhaps you would care to quit this area bedevilled by flying soots and noisy engines for its privacy.'

Charlotte turned towards the man dressed in a pearl-grey suit. She had last seen him at Knightshill when Sir Gilliard had ordered her to arouse his interest as a prospective suitor. Never having really liked or trusted Laurence Nicolardi, she could not now deny that he was extremely personable. His dark eyes glowed with vitality as he made a slight bow, and his smile made nonsense of her constraint.

'We are *all* glad that you accepted Margaret's invitation. I trust I may call you Charlotte. It would be absurd to stand on formality now that we are related, do you not think?'

How like him to speak with such candour . . . and how different he was from the surly, pious Philip! Yet she could not bring herself to address him in the same friendly vein, so merely nodded in reply.

'Allow me to escort you through the crush of hopeful passengers,' he said, offering both arms to the sisters. Telling Timothy to take Kate's hand and follow them closely, he led them across to where carriages were lined up for hire. Within seconds he had established his position as head of his new family. Charlotte was swept along in a daze induced by more than the noise and bustle of a capital city after the peace of Knightshill.

Once in the carriage, with the children sitting on each side of her, Charlotte's attention was held by Timothy pointing out sights as they passed and giving informed comments on each. How bright the boy had become in one year! Philip had refused to allow his son to take his place at the preparatory school attended by all Ashleigh boys, and had confined his education, and that of Kate, to religious teachings. Timothy was clearly receptive to each fresh experience.

'My goodness, is there any building in London about which you are ignorant?' asked Charlotte with a laugh.

'Quite a number. But we've only been here for two weeks. It's all so *fascinating*! The whole world is fascinating,' he added expansively. 'I want to see it all.'

'An explorer, eh? You always wanted an army career,' she reminded him.

His eyes danced with zest as he said, 'I still do, of course. I'll see the world as a soldier. Father has given me permission to join any regiment I choose, but it will be the West Wilts. I shan't mind too much being called Daulton because they'll know I'm an Ashleigh in all but name. I expect Val feels like that, even though he's known as Martin Havelock. I think he's tremendously courageous to do what he wanted to do even though he had to be just an ordinary soldier and give up his name.' His expression was reminiscent of his youthful uncle at his most defiant, as he added. '*I* was determined not to be a missionary, Aunt Lottie. As soon as I was old enough I would have run away and done what Val did.'

'We will speak of that later, old fellow,' put in Laurence calmly. 'Your aunt will be in London for several weeks. It's not necessary to cram into the first hour every piece of information you wish to impart to her.'

The boy grinned at the man he had willingly accepted as his parent. 'Sorry, sir. Talking too much as usual.'

'It used to be Kate who did that,' Charlotte declared, smiling down at the girl close against her side. 'But she has not said a word yet.'

Green eyes gazed back at her from a pale face. There was no sign that Kate shared the happiness evident in her mother and brother. Charlotte then grew aware that a curious silence had fallen and glanced up. Margaret's expression had shadowed; Laurence looked grave.

'You mentioned seeking medical advice for Kate,' she ventured. 'Why, Margaret?'

'We shall talk later, at the hotel. The noise of the traffic makes all but the lightest of conversation impossible.' Margaret gave a strained smile. 'Grandfather would have a great deal to say on the subject. Does he still grow irate when the mail train arrives late?'

'Most certainly.'

'How is he?'

'A little older, but much the same.'

The carriage was frequently halted by the mass of vehicles which made London's streets increasingly noisy and dangerous. Drivers cursed and cracked their whips, horses snorted and whinnied until they surged forward again with a rattle of wheels and a tattoo of hooves, only to meet with an immobile line of traffic at the next junction. It was afternoon. Shopping was a favourite pastime for ladies who then called upon each other for tea and gossip. There would be a lull after four-thirty until people set out for theatres or dinner parties. Then the streets would be congested once more.

Charlotte was relieved when they reached the hotel and went up to the floor housing the suite occupied by the Nicolardis and the rooms they had reserved for her. She was tired after her journey and glad to rest before taking tea. The country peace of Knightshill seemed far away in the elegant rooms where she discarded her fawn travelling-dress and unpinned the demure hat her milliner had made her for this trip. Clothes that had seemed right in Wiltshire looked drab in these surroundings. Laurence was clearly a man of wealth. Perhaps he received an income from the Nicolardi glass business in Verona. Margaret dressed with a brand of elegance rarely seen in the provinces; her children wore clothes expertly tailored from quality cloth. They were now living in premises affordable only by those of consequence, and they had also apparently travelled extensively over the past twelve months. It made nonsense of Charlotte's concept of a sinful, tawdry relationship.

Speculation was then banished by concern for Kate. Margaret's behaviour in the carriage had suggested a serious problem, yet the child seemed perfectly well apart from an unusual quietness which could be due to the significance of the occasion. When one was only eight partings and reunions could be emotionally formidable, and Kate had always taken things greatly to heart. Recollections flooded in of days at Knightshill when the children had built snowmen with Vere or pelted Val with snowballs as he pretended to escape them. Then of summer days when they had picnicked on the downs, run races across the lawns and made daisy chains with the Benson twins, or peeped through an opening in the double doors at guests in excessive finery arriving for the Waterloo Ball. Those days had gone forever.

This reminder of loneliness set Charlotte dressing with determination in her best blue silk afternoon-gown. Action banished introspection. She would spend the coming three weeks in London, in company with people she loved. There were so many places to visit, and it would be over soon enough. Wiser not to spoil it all with foolish yearning for the past. Putting the finishing touches to her appearance, she decided that a shopping expedition must be undertaken if she was not to be dubbed a country bumpkin wherever she went.

This decision was strengthened on entering the other rooms where a dainty tea had been delivered. With her hat and jacket removed, Margaret looked stunning. Her golden hair had been swept into a complicated arrangement which would have defied the fingers of anyone at Knightshill, and her semi-sheer blouse revealed a lace bodice beneath. Charlotte's silk gown looked dowdy against such finery.

It was certainly easier to converse with traffic noise deadened, and they talked of the times Charlotte had recalled earlier. Laurence sat patiently during these reminiscences from which he was excluded, and Charlotte began to warm to him. She hardly knew the man, of course. Perhaps her dislike and distrust had been unjustified. While Margaret and Timothy spoke with animation, Kate said nothing as she sat close beside Charlotte. The child drank a cup of milk but ate none of the sweet things that once used to tempt her.

After twenty minutes, Laurence announced that he would take the children to the park to feed the ducks, and rose to usher them from the room. Kate left without protest, but cast a longing backward glance at her aunt. Charlotte asked the nature of the girl's illness as soon as she was alone with her sister.

'We are endeavouring to find that out from Sir Peter Heywood, who is reputed to be infallable in these cases.'

'Which cases?'

There was a brief hesitation before Margaret sighed. 'I had better tell you the whole story. You deserve to hear it, Lottie. When I left Knightshill, we were afraid Philip might try to trace and claim the children, so Laurence felt it would be better not to stay in any one place for too long. We left the ship on the coast of North Africa, then travelled to Egypt, Turkey, Russia and, finally, to a small Greek island. It was there that Vere's letter caught up with us.' She shook her head sadly. 'News of Philip's murder caused me no grief, I'm afraid. I merely saw merciful release for us all. You will probably find that hard to understand, because you can have no idea of the pain and humiliation a wife suffers at the hands of a man who abandons her and her children for an overriding passion.' Another brief sigh punctuated her account. 'We married as soon as Laurence could arrange it and began to plan a wonderful future. Then, on the verge of sailing to Italy to join the Nicolardi family, we were all smitten with fever. Kate was so ill we thought she would not be able to go with us when recovered. The Greek doctor said her constitution was not strong enough to withstand all the travelling we had done through countries with extremes of climate. I immediately thought of Vere, Lottie, and was afraid Kate had inherited the same weakness.'

'I suppose it *is* possible,' said Charlotte, concerned by what she was hearing, 'although Vere was sickly from birth and Kate showed no signs of it at Knightshill. Sir Peter Heywood will surely set your mind at rest on *that* score.'

Margaret shook her head again. 'It's more complex than that. Since Kate's fever broke she has not spoken to anyone – not a single word in two months.'

Charlotte could hardly take it in. 'You mean she has been rendered *dumb*?'

'That is what Sir Peter will discover – whether she cannot or will not speak.'

'Will not?' Charlotte cried. 'Why would Kate do such a thing? Why would any child?'

Margaret's voice suddenly broke, revealing the true extent of her distress. 'Perhaps this is God's punishment for my lack of grief over Philip's death at the hands of those he felt driven to bring to Christianity. Or maybe . . . maybe my intense joy after misery has to be leavened by sadness because I sinned to achieve it. Either way, Kate is suffering.'

The following weeks were more eventful for Charlotte than the entire last year at Knightshill. Outings were planned each day by Laurence, who was skilled at arranging a timetable filled with variety and entertainment. Charlotte fell victim to his charm against her will, and then understood how Margaret had known her heart within so few weeks.

Her sister one day broached the subject of what story relatives and friends had been given of her whereabouts, and Charlotte told her, adding, 'I imagine Grandfather will allow sufficient time to pass before announcing that you have remarried and settled abroad. I'm afraid he was adamant that he would not receive you at Knightshill, because you left for reasons he cannot accept.'

'I suppose he *is* justified, Lottie.'

'The same applies to Val.'

Margaret gave a faint smile. 'That lad is too happily occupied to care. I wrote to "Martin Havelock" when Vere told me where his regiment is stationed. He replied with typical enthusiasm. He is now a sergeant hoping for a chance to be commissioned in the field if the present unrest out there develops into war – which I feverently pray it will not.

'According to Val, South Africa is the most spectacular

country posing the ultimate challenge to men unfamiliar with the tricks it can play on them. It's a somewhat enigmatic statement from our prosaic young brother, don't you think? I suppose experience has changed him as it has Vere. He, by the way, was fit and happy when we met. Not having seen him since he went off to the Sudan looking haggard and wretched over that Bourneville girl, I was delighted by the person he had become.'

Charlotte had read with mixed feelings Vere's letter sent via Margaret. Her brother was visiting galleries, sites of historic interest and so much that he had never expected to be able to see in person. There was no mention of Knightshill or of missing her. He wrote that he had found instant rapport with Laurence, who had effected introductions to several influential people interested in new artists. Vere expressed delight at Margaret's new lease of life with a man more worthy of her than Philip had ever been. He hoped Charlotte would find it possible to overcome her reservations and meet the Nicolardis in London, or she might forever regret a lost opportunity.

The letter dampened her spirits for a day or two with its reminder of a spinster who had little understanding of love, but she could not be long depressed in the company of those set on entertaining her to the utmost. Margaret led her into extravagance during several shopping excursions. She bought gowns in the latest fashion and in shades she had never before considered, not once dwelling on the likelihood of attending functions in Wiltshire which would justify the wearing of these elaborate clothes. Laurence knew a great many distinguished and cultured people so there were dinner parties, soirées and theatre visits in their company. Sir Gilliard was known, if only by repute, to most of Laurence's more senior acquaintances; Vorne's heroism outside Khartoum was revered by everyone. A great many people also had seen Vere's impressive pictures of war in the Sudan published by *The Illustrated Magazine.*

Speaking of her brothers and grandfather to these people revived Charlotte's natural vivacity. This was how life used to be at Knightshill when they were all there together and she was at ease with their guests.

Beneath all the pleasure, however, she constantly worried about the reasons for the Nicolardis' presence in London. Kate remained silent, although Sir Peter had established that her vocal chords were undamaged when she gave a cry of fright as he burst a balloon behind her. Each time Margaret and Laurence took the girl to the eminent doctor, Charlotte was left in Timothy's entertaining company. He made no secret of his pleasure in being with her but, although he spoke of Knightshill with great affection, he gave no sign of wanting to return there.

'I think Kate misses home,' he said one afternoon, while walking in the park. 'Before this happened to her she was always talking about it. Do you think it would help her to go to Knightshill?'

'She would have to leave again,' Charlotte pointed out.

'I forgot that. Poor Kate! I wish I knew what to do.'

'Sir Peter will know. We must rely on him.' She pointed in the direction of the lake. 'Shall we take this path?'

He grinned up at her. 'I'd rather go the other way and see the Guards outside the palace. Is that all right?'

'I suppose so.' She had known all along that was where he intended to walk. The lure of a military uniform was irresistible to him. Not for the first time she wished Sir Gilliard would relent and see them all. He would be proud of Timothy, who resembled both Vorne and Val so strongly and who matched their warrior spirit. Grandfather could indulge this boy who was every inch an Ashleigh, and stop living in the past.

As they strolled the paths where nursemaids pushed perambulators containing the heirs to fortunes and titles, and where smart soldiers promenaded with their sweet-hearts, Charlotte was beset by the thought of just one week of her visit remaining. She must then return to lone-liness; say goodbye to Margaret and the children without knowing when they might meet again. The halcyon days would end leaving more memories to haunt her.

'What is it, Aunt Lottie? You seem so sad.' Timothy was looking at her with such concern she longed to hug him close, but she knew he would be embarrassed by sudden affection in the park. Instead, she indicated one of the long benches.

'Shall we sit here for a moment? I should like to talk seriously to you.'

'All right,' he agreed. 'Are you feeling unwell? Mama does sometimes, and Father tells her to rest.'

As they settled on the warm wood, she asked, 'You think a lot of Mr Nicolardi, don't you?'

He seemed surprised. 'Of course. He's the most splen-did man I've ever met. He knows exactly how one feels about things, *and* the answers to any questions one asks. I think he is acquainted with every country of the world.' He moderated this exaggeration with a grin. 'At least, it seems that he is. He's a diplomat – but you know that – so I suppose he has to be on good terms with the people he meets.'

'He is on particularly good terms with you?'

'Oh, yes! We discussed, man to man, my wish to join the West Wilts and he approved right away. Not like my other father.'

Finding the boy more confiding than she expected, Charlotte decided to probe further. 'Have you never missed the Reverend Daulton?'

Timothy coloured slightly, and gave his reply while looking ahead to where two dogs were barking at ducks gliding past in a flotilla. 'I *am* sorry that he was killed by the heathens he wanted to help, but I always felt they meant more to him than we did. Kate was frightened of him, you know, and I was angry about not being allowed to go to Misleydale and then on to Chartfield like all Ashleigh boys.' His flush darkened. 'I would have run away and joined the regiment as soon as I was old enough. So, you see, it has all turned out well for me . . . and Mama is much happier with Father than she was with him.'

After waiting for a portly gentleman to pass with a very young woman in an astonishing yellow ensemble, who betrayed the fact that she was not his daughter by ogling him with a pair of brown eyes, Charlotte followed up Timothy's last statement.

'Is Kate as happy in her new life as you and Mama?'

Timothy was gazing at the swaying rear of the girl in yellow with a disconcerting amount of interest. Charlotte had to repeat her question before he collected himself and turned towards her.

'Father is very fond of her. He says she is more intelligent than he expected after being denied regular lessons by our other father. Kate learns quickly and seems to enjoy being taught something more interesting than religious tracts.'

When he stopped, Charlotte regarded his intent expression for a moment. 'You have not answered my question, Tim. *Is* Kate as happy as you and Mama?'

He frowned. 'Perhaps not. But she's not unhappy. She likes Father and obeys him without any fuss . . . but she's always talking about Knightshill. At least, she was before she caught fever and stopped speaking altogether.' His faced screwed into a pensive expression. 'She's never far from your side, is she? Do you think she would like to go home rather than visit all these fascinating foreign countries? Perhaps she's too young to appreciate them,' added the ten-year-old. When Charlotte made no immediate comment, he slid to the edge of his seat hopefully. 'Can we go to see the Guards now?'

*   *   *

Margaret and Laurence were unusually quiet when they returned from Kate's appointment with Sir Peter Heywood, saying merely that progress had been made. Charlotte did not press them for elaboration, guessing that it would be offered when the children had gone to bed. Her conversation with Timothy stayed in her mind whilst dressing in a gown of plum-red silk for an evening at Daly's Theatre. The boy was very discerning for his age. She had not the heart to tell him Sir Gilliard had forbidden him and his sister to enter their former home. He would be deeply hurt.

The Nicolardi carriage collected a former ambassador, his wife, son and daughter, so conversation was lively during the short drive. The musical play was entertaining and colourful, if not a little saucy, but Charlotte laughed with her companions who were more sophisticated than she. In this mood of conviviality they all enjoyed the dinner Laurence had chosen to round off another evening which brought Charlotte's departure nearer.

During the return drive she fell silent amidst the merry group. Thoughts of the empty rooms and corridors of Knightshill invaded her, and the spectre of loneliness drove away the pleasure she had known that evening. On reaching their hotel Margaret asked her to join them as she and Laurence wished to discuss something important. Suspecting that it concerned their meeting with Sir Peter, Charlotte walked with her sister to their suite furnished lavishly in blue and gold which had become a familiar venue after two weeks. Declining Laurence's offer of a nightcap, she leaned back against brocaded cushions and waited for Margaret to begin. When she did, it did not appear to be about Kate at all.

Standing beside her husband, Margaret said, 'When we left England last year Laurence resigned from the Diplomatic Service. He did not relish doing so but he had little choice under the circumstances. It was his intention to join his Italian family's business, when we felt the situation allowed such a move. Philip's death enabled us to go to them in Verona sooner than we anticipated.'

Charlotte was taken aback by talk of matters which should be confidential between husband and wife. She was further surprised when Margaret glanced at Laurence and said, 'Perhaps you should continue, dearest.'

He nodded. 'Charlotte, you have been made aware that I have acquaintances in high office in London, so it may not surprise you to learn that my presence has given rise to some discussion of my affairs.' His eyes narrowed speculatively. 'Although my marriage to a beautiful widow followed rather too soon after the death of her husband, it has been decided that the haste may be overlooked as my bride is the granddaughter of a renowned general who earned the gracious approval of Her Majesty during his years at Horse Guards. In short, my former masters have asked, nay, *begged* me to accept a diplomatic post for which I appear to them to be uniquely suited.'

Margaret spoke before he could continue. 'Laurence will not tell you this, so I must. He is fluent in eight languages and has a distinguished record of service to this country. His mother remarried on the death of Antonio Nicolardi, so Laurence was reared as an Englishman despite having two Italian parents.' She took her husband's arm affectionately. 'Lottie, he would never be happy as an Italian glassmaker. He is a talented diplomat and his resignation was the greatest of sacrifices for my sake. With all my heart I want him to accept this post.'

Charlotte was bewildered by their request to be present while they discussed Laurence's future. All she could manage was a rather embarrassed comment. 'Oh, I see.'

'I think perhaps you do not,' Laurence told her quietly. 'We are describing this badly because we are allowing our emotions to colour our words.' The look he gave his wife was so full of adoration, Charlotte felt even more uncomfortable. 'Thank you for your flattering resumé of my career, darling, but we should set this problem before your sister in a more concise manner.'

'Problem?' echoed Charlotte.

Laurence led his wife to a settee where they sat together, a darkly attractive man in his mid-thirties, and a woman in black moiré and emeralds whose beauty was enhanced by her husband's love for her. Charlotte now perceived the exact depth of passion between them, and envied her sister as she never had before.

'A post has fallen vacant in South America,' Laurence said. 'It is a particularly sensitive period out there, so the man who fills it must be experienced and familiar with the political complexities of the many countries comprising that continent. I know South America. I speak fluent Spanish as well as the languages of other major nations with interests there. I *am* the ideal man for the post, and I very much wish to accept it – not only for myself but for my family. They deserve the best in life I can give them.'

Margaret took her husband's hand, saying, 'Laurence would have accepted immediately, but for Kate. We asked Sir Peter this afternoon for his verdict on her condition. He told us he was not ready to give one but, on hearing our reasons, offered an *opinion*. It is this: tearing a child from her roots at an age when she has been able to build an understanding of every-thing around her, yet is not old enough to accept the need to change what she knows and trusts, can some-times produce in that child fear that she will never find roots again. All our travelling has fed that fear, and the severity of the fever she suffered may also suggest to Kate that pain is an integral part of her new life.'

'How can he possibly know all that?' demanded Char-lotte. 'Has Kate spoken to him?'

Laurence shook his head. 'He is a clever man and his opinion makes good sense. Would you not agree?'

'I . . . no, not entirely. Only Kate can tell us what ails her, and this man does not know her as we do.'

'But he knows his profession, Lottie,' said Margaret on a sigh. 'We believe he is right.'

Laurence continued. 'Taking Kate to South America would not only be inadvisable, it could worsen her condition. We cannot take that risk.'

'Tim would benefit from all Laurence could give him by accepting the post, however,' said Margaret. 'There is an excellent European school he could attend until going up to Oxford, and the experience he would gain as the son of a high-ranking diplomat would be invaluable to his chosen career.' She glanced swiftly at the man beside her, then turned back to Charlotte with a smile. '*I* have the very best of reasons for wishing to stay with Laurence. I am to have a child at the end of the year.'

These confidences were too much for Charlotte. Another child – half-Italian, and so soon! Were they telling her they were bound for South America, or not? What of Kate? Laurence had admitted it might be dangerous to take her there, yet they both appeared to be expressing their eagerness to go. As she tried to assemble her wits, Margaret came across to sink before the chair and take her hands.

'Dear Lottie, what we wish to ask is whether you would consider looking after Kate at Knightshill until she has recovered and is old enough to join us.'

Charlotte's confused thoughts suddenly fell into place to produce the most wonderful pattern. Here was the absorbing occupation she had been seeking; the purpose to her life. She would have a child to rear; a sweet, loving companion who was dependent on her. Loneliness would be at an end. Bringing up Kate would turn the empty hours into ones of delight. Knightshill would again ring with laughter. There would be snowmen, daisy chains and summer picnics. A lump gathered in her throat as she gazed back at her sister.

'Nothing would make me happier. *Nothing*. To the devil with Grandfather! *You* have all defied him. Now it is my turn. Kate will recover in familiar surroundings, I *know* she will.' She began to laugh with delight. 'She will be the first of the Ashleighs to come home. The rest of you will follow, in time.'

Vere sat beneath a shady tree with a sketch-pad on his knee, his hands idle. It was September and excessively hot on the island. He was lodging in a crumbling establishment run by a Greek who rated food above décor. It was idyllic – overgrown gardens wonderfully perfumed during indigo nights scattered with stars, old stone columns hung with flowering vines, spartan airy rooms which seemed to sleep along with their occupants during the heavy afternoons and, best of all, a sweeping view of the sea.

When the sun went down the courtyard filled with those seeking a first-rate meal, a bottle of wine and good conversation. Vere had made friends with many local people. Artists were welcomed on this isle of vistas and valleys. The penniless ones paid for their food and lodging with small samples of their work. Wealthy ones were expected to show appreciation by bestowing gifts of theirs. Vere had done so willingly. The watercolours and pen-drawings he had done since arriving here were skilled, but none had truly satisfied him.

During his six-month search for culture, he had worked unceasingly. The Mediterranean countries contained some of the most beautiful aspects an artist could desire, with colours found only in lands washed by sea and sun. Vere had developed his talent considerably by attempting every form of art without considering the commercial aspect, or confining himself to the skills he preferred. He intended this period to be one of experiment in which to discover his strengths and weaknesses. Yet, despite freedom to devote himself to something he had been obliged to suppress in the past, despite inspiration gained from studying many of the greatest works of art in the world, despite his itinerant life, the restlessness he had known on returning to Knightshill had not been banished. The first few months had subdued it, but it was returning to full strength. Seductive nights had him lying awake seeking reasons. Somnolent sun-drenched days brought indolence. He had become a lotus-eater without understanding why.

Sitting beneath the tree on that day at the end of September he felt no inclination to work. The malaise was starting to worry him so he attempted to analyse it. He certainly had no desire to go home to the company of a possessive sister, and an old man who saw just one virtue in his heir: the ability to produce another. There had been ample opportunity during his travels to enter into the kind of liaison easily begun, and just as easily discontinued. Why no woman had captured his interest for long he could not tell. Perhaps his lethargy extended to sexual desire. He was in an artists' paradise, yet neither man nor painter was fulfilled.

Dropping his sketch-pad at his feet, Vere frowned at the sparkling blue water stretching away to a misty horizon. What was wrong? For some minutes he stared across the Mediterranean wondering if he had lost his muse along with his zest for life. Then, as the horizon started to shimmer like a mirage before his eyes, he suddenly saw the answer. He was here to paint the exotic wild beauty of these lands but was more and more often facing the sea instead, watching that distant horizon. He got up slowly and walked to the edge of the dusty rise which hung out over crystal-clear depths hugging the shore. A boat could take him across to Alexandria and the Nile. A train could get him to Cairo. He would be there within a week.

Dreaminess vanished beneath a charge of excitement.

The desert was calling him. It had been calling for six months and it was not until now that he had recognized its voice. Only when he was again gazing across the enduring sands would he find release from this yearning, and rediscover his true talent.

He made the crossing to Alexandria the following evening and, when the ship drew alongside the shore of that vast continent, he owned to himself that it was not only the desert singing a siren song. Memories of Floria Pallini still lingered in his heart. Leaning on the rail to gaze at the lights of Alexandria, he allowed those memories full rein as he recalled her large amber eyes gazing at him with compassion, and her soft caressing voice saying, 'I will silence the cry in your heart.' She had tried too well, and he had come near to loving her before he left Cairo to march to Omdurman.

Floria had drifted into the life of a courtesan after her husband disappeared during a desert expedition when she was only eighteen. As the years passed she had earned acceptance from the wealthy and distinguished, her villa becoming the venue for elaborate parties which all but the sticklers for propriety had attended. It was not her legion of lovers who had stood between Floria and Vere, however; it had been the fact that she had given her heart to another Ashleigh. His brother Vorne's ghost, which had also captivated Annabel Bourneville, continued to possess the devotion of the second woman Vere had cared for.

Yet Floria had loved Vere in her fashion. Her appreciation of his talent had opened the way to its present popularity. She had introduced him to Armand Lisère, who owned galleries in Alexandria and Cairo patronized by collectors of standing in the Middle East. Lisère had recognized Vere's worth and had bought his set of sepia paintings of desert warfare with a request for more; so he was now the man to show selected canvases of Mediterranean scenes. From the gallery owner Vere would also learn of Floria's present situation.

Guilt washed over Vere as he stood on that ship recalling another moored on the Nile ready to transport the European captives found in the dungeons of Omdurman by British officers. Roberto Pallini, captured thirteen years earlier like many of his fellow prisoners, had been suffering terrible deprivation chained to the walls of his cell while other men had been enjoying the generosity of his wife who had believed she was a widow. Vere had suffered the guilt of two Ashleighs on that score, and yet he could not forget the plight of poor Floria when her husband returned to learn of the life she had been leading.

Armand Lisère was not in Alexandria, so Vere purchased a small trunk in which to pack his heavier clothing and those items of his work he knew the man would not consider, then left it at the shipping office, to be transported to Knightshill via Southampton, before taking the train to Cairo. As it wended its way across terrain sectioned by the many tributaries at the mouth of the river Nile, Vere again smelt the undeniable whiff of the East, saw camels and palms and brown men navigating every kind of craft along the muddy waterways. He also renewed acquaintance with the multitude of rogues eager to sell anything from hair bracelets to bottles of Nile water, and he rejoiced in it all as memories flooded back.

On reaching Cairo he was not the innocent abroad that he had been last year, so he was soon in an open carriage with his baggage, being taken to the hotel in which he had spent his leave. He was welcomed there with the exaggerated pleasure of men of the East, and was conducted to a room with a view of the residential area in which Floria's villa was situated. Standing by the window he longed to see her, hear her low laugh, touch her warm skin, and he knew she was not yet out of his heart.

But she was out of his reach. Armand Lisère revealed that Floria had departed before her husband arrived on the steamer from Omdurman. What Cairo society had been prepared to accept from a supposed widow, they condemned in a married woman. The villa had been so hurriedly vacated most of the treasures were there when Pallini arrived to hear the scandalous truth about someone he had last seen as his bride of eighteen. He had returned to Italy and died there several months later. Floria's whereabouts were unknown, but those who retained their affection for her hoped she was queen of some distant appreciative court.

Ridiculously disappointed by news he should have expected, Vere felt little delight at the gallery owner's immediate acceptance of a set of Italian twilight scenes in mauves and blues, another set painted in Sicily which evoked the barren landscape with remarkable economy of colour, and three pen-pictures of village life high in the hills. One canvas remained in Vere's case: the portrait of a Neopolitan woman with dark fiery eyes and sensual curves who had posed for him in exchange for a mangy donkey he purchased for her from the market. Despite her peasant's clothes, the woman too closely resembled Floria for Vere now to allow the picture to be exhibited in a city where she had been so well known.

Floria's absence was not Vere's only disappointment. Last year, Cairo had been home to many British regiments; cafés and markets had been filled with soldiers relaxing on leave or acclimatizing after arriving from England to reinforce the army which had already fought half-way to Omdurman. In the more elegant restaurants, the superior hotels, the clubs and banks, there had been affluent British officers whose voices rang with authority as they demanded the attention they regarded as their due. There was still a small British presence provided by officers of the Camel Corps and various other Egyptian regiments, but Cairo became an alien spot now the war was over. Even the desert seemed hostile when Vere stood gazing across the eternal sands trying to recapture what

it had meant to him before. Where were the neat rows of
tents, the compounds filled with camels and horses, the
constant movement of men in khaki? There was nothing
before him but miles of dun-coloured terrain baking
beneath the sun, where the only sign of motion was the
heat shimmering several feet above it. After two weeks in
Cairo, Vere's excitement was replaced by surprising and
unexpected sensations of raw loneliness.

Wandering moodily along the banks of the Nile, where
urchins' and pedlars' pleas fell on his deaf ears, Vere
decided that trying to relive the most momentous year
in his life was futile. Perhaps Sir Gilliard had been right
to insist that he marry and start a family. He was
twenty-seven. It was his duty as heir to a large estate
to ensure the continuation of the line. A wife and children
would make Knightshill a happy and lively place again;
they might ease his restlessness so that he would again be
content there. But he would not marry without love.

'By God, it can't be!' exclaimed a voice from a passing carriage. 'The pre-Raphaelite with a sword, or I'm
damned forever!'

That last sentence brought Vere from introspection and
he swung round. The carriage had halted and its passenger
was leaping from it with disbelief written all over his
broad sun-browned face. Vere took several giant strides
to seize his outstretched hand with matching disbelief.

'*Ross*! This is incredible. What are you doing in
Cairo?'

'Acting on Her Majesty's service, of course,' came
the laughing reply. 'Have you forgotten that we went
to Fashoda with Kitchener after you left Omdurman?
When we settled that affair, I was asked to stay on for
another year attached to Headquarters. What is more to
the point is what *you* are doing here when your regiment
is barracked in Lincolnshire.'

The pleasure of this encounter with a friend who had
shared those times he had been trying to recapture

brought a return of hope. 'The pre-Raphaelite hung up his sword in January. I'm on a tour of the Mediterranean as an artist, seeking to further my career,' Vere told him heartily.

Ross gave his inimitable grin. 'The Mediterranean? You're a trifle off course, aren't you?'

'Oh . . . yes. Yes, I am.' Vere laughed. 'You have no idea how good it is to see you. Let's lunch together and exchange news.'

Ross indicated the carriage. 'I was on my way to lunch when I spotted you.'

The day immediately turned brighter for Vere. Cairo was now welcoming and familiar. Ross Majors had befriended him on his arrival in Egypt and tried to save him from the certain humiliation awaiting any artist who attempted to become an instant warrior. They had fought their way to Omdurman together, and parted regretfully when their regiments went their separate ways a year ago.

'So you decided the army was not for *this* particular Ashleigh after all,' said Ross, leaning back against the squabs as the carriage headed for the bustle of central Cairo. 'A wise decision, although you were growing into the role very well.'

'A compliment, coming from you,' Vere replied. 'I returned to England thinking I could take up life where I had left it, as a prosperous landowner.'

'And?'

'I kept hearing phantom bugles across my meadows, and saw the Nile instead of waving wheat when the moon shone down on it. If I'm honest, I must admit I also imagined camp fires amid a bivouac when I gazed into the valley where the lights of the village were twinkling.'

'So you embarked on a tour of the Mediterranean as an excuse to come back, hoping to find it just as it was?'

'Dear God, you've grown amazingly perceptive since

we last met! I wasn't aware of that myself until several weeks ago!'

Ross grinned. 'My powers of perception gained me this post at Headquarters. It also gained me promotion.'

'*Captain* Majors? Congratulations.'

'I may have to call a halt now. *Major* Majors might cause difficulties, don't you think?'

'I have never known you to worry about making difficulties. You damn well enjoy the occupation.'

Laughing and reminiscing the pair arrived at their destination, and made their way through to the airy restaurant where Ross had arranged to meet up with some of his fellow-officers. Vere was accorded a warm welcome when Ross explained that his companion had also participated in the Sudanese campaign, and the inevitable question regarding his name was asked.

'Yes, Vorne Ashleigh was my brother,' he said as lightly as he could, then hastened to explain that he had left the army in order to pursue his career as an artist. He had no wish to discuss a hero he knew to have feet of clay. His table companions then recalled the pictures he had done of the war for *The Illustrated Magazine*, and the awkward moment passed.

An hour flew as they spoke of last year's campaign, followed by the show of strength at Fashoda to prevent the French gaining territory along the banks of the Nile. With brandy and cigars on the table before them, the senior man present predicted war in South Africa very soon. Opinions were divided on whether or not a mere show of strength there would deter the Boers, as it had the French.

'At Fashoda we had a considerable force and some useful artillery,' Ross pointed out. 'The French consisted merely of a handful of men who had hoisted a tricolour over a collection of mud huts and claimed them for their country. Faced with our cannon they could do little else but take the flag down when Kitchener ordered them to. In South Africa we're confronting an entire race of Dutchmen, not a handful. They are challenging us over their own territory, not a tiny native village in a land miles from their own.'

'It's not a challenge, it's a bluff,' declared a captain of the Camel Corps, puffing at his cigar.

'They may find themselves deep in a strategy which rebounds if we decide to take them seriously,' a dark-haired subaltern pointed out.

'No chance of that,' the captain returned. 'The Boers are farmers who live by the word of God. We would never take up arms against such people.'

'We did just that not so long ago,' the senior officer reminded them. 'My brother was at Majuba Hill. He almost died of shame when his regiment was cut down by armed civilians and forced to retreat.'

'But they were at the greatest disadvantage, sir,' protested the subaltern. 'They should never have been ordered to advance uphill in red coats through spiky aloes, when riflemen in dun-coloured clothes were easily hidden at the crest.'

The greying major sipped his brandy, then nodded. 'Yes, they were at the very worst disadvantage. Even so, Boers used a recognized military tactic to supreme effect. We should not dismiss them too hastily. I believe it must come to war before we can settle harmoniously with them in a country more than large enough for both races.'

Vere heard all this with growing disquiet. While he had been lotus-eating in countries with little interest in possible war at the tip of the African continent, a situation which would certainly effect his young brother had developed. For six months he had drifted in search of elusive fulfilment, and finally saw where it was to be found. Artist, he might be, but it was with these men he knew accord. It was not Cairo, not the desert, which had been beckoning to him, but the company of others who had known war in all its unforgettable guises. The beauty of Mediterranean vistas had failed to inspire him because he was seeking subjects which fired his true talent. He was inspired already. A group of men around a table, talking of distant heroes and past glories, as fans circled slowly above a starched cloth littered with glasses and cigar-ash. Paint this scene with another canvas of these same men around a table set up in haste near some battlefield, their warriors' uniforms now stained and torn, their faces lined by fear and exhaustion, and Vere would have a pair of pictures worthy of those which had been so highly praised last year.

He encouraged further discussion on the subject of South Africa. 'If, as you say, the confrontation has arisen over the Boers' refusal to allow foreigners the right to citizenship in their province of Transvaal, is it not a political rather than military dispute?'

The senior man crushed out his cigar before answering. 'Yes, Ashleigh, but politicians seem unable to solve their difficulties without lining up soldiers in neat rows opposite each other. When enough of them are dead, agreement will be reached. It was ever so.'

Ross poured himself another brandy. 'You have no doubt that it will come to exchanging shots, sir?'

'None at all. I heard last night that the Government has ordered reinforcements to the count of ten thousand to be hurried there. Regiments from India are favoured because of their proximity, but others are being shipped from home stations.'

Unable to reveal that his brother was serving under a false name with the 57th Lancers in a small garrison town in Natal, Vere asked, 'Is that fact, or merely a contingency plan?'

'A fact. Our ambassador was informed through diplomatic channels.'

Ross turned to Vere with a wry expression. 'Now, *that's* the war we should have chosen rather than struggle through the Sudan and its horrors to recapture a city in ruins! I've heard the country is stunningly lovely with clean air, civilized cities boasting social amenities of high standard, an abundance of excellent food and wines, ladies who appreciate gentlemen of refinement like us and, best of all, the most marvellous hunting terrain teaming with antelope.'

'With a parcel of farmers to fight, the affair would soon be settled,' drawled the Camel Corps captain.

'Not so,' put in a staff officer who had remained on the periphery of the discussion. 'The Boers are people of great determination. They believe the Good Book has decreed that they should seek and settle in their Promised Land. South Africa is it, in their opinion. There is no enemy more unpredictable and dangerous than one driven by the belief that the Lord is on his side. Good God, you fought just such a one last year.'

'And thrashed them soundly,' Ross pointed out.

'Only because Dervish weapons were antique and tactics badly executed,' Vere reminded his friend. 'Their courage was outstanding.'

'So was their faith in Mohammed's participation in the battle, or they would never have continued to advance when their comrades were falling in thousands before your guns,' said the staff-captain. 'The Boers have more than religious faith to spur them on, however. They have been attempting for two hundred years to settle peacefully down there, and I fear we have followed behind them every time they moved north away from our rule. They are set on making a stand to establish a national territory. God *and* Justice on its side makes a foe more formidable than the fanatics you took on last year, Majors.'

'Quite possibly,' said the irrepressible Ross, 'but I would still give anything to receive orders to proceed southward to Pretoria.'

'And I,' chorused the two younger officers.

Vere regarded them all with a smile. 'As the only civilian amongst you, I am not governed by orders, gentlemen. *The Illustrated Magazine* is eager to publish any pictures I do of military campaigns. If all you have told me about gathering war clouds is true, South Africa seems to be the ideal country for me to visit next.'

4

WHILE TROOPS LOADED a waggon with supplies that had come up on the train from Cape Town, their sergeant led a dozen horses one by one down the ramp from an open truck, inspected them thoroughly, then took them across the railyard to where the regimental horses were tethered. Leaving a corporal and a brawny trooper watching over them, he crossed to the office to sign for several sacks of mail which were as vital as supplies to men far from home. Four soldiers went to collect them and heave them into their waggons now waiting to leave. With two men on the box of the vehicle, the remaining twelve swung into their saddles and each took one of the remounts on a leading rein.

The small procession set off through a South African town no larger than an English village. At its head was the sergeant who sat his tall stallion with an air of élan. He was young and powerfully built with a broad, deeply tanned face made particularly striking by clear, vivid blue eyes; an impressive figure in a smart uniform in two tones of grey with the cap set at a jaunty angle on his thick blond hair. The people of Mariensberg were used to the sight of British soldiers for they had been garrisoned there for some years. They either admired the troops or cursed them, but the burghers walking in the main street could not help but watch this sergeant who rode past in the manner of a general. Young girls were dallying by their front doors to await his return from the station, but their eager blushes faded when he rode past without a glance in their direction. Their only consolation was that he had held aloof from them all throughout the eight months that his regiment had been stationed there. Whoever it was that he remained faithful to in England must be a truly exceptional person, they thought, and envied her such loyal devotion.

Val Ashleigh's thoughts were far from romance as he rode back to the garrison occupied by the 57th Lancers. The remounts he had collected were splendid beasts, but he would have preferred a dozen sturdy 'whalers' from Australia to these cavalry horses straight from home. The regiment had come to realize that the South African terrain better suited animals with shorter legs and greater staying power than those bred to carry large men, heavy equipment, and lances weighing almost five pounds. In this country horsemen travelled light. Distances between hamlets were vast and to linger on the veld was dangerous. It was a land of undeniable splendour, with sobering vistas and exciting wild creatures, but these could kill as well as charm and the lure of clear unhindered views could deceive a man into seeking horizons which were further off than they appeared.

Their progress along the main street raised dust that would hang in the still air long after they had passed. Winter had been dry and sunny, pleasantly warm by day and cold during nights with skies full of stars. Spring was almost here. According to several young men of Mariensberg who had become Val's friends, the coming season would bring storms to turn dust roads to mud and swell rivers so the *drifts*, where men were able to cross in winter, often rose by as much as eight feet within a short time. Many had drowned at these deceptive, treacherous fords, their horses with them. As spring lengthened into summer, temperatures would soar and the veld would bake beneath the sun. Those obliged to travel during summer did so with a good supply of water and emergency rations. They also learned in advance the vagaries of the terrain and the location of isolated farms where help could be sought. There were few maps of this tip of Africa, so the only travellers who went forth with confidence were those who knew the veld and respected it.

The troops left the town and followed the narrow track leading to their military outstation. The waggon creaked as its wheels crossed ruts, and the horses began picking their way with care over uneven ground. Val studied the cluster of tin-roofed stone buildings lying beneath a cloudless azure sky and wondered if there would be a war. It was what he had yearned for. Only on a battlefield would he have the opportunity to redeem himself, as he had vowed to do. Only if war came could he wipe out the shadow over his past and earn the right to be where an Ashleigh should be. The usual pang of regret over forfeiting his identity touched him, reminding him that no matter how heroic Martin Havelock became, Sir Gilliard might never accept him in place of V. M. H. Ashleigh.

The affair at Chartfield School had brought Val humiliation, dishonourable dismissal, and the burden of knowing that he had badly let down a family of which he was inordinately proud. Julia Grieves, the young second wife of Val's housemaster, had coaxed from him the confession that he was determined to join the cavalry in spite of his grandfather's threat to use his influence to prevent him from doing so. Then she had revealed that her uncle was about to take over command of the 57th Lancers. She had offered to recommend Val to Max Beecham as a prospective officer of his regiment. His gratitude and eagerness to earn her continuing help had unwittingly led Val into her cat and mouse game until she seduced him on an evening when he was shattered by the tragic death of his closest friend.

Luring him with the promise of an introduction to her uncle, Julia had intensified her campaign for total control.

Somewhere along the way Val had lost sight of the 57th Lancers and become sexually obsessed with her. That was when she had played her ace. Too late he had recognized the true nature of her plan to strip him of all pride and self-respect. When he had turned from her in horror and disgust, Julia had cried attempted rape.

Believing that Sir Gilliard would find his presence at Knightshill a constant distressing reminder of his disgrace, Val had lived rough for several days, nursing his pain and coming to terms with the loss of all he held dear. Longing to hit back at Julia, he had thought of a means to do so. He *would* join the 57th Lancers; gain the prize she had promised him. Unable to use his real name because Max Beecham would know him as the senior prefect who had assaulted his niece, Val had taken his two middle names and enlisted as a trooper. Julia remained the victor, however. When Colonel Beecham had offered Martin Havelock the chance to go to Sandhurst and take a commission, Val had had to admit his true identity. It had then become clear to him that Max Beecham had never been approached by Julia on his behalf, nor had he heard of the Chartfield scandal. His alias had been unneccessary. Giving as his reason for it Sir Gilliard's vow to prevent him from joining the cavalry, Val had won Max Beecham's silence on his false enlistment – a court martial offence – and a promise to give him commissioned rank in the field if Val proved himself deserving of it in battle. Even as a sergeant, Martin Havelock could not forget his right as an Ashleigh to be an officer, nor could he forgive Julia Grieves for robbing him of that right. As a result, he viewed the entire female sex with cynicism and deep mistrust.

Glancing over his shoulder to check that all was well with his men, Val's thoughts returned to a more welcome subject. His ancestors had fought in wars all over the world, and he had been inspired from childhood by their exploits. He longed to emulate them, but had never imagined the kind of situation that politicians were creating here in South Africa. Daydreams had invariably had him facing hordes of fanatical natives, or the disciplined ranks of crack European troops. There was a brand of glory in that concept but, in Val's eyes, the Boers did not constitute an acceptable enemy. They had no professional army as such; they lived alongside settlers from many nations. How did a soldier distinguish an enemy when he was surrounded by friends? How did he challenge and fight him under such conditions? For decades the British had conducted their wars in the lands of their foes, but South Africa was peopled by many races with whom Britain had no dispute. Val was uneasy about the notion of loosing his professional aggression against civilians; of charging, with his nine-foot lance, men who farmed the land and lived by the word of God. Many of the 57th Lancers shared that unease.

They reached the perimeter and turned up the track leading to the stores. Half-way along it those men handling the remounts branched to the right, heading for the horse lines. Val went on with the waggon to hand over the mailbags. They often contained official communiqués or items of value, so he must sign a guarantee that the sacks which had travelled up from Durban under armed guard had been in his sight from the moment he had received them. Once this had been done, he mounted Samson and headed for the horse lines. So keen was he to claim for his own troop two he had judged the best of the twelve remounts, he defied regulations and rode at a speed that sent dust rising to the open windows. Cries of protest from inside merely made him grin. He had cursed sergeants in *his* days as a trooper.

Almost leaping from his saddle, Val tossed the bridle to a soldier and crossed to where the Sergeant Roughrider was squatting beside one of the animals he wanted. The man glanced up and smiled.

'I thought you'd be here like a shot. I know what you're after.'

Val squatted beside him. 'As I collected them, I'm entitled to first choice. This is one.' He nodded to the left. 'That's the other.'

The sergeant shook his head. 'It's up to the officers to choose which they want, not sergeants with too much cheek. Mr Pickering is coming to look them over shortly.'

'He doesn't know a horse's head from its arse,' Val claimed in disgust.

'Watch that, young Havelock. It's well known you have it in for a certain subaltern who had you consigned to the cells for twenty-eight days last year, but it's a wise man who keeps a still tongue in his head. You have more to lose now. He could break you to the ranks.'

Val was engrossed in studying the animals which were the major passion of his life. The man's warning went over his head. Running his hands over the glossy flanks of the chestnut gelding, he thrilled to the feel of muscles beneath its warm coat and the smell of straw and sweat which clung to it. He was a skilled horseman, one of the best in the regiment, and was at his happiest on or with the beasts with whom he felt as one. He wanted this one badly; wanted it for men who liked and trusted him. The other gelding he could bear to lose, but this creature was a beauty.

He straightened and went to gaze into intelligent brown eyes, presently betraying confusion. 'It's all right, boy,' he said softly, stroking the animal's cheeks with his square brown hand. 'You're with friends. Steady, *steady*! No more travelling, no more rattling rail trucks. A few days for you to rest and get used to this place, then you and I will explore the great paradise you can see stretching away into the distance.'

The Riding Master came alongside him, his thin, dark-moustached face showing exasperation. 'Never give up, do you, Havelock!'

'It's the only way to secure what one wants,' said Val turning and saluting Lieutenant Tomms.

'I heard you had gone to meet the train today. You had no ulterior motive in volunteering for the duty, I suppose.'

'You malign me,' he cried in mock protest. 'I didn't volunteer.'

Tomms grinned. 'My mistake. You invariably do when the duty concerns horses. Well, have you sized them up?'

The three men talked for a while about the qualities of the beasts they had been sent, agreeing that 'whalers' would have been preferable. When Val rode back to his quarters he had persuaded the Riding Master to ask Colonel Beecham to request some of the Australian animals. He might manage a miracle. All that Val could hope for otherwise was that his own troop captain would select the chestnut gelding before someone else did.

His servant brought him a cup of tea in the single-storey block he shared with three other sergeants, and he stretched out on his bed for half an hour before going to supervize evening 'stables'. It was a routine he loved and when it was time for dinner he reflected on his present situation as he washed and dressed in mess kit.

Life was full and satisfying. His longing for officer status was tempered by the knowledge that his forced enlistment in the ranks had enabled him to learn his profession most thoroughly. The nine months he had spent as a trooper had taught him an appreciation of the men he hoped one day to lead as their commander. He had suffered the rigours of day-to-day life, and learned the difference made to it by good or bad officers. An invaluable experience. After a deeply hostile initiation, Val had been accepted by his rough and ready companions. They had quickly made him their hero after he led the rescue of their troop horses from a burning stable. In a cavalry regiment, any champion of the regimental animals was regarded a hero. In return, Val had grown to like and understand men from backgrounds vastly different from his own. As their sergeant, he still earned their respect, and returned it. He knew it would be the same when he eventually gained the commission he so wanted.

As he brushed his thick blond hair into place his hand stilled. He no longer looked a schoolboy. His face had grown firmer and regained the air of confidence Julia had banished. Not yet twenty-one, he nevertheless looked sufficiently responsible to hold his present rank. His moustache had now thickened enough to silence tormenting on infant whiskers which had not grown swiftly enough. It made him look older than his years, which pleased him. All in all, life was good. The Ghost Lancers provided all he wanted; the regiment was his kind of world. His spirits soared at the sound of bugles on still air, the laughter and banter of soldiers around a camp fire, the roared commands that turned six hundred individuals into a single, highly efficient force. All this was in his Ashleigh blood.

Many of the men found their present posting unbearably boring despite Max Beecham's efforts to create diversions which involved the residents of Mariensberg. There had been football and cricket matches, field entertainments, picnics, fêtes and parties, but those men with wives and children in England, and those who had no interest in sport, found time hanging heavily in this tiny garrison.

Val was in his element, however. An avid cricketer, he could always get together enough volunteers for a game. He had learned to play football quite well. Rugby was his first love but that was the sport of officers and would have to wait a while. Each morning and evening he could be found running around the perimeter to keep fit, and his off-duty hours were spent riding the veld with his friends from the town. Being a troop-sergeant fulfilled his inborn military talent, and the company of others who could talk for hours on martial subjects completed his contentment. He had always got on famously with his fellows; it was with females that he invariably came to grief. Thank God there were none in the 57th Lancers!

When Val emerged from his quarters in the early evening glow he saw the error of that heartfelt belief. Coming towards him from the direction of the horse-lines on a tall roan mare was a thin, red-haired girl dressed in a green riding-habit. His heart sank at the sight of his colonel's daughter. Vivienne Beecham was a thorn in his side; had been since his first days with the regiment. It was her persistent interest in him that had led her father to demand his true identity last Christmas. She was an impossibly unconventional girl determined to force her company on someone so obviously from her own social class. Val was angered by her attempts to trap him into revealing the truth about his background, and by her refusal to recognize the barrier of military rank which made their friendship unacceptable. She had resolutely pursued it when he was a trooper. Now he had gained swift promotion, there was no stopping her.

The sky behind the girl was changing from orange to a vivid yellow shot with silver streaks. The light dazzled him so that he could not tell whether or not she had recognized him until they drew level on the path leading to the Sergeants' Mess.

She greeted him in unusually subdued manner. 'Hallo, Havelock.'

'Good evening, Miss Beecham.'

She turned Dinah across his path as he would have walked on. 'Why do you consistently refuse to call me Vivienne?'

'Probably for the same reason you refuse to call me

Sergeant Havelock,' he said, feeling irritation rise as he studied her freckled face.

'You know why. The first time we met you told me your name was Havelock. That's how I always think of you.'

'I always think of you as Miss Beecham.'

She sighed. 'Oh dear, you are in one of your truculent moods.'

'I am on my way to dinner,' he told her firmly. 'Shouldn't you be heading home for yours?'

Undergoing one of her swift changes of mood she held out her arms, saying, 'Help me down. I have something to tell you.'

He had no intention of doing as she commanded. Once standing beside him she would have him trapped. 'Tell me from there. It will save time.'

Vivienne raised her leg over the pommel and prepared to jump. Resigned to the inevitable, Val put up his hands to steady her descent then, when she was standing before him, stepped back to put greater distance between them. She seemed uncharacteristically reluctant to impart her news, so he had to prompt her.

'Well, what have you to tell me?'

'I've just been to the horse-lines. Father sent me to choose for myself one of the remounts you brought in today.'

He then understood her hesitation. Words burst from him in accusation. 'You've taken the chestnut.'

'I knew you'd be angry. They told me you wanted him.'

'I am, and I did,' he retaliated heatedly. 'Those animals were shipped out for the regiment, not for you to use for morning calls around Mariensberg. You can't have him!'

'I can, and I will,' she flashed back. 'You have no control over what I do.'

'If I had you would have been shipped home long ago.'

A stormy silence ensued for some moments, then she said heavily, 'If you were not always so prickly you'd give me time to explain the things I do.'

'The only explanation of this is that I've lost a splendid beast due to the colonel's daughter's desire to show off to the residents of Mariensberg.'

'It is *not* the only explanation. If you'll remove that mulish expression and walk with me to the perimeter gate, as a proper escort for the colonel's daughter, I promise you'll be pleased by what I have to say.'

Val hesitated. They were very near the Sergeants' Mess. Men were beginning to arrive for dinner. If he simply walked away from her, there was no knowing what she might do to cause a scene. To remain where they were would mean that their conversation would be overheard and speculated on. He had no choice but to do as she wished, but he made clear his mood by taking Dinah's bridle and leading the mare into the growing dusk at a pace dictated by his anger. The black orderlies were already out lighting wicks in the saucers of tallow at each corner of the huts. Darkness came swiftly in this land of brief twilights. If no moon brightened the night it was pitch black only a few yards from the perimeter. Val had no desire to be forced to escort Vivienne all the way to the house in town rented by her father.

'Must you go so fast?' she complained from several feet behind him. When he gave no response, she said, 'I have Dinah for making morning calls . . . and I would *never* show off to the people of Mariensberg. So many of them are my friend.' When he still would not relent, she spoke again into the silence. 'Father intends to replace the chestnut with one of his personal chargers. I think it will be Riptide.' She walked on, struggling to match the fast pace he deliberately maintained. 'If it is, I'll persuade him to give the stallion to A Troop. You'd like that, wouldn't you?'

As usual, she had taken him unawares. Riptide was a

splendid animal. He was getting on in years but had seen battle twice and was reputedly very steady under fire. Of course he would like the stallion for his troop.

'Aren't you going to answer?'

'You haven't told me everything yet,' he returned over his shoulder. 'What are you intending to do with the chestnut?'

'Father believes Mama and I should each have a reliable spare mount. You see, with the official mail you brought in today there was a notice sent out to every garrison. Regiments in India and at home are being mobilized. Troopships are preparing for the transportation here of ten thousand troop reinforcements, large numbers of rifles and ammunition, batteries of field guns and enough supplies to maintain an army for months. Father says war is now inevitable. There has never been such a massive movement of men and stores, especially over a great distance, and the Government would hardly make such a decision then settle the dispute without a shot being fired. And it cannot possibly be merely a show of strength,' she went on rather breathlessly, as he slowed his energetic pace. 'The cost of such an operation is too great for it to be mere bluff. Besides, prestige is at stake. We would look foolish if we paraded a vast army then sent it home again.'

Stopping beside him, the long skirt of her green habit still held free of the dust, she gave him a frank look. 'The railways are acutely vulnerable to attack – we all know that – so the only means of transport might be a pair of good horses. Mama has Velvet and Desirée. I have only Dinah. Now do you see why I need the chestnut?'

Val hardly heard her last words. The news she had related sent excitement through him and took his full attention. 'Is this true? They really are shipping out that number of troops with sufficient stores?'

'The details will be public knowledge by morning. Father would not have spoken of it openly if it was secret information. He called a meeting of all officers just before I left. The news is intended to boost the morale of our troops and lower that of the Boers.'

Val was beset with conflicting emotions. War would bring him his greatest opportunity to regain Ashleigh honour, yet he was not keen on a conflict of this nature. Having been a passionate sportsman all his young life, he was reluctant to take on an opponent ill-equipped for the contest.

'I suppose you are thrilled by the news?'

Vivienne's face swam back into focus, banishing his visions of combat. 'Naturally.'

'I'm not.'

'You're a girl. You wouldn't be.' He frowned in concentration. 'Let us suppose they sail by the end of this month. It will take them three weeks to reach the Cape, possibly another four days up to Durban. Allow time to send them out to all garrisons by special trains – I have no notion how long that would take – and it seems likely that we shall be ready to challenge the Boers by November.'

She looked dismayed. 'In less than two months? I hadn't expected it to be so soon.'

'It's still a long way off and summer will be well advanced. We missed the worst of it last year, but the tail end was hot enough. The doctor's son warned me that temperatures rise to over a hundred and the rivers dry up in high summer. It will make long marches difficult, especially for the horses. God knows where we shall get sufficient fodder for them at that time of year.'

He was away on a flight of speculation, but her words brought him back to earth. 'You speak as if you'll be responsible for the whole regiment. All sergeants will have to concern themselves with is keeping their troopers under control.'

Anger flared in him. She took delight in reminding him that his behaviour did not match his rank. If he could only reveal the truth, she would be mortified by her high-handed treatment of a grandson of General Sir Gilliard Ashleigh.

'It's getting dark,' he told her frostily. 'You had better hurry or night will overtake you before you reach the town.' Stooping, he linked his hands to form a foothold to help her mount. When she made no move, he glanced up to discover a surprisingly soft expression on her plain face.

'I wasn't trying to belittle you, silly. I was attempting to console myself with the thought that you won't hold command in the coming days.'

He straightened. 'Sergeants also have to concern themselves with fighting the enemy at the head of their troopers, Miss Beecham.'

She moved towards him. 'Don't be angry, Havelock. I hate it when you grow haughty and unapproachable.'

Always out of his depth when she adopted this coaxing manner, he instinctively veered away from intimacy. 'I suppose your father will send you and Mrs Beecham to the rear well before November.'

'Of course not.'

'Then why the need for the chestnut?'

'To follow the regiment's triumphant advance.'

He frowned. 'Does you father approve of that?'

She smiled. 'He knows Mama. She is very determined on matters of that nature.'

Val could not believe Max Beecham would allow himself to be dictated to by a pair of females, for Vivienne was as determined as her mother. Then he recalled his own submission to a strong-willed woman and accepted that his commanding officer might well bow to superior numbers. He attempted to bring the meeting to an end on that thought.

'I *am* grateful for the information about reinforcements, and so on. Thank you for telling me.'

'I did so because you are my special friend, although

you always fight the fact. I do wish you wouldn't. It's very lonely being a colonel's daughter.'

'Nonsense,' he said awkwardly, 'you have all the officers dancing attendance on you.'

'Only because they hope for advancement. None of them is a real friend. The married ones are meticulous in their treatment of me for fear of endangering their chances for promotion; the single ones see me as someone who could impress upon father their true worth. Several of the subalterns even have hopes of an advantageous marriage . . . including Audley Pickering,' she added slyly.

Mention of Val's prime enemy provoked his heated response. 'You surely don't believe that! With his pedigree he has no need to court you in the hope of advancement.' Seeing her expression, he felt his colour rise. 'I'm sorry. That sounded very ill mannered.'

'Yes, it did.'

'I simply meant . . .'

'I know what you meant. I was only teasing you. He is an insufferable prig and a useless member of the regiment, but he will rise to high rank on the strength of his royal connections alone.'

'Not if I have my way,' Val said grimly. 'When I bring him down it will be with as painful a bump as I can contrive.'

'Be careful, he has many influential friends.'

'So have I,' he said without thinking.

'Other former stable-boys like yourself?' she asked, taunting him with the lies he had once told her about his background.

Recognizing the trap into which he had fallen, Val changed the subject. 'Your mother will be growing anxious over you, and my dinner is waiting.'

Her glance was warm and intimate. 'That's exactly why you're my special friend. You are not in the least concerned with my influence over your colonel, so you say what you choose to me. It can be infuriating, but it's curiously refreshing after so much flattery from the officers.'

This subtle reminder that he was not one of them led him once more to offer his linked hands as an aid to mounting. She put her small boot into them and was soon in the saddle looking down at him.

'I'm so pleased that you happened to come from your quarters as I was passing, so that I had the chance to explain about the chestnut. Thank you for walking to the gate with me. We don't meet very often, so I have to make the most of the times that we do.'

He was not prepared to respond to that, and was about to walk away when she suddenly bent to touch his cheek with a swift kiss. '*Dearest* Havelock, please promise not to get yourself killed in this war you want so badly.'

She was off, leaving him to watch with a sense of shock because she had been in tears as she turned away. Damn the girl! He never knew what to make of her, but of one thing he was certain: it was more than friendship she wanted from him.

The first person Val encountered on entering the Mess was Toby Robbins, another sergeant who was only a year or two older than himself. They had become friends due to a shared interest in team games and a mutual reluctance for female company. Toby had been jilted at the altar by a bride who did not relish being deserted for four years by a soldier husband. He had sailed with hatred in his heart, and saw all women as the one who had let him down. An educated young man who took his profession seriously, Toby accepted Val's lies about his past and never pushed him for further details even when the occasional revealing remark slipped past his guard.

'There you are at last,' Toby greeted, waving a tankard of ale in Val's direction. 'I'm two up on you already. Turner, ale for Sergeant Havelock, at the double!'

Val crossed to him eagerly. This was his environment. He was happy and comfortable in Toby's company, and he could not wait to break his news to those gathered there. He was initially forestalled by the arrival of a pint of ale, which he drank in almost a single draught. It made him feel even more elated, so that he returned laughing retorts to comments about a certain sergeant trying to nab the best remounts for himself.

'I'm the only one here who knows decent horseflesh when he sees it. Besides, I brought them in and earned the privilege of first choice. A Troop deserves the best. With war only two months off, a fellow has to look after his men.'

'Nah,' said a senior sergeant as tough as they came. 'The Boers would never get themselves into that situation because of some damn fool politicians. We'd make mince-meat of them, and they know it. A spade's no defence against a lance.'

Uneasiness pierced Val's thoughts momentarily, but he was too eager to make his announcement. 'Nor is it a defence against field artillery and ten thousand reinforce-ments arriving from home and India very shortly.'

'Eh?' queried a quiet man named Hobson. 'What are you talking about, young Havelock?'

'Notice came in with the mail. Troop-ships are stand-ing by to bring men, supplies and field-pieces. It's war without a doubt, and it's not difficult to estimate when it will start.'

Men gathered round to bombard him with questions, none of which asked how a sergeant knew the text of a notice sent to their colonel who had not yet made it public. The discussion lasted throughout an excellent dinner guaranteed to satisfy the largest appetite. Val did justice to it, then returned to the bar for more ale with four of the junior sergeants. He had cultivated a liking for the drink favoured by the rank and file, and could now down a great deal of it without having to be carried to his quarters. He did so this evening and was soon in the thick of a rowdy argument on how quickly they would wrest from the Boers control of the Transvaal and the Orange Free State.

'If we call their bluff in November, we'll be in Johannesburg and Pretoria by Christmas,' claimed Toby with alcoholic bravado.

'Don't be too sure,' Val warned. 'They have the advantage of knowing their own country, and how to move around it. Forbes maintains they have been preparing for months to take us on. He says he was told by a reliable source that arms have been arriving from Germany, France and Ireland so that there is now a veritable arsenal of weapons ready for them to use.'

'I heard that story, Havelock,' sneered a sandy-haired former boxer. 'The Boers have put it out to scare us. There's no truth in it.'

'It'd take more than that to scare the 57th, eh lads?' boomed one of their members well on the way to intoxication.

So the evening passed until the Mess began to empty. Toby and Val lived in adjacent rooms, and were heading for them when Val noticed a letter lying on the table by the door.

'Forgot to tell you about it, Martin,' mumbled Toby. 'It's for you. That writing looks like a girl's, you old slyboots!'

The handwriting was that of his sister Charlotte. Val picked up the envelope with a sensation of dread. There could be only one reason why she should write to him after all this time. Grandfather was dead! Waves of regret washed over him. That grand old man would never witness the redemption he had been promised, would not learn of Val's valiant attempt to regain the respect of his family and honour the name of Ashleigh. He might have to do it as Martin Havelock, but he would still be upholding an inbred obligation to live up to the memory of his brother Vorne. Sir Gilliard would surely have recognized that and been mollified.

Val tore open the envelope and began to read. In growing confusion he scanned the three pages. It appeared to be no more than a friendly letter from the sister with whom he had often argued and who was almost as unforgiving as Sir Gilliard. He could not make head or tail of it. She wrote as if nothing had happened between himself and his family, as if he had never been sacked from Chartfield. The tone of the letter was too generous for the Charlotte he knew, yet it was certainly her handwriting. There seemed to be no reason for sending it other than to tell him news of Knightshill and the family.

Val already knew Vere was in Italy; there had been a letter from him a month ago after he had met up with Margaret. He also knew Kate had been ill – Margaret had written, too – but he had not realized how ill. Poor little girl! He could not imagine a silent Kate. She had always let her tongue run away with her. It *was* news to him that the Nicolardis were sailing for South America and leaving Kate with Charlotte. His sister wrote that Grandfather had been angry initially when she arrived with Kate, but had bowed to the inevitable because he could not refuse his great-granddaughter a home. The letter ended on the same loving note used throughout by wishing him well and asking him to reply when he found the time. Totally mystified, he was brought back from his thoughts by Toby.

'Your expression suggests that you've lost a shilling and found a sixpence.'

He looked up. 'That's a good description of how I feel. I'm either drunk or I need to sleep off the effects of today's surprises. Come on, let's turn in.'

Sleep did not come immediately. Val's head spun with all manner of thoughts as he stared at the ceiling washed by moonlight. The letter from Charlotte revived memories of Knightshill in a way those from Vere and Margaret had not. His brother and elder sister were away from home so their news was of other countries and their exploits there.

The unexpected olive branch from a sister who had been swift to condemn even his mildest indiscretion unsettled him. He saw his home so clearly and was startled to recognize an ache of homesickness. That brief moment during which he had believed his grandfather was dead remained with him. If the old man went before he had proved himself a worthy successor to the hero who had been lost outside Khartoum, all he did from then on would surely be empty of glory.

Time was against him. Sir Gilliard was eighty-nine and his weakening heart had already once caused him to collapse. Rolling from his bed, Val stepped across to the window to gaze out at the moonwashed veld. He must put aside any scruples he might have about an unequal foe. When this conflict began he would fight the Boers as a true Ashleigh, sparing no one, least of all himself.

Two weeks later the 57th Lancers received orders to move north to Ellinsdorp beside the Orange River, where a consignment of tents would be sent up to the nearest railway halt to await their arrival. The Mariensberg outstation was to be taken over by a regiment coming from India. Colonel Beecham was advised to buy as many provisions as possible to take with him on the three-day march. Ellinsdorp apparently had few, and supplies from Cape Town were likely to be late due to preparations to receive an influx of additional troops. The orders concluded with the notice that khaki uniforms were to be issued as soon as they were available to all British regiments already in South Africa. This news brought war a step nearer. The men of the 57th were elated. They longed for action. They also welcomed the move from an outstation where there was little to do and where time dragged. Val was eager to experience the mysteries of full-scale battle, which his forbears had known and endured. The advance towards Boer territory was the answer to his prayers. With his own equipment packed, he went to A Troop lines to see how his men were faring. It was an unusually warm afternoon for September and there were a few grumbles about how stifling it was indoors. Val walked between the two rows of beds, as hot as anyone in his serge uniform, but his spirits were too high to be dampened by discomfort.

'Come on, lads, you'll have to get used to temperatures higher than this,' he said cheerfully. 'When summer comes you'll know what heat really is.'

'You're a proper Job's comforter, Sarge,' commented the troop pessimist. 'We'll be dead before summer comes. I heard as how they've got a good arsenal of guns hid in the heart of one of them flat-topped hills, and there's more'n five thousand veld ponies in a corral in Johannesburg.'

Val stopped beside the man's bed, laughing. 'If you believe that, Potts, you'll believe anything. In Johannesburg they are too busy digging up gold to look after five thousand horses, and if you had ever ridden to the top of a *kopje*, as I have, you would know they don't have hollow centres in which to hide field artillery.'

'I 'eard it was *six* thahsand 'orses and 'eavy cannons used by the Rooshans at Sebastopol,' said a wiry man named Jakes.

Several others gave details of the versions they had been told, then the comedian of the troop said solemnly, 'I can tell you all wot was told ter me by Kruger, personal like. They got twenty-seven spades, eighteen pitchforks, thirty-nine milking-stools and five 'undred moo-cows. It's the troof, honest.'

By the time the laughter died down, Val had reached the end bed covered with the kit of a giant named Deadman. As rough as they come, the man nevertheless had a curious bond of comradeship with someone he had once cruelly persecuted for being too gentlemanly. During the stable fire last November, Val and Deadman had between them saved most of the troop horses. Having been pulled away from danger by Val just before the building collapsed, the massive trooper would now defend with his life the young man who had become his sergeant.

Val smiled at him. 'I suppose you have been taking bets on all these ridiculous stories and will rake in a fortune.'

The ugly features registered innocence. 'Wouldn't do nuffink like that. Get meself on a charge for that, I could.'

'I'm glad you realize it.' Val's smile broadened. 'Just ensure that you collect your winnings when I'm not around.'

After five more minutes of light-hearted banter with his former barrack room fellows, Val walked out into the sunshine wondering if there really was any truth in the stories circulating the area. He asked Jonathan Forbes during a farewell dinner at his home that evening, but the doctor's son would not commit himself to more than a guess that there might be some substance in the rumours. Val was sorry to say goodbye to the Forbes family, and to several others who had made him welcome in their homes. They all wished him well and vowed he would be back round their tables to celebrate Christmas or, certainly, to herald in the twentieth century.

The regiment left Mariensberg at first light. They had no maps of the route so had to rely on a civilian guide who knew the terrain between the town and Ellinsdorp. It was a cumbersome procession that set out across rough veld, where giant anthills and stunted bushes erupted like blemishes on harsh skin. The distant hills were further off than they looked. These would be encountered on their second day's march. Beyond that the nature of the country was unknown, although the guide assured them that it would be easy going all the way. They were to discover that what a man of South Africa regarded as easy going was considered arduous by soldiers in thick uniforms whose horses were burdened with their weapons and all the necessities for bivouacking.

The first day's march was long because the overnight halt must be made near drinking water for the animals. There were almost two thousand. Aside from six hundred troop horses, there were a number of remounts, several hundred pack mules, and teams of oxen that pulled the waggons. It was always a tricky business trying to control very thirsty animals. The narrow stream soon darkened and grew cloudy as hooves tramped through it in their thousands. Everyone was weary and ready for a meal, but it took time to light fires and prepare food which had inadvertently been loaded in the rear waggon. Stars were starting to show in the translucent blue-grey sky overhead before stomachs were full, and the quietness which always fell when men relaxed aching limbs and faced the coming night on a blanket beneath the sky descended on soldiers and animals alike.

Val drank ale seated on the ground beside Toby in companionable silence. He knew a sense of destiny awaiting him and was sobered by it. How would it feel to settle thus, when there were men nearby determined to put an end to one's life? He gazed around at the silvered shadows and told himself there would soon be figures creeping silently through the moonlight intent on killing. What was it like to run a lance through a human body instead of straw? Why did he suddenly feel very alone surrounded by an entire regiment?

'Are you thinking what I'm thinking?' asked Toby quietly.

Val continued to look at the emptiness beyond. 'Quite possibly.'

'It's a funny sort of sensation, isn't it?'

'Mmm,' agreed Val, lost in it. Then, after a short silence, he said, 'I know a man who was an artist; a gentle, laughing person who loved beautiful things and to whom killing must have seemed utterly repugnant. He had been an invalid all his life and none of us expected him to survive beyond thirty.'

'So what about him?' asked Toby.

'He joined Kitchener's army in the Sudan, fought at Atbara and Omdurman, then returned home to become an artist again having survived everything the desert produced.'

Toby drained his tin cup and wiped his lips with the back of his hand. 'Seems a funny thing for him to have done?'

'Mmm, wasn't it.'

'Well, why did he?'

Val sighed. 'For the sake of a girl.'

'Ha! Might have known.'

'I was just thinking that if *he* could do it, so can I.'

'Ah, I was wondering about the point of the story.' Toby lay back on his blanket and belched loudly. Val was still sitting up when his friend asked a few minutes later, 'Who is he, this artist fellow?'

'Vere Ashleigh.'

'Never heard of him,' said Toby, and soon fell asleep.

The second day's march took them up to the hills. To go around them meant a detour of many miles and the guide assured Max Beecham that there were easy tracks which would take them over the ridge to a pleasant stretch beyond. The 57th had their first real taste of the challenge South Africa offered strangers. The 'easy' tracks presented problems to heavy cavalry chargers and proved impossible for ox-waggons to negotiate. Steep paths wound tortuously upward. They were so narrow, in parts, they allowed only single files through cuttings bordered by giant spiky aloes, and the stony surface made progress slow. On the descent, animals frequently slid on the loose shale and caused temporary panic by cannoning into those ahead. In every man's mind was the sobering thought of crossing such hills with an enemy in the vicinity; in every man's mind was repugnance for such terrain. Cavalrymen charged at the foe, lances dipped, and the combined thunder of two and a half thousand hooves added to the awesome sight of grim expressions above a mass of wickedly sharp points were guaranteed to instill terror. Crossing hills like this would put them at the mercy of an enemy with every advantage. They were extremely unhappy.

Colonel Beecham had sent the waggons on the long route around the hills, which meant the men would have to wait for a meal until they arrived. There would be ample water from the stream and that was more essential than food. He was beginning to question the loyalties of his guide, but had to use him because there was no other. It was coming home to them all that they would have two enemies in the coming conflict – the Boers, and the country they had claimed as their Promised Land.

The waggons rolled in long after the troops had fallen asleep. Cooks set about preparing a double-sized breakfast instead, but no sooner had fires been lit and pots hung over them on the tripods than it began to rain. It cascaded down to put out the fires and waken the sleepers, who could do no more than crouch beneath their cloaks until dawn brought pale sunshine. Soaked to the skin, hungry, and facing another long march, the men of the 57th wore doleful expressions as they ate thick tinned-meat sandwiches washed down with water from the stream.

'If this is peacetime in Sarth Afreeka, Gawd 'elp us when war comes,' was an oft-heard sentiment as the men saddled their wet horses and prepared to move off.

Val was thoughtful as he rode beside Second-Lieutenant Manning at the head of A Troop. He was still hungry and felt uncomfortable in his wet uniform. He was also beginning to amend his assessment of the coming conflict, which he had likened to a sporting contest. The other side might well be inexperienced and ill equipped, but the British could find themselves batting with the sun full in their eyes on an unfamiliar pitch full of lumps and dips. It might not be easy for him to earn the commission Max Beecham had promised him. The training he had received, the inborn warrior instincts, the advice on manoeuvres and tactics his family had given him during his childhood years might well be of little use to him in the days ahead.

During that final long ride over terrain as flat and dry as a desert, Val tried to find optimism. Time was passing; Sir Gilliard was an old man. If no opportunity to be a hero in this war presented itself he might never regain his grandfather's recognition and blessing.

'Good God!' exclaimed the young subaltern beside him, just as the sun was starting to go down. 'That surely can't be Ellinsdorp.'

Val glanced up to see no more than a dozen tin-roofed dwellings along a shallow river bank. At the end was one with a bell-tower which marked it as the inevitable church. 'That can't be all, sir,' he said with conviction. 'They wouldn't send us to defend a cluster of native huts occupied by the black people of the town. The main part of Ellinsdorp must be a little further on.'

He was wrong. Their new garrison was a mere hamlet containing eight white families, a handful of black workers, a store and a church. What was more, the river here was no more than a trickle of water on the stony bed.

5

WHILE VERE WAS voyaging down the east coast of the African continent, the British were presented with an ultimatum demanding withdrawal of their troops from the borders of Transvaal and the Orange Free State, both areas under Boer jurisdiction. It also demanded the return of all reinforcements newly arrived or aboard troopships bound for South Africa. This move was designed to instigate the war for which Boers had been secretly preparing throughout their winter months.

It was October. Spring weather would be perfect for men of the country to take on those unused to soaring temperatures in vast, unmapped areas offering little or no shade. British military horses lacked the stamina of veld ponies, so mounted troops would be less effective in this terrain. British guns were impressive, but unsuitable for hauling great distances across a country boasting few roads and scored by rivers with bridges that would be difficult to defend. The fords, known locally as *drifts*, could be treacherous when rivers rose during sudden storms. Roads which wound between flat-topped hills whose slopes were covered by tall spiky aloes turned to mud when it rained. A lone horseman, even a small group on lightweight beasts, could travel on them with care. Battalions of infantry and cavalry, accompanied by heavy cannon and commissariat waggons forming long columns, would flounder in the mire. Riflemen hiding in surrounding hills would be able to pick them off with ease. Yes, the God-fearing Boer pioneers knew

October was the perfect time to confront their hated neighbours.

The British had no alternative but to refuse the ultimatum, playing the hand their enemies wanted. Within two weeks the British public was stunned by news that the so-called 'farmer army' had driven Queen Victoria's soldiers from their borders and held them under seige in the garrisons of Mafeking, Kimberley and Ladysmith. Not only was this a humiliating reverse for one of the best armies in the world, it rendered ineffective many thousands of crack troops and left the British states of Natal and Cape Colony only thinly defended. Reinforcements were still arriving and relief of the beleaguered garrisons could not be organized until regiments and stores were ready to be moved from dock areas.

As Boers surrounding the three towns gave no immediate sign of intending to overrun and capture them, and as the commanders of each invested garrison signalled assurance of adequate supplies, it seemed reasonable enough to take time over the formation of columns which would march across country to lift the sieges and rout the enemy. Generals estimated that it would take only a week or so to set free regiments presently cooped up in settlements which were little more than clusters of tin-roofed huts bordering dust roads. Once the Boers faced the massive numbers which would then oppose them, the war would be over swiftly. Britain would be celebrating final settlement of this gold and diamond dominion when she heralded in the new century, the generals assured the Government and their officers. The officers passed the message to their men and everyone relaxed.

When Vere's ship approached Durban he was on deck, anxious for his first sight of the port. After the sweltering heat of a voyage through the Red Sea, along the fever coast and down past Zanzibar, he found the balmy pre-dawn air wonderfully refreshing. His restlessness had been replaced by energy waiting to be released. News he had heard *en route* confirmed the wisdom of his decision to head south from Cairo: a cable from *The Illustrated Magazine* received at Zanzibar told him a contract for all his war sketches would be drawn up ready by their representative in Durban.

Vere gazed shoreward as he leaned on the rail, straining his eyes as the sky began to lighten. A sudden inexplicable sensation of coming excitement touched him as he heard the engines slow, and it quickly consumed him. He had experienced a similar, curious premonition once before in the Sudan. There, it had taken the form of violent reluctance to go ashore to visit Vorne's grave. On reaching the spot he had found it desecrated, the bones scattered among those of his brother's enemies. The sense of foreboding had been fully justified. Today it was quite the reverse. He was overwhelmed by eagerness to set foot on this tip of Africa which had beckoned his artistic soul.

As Durban slowly materialized in the gilded dawn, his sense of excitement doubled. A city of considerable size with impressive colonial-style buildings, highlighted by a cloudless aquamarine sky, and fronted by commercial docks, it was a pleasing sight as the ship stood-to a short distance off. Due to the late arrival of a troop-ship still alongside the jetty, disembarkation could not take place until early afternoon, so Vere returned to the deck after luncheon to watch the milling confusion of khaki-clad troops, black labourers off-loading stores and artillery, and waggons criss-crossing ceaselessly as they set off burdened and returned empty. It was a familiar sight to a man who had lived as a fighting soldier for almost two years, and his sense of still being a part of it surprised Vere.

When the gangplank was eventually lowered, he went ashore with the thought that he was once more setting foot on a land one of his brothers had trodden before him. Val had been here for almost nine months with the 57th Lancers. Vowing to seek out the regiment as soon as possible, Vere knew it would be good to meet up with the boy he had last seen at Chartfield School before leaving for Cairo. He had then given Val the responsibilities of being Sir Gilliard's heir to Knightshill in the belief that the desert would cover his own bones as it did Vorne's. Now he had resumed the rôle that was his by right of birth, it was only fair to apologize to his young brother.

Threading his way through the miltary mêlée, Vere stopped to question several young officers grouped beside a laden waggon. Two had arrived only that day and could be of no help. A third had been in Durban two months and knew something of the deployment of regiments, but he could not say where the 57th Lancers were at the moment.

'Everything happened so fast, we were all taken by surprise,' he explained above the noise of winches and irate commands. 'Most of our smaller garrisons were awaiting orders when the Boers swept across the borders and set three seiges. So far as I know, they could all still be awaiting them. Until we sort out this influx of men and equipment, no orders can be issued. Luckily our enemies seem happy enough to sit tight in the hills surrounding the besieged towns.' He turned away to instruct a waggon driver, then called out as Vere moved off. 'Try the Transport Office. Someone there might know where the Fifty-seventh is.'

Vere had a long wait before a carriage was free to take him to a hotel overlooking a deserted bay ringed by wild shrubs in flower. Their perfume hung on the early evening air, and the gentle aromatic shoreline was soft on the eye of someone who had gazed at endless sea for too many days, his only glimpses of land showing desolation beneath harsh, relentless sun. This southern area of the great African continent was green and benign.

Small wonder it was coveted by those who had settled here and brought civilization.

So charmed was Vere by this haven that he wandered paths within the hotel grounds to watch birds with the most glorious plumage and liquid song as they indulged in courtship antics. The artist in him longed to paint the exotic plants and shrubs, the aesthete was fired by the vivid shimmering feathers, the heady scent of blooms he could not identify, and by a strange sense of having come home to a place he had never before visited. He felt a strong harmony with his surroundings which had been absent in those Mediterranean countries that traditionally inspired artists. Curious contentment for a man seeking war.

Morning brought a continuation of Vere's mood. He walked for an hour, descending to the sands patterned by trails of tiny footprints left by yellow and buff birds who ran over the tideline searching for food. The tranquillity was enchanting enough to keep him from the breakfast table until it was almost too late. By mid-morning he was in a carriage heading for the centre of town, where the office of *The Illustrated Magazine* was sited. Broad streets were busy with parties of mounted troops and military waggons which mingled with the more elegant vehicles of residents making morning calls or transacting business. Soldiers whose rosy cheeks betrayed them as new arrivals from England, and others browned by the Indian sun, walked amidst ladies in pale muslins or silks and gentlemen wearing lightweight suits. There was an air of festivity rather than purpose, as if the war were merely a distant diversion to be discussed only when drawing-room conversation had palled. It almost made nonsense of the frenzied activity at the docks.

The tiny office of the magazine for which Vere would work was in a side street, next to a ramshackle store selling cheap, brightly coloured cloth by the yard. The stern, bewhiskered man who gave Vere a contract to read and sign treated him to an impassioned speech on the evils of war while he did so.

'I read that your kinsmen have lived by the sword for thirteen generations, Mr Ashleigh. To kill is a sin against the scriptures, yet your family parades it as a virtue.'

Vere glanced up at the face glowering with self-righteousness. Although he had never regarded soldiering as a sin, he had once deplored those who lauded the profession. Experience had honed his opinion on many things.

'All we parade as a virtue is sympathy for our fellows, sir. When I and my family see them being mercilessly massacred in the name of some madman's bid for power, we are prepared to defend them. Is that a sin?'

The man's eyes narrowed. 'Who is being massacred in the name of a madman here?'

Dropping the pen on to a desk stained by printer's ink, Vere got to his feet. 'I hope to God there will be no massacre. I have a close relative in the cavalry who is committed to serving Queen and country.'

'Pah!' came the explosive comment. 'He is serving the madman Cecil Rhodes, who aims to rule the whole African continent. Your queen is merely his pawn.'

Vere pocketed one copy of the contract and prepared to leave. 'Africa is a huge continent. I have just travelled the length of it. No man in his wildest ravings could believe in its entire conquest. Mr Rhodes is by no means mad, and he is a loyal subject of Queen Victoria, I assure you.' At the doorway he turned. 'You referred to her as *my* sovereign, which suggests that you are not her loyal subject, sir. I read that *your* kinfolk are God-fearing, peaceful farmers. Why, then, are they bombarding civilian residents in Ladysmith, Kimberley and Mafeking in an attempt to starve or frighten them into surrender, and parading *that* as a virtue? Good day to you.'

The mild shock of finding a Boer running the office of a patriotic British magazine brought home to Vere the uniqueness of a war where people continued to live side by side while their compatriots were killing each other. In the Sudan, Dervishes had slain anyone in their path and had, in turn, been slain on sight by their foes. The incident impressed upon Vere how integrated the two warring races here had become. It was tragic that the discovery of gold and diamonds might put an end to peaceful dual existence in this land of rich promise. Whatever the outcome of hostilities, it must create between neighbours a rift that would be difficult to heal.

The Transport Officer was not only disinclined to give his precious time to a civilian, he made it clear that a man waving at him a paper commissioning paintings of military activities was highly suspicious. Vere was advised to report to an address in town used as a temporary headquarters where he should ask for Captain Harmesworth. Telling the driver to head back to the main street of Durban, Vere settled in the carriage seat resigned to travelling to and fro all day. Last year he had been an active member of the army he portrayed in his pictures. He suspected that he might not be so willingly accepted by the military now. This was confirmed the moment he entered a large stone house with a façade of tall pillars and a balustrade depicting leaping antelope. A pink-faced subaltern glanced at Vere's card, but refused to take it through to his superior.

'We are at *war*, Mr Ashmead,' he said, still seated at his desk. 'Captain Harmesworth has no time to consider purchasing your paintings.'

'I have yet to create them, by courtesy of the military authorities,' Vere told him. 'And my name is Ash*leigh*.'

'Ah, I see,' said the young man in relief, finding a way to rid himself of this artist fellow. 'Why don't you come back when you have something to show us? The war will be over by then, and Captain Harmesworth will have more time.'

Used to this breed of rather pompous junior officer, Vere knew he would get nowhere until he spoke to

Harmesworth, or to someone else in authority. He was also aware that civilians were not welcomed by uniformed men conducting a war. Having been one he appreciated their point, so he walked to a chair giving a view of Harmesworth's door and settled down to wait. While he did so he took out his sketch-pad to record a scene he found interesting. The interior of this imposing entrance hall suggested a woman's touch. Walls washed in pale lilac bore several large canvases of interiors featuring ladies in silk gowns wonderfully conveyed by use of light and shade. The chair upon which he sat, and others dotted around the open area, had gilded legs with lilac and cream upholstery. The marbled staircase curved away from Vere's scope of vision, but the lower steps were enhanced by a carpet of rich dark green.

Whilst sketching the elegance marred by military intrusion, Vere grew aware that a man was standing beside the subaltern who had been watching him with covert suspicion. The pair were clearly discussing him, and it seemed likely that the captain was Harmesworth. Next minute, Vere recognized someone he had seen only once and then more than a year ago. Yet he remembered their meeting with clarity, and crossed to the desk with a smile.

'Had I known it was you I would have insisted on seeing you right away, Harmesworth,' he said warmly. 'Your name had slipped to the recesses of my mind.'

Having heard part of his junior's story, the fair-haired captain was clearly resistant to Vere's approach. 'Yours has done likewise, sir.'

Vere quoted the man's words to him on the jetty at Berber as they had both awaited a steamer rumoured to have been captured by the enemy who had slaughtered all passengers. '*Only a bally fool would wait here with just a sergeant if a boatload of Dervishes was about to arrive.*'

Harmesworth's brow furrowed as he studied Vere's

face. Then recollection dawned. 'You had a packet to send up to Wad Hamed in the military bag!'

'Sketches I had made of the terrain between there and Berber.'

Harmesworth glanced again at Vere's card, picking it up with growing interest. 'Didn't I ask if you were related to Vorne Ashleigh of the West Wilts?'

'That's right. I was prevented from answering at the time but, yes, I'm his brother.'

The subaltern rose, his pink cheeks deepening to red. 'I beg your pardon, sir. You spoke about paintings, so I had the impression that you were an artist.'

Vere felt sorry for the boy. He had only claimed brotherhood with a supposed hero in the hope of gaining Harmesworth's assistance. 'I *am* an artist, Mr . . .?' He glanced at the name-plate on the desk, 'Mr Frankham. I resigned my commission in January.' He turned back to the senior man. '*The Illustrated Magazine* has asked me to make a pictorial record of a war which will be vastly different from the one in which we both fought two years ago. I was hoping to learn from you where best to find the forward troops, in particular the Fifty-seventh Lancers. I have a cousin in the regiment.' That lie had to be told for the sake of 'Martin Havelock'.

Harmesworth's memory was working hard. 'Of course, you did those pictures that caused such a stir at home! My fiancée was terribly impressed, especially by that large one showing the released captives sitting beside the Nile with a gunboat in the background. Its poignancy brought tears, she told me.'

'Your fiancée clearly has a compassionate nature.'

'She is now my wife,' Harmesworth revealed with a grin. 'Her ship docked last month and we married a week later.'

'Congratulations,' said Vere, thinking of Sir Gilliard's tale of regimental marriages in China. He should have had this man as his heir.

'Have you plans for luncheon?' Harmesworth asked. 'If not, be our guest. I'm off home now. It's just a short walk away. Join me and we'll have a chat as we go along.'

Thanking God for that fleeting encounter in Berber, Vere accepted the invitation and went out into the bright day knowing his path would be eased by this chance reunion.

'The Fifty-seventh were at Ellinsdorp when war was declared,' Harmesworth said as they reached the bottom of the steps. 'The Boers moved so fast on Kimberley they were in danger of being encircled, so they were told to fall back and make a stand at Brookman's Bridge. I suppose they're still there waiting to be augmented by troops arriving almost daily. It's a nightmare, Ashleigh.' He grinned. 'A worse nightmare than wondering if the steamer *would* arrive filled with Dervishes.'

Vere grinned back. 'I also wondered that, at the time. If it had we would now be two piles of bleached bones.'

'There appears to be no real plan of campaign yet,' Harmesworth went on in more serious vein. 'Our commanders have an astonishing attitude of "tomorrow will do".'

'More haste, less speed, perhaps,' Vere suggested as they turned a corner leading to a line of grand houses with wrought-iron balconies.

'We have no knowledge of the damned terrain, that's half the problem. It's impossible to estimate how long it will take troops to march from camp to camp. Local guides give distances in the number of days' riding, which is scant assistance to heavily laden cavalry and even less to men on foot.'

'What about the railway?' asked Vere.

'The Boers keep blowing it up. It has its limitations.'

Once again Vere was reminded of Sir Gilliard, who did not approve of trains. Yes, Harmesworth should have been his heir, without doubt.

'They blow the track in a cutting, or where it runs close

beneath the hills, then lie hidden from view so that we are at every disadvantage trying to repair it. It's impossible to defend the whole damned line, and they dash from spot to spot on small strong horses. Your cousin is in the Fifty-seventh, you said? I don't envy him and his fellow officers trying to lead cavalry in a war like this.'

Vere did not elaborate on details of his supposed cousin, but he heard the man's comment with anxiety for Val. It would be his first experience of battle and the dice appeared to be loaded against him.

Harmesworth's bride was young and pretty, with much common sense. Vere envied her husband his good fortune and wished he could also find a woman to captivate him so completely. During the light meal, Peter Harmesworth revealed that General Buller was setting up his headquarters at Frere, a small town twenty miles from Ladysmith, and suggested that it might be the best destination for someone seeking the centre of military activity. He promised to give Vere a docket for a seat on one of the troop trains, providing he travelled light and saw to his own equipment and accommodation. At the end of a very pleasant hour of conversation with a charming couple who treated him as an honoured friend, Felicity Harmesworth then disconcerted her departing guest.

'Goodbye and good luck, Mr Ashleigh. I look forward to seeing your work in *The Illustrated Magazine*, but I confess to being rather puzzled. You claim to have resigned your commission because you are an artist, yet you converse with Peter like a dedicated soldier. Are you quite certain that is not what you really are in your heart?'

Vere went up the line two days later on a troop train fully laden with Riflemen, horses and stores. Harmesworth's permit allowed the holder to occupy a seat in a carriage reserved for officers, for which Vere was initially grateful.

He felt sorry for troops packed into open waggons. Rolling stock was scarce as the Boers now prevented passage of trains in both directions through the major junction of Ladysmith. Equipment, horses and men had to be transported in goods-waggons shunted back and forth between the port and various garrisons. Officers were fortunate to find a normal passenger carriage attached to the train. Many had to travel like their men, but in less cramped conditions.

Taking a seat in a compartment with five junior officers, Vere was quickly dismissed by arrogant young men who had little time for a civilian in the employ of a popular magazine. Incompatibility was mutual, so Vere left them for the solitude and peace of an observation platform at the rear of the carriage.

The sense of excitement which had been subdued during preparations for the journey returned in full as Vere studied the passing scene. This was a spectacular country in all its aspects. The lushness of the coastal belt gave way to open, rolling terrain quite soon. Small settlements were scattered and comprised no more than several huts around a large farmhouse. Yet there was a grandeur in the uninhabited vastness, in high ridges and long valleys, and in meandering rivers which the railway crossed and re-crossed over a series of bridges. Vere understood Peter Harmesworth's statement that it was impossible to defend the track. It would take an entire army to do it. Yet he saw how easily a few horsemen could destroy a bridge or section of line in the most vulnerable spot, and gain military advantage over troops crammed into open trucks which made them sitting targets for snipers. Even so, it was difficult to dwell on death and destruction in this present perfect peace.

Rivers sometimes flowed a few feet below girders of bridges; often the glint of water was deep in a ravine haunted by a rainbow of birds. Antelope roamed freely in herds, some as large as horses, others as dainty as the dear that grazed Britain's parklands. Vere occasionally spotted solitary members of a species as small as a hare, that leapt with agility along the rocky sides of a ravine. Once, he thought he saw a leopard moving between trees near water, but in the dappled shade he could not be sure. The great distances populated by wildlife undisturbed by man, and the deep, deep blue of the sky which overhung them, gave Vere immense pleasure. He sensed that the veld might match the haunting lure of the desert, and acknowledged that this was what he had been seeking since leaving Knightshill. Felicity Harmesworth's provocative remark no longer troubled him. Vere Ashleigh was at peace with himself.

For several hours Vere remained on the platform. Officers sometimes joined him to smoke a cigar and exchange a few words, but they mostly saw their surroundings in military terms and missed the overwhelming beauty of them. Vere preferred it when they left him to his solitude. He leant on the rail, listening to the slow rhythmic click of wheels passing over joints in the track as a long line of waggons was hauled by an over-burdened engine, and to the distant voices of soldiers whose helmeted heads were all he could see of them whenever the line ran around a curve. Often they were so close to the hills Vere felt he could reach out and touch them, and when they ran through narrow *neks* with rocky heights rearing up on each side of the track, he was awed by a sense of insignificance.

So lost was he in contemplating this land of spectacle and pure exhilarating air, it was a little while before he realized the sun was setting. In the Sudan, the horizon had been straight and an eternity away, so the burning ball of light had dropped away as if sinking into a yellow sea. Here, the sky changed from azure through turquoise, misty green, lemon, pink and carmine until the tranqil evening was pied with mauve and blood red as the sun vanished behind a distant ridge.

He took out his watch and peered at it in the half-light. Half an hour to go before they reached their destination. The troop would be glad to leave their uncomfortable trucks, pitch their tents and enjoy a meal. He realized he was hungry, too, and faced the prospect of finding accommodation for himself. Harmesworth's help had covered only transportation. Taking the man's advice, Vere had left the bulk of his luggage in his hotel. He had brought with him a small tent, camp bed, oil lamp and collapsible table, in addition to two sets of drab breeches and coats, as worn by local burghers, together with a wide felt hat. He was wearing the khaki clothes now and, but for the absence of badges and polished buttons, he could be an army man. In the desert he had had a batman to look after him, and an officers' mess to provide his meals. He must now find a civilian alternative.

The train began to slow, then stopped with a series of high-pitched clangs as bumper hit bumper. Leaning out, Vere saw lights alongside the track ahead. They appeared to be at a siding or small halt. He could make out uniformed figures moving about in the dim lamplight. One rode along to the carriage where officers' heads poked through open windows.

'What's the trouble?' called one of them.

'Sorry, sir, the track's bin blown 'arf a mile ahead. Nothing can't be done 'til morning. It's certain to be a trap,' replied the mounted corporal. 'Colonel Dodds'll send down an armoured train soon as it's light. 'E says you'll 'ave to stay where you are 'til it's bin repaired.'

'Oh God, what are we expected to do about feeding ourselves meantime?'

The corporal shunned responsibility for that. 'There's an 'otel, sich as it is. They might be able to do somethink, sir,'

'A hotel, you say? Good-oh,' exclaimed another officer. 'They're sure to have stabling for our horses, too.'

'Out here, Tancott? There's no one but peasants and

blacks once one leaves the cities. What a cursed nuisance!'

The N.C.O. saluted and wisely rode off having delivered his message. Vere was thoughtful. In his baggage he had several tins of meat, some biscuits and two bottles of wine – his emergency rations. This might constitute an emergency, but he had no intention of sharing his food. Let them solve their dilemma as best they could. The situation could provide him with lively material for sketches 'on active service in Natal'.

He stepped down from the platform and sauntered beside the train to reach the lighted area. Oil lamps hung from six evenly-spaced posts forming a stopping-place too primitive to be called a station. Yet there was a water tower and a lean-to containing ample supplies of wood. A shack beside it served as an office, where a plump burgher watched the proceedings with undisguised resentment. Vere was delighted and swiftly sketched a scene showing him, and the grouped officers in discussion, with a background of disgruntled faces peering over the rim of one of the trucks. This was an aspect of war civilians knew little of. It was the human side of conflict, the side that concerned wives, mothers and sweethearts. There was no glory here, no patriotic endeavour, yet it was part of a life spent following the flag. The greater part, in fact.

It was some minutes before Vere glanced up from his pad to look around. A sign hanging free of one of its hinges told him he was at Vrymanskop. By the dying light of day he made out a row of buildings some fifty yards away, one of which had lamps in windows of both storeys. The hotel mentioned by the corporal? As the officers moved off towards it, he decided it constituted his own best hope of a meal and a bed, so he trudged back to where he had left half his luggage on a rack above his seat, and the other half beneath it.

Taking only those things he would need for the night,

he returned to where troops were spilling from trucks to stretch their legs and toss coins to decide who would sleep on the train, and who on the earth beside it. They all wanted tea and something to eat. Sergeants promised to get permission to break open stores aboard which would provide a cold supper. There were grumbles and curses, arguments and accusations. It helped men make the best of things. There was worse to come.

The hotel had no name. As it was the only one in Vrymanskop Vere supposed it did not matter. A lamp over the entrance was now alight and he ducked beneath it as he entered. The scent of lavender polish pervaded a vestibule containing a *chaise longue*, four matching chairs and an oval table. Against faded wallpaper hung sepia portraits of stern-faced men and women in working clothes. Former owners? Ancestors? The well-worn rug on which the table stood did not do justice to the floor, which gleamed from the results of loving care, as did the furniture. The small lobby was ill lit save for one bright light above a corner reception desk. Officers were crowding around it, making it impossible for Vere to advance beyond the table. The atmosphere was unbearably close even with the door open, and he was on the point of returning to the train to break open his emergency rations when his attention was caught by an altercation.

'Look here, you must fetch the proprietor,' demanded an irate captain. 'We'll sort this out with him.'

'I have already told you that *I* am the proprietor,' said a crisp female voice.

'Seems odd in a back-of-beyond place like this,' the captain returned suspiciously. 'You'd get some rough characters passing through.'

'Rough, but genuine. They respect my word. If I tell *them* I have only four rooms vacant, they believe me. As I said a moment ago, the beds are very wide and well able to provide comfort for two.'

'I'd sooner sleep on the train,' said one in disgust. 'I can keep an eye on my baggage there.'

'I'll join you, Jarvis,' said another. 'The idea of two to a bed!'

'That's quite out of the question,' said a blond major firmly. 'The four most senior among us will take the rooms. The rest of you will have to find what comfort you can on the train or, if you feel hardy, bivouac beside it. However, this woman says she can provide some sort of meal if we organize two sittings.'

The proprietor hidden from Vere's view was vocally annoyed. 'Please refer to me as Mrs Munroe, not as "this woman". My other guests, rough though you may consider them to be, always address me by name. I have told you my terms, gentlemen, which are payable in advance. When we have settled that, I will send girls to your rooms with hot water.'

'Are the beds properly aired?' asked the captain, who clearly did not like dealing with a businesslike woman.

'Of course,' came the frosty reply, 'and they are free of lice, if that was to be your next question. We might be in a remote area of Natal, but we are civilized, sir. If you find that impossble to believe, you are welcome to sleep on the bare bed frames . . . or on the floor. There'll be no reduction in my terms, however.'

Vere was amused by this attitude from men who thought nothing of sleeping rough in even the foulest weather on the march, but who were fastidious to a fault when about to occupy a bed in a hotel. Although he was resigned to spending a night beneath the stars, he remained where he was until the rest began to leave. Not only did he hope to partake of a meal during one of the sittings, he was curious to see this woman who could manage an isolated veld hotel *and* get the better of a group of military officers in such formidable style.

Mrs Munroe was not in the least the person Vere

expected to see. Surprisingly young, she had dark, challenging eyes in a pale oval face, and the lamp above her desk highlighted titian hair drawn back to leave a halo of fine, untamable threads gleaming like rich gold. In a high-necked gown of bottle-green silk, and framed by an arch of dark wood, she presented a vision which deeply touched Vere's senses.

Growing aware of his presence by the table, she said briskly, 'If you hope for a bed you are too late. Your friends have grudgingly taken all I have available, and they refuse to share. You'll want a meal, I suppose?'

Vere walked slowly towards her feeling that he had stepped into another time, another place. The sensation of having come home to somewhere he had never before visited returned in full strength.

'Are you all right?' she asked with a frown.

'I am enchanted,' he replied impulsively. 'I step from a train filled with men heading for war and, in the heart of wilderness, I discover a living cameo.'

She studied him warily from head to foot while a nearby clock struck seven. 'You were on the train? You're dressed like a burgher rather than a soldier.'

'I am with the troops, but not one of them.'

Her wariness increased. 'I don't understand. Who are you?'

'Vere Ashleigh, an artist.'

'I now understand even less. Men come to South Africa to dig for gold or diamonds, to claim land, to trade or to farm. There's nothing here for an artist. It's a harsh country. It should be squarely faced, not viewed through a rosy glass.'

Now that he had drawn nearer Vere saw strength of character in a face he found arresting despite its lack of real beauty. He guessed this woman faced life as squarely as she faced her country, and enchantment remained as he said, 'I have no rosy glass, merely the ability to look beyond what others see. Those fellows came in here and found only someone to provide them with food and shelter. I discovered something entirely different.'

'Then you were deceived,' she told him firmly. 'I am no artistic vision, simply an innkeeper who has to find enough food in her larders to feed thirty-six hungry men within the next two hours.'

'Thirty-seven, if you will be good enough to accept a bemused artist along with all those brawny military fellows.'

She hesitated, apparently not too anxious to begin the task awaiting her, and Vere sensed a partial softening of her mood when she asked, 'What can you hope to paint here on the veld?'

'You believe there is nothing? Then you could not have noticed the sunset this evening which splashed across the sky colours that will be dificult to capture on paper or canvas. Our train passed deep ravines where iridescent birds sang sweetly to pierce the stillness, and herds of graceful antelope were silhouetted against the rich blue of the sky. You must have seen *them*. Add all that to stark, awesome hills and great rolling green distances, and any man who can wield a brush will be in his seventh heaven.'

She gave a faint smile. 'You have missed your vocation, Mr Ashleigh. You possess eloquence many an aspiring actor would envy. But still I say you look at everything through a rosy glass.'

'If I do, it will be of little help in the coming days. There is only one possible way to view battle.'

It took a moment for her to absorb that remark, then her eyes widened in disbelief. 'You mean to paint *war*?'

'You find that difficult to accept?'

'I do, indeed,' she said with spirit. 'You spoke of colour and nature's spectacle a moment ago; the glory of the sunset. You surely cannot also regard human suffering as a subject for a picture. What kind of an artist are you? What sort of man?'

Driven to vindicate himself Vere began to tell her of something he had never revealed to anyone. 'I once went into battle alongside a man who was everything I was then attempting to be. A sense of inadequacy on my part and contempt on his kept us strangers. When the fighting ended I passed this perfect warrior transfixed by a spear through his breast. His open, sightless eyes appeared to accuse me, seemed to convey that I should rightly be in his place. I grieved for him because I had not bothered to know him well enough to write words of comfort to his family.'

Her dark eyes regarded him shrewdly. 'Because of that man you abandoned your life as a soldier and became an artist?'

He shook his head. 'I have always been an artist, but the effect of seeing his young life terminated by a single blow on a morning when natural beauty was all around us gave me the desire to paint humanity rather than mere prettiness. My pictures for publication will show ordinary men rather than uniformed heroes posing for the best effect. The people at home deserve reality, not war seen through the rosy glass you claim I carry.'

Faint colour touched her cheeks. 'I should not have said that.'

'No,' he agreed gently. 'You obliged me to reveal a great deal more about myself than I have confessed to anyone else.' Studying her intently as she faced him, uncertain how to counter such an admission, he then asked, 'May I learn a little about my living cameo?'

She slowly shook her head. 'On the veld strangers meet, then travel on as strangers still. It's better that way.'

'I disagree. If strangers had become friends there might not now be war in this country of yours.'

After a moment of silence she gave a half smile. 'A philosopher as well as an artist?'

'Am I forbidden to question my hostess . . . in pursuit of humanity?' he persisted.

121

She glanced at the watch pinned to her dress. 'The evening is racing past. I must prepare dinner.'

As she turned away, Vere asked swiftly, 'After dinner, perhaps?'

Glancing back at him, she nodded. 'Perhaps.'

A meal of soup, sliced cold meat, pies and great platters of sweet potatoes, followed by fruit and cheese was served in the cosy dining-room containing two long tables of sturdy rather than elegant design. Vere chose the second sitting so had only a glimpse of the several civilians staying at the hotel. They were dour, rugged men who gave no more than a nod in return to his polite greeting. His military companions, on the other hand, grew mellow and voluble during a meal that was satisfying if not what they were used to. The wines in the cellar were unfamiliar and therefore considered inferior, but Mrs Munroe refused to allow them to bring into her hotel some vintage bottles from the train. They promptly agreed to seek the wine and drink it on site to round off the evening.

During the meal Vere watched their hostess supervise the two girls who served at the tables. It was quite evident that she had been doing this work for some time, yet he had never before come across anyone in quite her style. Her voice was cultured, her features and grace suggested a genteel background. Yet there was an undeniable assertiveness in her manner which hinted that she was used to holding her own in the world – a world vastly different from the one he knew. Convinced that she was a widow, or had assumed the title of a married woman to protect herself and maintain respectability, Vere wondered why so fascinating a woman should be living in such an isolated settlement. Surely she could do better for herself than this?

It had been no exaggeration when he had admitted to being enchanted, and not only with the cameo image she had presented. Reason told him it was absurd to feel as he did; that the haunting quality of the train journey through a hushed wilderness to arrive at dusk in a tiny hamlet housing a titian-haired woman of disturbing attraction had hazed his judgement. Meeting Mrs Munroe under ordinary circumstances – at the rector's tea party, on the board of some charitable body, shepherding schoolchildren on an outing, or even running a discreet hotel in an English seaside resort – would surely not have had the same stunning effect upon him. Reason told him many things, but he paid no heed and continued to watch her, deriving great pleasure from doing so.

When fruit and cheese were placed on the tables by the two girls, the subject of Vere's reverie left the dining-room. He was deeply disappointed, believing that she had reconsidered her hint that she might talk to him for a while after dinner. Soon, however, he heard music from an adjoining room and discovered another surprising facet of someone who intrigued him in a way no other woman had. As the officers departed in search of cases of wine intended to stock their Mess at Frere, he wandered to stand in the doorway to watch her playing Brahms on an upright piano. Candles in the brackets threw flickering light on the curve of her cheek and on the smooth silk of her dress, which then fell in darker folds from stool to floor. Her capable hands moved with grace over the keys to produce music Vere was more used to hearing in the elegant salons of England's mansions. Caution fled as he silenced reason and surrendered to enchantment, remaining there until she grew aware of his presence and glanced up.

'Do you not care to drink with your companions, Mr Ashleigh?'

'Certainly, but I care more for music when it is scarcer than wine.'

She smiled in the flameglow. 'A man with a romantic

123

soul can never become the perfect warrior. How wise you were to abandon the profession.'

He might well have regretted telling her how Colin Steadman's death at Atbara had affected his approach to his work, but the fact that she remembered his words pleased him. She was very astute. He went into the dim parlour where lace curtains hung over windows curtained by red plush. A chair stood on each side of a huge horsehair sofa; a tallboy in the corner bore a heavy porcelain epergne. There was space for little else but a square table covered with a tasselled red-plush cloth on which stood a tray with crystal decanters. Compared with the rooms in his Wiltshire home it was minute, yet he felt at ease there.

When the piece finished he begged her to continue, adding, 'You play very well.'

'I was very well taught.'

'By whom?'

'My mother.' She selected music from a pile beside her. 'Do you care for Liszt?'

'Very much. My sister finds his style too extravagant for her taste and has to be persuaded to play it for me.'

Propping the music on the stand, she said, 'I imagine you have no difficulty in getting your wish.'

He smiled at her words, but a cascade of forceful notes prevented any reply. As he watched her fingers race over the keys he wondered about her mother. Did a family exist out here? He sensed it would not be easy to find out all he wished to know about her, but music was a great softener of moods. He must allow it to smooth a difficult path before venturing on it.

She played two further pieces after the Liszt, then closed the lid and turned to him. 'Would you care for a glass of port? Most of my guests are people with simple tastes or religious scruples, but I keep a bottle or two for several gentlemen who come regularly and appreciate more sophisticated customs.'

Vere accepted her offer of port, but shook his head when she held out a box of cigars. Having for years been denied them by order of Dr Alderton, he was happy to continue his abstinence. Her generosity deepened his speculation. It was customary for a certain kind of female to pour port and light cigars for a male companion – Floria had done so with surprising sensuality – but he could not believe he was presently in the company of a courtesan. Her manner was too calm, her gaze too frank, her dress too demure. Yet she was clearly accustomed to this masculine ritual. The mystery surrounding this woman intrigued him so much he began probing it as soon as they settled on the two chairs flanking the sofa.

'You spoke of your mother's tuition in music. Have you brothers or sisters who play with matching skill?'

After brief hesitation, she said, 'I have a half-brother who is a mining engineer. I imagine his notion of music is the squealing of winches in a diamond field.'

'So your mother or father was twice married?'

She gazed at him uncertainly for a while as if fighting an inner battle, then said with the frankness he admired, 'It's rare for me to be in the company of a cultured artist, someone with finer manners and deeper understanding than the majority of my guests. As I said before, you have a very persuasive manner, Mr Ashleigh. It must be that, and the influence of this rather unusual evening, which persuades me to satisfy your evident curiosity over an innkeeper you treat as a lady. You spoke most sincerely of humanity. Perhaps *you* will understand what your carousing friends would not.'

He had expected to be obliged to overcome her reticence with care, but she now appeared ready to tell him all he wanted to know. 'I'm honoured by your trust, but curiosity is the wrong word. My interest is far more flattering, I assure you.'

She was disconcerted by the compliment, and he feared

he had misjudged her mood. However, after a brief silence, she surprised him with her first sentence.

'My mother was the only child of Sir Ralph and Lady Brinley. She fell hopelessly in love with an actor as handsome as he was talented, and ran off with him because she knew her father would come between them. The Brinleys disowned her, of course, but she found happiness in her new life and believed she needed nothing more. I was born a year later. My grandparents were informed but remained aloof, much as Mama had expected.' She smiled rather sadly. 'Papa was attracting much acclaim, and both my parents were determined that I should be reared to take my place in society. I had a private tutor – an impoverished young man willing to travel with us in return for meals, a roof over his head, and a very small wage. I took dancing lessons from a member of Papa's theatrical company, and my mother taught me to appreciate music. She used to say, "Kitty, you are a Brinley as well as a Kellaway, never forget that".'

Vere sat forward with rapt interest. 'You are Monkford Kellaway's daughter?'

'You know of him?'

Vere nodded. 'He died young. Theatres all over England closed that night in respect for a talent lost so soon.'

'And as soon forgotten, I fear. You must also have been a child at the time. How is it that you are so well informed?'

'I am closely acquainted with Gilbert Dessinger, the stage designer. He introduced me to a number of people connected with the theatre, and I promise you your father has not been forgotten by them.'

Her smile in the low light was wide and warm. 'First an artist, then a philosopher, former soldier and now a friend of thespians. What a very surprising person you are, Mr Ashleigh.'

He smiled back at her. 'No more than you, Mrs Munroe.'

'I have no claim to renown other than successfully performing a task that was forced upon me.'

'*Forced* upon you?'

Her expression suggested that she regretted her words. 'Dear me, how foolish to suggest a form of drudgery. I haven't your elegant turn of phrase. Eloquence becomes a dying art when there is little need for it. Please pour yourself another glass of port. I left the decanter beside you for that purpose.' Silent while he did as she suggested, she then continued. 'When Monkford Kellaway died the news was widely publicized. My mother waited for her family to offer a home to her child. She had too much pride to beg for their support and, after twelve months passed without word, she married a counting-house clerk who promised her a fortune if she would go with him to prospect for diamonds in South Africa. My half-brother was born in Kimberley a year later.'

'But the fortune was never forthcoming?'

'Yes, certainly it was. My stepfather worked like a slave, and we were soon living in a house with four rooms and a *stoep* away from the hovels and taverns which housed the growing flood of prospectors.' She sighed. 'It was like a huge terrible casino, you know, except that *those* men who gambled all they had in the hope of gaining a fortune were filthy and hungry, scavenging in the blue clay, desperate to find even the smallest hard pebble that glinted dully when polished by a shirt tail. Fortunes were made and lost overnight. Hardly a week passed without the death of someone in an accident, or by his own despairing hand. We were fortunate. My stepfather was a good man who steadily grew richer and looked after his family well.'

Vere was fascinated by all she was telling him, and even more so by Kitty Munroe herself. 'You did yourself an injustice just now. You are very eloquent. I can see quite vividly all you describe.'

'You would, because you are a champion of humanity.

There was much in Kimberley to inspire compassion in those early days.'

She rose and crossed to fill a glass from the carafe of water. When she returned she sat on the sofa, nearer to him. Vere admired anew her grace of movement; reason stood no chance as he told himself a Brinley who was also Monkford Kellaway's daughter should not be in a place like Vrymanskop, running an inn for the brand of characters who travelled the remote areas of this land. She had charm, intelligence, wit, courage and greater personality than many women he had met in the social circle he frequented. What was more, her undeniable physical appeal was arousing in him a response which had been dormant for too long. It was imperative to discover whether or not there was, or ever had been, a husband named Munroe. He began cautiously.

'You mentioned a brother who is a mining engineer. Is your entire family presently besieged in Kimberley?'

Her hair gleamed in the lamplight as she shook her head. 'My mother died when I was eighteen. As the stepdaughter of a wealthy prospector, I was attractive to a number of men eager to share our comfortable home and the patronage of a burgher of stature in a growing town. My stepfather chose William Munroe because his early good fortune suggested that he would have a prosperous future.' She sighed. 'My brother could not take to Bill. In truth, Gerald would have resented any husband of mine. He mistakenly believed his position as son of the house had been usurped, and he soon moved out to live with the family of the engineer who was training him. I missed Gerald a great deal. So did my stepfather.' She gave Vere another of her frank looks. 'But Bartholemew Jakes needed a housekeeper more than he needed a son, so he would not upset Bill in case he moved out, taking me with him. How little he knew the man he had chosen to be my husband!'

'It was not a successful marriage?' asked Vere, burning to know the present whereabouts of Munroe.

'His early luck gave way to diamond fever. A common affliction, believe me. It takes the form of an obsession to find the one big stone which will make the owner a millionaire and intimate of the great Barney Barnato. Bill spent every penny he earnt buying bigger and bigger claims, disregarding the fact that these claims were sold to him by men who had become bankrupt because there were few diamonds left on them. When my stepfather was killed in one of the frequent landslides caused by underdigging, Bill sold our house and everything in it to buy yet another large claim. He left himself no money to pay labourers to work it, and quickly slid into debt. It was merely a matter of time before he was bought out by Barnato for a pittance.' She shrugged fatalistically. 'Only a giant can take on another in this country.'

For a moment or two Vere thought she did not mean to continue, because she fell into a pensive silence which suggested that he had been forgotten. He prompted her with an intense leading question. 'Where is your husband now?'

When she looked back at him it was as if she was returning from another time. 'All the mines very soon came under the control of just three men – Cecil Rhodes, Barney Barnato and Alfred Beit – so diamond fever became a disease of the past. All hopes were over of an individual prospector finding a stone so big he would become a diamond baron overnight, but Bill still yearned for the elusive fortune. He exchanged the last of his personal possessions for an old waggon and we set off into the unknown, but he had lost his self-esteem in Kimberley and grew more and more morose as we travelled on.'

She drank water from the glass in calm manner. 'We finally reached Vrymanskop and Bill chopped wood in return for a meal here at the inn. That night we slept in the waggon, as usual, with the intention of moving on in the morning. When I awoke I was alone. The two horses had gone and I knew I would never see Bill again. He left no note. His self-disgust was too deep to offer more excuses for what he was doing.'

Vere remained silent, anger within him too strong to trust himself with words. Kitty Munroe's experience was one known by many wives of pioneers but the fact did not diminish for him the tragedy of her story. Admiration for her overwhelmed Vere to strengthen the growing truth that here was the woman he had been seeking.

'I had never been fond of William Munroe,' she said quietly. 'He had gone in the belief that I would fare better without him, and I did. Amos Drurie took me on here as cook and housekeeper, giving me a room and food in return for my work. When he died, he left the inn to me: the greatest piece of good fortune I could have. A month after his funeral I received a letter from a solicitor notifying me of my husband's death. It provided no details except that he had died a pauper, so there was no estate to settle. I imagine the man had little hope of the letter ever reaching me. There was a request on the envelope for it to be forwarded if another address should be known.' A small frown creased her brow. 'In this country people are always moving on. They are swallowed up by the vastness of it. It's impossible to keep track of them.'

'Unless one is determined to do so,' put in Vere, relieved by the news of Munroe's death. 'You are still in contact with your brother?'

'I was until the siege. Gerald wrote that he had joined the Diamond Fields Horse in defence of the town he regards as home. I know I may not see him again. Everything is changing. It will never return to how it was.' She sighed. 'An army arrives here by train tonight destined for a war being fought no more than a few miles from Vrymanskop. Peaceable men who have slept in my inn and eaten at my tables are now arming themselves to defend their farms from British troops who have no wish to rob them of what they own. When this conflict ends *I* may be obliged to move on and be swallowed up by a land that does not contain my roots.'

Vere was driven to say, 'You should return to that which does, Kitty Kellaway.'

She studied him for several moments, her eyes further darkened by an emotion Vere recognized too well. Then she got to her feet. He did the same, sensing with regret that the evening was over.

'I have told no one what you have somehow coaxed from me tonight, not even Amos Drurie. He took me in on trust and never probed my past. It must be due to the poignancy of the present times that I was foolish enough to speak as I have to you.' As Vere moved towards her she halted him with further words. 'I know little of you save that you have a sister who must be coaxed to play Liszt, and that you once hoped in vain to become a perfect warrior. You will depart tomorrow a stranger still. In the coming days your search for humanity will touch you so deeply you will soon forget a commonplace story told by a widow running an inn in the wild heart of Natal.'

'No,' he said urgently. 'I shall return as soon as I'm free to do so.'

'That would be very foolish and prove that you do, indeed, see through a rosy glass. In the cold light of morning you will realize that I only spoke about things long forgotten because you will not be here to confront me with my indiscretion.' At the door she hesitated long enough to say, 'God go with you in the days ahead.'

The room seemed alien without her presence. He swiftly left it for the chilly night. The ground outside was covered by soldiers wrapped in their cloaks, some asleep and others smoking or talking quietly beneath a spread of brilliant stars. Vere stepped around them with care on his way to where the officers were still enjoying their wine in the railway carriage. Sentries had been posted. A forlorn subaltern on duty wandered back and forth, pistol in hand. A state of war existed and the mobile Boers could appear anywhere, at any time.

If they had come to Vrymanskop that night they would have found Vere awake. He lay on his folding bed alongside the train thinking of all Kitty had told him, cursing the need to leave so soon. She had hinted that there had been little affection between herself and the husband chosen for her, so love was possibly unknown to her. How, in God's name, was he to induce it in his absence? He must leave with the train in the morning – he had a contract with *The Illustrated Magazine* to fulfil – and there was no way of knowing when another might pass through and halt at this hamlet. Reason returned with a vengeance to tell him he had chosen an uphill task in deciding to make Sir Ralph and Lady Brinley's granddaughter the next mistress of Knightshill. The problem kept him awake until just before dawn, so he was in a deeply comatose state when an officer shook him vigorously and advised him to get breakfast before it was all eaten.

Vrymanskop was a daylight surprise. The settlement lay surrounded by flat-topped hills standing in bold relief against a deep-blue cloudless sky. Palm trees grew like sentinels on each side of the dust road running between the hotel, several stores, a church, a bank and a doctor's surgery. Beyond these was a large building resembling a warehouse, and this was later revealed to be the reason for the existence of the hamlet. While Vere washed and attempted to shave using the carriage window as a mirror, a talkative captain similarly engaged beside him gave out some facts he had gleaned. People from many miles around ordered goods from catalogues kept at Millbrook's Distribution Centre – the warehouse now visible. Furniture, clothes, books, wearing apparel, cooking pots, farming implements, food and rifles were just some of the merchandise which came up the line to be stored at Millbrook's until collected. The hotel thrived because customers from distant farms invariably stayed overnight before driving home with their purchases. The war had changed everything. Most trains had been commandeered for military use so goods could no longer be sent. In addition, people were wary about leaving their homes to cross the veld. Farms could be occupied and ransacked by soldiers during even a short absence. This explained why there had been ample food available for so many unexpected diners last night. Times were hard for Vrymanskop, and might get harder still before long.

In the hotel, officers were eating porridge, eggs and fried potatoes. There was no sign of the civilian guests, nor of Kitty. When Vere asked where she was, the two serving girls said she was busy upstairs. He wondered if her absence was deliberate. If so, he could do little about the situation. A note would have to reiterate his promise to return. Half an hour later he abandoned his fifth attempt to write what could be better said, and decided on a different approach. Perching on a step of the railway carriage he made a sketch of the scene before him – the peaceful street of Vrymanskop fronted by soldiers grouped around an open truck containing two light guns. When it was finished, he wrote a single sentence at the foot of the page. *I believe strangers should become friends to prevent this from happening.*

When the morning was well advanced, news that the line was again open was delivered. The troops raised a cheer and the engine driver set about getting up steam. The officers began wandering to the rear to take their seats, but Vere waited half-way between the hotel and the track hoping Kitty would appear to wave goodbye. Only when the burgher who ran the halt single-handedly emerged from his hut with flag in hand was Vere rewarded. He strode towards her thinking how good she looked in a gown of blue and white cambric, but his smile slowly faded when she drew

forward a boy of around eight with hair as darkly red
as her own.

'Perhaps you'll understand why Bill left as he did . . .
and why it would be foolish of you to return,' she said,
as Vere halted a few feet from them.

He had no time to study the boy, or the implication
of her words, because a whistle announced the train's
departure. Thrusting the rolled sketch into her hand, he
said, 'I *shall* be back, and it will be the wisest thing I've
ever done.'

Turning to run for the step of the rear carriage, Vere
hauled himself aboard as the train gathered momentum.
Kitty did not wave, but she and her son watched intently
until the carriage rattled around the base of one of the
hills cutting off all sight of them.

6

BETWEEN FRERE AND Ladysmith lay wild, hilly terrain difficult to cross by an army burdened with the necessity to take with it food, ammunition, stores, accommodation, medical supplies, fodder, field kitchens, and a laundry, to say nothing of several hundred spare horses, and heavy guns requiring eight oxen to drag them at snails' pace. If Ladysmith were to be relieved the terrain had to be crossed, however, with the added disadvantage of knowing enemies were in the hills determined to prevent the operation.

The road and the railway ran through the vital junction presently rendered helpless by siege. Both crossed the River Tugela at a small settlement called Colenso, a few miles from Frere. The Boers had blown the rail bridge at the end of November, after dispersing a small British force which had managed to escape being driven in to Ladysmith and trapped along with the garrison. That the Boers had then chosen to halt at Colenso, leaving these few thousand troops at liberty in the area, was seen by the British as lack of tactical soundness. They also chose to regard the enemy's successful investment of three vital garrisons as beginner's luck.

Even more heartening to the small force still at large was the arrival of almost twenty thousand reinforcements to form a relief column under the command of General Sir Redvers Buller. This much-decorated warrior had been awarded a V.C. in the war against the Zulus twenty-two years earlier, when Boers and British had been allies.

Everyone, including Sir Redvers, believed he would enter Ladysmith within a week of assembling his troops into a marching column. A message to this effect was sent by heliograph and by carrier pigeon to the beleaguered garrison, whose commander then made plans for an attack from within in support of the advance. Soldiers who had come from autumn days in dark, gloomy barracks at home revelled in the sparkling warmth of the vast tented camp outside Frere. They provided an air of zestful confidence as they moved about the place in their new khaki uniforms, calling to each other in vigorous cheerful voices. If they knew dread of coming battle, they hid it well.

Vere arrived at Frere to find a variation on an original theme. Instead of desert sands, the familiar neat rows of tents stretched over a grassy plain surrounded by a succession of distant ridges hinting at an impenetrable barrier. There was no lost horizon here as there had been in the Sudan, no clusters of palms, no far-off caravans moving against a brassy sunset, no Nile to provide reluctant fascination. Yet the sounds, the aromas, the disciplined routine and the sight of men in khaki were so familiar, Vere sensed continuation of an experience he had been unable to surrender at Knightshill. It made him wonder uneasily if Felicity Harmesworth had been right in asking if he were not really a soldier at heart.

Contrary to Vere's reservations he was welcomed by those he had come to paint. The Ashleigh name, and the fact that one of the generals at Frere was a close acquaintance of Sir Gilliard, made it easy for an ex-officer turned war artist to settle into the huge camp as an integral member. His tent was erected in the lines of a Fusilier regiment. He was made an honorary member of the Officers' Mess, and he was looked after by a cheerful soldier who was also batman to Lieutenant Pickering – the younger grandson of Lord Garnier who was another acquaintance of Sir Gilliard.

Vere struck up an immediate friendship with Edward Pickering, an amiable, well-read man about his own age who occupied a tent facing his in the same lines. The two soon discovered the link between their respective grandparents, but more than a week passed before Vere learned of a second concerning their families. They were riding back from Frere station on a hot afternoon when the subject arose of cavalry finding hilly terrain difficult.

'I never had the slightest inclination to race into battle with six hundred or so horsemen, striking and slashing with cold steel,' confessed Edward heartily. 'The most frightful mêlée ensues so that it appears possible for men to accidentally cut down some of their own number. No, that's not for me, and I envy them even less out here. The charge at Elandslaagte soon after the start of the war is said to have been effective in that it instilled in the Boers a dread of the lance as a weapon, but cavalry are being issued with carbines now. More useful than steel when hills prevent a full-blooded charge, don't you agree?'

'I know little about mounted tactics,' Vere said, 'but my young . . .' He remembered just in time. 'My cousin can quote even the most complicated of them. He's out here with the Fifty-seventh.'

Edward's lean face registered amusement. 'By George, so is mine! Another happy coincidence, although I trust that your kinsman is a finer example of a military man than Cousin Audley. I regret to admit that the fellow is a nincompoop of the first order, who claims connections with minor royalty through his mama's family. I believe it is true, but there is nothing in the least regal about Audley. The blue blood must have thinned disastrously in *his* veins.' He laughed, then said, 'He has never mentioned an Ashleigh in the Mess. Knowing his penchant for cultivating the acquaintance of anyone with even distant claims to fame or fortune, I cannot understand it.'

Vere regretted having mentioned Val's regiment. It was an unfortunate coincidence, particularly as Audley

Pickering was his young brother's hated adversary. He hastened to find safer ground. 'Do you know where the Fifty-seventh are now?'

'Last week they were at Brookman's Bridge on the Orange River, waiting for the main force to come up in the push to relieve Kimberley. They were fortunate to avoid being driven into the Diamond City and trapped during the first few days of war. Audley persists in sending me communiqués I have little wish to receive. It's my fervent hope that a Boer will put a bullet in some part of his anatomy which requires shipping him home at the earliest moment.'

Vere laughed and pursued that topic. 'I believe a number of high-born ladies have come out from England at their own expense, to assist friends who mean to turn their houses into convalescent homes for officers. If your cousin is a bachelor he might well meet his match before being shipped to England.'

'Not he! No female of generosity and compassion would accept the responsibility of such a husband, and genteel ladies prepared to nurse the wounded must surely be of that ilk.'

'Ministering angels? I wonder,' mused Vere. 'Could they instead, perhaps, be of my Aunt Maud's mould with the desire to dominate any man at his most vulnerable? As it happens, I have instructions from my publisher to seek out these paragons of mercy when the chance arises and submit a series of sketches depicting them at work. Would you like me to send you a communiqué so that you can either avoid being wounded, or ensure that you are?'

Edward grinned as he reined in and prepared to dismount at the regimental horse-lines. 'I have no wish to dally with the fair sex until I return to England. I've known too many fellows who found "the perfect partner" in some exotic foreign posting only to see enchantment vanish on introducing the creature to home and family.' He handed the reins to an orderly as Vere swung to the ground. 'It's a known fact that a fellow's passions are too easily aroused in hot countries. I aim to keep mine cool, Vere.' They fell in together to walk to their tents, Edward adding a caution. 'Bear my words in mind when you seek out and sketch those ladies of compassion. An artist's emotions are more easily inflamed than most, I've heard.'

During the interval prior to dinner, Vere sat at the entrance to his tent watching the surrounding hills change from grey-green to mauve. They reputedly contained enemy lookouts watching every movement of the troops encamped on this open plain. What were they thinking of as they watched the mass of white tents turn into a ghostly settlement in the paling light? Did some worry about the dangers facing a young brother? Did they gaze around at the awesome splendour of this land and wonder what their own destinies would be? Were some minds filled with recollections of a soft voice, a hesitant smile, eyes glowing in the candlelight and an unforgettable face?

In the ten days since leaving Vrymanskop, Kitty had never for long been out of Vere's thoughts. The story she had told haunted the period before sleep overtook him each night. He was filled with admiration for her courage and longed to tell her so. She had had a hard life; one containing sadness and disappointments, with intermittent wealth. A life which had apparently offered little constant affection. She faced an uncertain future for herself and her son, abandoned by a man who had lacked the strength of character she possessed. In the face of many setbacks, Kitty had survived and triumphed, retaining her Brinley heritage of dignity and good taste while understanding her adopted country and its people with commendable insight.

Each day brought deeper appreciation of her qualities to strengthen Vere's conviction that he had found the future mistress of Knightshill. Edward's words about partners from abroad proving to be embarrassments when taken home did not deter him. There would certainly be initial disapproval from Sir Gilliard, and possibly from Charlotte, but Kitty would soon win the love and respect of everyone at Knightshill. In addition, her son would grow happy and strong in the gentle climate of Wiltshire, discovering the family security he had never known.

One aspect of his determination to make Kitty his wife constantly plagued Vere. Before Annabel had compared him with a legendary hero and found him wanting, he had been supremely content as heir apparent to a large country estate. The Sudan had changed him so that he was now uncertain of his true self. On his return to Wiltshire, his home had no longer provided all he sought from life. Revival of the military link had reduced his restlessness; he was at ease with men who travelled the world staring death in the face. When he took up crayons or brush he became alive with the desire to express himself through images that spoke more eloquently than words. Yet, since meeting a woman who advised him to forget her, his thoughts were forever imagining himself with her at that lovely old grey-stone house on a hill in England.

When he asked Kitty to make her future with him what kind of marriage would he be offering her? One in which she must emulate Ashleigh wives in spending years in that great mansion while her husband chased wars in all parts of the world, or one which required her to sit at home while her Bohemian husband was fêted by artisans and wealthy collectors in the cultural capitals of Europe? He was presently a mixture of soldier and painter, enjoying the best of two worlds, but at any time he could receive a summons to return to Knightshill as the new head of the Ashleigh family. He must decide who that man would be before asking Kitty to become his bride. As yet he did not know the answer.

The brooding dusk atmosphere of that plain surrounded by hills containing hostile men presently heightened his uncertainty. To counteract it he turned away
from the scene outside, put a match to the wick of his
lamp, and wrote a letter to Kitty. It contained nothing
more romantic than an account of his life at Frere,
but he concluded by stating his intention to travel to
Vrymanskop as soon as conditions allowed. He enclosed
a small drawing of the regimental goat in his tartan
saddlecloth for the boy, then sealed and addressed it in
the hope that it would eventually reach its destination.
After that he rolled up his completed sketches, inserted
them into a tube and addressed it to the bearded Boer
manning *The Illustrated Magazine*'s Durban office. He
thought it ironic to be sending his work to one Dutchman
while waiting to attack the man's brethren.

The waiting ended two days later. The Fusiliers were
ordered to Chieveley to prepare an advance camp. The
remainder of the force would arrive within forty-eight
hours for an attack on Colenso, known to be held by
an indeterminate number of Boers. Vere rode out with
this forward brigade, sharing their relief from inactivity.
But, once settled in their new position, there was little to
do but wander the limits of the camp. To venture beyond
the perimeter was to risk being shot at.

Vere kept himself busy sketching the scene. He did several good watercolours showing the hills stretching away
in a formidable array of ridges, with the tiny settlement
of Colenso nestling beside the river. Nothing could look
more peaceful. The atmosphere was so wonderfully clear
he could easily make out the typical tin-roofed buildings
and the people walking between them. It was an ideal
time for him to embark on a series of sketches around the
camp before the big push began. Simple activities such as
queueing to collect letters from home, cutting a comrade's
hair, teaching a dog to beg, and men telling yarns around
a fire where danger could be lurking beyond the circle

of light thrown by the flames; all these familiar things became invested with poignancy beneath his crayon. During these periods he was the complete artist.

When he joined the officers for dinner, Vere Ashleigh became as much a soldier as any one of them. The hush of pre-battle haunted him as it did his companions. He knew their tension, his throat was as dry as theirs, his eyes also strained to catch the flash of sun on rifles in the hills. Then, all at once, he would remember that he must remain behind when his companions went to meet the enemy, and his words to Sir Gilliard smote him. *I shall endeavour to bring distinction to the Ashleigh name with the brush rather than with the sword. There's no dishonour in that, surely.* But was there not a *touch* of dishonour in an Ashleigh watching his fellows being slaughtered so that he could capture their ordeal on paper? It had not seemed so when he had risked his life alongside theirs in the Sudan. But now? This doubt augmented others besetting him while the waiting hours dragged passed.

Prior to the arrival of the major part of Buller's force, the naval guns in the advance camp pounded the hills throughout daylight hours. The plain reverberated with deafening sound making conversation impossible until nightfall. In the blessed quietness of the second evening, the officers sat in a large tent and ate dinner by the yellow light of lamps. It was a scene familiar to someone who had been Second-Lieutenant Ashleigh until January of that year, and Vere listened with interest to speculations on the absence of return fire.

'We've scared the Boers off,' declared a young subaltern heartily. 'They're not prepared to take what we can deal out to them.'

'Wait until they see the rest arrive tomorrow,' said another. 'The few brave ones who might still be up there will ride out damn quickly. I wager we'll be in Ladysmith within a week.'

'I have friends living there with a dashed pretty daughter,' volunteered a third with a wink. 'I have high hopes of being greeted as the conquering hero when I have fought my way through to her.'

Edward glanced at Vere who was sitting beside him. 'I suppose you heard this brand of nonsense in your war, too.'

Disliking the inference that this was *not* his war, Vere said, 'They may be right. We've been sitting targets here for all of thirty-six hours. If Boers *are* up in the hills, why haven't we been attacked?'

'Because they have more military sense than we give them credit for. Their spies must have told them we are simply a small advance force, so they're holding their fire until the rest arrive. Then we shall discover whether or not they have been scared off. My guess is that they have not.' When Vere said nothing, his friend gave him a shrewd glance. 'It must be unnerving being a sitting target and having no means of defending yourself. How do you cope with that?'

His friend had touched a sensitive spot. The familiar atmosphere of camaraderie, wine and cigar smoke led Vere impulsively to confess his doubts. 'I think I possibly made an error of judgement at the start of this year.'

'When you were faced with a choice between the army and art?'

'I had the best of both worlds in the Sudan, and I could have had it still in China. I'm finding this very difficult, Edward. I may not be a typical Ashleigh, but I'm enough of one to feel there's something rather shabby about being here to create pictures while you all get on with the fighting.'

'Nonsense!' Edward declared. 'There are a vast number of men here to cook, and others to launder, while we get on with the fighting. You did your duty when a serving officer. Now you're here to do something different. If you want my advice, you'll seek out those ladies of mercy

you've been instructed to sketch, and keep well away from battlefields.'

'I've committed myself to accompanying you all the way to Ladysmith,' said Vere heavily.

'Then keep well to the rear, man, and you might arrive there whole. This business is going to be bloody, believe me.' He nodded his sleek dark head at a rowdy group nearby. 'They're only talking so optimistically because they know it too.'

The battle for Colenso, a tiny settlement housing families whose simple lives were in no way concerned with the political issues being contested, was to begin before daylight on December 15th. Vere slept little that night, unable to forget Edward's advice to keep well to the rear – advice never before given to an Ashleigh. His ancestors had traditionally gone into battle at the head of their men, and an inner voice repeatedly told him that was where he should be during the coming engagement.

In the early hours of the morning the sound of boots swishing across grass told Vere that men were on the move. He rolled from his camp bed and lifted the tent flap. Dark shadows bobbed for as far as the eye could see against the paler darkness of pre-dawn. Twenty thousand troops and half as many beasts were getting into their positions, ready for the sunrise.

A surge of fear-excitement took hold of Vere as he recalled being part of such a manouevre before his very first battle at Atbara. The urge to join these men was irresistible. Having lain on his bed in shirt and breeches, he pulled on boots and the drab jacket, then took up his slouch hat and made his way through the press of men to where his two horses were tethered with the regimental remounts. A groom swiftly saddled one – a sturdy grey gelding – and Vere mounted to join the moving battalions, the only unarmed man among them.

The tide of troops flowed ever onward, occasionally concertina-ing when front ranks unexpectedly halted, then surged forward again. All around Vere cigarettes glowed in the growing light, men coughed nervously and horses blew through their nostrils as they sensed the tension. His throat grew dry as he wondered what he was doing where he had no right to be, yet he knew he *had* to be there. The air was cold enough to set him shivering, or perhaps it was anticipation of battle. His Ashleigh blood was stirred by the sounds of tramping boots, the squeak of saddles, the groaning of laden waggons as infantry, cavalry and heavy guns moved into battle positions to await the dawn.

When it broke, Vere gazed around at the terrain that had slumbered beneath the sun for the past few days. It was now smothered with khaki dots in neat ranks facing the River Tugela. Away to the left the railway ran down a gentle slope to the blown bridge. Motionless on the track, steam drifting from its funnel in a thin spiral, stood an armoured train filled with troops ready to advance in defence of that flank. Even further off to the right Vere could make out masses of cavalry, positioned ready to storm the hill from which any Boer marksmen remaining there could pick off infantry attempting to cross the single ford giving access to the town below.

The Tugela ran between high banks which cut off all view of the water. Those banks, together with British ignorance of the present depth of the Tugela, made the ford the only probable means of successfully capturing Colenso. It was, therefore, essential for any enemy snipers on the hill to be captured or driven off. As Vere studied the waiting cavalry, his thoughts flew to his brother, and to Edward's comments on the difficulties for mounted regiments in this country. Poor Val! Not for him – or for these poor devils – the advantage of a full-blooded charge at the enemy. Vere did not envy them their dangerous job of flushing out, with carbines rather than with the more usual cold steel, an enemy hiding among the rocks.

His gaze then travelled on to where a formidable army of artillery had been sited on several slight rises across the plain. To the rear was a long line of waggons. Some bore a red cross, some carried supplies of water, a few contained staple rations, but many more were laden with ammunition. The entire scene simultaneously stirred and sobered Vere. If the optimists were right, Colenso would be in British hands by noon. If they were wrong, and the Boers had *not* been driven away by the daily bombardment, these waiting men might soon face the bloodbath Edward predicted. Totally exposed to the surrounding high ground, they could be mown down without mercy when they rushed that river. Yet it had to be crossed to take Colenso.

With that thought in his mind, Vere jumped nervously as nearby artillery began to bombard the hills once more. Shells burst all along the ridges, sending up showers of red dust until the heights disappeared behind a pall of smoke and debris. The thunder of guns continued relentlessly until it seemed they must have blown the hills right away, and still there was no return fire. The troops sitting patiently on the ground began clapping each other on the shoulder with glee. The Boers must certainly have vanished overnight or they would be joining the battle now.

Knowing all too well that bombardment usually preceded a general advance, Vere's heartbeat began to accelerate when it ceased to leave an unnerving silence across a morning already growing warm from early sunshine. The sudden stillness was quickly broken by a chorus of sharp commands. The khaki horde rose in a concerted movement, then set off across the sloping plain towards the river. Despite general confidence, the troops approached in textbook manner, making a succession of short advances, dropping to the ground between them for several watchful minutes, then rising to move on again.

Sweat sprang up on Vere's brow as he watched ruler – straight ranks cover the ground unimpeded, the only sounds now being the orders of officers and N.C.O.'s whose tense voices carried on the still air. He was there in spirit advancing with them. He shared their fearful eagerness, knew the unbearable tension and the tautness of every nerve as one waited for the first shot from an unseen enemy. Yet they flowed on towards the high banks they must scale to reach the river, and there was no opposition. The optimists were right. Colenso *had* been vacated.

The advance regiments were mere yards from the river when all hell suddenly broke loose, turning the morning into a deafening massacre. Heavy guns opened fire in the hills sending shells down one after the other into their midst. Vere's blood grew cold as he watched the plain disintegrate into rising spirals of earth containing the bodies of men who had fallen into the deadly trap set for them. The ranks began to thin, then broke up, as troops fell like ninepins to leave huge gaps in the lines which nevertheless relentlessly rolled onward, urged on by those commanders left alive.

Most of these then fell as a hail of thunderous rifle fire suddenly descended on them from Boers hiding in the hills giving excellent views of the Tugela. Confusion replaced confidence. Those of the advance regiments who had reached the river and mounted the nearest bank were then met by concentrated fire of enemies hidden behind the rim. The Tugela became a complete deathtrap within minutes. Soldiers were falling as soon as they appeared at the top of the rise. Some pitched backwards into those following up the slope, causing further confusion. Many tumbled to drown in the river, others were mown down as they attempted to retrieve the wounded. A few survived long enough to reach the far bank, only to die from the bullets of snipers hiding in Colenso itself. Unable to assess the full danger, commanders of rear regiments continued to advance so that strategic retreat was impossible and the area approaching the Tugela became covered by a seething, bewildered mass of men under attack from all directions.

Sickened by this evidence of disaster, Vere turned away only to witness another on the right flank. Several big guns had been moved forward within range of the river, their teams being unaware that the new position was close to a concealed trench filled with Boers. Once they were in position, the hidden marksmen rose and opened fire. Gunners and horses dropped dead before a shell could be fired. Replacement teams galloped out only to join those sprawling lifeless beside the guns.

Vere watched with a sense of angry helplessness. It was clear the position was untenable, yet the cannon could not even be withdrawn while the enemy occupied that trench. Successive attempts to limber up and bring them to the rear failed, yet gallant men continued to try and paid the ultimate price. A lump formed in Vere's throat as he thought of Vorne Ashleigh wrongly revered as a hero. The true heroes were dying here before his eyes.

As the day progressed it became intensely hot with a scorching clarity that enabled him to identify numerous further failures because of superior tactics by the Boers. The forward guns now stood in danger of falling into enemy hands, the few artillerymen left alive sheltering in a *donga*, unable even to raise their heads without drawing rifle fire. To the far right the cavalry were being driven from the hill they desperately needed to take; driven in greatly depleted numbers. Infantry regiments were still pinned down on the lower slopes of the plain without water and shelter from the merciless sun. It was impossible to withdraw. To move at all meant certain death.

As Vere observed all this through eyes aching from the blinding sunlight and the irritation of cordite and smoke, a pain grew in his chest. To watch battle was far worse than taking part in it. In the Sudan all his senses had been in hiatus until the fighting had ceased. He had seen the outcome of aggression after it had happened. The full agony and glory being enacted before him now made each and every one of his senses suffer while an unwelcome feeling of shame that an Ashleigh should stand aside and do nothing rose to unbearable proportions.

There was a sudden rush of activity behind him and Vere turned to see a small group of sturdy, sun-browned men, dressed much as he was in drab coats and breeches, and with slouch hats. Without a doubt they were members of one of the English-speaking South African volunteer companies fighting the Boers. Their veld ponies were restive, rearing and sidling while their riders halted briefly in heated argument. Their leader, a huge swarthy man with a resonant voice, yelled at them above the noise of battle.

'That waggon *must* be brought off, I tell you.'

'It's certain death, man,' argued another giant. 'Two teams have already fallen trying to dislodge it.'

'He's right,' averred a third, wiping his wet face with his sleeve. 'It's more important to stay alive and fight another day.'

Their leader was furious. 'If those Boer bastards get it they'll use the stuff against us, and you won't live until sundown today. How would you rather die, bravely or as a sitting duck? Get moving!'

The men turned and swept off across the plain, their beasts covering the ground with long strides. Before he had time to think, the martial side of Vere Ashleigh obeyed instinct. His gelding had been inactive for too long and moved off only slowly in pursuit, but it valiantly pounded the grass with accelerating speed as Vere urged it onwards. All sounds other than the thunder of galloping hooves and his own heartbeat faded. Images floated past him as if unreal and part of another world. Vere saw

149

only the reality of those men he chased with the inbred urge to join them. When they swerved to fan out and surround a covered waggon tilting at a crazy angle on a small rock, Vere hauled on the reins to bring his gelding to a skidding halt near to where the bodies of other volunteers lay scattered after their abortive attempts to free the vehicle.

The leader leapt from his saddle shouting orders. 'Cut the traces and drag the live beasts clear.' He swung round and pointed to a hefty lad no older than sixteen. 'Detach those two dead oxen as quickly as you can. We can't do anything until they're out of the way.'

The boy jumped to the ground and crossed to two animals which were now no more than bloody pulped flesh hanging from the crossbar of the yoke. After only brief hesitation Vere did the same, driven by a continuing undeniable instinct. The boy showed no surprise – there was no time for anything save the gory task in hand – when Vere embarked upon it as if acting in a bizarre kind of dream over which he had no control. The others were doing the same with four more oxen badly injured, while the two beasts left alive were unyoked and led aside. Still as if in a dream Vere worked fast, his hands growing slippery with ox blood, his clothes slowly becoming stained with it. Then, just as it was possible to swing the yokes free of the carcases, the boy beside him gave a terrible cry and keeled over to sprawl face down over one of them. Vere bent quickly to help him up, then froze as he saw a broad stripe of blood oozing through the tattered khaki jacket. The young, vital stranger was dead.

The dreamlike quality vanished; awareness returned to Vere with a deafening rush. The world around him was no longer silent. Guns were thundering in the hills, the rattle of musketry was everywhere. Horses were screaming in pain, dying men were crying with the anguish of their wounds and of defeat. Bugle calls echoed in every direction in a confusion of contradictory commands and the very ground beneath Vere's feet shuddered from the force of continuous explosions. The peace-loving artist realized he was in the thick of battle. Only now did he hear the whine of shells passing overhead and recognize the whistle of bullets raining down upon them. Only now did he see that the waggon was laden with ammunition. Dear God, one shell finding its mark and they would all be blown sky high.

The swarthy madman, set on dragging off the waggon before it fell into the hands of the Boers, strode across with a set face to pick up the body and drape it across the lad's own saddle. Then he stood beside Vere to seize the heavy yoke and help him to drag it clear of the carcases.

'Soon as we can, we'll harness up the horses and pull the waggon to level ground,' he said, accepting Vere's presence with no sense of surprise. In war, strangers replaced comrades as soon as they fell. 'Get over there and help with the two ponies that are nervy. They'll bolt if we don't calm them down.'

Working alongside men who believed he was one of their number, Vere struggled under fire to help replace the useless oxen with their own horses. Sweating, breathing laboriously, incredibly tense and far too aware of the dangerous load within the waggon, he obeyed all orders until they were ready for the bid to shift the waggon. One horse had been slightly wounded in the neck, another was bleeding profusely where an ear had been shot away, but they were finally harnessed as a team with two oxen. They would be encouraged to drag the heavy waggon while four men — two of them extremely powerful — would try to prevent the vehicle from overturning as it came off the rock. It would be a tremendous feat if successful . . . and if they were not all blown up in the process.

Alongside three of the South Africans, Vere put his back against the waggon and braced his feet on the blood-stained ground as they all prepared to take incredible weight. *I am the weakling of the Ashleigh family. I wonder if they are aware of that*, he thought wildly, trying to forget the ammunition on the other side of the canvas cover at his back.

Heaving, straining, and nervously watching shells passing overhead, they all shuffled sideways as the animals began pulling the load to which they were harnessed. There was an ominous scraping sound as the rock scored the underside of the waggon, but it continued slowly to move forward while they all fought to keep it upright. Vere thought his back would break beneath the impossible burden, that his knees would surely fold, but the example of the rest kept him going in superhuman fashion.

When the waggon cleared the rock, the horses panicked and one slipped because the vehicle progressed with a rush into the rear beasts, who then cannoned forward into the pair in front. A few minutes had to be spent calming them for the next phase, then Vere and his companions moved behind the waggon to add their strength to the effort of getting the precious ammunition out of range of Boer shells. Their route lay uphill across ground covered with shell craters and the bodies of men who had believed Colenso was theirs for the taking.

Vere pushed on his outstretched arms, while his boots found purchase on the rough ground for each laboured step as the waggon rolled upwards towards safety. A few minutes later, one of his companions slid to the ground either dead or wounded. The remaining two closed up on Vere and they continued to push the tiny vulnerable arsenal with all their combined might.

It then became clear that the Boers had spotted what was happening. Shells began falling much nearer, and more frequently. The horses fought to free themselves of the yoke. They had not been trained for draught work and hated the restriction under such dangerous conditions. The man leading them yelled for assistance, and Vere was then left with only the massive, determined leader to help him push from the rear.

Those leading the curious team of oxen and frightened horses had to swerve to avoid craters, only to find another opening right ahead as shells continued to explode just off target. Progress was agonizingly slow as the sounds of heartbreaking defeat continued all around them. Vere began to believe they would never reach safety. He seemed to have been pushing or heaving for an eternity. Would he ever again see something other than the rear flap of a waggon, or his own dusty boots moving painfully one after the other? His elbows had surely locked and would never bend again; his knees would never straighten. His head was pounding, his eyes were sore and filled with dust. He was so exhausted he could surely go no further. A shell exploding just to his left so deafened him that the tumult of battle ceased. He was just comforting himself with the thought that he would be spared the thunder of the ammunition waggon exploding, and thus would end his life in blessed silence, when a roaring hurricane knocked him off his feet and he began falling into gathering darkness.

Vere lay gazing at stars faintly discernable in a sky which was starting to darken. He felt no pain, but the slightest movement of his head set everything whirling in sickening fashion. Men lay on stretchers all around him. Most of them also lay still and silent. Only the mortally wounded, and the young frightened ones, moaned softly as they waited for their names to be called by doctors in tents being used for emergency treatment or operations. Vere had no idea why he was there.

Orderlies constantly moved among the wounded. It was from their conversation that Vere learned the battle for Colenso had been a costly failure which had included much individual heroism, but many gross errors of judgement at the highest level. Guns had been left unspiked to fall into Boer hands after a number of valiant attempts had been made to bring them in. Among those killed beside the guns was the young son of Field Marshal Lord Roberts, a much revered commander whom, according to the medical orderlies, would have led them so wisely they would have been occupying Colenso tonight. Rumour had it that prisoners had been taken by the Boers, who had walked unmolested back to the places in which they had been hiding prior to the battle. It was impossible to guess their losses.

Vere must have slept, for it was fully dark when he next looked at the sky. The work of healing was continuing around him, and food was being offered to those fit enough to eat. He refused the meal but accepted a mug of strong tea. Shortly afterwards he wished he had not. The world spun madly for a while bringing acute nausea, so he lay back again and kept very still until he saw Edward Pickering smiling down at him. Vere was immensely glad to see his friend alive and whole.

'This is what comes of ignoring my advice,' said Edward, squatting beside him. 'You should have stayed at the rear.'

'I did.'

'Then how did you become involved in that courageously foolhardy attempt to bring in a waggon full of ammunition under heavy fire?'

Vere had no idea what he was talking about and listened in growing confusion as his friend assured him that the action had been successful, despite two men being killed, and the remainder wounded in a shell explosion.

'I've spoken to the doctor about you,' he continued. 'All you are suffering from is concussion, and a touch of heatstroke like the majority of our poor men. Ashleighs must have charmed lives.'

'I pray that applies to my brother,' Vere murmured.

'Your brother?'

'In the Fifty-seventh.'

'Mmm!' Edward gave him a considering look before
adding, 'I heard a few minutes ago that the Fifty-seventh
have not yet engaged the enemy, but that a big push
towards Kimberley is to be made soon when they are
certain to be used. I trust their commanders are men
of greater wisdom than ours, and are furnished with
accurate information concerning enemy positions and
strength. We had no notion Colenso was so heavily
defended. Our spies are either too timid or they are in
the pay of the enemy.'

Edward recounted in bitter terms his regiment's part in
the battle, and vague images of that terrible day began to
return to Vere while he spoke. When his friend departed
and Vere fell asleep, they continued as garish, desperate
dreams. At some time during the night he was half aware
of being coaxed to drink a slightly bitter liquid, before
hands bathed his face and torso with tepid water. His
brain was too troubled to allow him full consciousness.
Visions floated through his sleeping mind to torment him.
He saw his older brother's desecrated grave superimposed
upon the face of the man who had revealed the truth about
Vorne. He saw Colin Steadman's corpse transfixed by
a spear, and heard Charlotte asking repeatedly: *Is that
what you want*? Sir Gilliard's stern features appeared,
then vanished, throughout these confused images. But
his voice seemed ever present. *You refused Dunwoody's
offer to serve your queen and country merely to become
an effeminate wielder of brushes? Have you no honour?*

The desert and a dry, dusty plain became one as
his grandfather's voice was drowned by gunfire and
the screams of battling men. One moment there were
Dervishes rushing towards him, mouths open as they
uttered their unnerving war cry; then white robes became
khaki uniforms and the black faces turned white as they
grimaced in agony. His knees and elbows were surely

broken. He was supporting an unbearable weight on his back as he trod over the mutilated carcases of oxen which lay for as far as he could see. The young lad shot at his side fell to reveal that he was, in reality, Val. Yet, when Vere bent in distress to hold him close, his brother's body floated away on a river lined by men with rifles.

It was daylight when the nightmares faded and a brand of sanity returned. Vere was depressed and immensely disturbed over Edward's remarks about bringing in an ammunition waggon. How could he have been involved in the battle? He had been watching it all from the rear.

A doctor came asking how he felt, then added, 'Don't worry too much, Mr Ashleigh. The symptoms you are suffering from will only be temporary. It is essential for you to rest quietly for a couple of days, sleeping whenever you feel like doing so. Drink nothing stronger than water, and keep cool. As soon as I have orderlies to spare, you'll be carried back to your tent where I can look in on you now and then. It may be a while yet, however. We have to put all the serious cases aboard the hospital train by midday, when it's due to leave for Durban. Relax and be patient. We were not prepared for such numbers of casualties.'

The sun rose and the temperature rose with it. As the treatment tents were gradually vacated by men being sent down the line to hospital ships lying at Durban, Vere was shifted beneath the shade of one with others waiting for minor treatment. They chatted with the bravado of men who emerge from battle with only slight wounds, and their words deepened Vere's confusion. He was excluded from their conversation, and yet he had apparently fought in their battle. How could he have done that? He was no longer a soldier.

From his position by the entrance to the tent he could see a train standing on the line a hundred yards distant. He lay watching smoke drift from an engine at the head of carriages clearly marked with a red cross. It was due to depart at noon. With a rhythmic click-click of wheels, it would head through the splendid terrain he had seen from the observation platform on the way up, to arrive in Durban late this afternoon . . . if the Boers had not blown the track to force a halt somewhere in the heart of Natal.

That thought remained to blot out all others as Vere continued to watch the thin grey curl of smoke drift up into the blue. If anyone protested as he slowly rolled from the stretcher, got to his feet and staggered from the tent, he did not hear. The ground resembled a sponge into which his boots sunk with every step: the train seemed to shift its position each time he looked up. It took him a long time to reach it. Medical staff were busy at the rear so did not notice him haul himself up the three iron steps of the leading carriage, then sink on to the iron platform. Grasping the rail with shaking hands to stop himself rising, falling and spinning around in giddy fashion, he then found the entire train moving with him. He closed his eyes and pressed his body against the solid comfort of the carriage.

Constant gliding movement had replaced the see-sawing when awareness returned. The passing scene told Vere little. He had no idea how long they had been travelling. The train was progressing slowly to avoid jolting the patients, so Vere managed to struggle to a sitting position, then waited for everything to settle into place before peering round the edge of the carriage to look ahead. Hills and more hills! He prayed they had not already passed his destination. Clinging to the rail, he stared beyond the engine as it ran between the heights and told himself he might still be there when it puffed into Durban. An age later, as the train rounded a bend, he saw buildings clustered beside the track where a row of lamps had illuminated Vrymanskop two weeks earlier, and knew he had arrived where he most wanted to be.

There was no alternative but to lower himself down

the steps then tumble to the ground on the far side of the track. He lay where he fell for some time, trying to summon enough energy to get up. His weakness appalled him. The temptation to stay where he was was so strong, only the image of her face drove him to seek it. He raised his head with an effort and squinted along the track. The train was no longer even a shimmering blot in the distance.

The sun was at its zenith; the air was heavy and still. There was no sign of movement in the main street. He struggled to his feet and began to stagger towards it. The fat burgher in his hut beside the track had either resumed his doze after seeing the train pass, or had slept soundly throughout. He was snoring as Vere made for the hotel, where a lion-coloured dog also slumbered in the shade cast by its entrance. It ignored Vere.

The door stood open. Inside, the atmosphere was still hot but thankfully dim after the glaring brightness. Vere was blinded for a while until his eyes adjusted to the change of light. The scent of lavender still pervaded the vestibule; the furniture shone with polish. The sepia portraits on the walls were now old friends. It was like coming home after being lost. He felt tears well up as he gazed at the empty rooms and told himself everyone in Vrymanskop must be asleep.

The old clock was not. With musical notes it proclaimed the time to be one-thirty. As the chimes ceased, the rear door opened and she came through with some papers in her hands. She looked very cool and fresh in pale green with white lace trimming. Her hair was defying confinement and lay against her cheeks and neck in bright curling tendrils. He longed to touch them, let them encircle his fingers. Wanting to go to her, he nevertheless found it impossible.

As she took a file from a shelf beneath the desk she grew aware of a presence and glanced up. Her hands stilled, her whole body stilled with momentary shock.

She soon conquered it to say, 'You are using your rosy glass most unwisely. Can you really be so foolish?'

Words would not come. He could only gaze with heartfelt relief at the one person who played no part in his present confusion. She represented sanity and peace.

Her expression began to change as she came around the desk. Two yards from him her eyes widened with alarm. 'Oh, my dear, whatever has happened to you?'

Her arms reached out for him as he began to fall, but darkness returned before their softness had encircled him.

Several days passed during which sleep brought nightmares, and waking continued the sensation of being lost in one of them. His head pounded intermittently; his arms and knees ached even in sleep. He believed he must be suffering from the fever that had plagued his early years, yet the person who was never far from his side was calm and encouraging, unlike those who had tut-tutted over him at Knightshill. A doctor came each morning and evening. He was reassuring and nodded satisfaction as he departed. So he might; he was not wandering in a land of pain and mystery.

The headache was absent when Vere awoke on his fourth day, and as he turned his head on the pillow to look around the room everything remained where it should be. He sighed with relief. There was still dull pain in his arms and legs and he felt incredibly weary, but reality appeared to have returned. He was lying in a wide bed set against one wall of a room furnished very simply. Lace curtains were closed to minimize the brightness of morning well advanced, but checkered sunshine glossed a jug and basin patterned with yellow and blue flowers which stood on a table before the window, and it lay in a broad filigree stripe across the white counterpane folded at the foot of the bed. Contentment washed over him. This was an oasis in the midst of a desert in which Vere Ashleigh had been wandering unable to find a destination.

A woman entered quietly, then smiled when she saw his eyes were open. 'You look much better. The worst should now be over.'

Words eluded him. He studied the face he considered so striking; the neat figure in cream figured cambric, and the vivid hair he longed to release from its chignon.

She crossed to sit on a chair near the bed. The scent of cologne wafted to him. 'Are you still in pain?'

He shook his head. There was nothing but a wonderful warmth enveloping his body now she was there.

'No nightmares?' She smiled again at his expression. 'You mutter almost non-stop in your sleep, so it's small wonder you have run out of words.'

He found some swiftly. 'I've put you to a great deal of trouble. I'm sorry.'

'Business is quiet. The war has kept most people in their homes. Boer families shelter anyone fighting their cause; provide them with food, fresh horses, spare rifles. Those who have no love of Dutchmen are afraid to leave their farms in case they are robbed of these things while away. Looking after you has been no hardship.' Her mouth twitched with amusement. 'I have often put to bed the men of my family when they were drunk. You arrived in a state remarkably similar.'

'I have little recollection of it,' he admitted.

'A train bearing red crosses passed through Vrymanskop a short while before I found you in a dazed state downstairs. I imagine you must have tumbled from it,' she told him with a twinkle in her eyes. 'How fortunate that your fall occurred at the very place you vowed to revisit.'

'Very fortunate,' he agreed, enjoying the way sunlight played on the curve of her cheek to emphasize her pale skin.

'The military at Durban have been informed that you are here with a doctor in attendance.'

'I am no concern of theirs, in effect. I'm a civilian.'

She maintained a short silence as she studied him. Then she said, 'You were surely not attempting to emulate the perfect warrior again.'

Pleased that she recalled their conversation on that other occasion, he managed a faint smile. 'I hope I'm wise enough not to make the same mistake twice.'

'Then how did you receive a wound that has given you quite severe concussion?'

'I have no idea,' he told her frankly. 'According to my friend, I assisted in an attempt to recover an ammunition waggon under fire. He would hardly lie to me, and yet it seems incredible. I watched the battle from the rear. I remember *that* quite well. Why would I have done such a thing?'

'I cannot possibly answer that. I know too little about you.' After slight hesitation she added, 'From your delirious ramblings it seems you might be suffering from that same problem.'

He thought about that for a moment or two. 'Perhaps I tumbled from the train to solve it.'

She looked him steadily in the eye. 'There's no answer to be found here.'

Returning her look he said, 'I believe there is. Why else would I have made my way to this place when I was hardly aware of what I was doing?'

'You have answered that with your last words.'

'No. One thing I do know about myself is that I was determined to return, and if I am using a rosy glass I must persuade you to use it also.'

She shook her head. 'I must persuade *you* to look through my darker one.'

His smile reflected the happiness he felt at being with her again. 'The colour of the glass is unimportant so long as we both look through the same one.'

7

A WEEK PASSED before Vere's concussion diminished to allow him full recollection, but present happiness softened memory of that disastrous battle. His troublesome warrior instinct subsided in the peace of Vrymanskop. The doctor encouraged a period of rest and tranquillity, so Vere immersed himself in the simple life of that small Natal settlement surrounded by distant flat-topped hills that stood out so clearly against the deep blue of a sky that seemed to go on forever.

During the week, two men had ridden in at dusk to ask for a meal and a bed, then departed before anyone stirred in the morning. Stern, uncommunicative creatures, they had personified Kitty's maxim of remaining strangers in this spectacular, dangerous land. Her response to Vere suggested that she had abandoned it where he was concerned. The nurse-patient relationship had broken the barriers of convention to allow a familiarity Vere could not otherwise have hoped for in such a short time. Indeed, they might have been a contented small family if they had not all dispersed to separate rooms at night, for Simon Munroe was soon following at Vere's heels as faithfully as the lion-coloured dog.

Kitty's son was a complex boy. Sturdy, active and well used to roaming the surrounding hills alone without fear, Vere sensed that he was nevertheless too dependent on his mother. Perhaps the dependence was mutual. They had both been deserted by Munroe and left to fend for themselves in a country where the weak often failed to survive. In a community boasting no more than twenty childen between the ages of eighteen months and fifteen years, each one was obliged to mingle with those older or younger, according to temperament. Simon apparently did not fit easily into either group, but he was a rapt companion when Vere read aloud from a selection of classics Kitty had on her shelves, and when he described the haunting quality of the desert or the lush green tranquillity of the countryside of England. Vere spoke merely of a grey-stone house and a productive farm when describing Knightshill. Prudence warned him to say no more on the subject until Kitty agreed to marry him.

Fondness of Simon led him to seek the cause of the boy's isolation from other children. In doing so he was soon made aware that Kitty was generally regarded with suspicion. A woman from the diamond fields, deserted by a man who might or might not have been her husband, who is then bequeathed a thriving hotel by the old bachelor who had taken her in, was not easily accepted by sober, hardworking settlers. Such a woman's child suffered the consequences of being different from those around him. Knowing that penalty all too well, Vere casually tackled the subject as he sat with Simon on the *stoep* one morning waiting for Kitty to bring cups of tea. He was drawing the dog, named Kimber as an abbreviation for the diamond city, and spoke as he concentrated on his sketch-pad.

'Isn't it curious how one dog in a litter can look nothing like the rest? I know you chose him because he resembled a lion cub more than a puppy, but I wonder why he is this wonderful tawny shade when the others are black.'

Simon was studying his pet as the animal lay, nose on paws, watching the welcome masculine addition to his world. 'Kim is special, that's why.'

'Of course he's special,' Vere agreed, pleased by the boy's train of thought. 'Do you think he realizes that?'

Simon sounded surprised by such a question. 'How can

he? *We* can tell he's special because we compare him with other dogs, but *he* only knows that he is himself.'

Vere continued to draw swift lines. 'But he's happy.'

'That's because I love him.'

Glancing at the earnest freckled face topped by dark-red hair, Vere smiled. 'It's really all that matters, isn't it, Simon? Your mother loves *you* very much.'

'And Kimber does.'

'Yes . . . and Kimber.'

The boy frowned up at Vere. 'Does anybody love you, sir?'

'I certainly hope so,' he replied with secret amusement.

Growing diffident, Simon said, 'I like you *very* much . . . and so does Kimber. I'm sure Mother does too. Only, you see . . . well, you don't seem to *be* with anyone. Don't you sometimes feel sad?'

Seeing the perfect opening for what he wanted to say, Vere leaned back in the sagging chair to gaze at the scene so starkly different from home.

'My grandfather is a great man, a general with so many medals he can scarcely fit them on his chest. My father was a brave officer killed by the enemy in a bloody battle. My elder brother is known as a famous hero. The younger one is certain one day to exceed his gallantry.' He smiled at Simon's rapt expression. 'You could say I am like Kimber. Because I love to sketch and paint, I am different from the others. I once believed I should try to be like them, but if one is a wonderful tawny colour it is impossible suddenly to become black. One has to decide whether it is better to be like the others, not as happy but universally accepted, or to remain tawny and special.'

'And have you yet decided?' Kitty asked softly from the doorway.

Vere turned, wondering in dismay how long she had been listening, then got to his feet to take from her the tray bearing tea and little scones. He avoided a reply, but he had forgotten how persistent children could be.

'Yes, *have* you, sir?' demanded Simon, eager to bring the curious conversation to a satisfactory conclusion.

Avoiding Kitty's eyes Vere said, 'I'll tell you my decision when you have made yours, Simon.'

They sat together in the shade looking out over a garden filled with gold, pink and cream rioting shrubs which contrasted in striking fashion with the awesome environs. They were a contented group – a man and a woman, a boy with his beloved dog. As the sun rose higher to intensify the colours of the blossoms around them, Vere slowly became aware that his attempt to help Simon had somehow cleared his own confusion. Two certainties had become linked in his mind: his love for Kitty, and the fact that he would inherit a thriving estate with a considerable fortune before too long. He was experienced enough to sense that the woman he planned to make his wife was gradually capitulating to something she had initially resisted. If this present contentment and peace were transferred to Knightshill he would surely demand nothing more from life.

There might be times when a trick of light turned ripe waving wheat into rippling sands, when the cawing of crows reminded him of a Dervish war cry; when the ring of a hunting horn on a crisp, clear morning would wing him, in imagination, to this country and a tented camp spread before the river Tugela; or when the assured voices of scarlet-jacketed men gathered in a room hung with portraits of Ashleigh ancestors would kindle a momentary spark within him. But a man without vivid memories was only half alive. They had been the missing elements in the Vere of two years ago, when he had believed the shallow Annabel capable of fulfilling his future in the home he loved.

With Kitty as his wife, Knightshill would provide an entirely different challenge. Simon reminded him very much of young Timothy. It would delight Vere to show him the green Wiltshire landscape and introduce him to the world of literature and art. He was an intelligent lad who would prove an apt pupil.

Vere recalled once telling a disapproving Annabel he would fill his home with artists, musicians and writers to chase away the warrior shades presently filling it. He had vowed to cease holding the annual Khartoum Dinner and the Waterloo Ball. The evening designed to honour Vorne as a hero would definitely have to be discontinued, but he no longer wished to remove reminders of his illustrious ancestry. He would create an exciting life for Kitty in which her new home would welcome friends of *any* profession or inclination. Knightshill would stretch its walls to embrace not only soldiers but men of learning, women of wit and beauty, artists, statesmen, financiers, actors and anyone with a tale to tell. None would arrive as a stranger and depart as such. He wanted the whole world to know and appreciate his wife . . . and he wanted to be constantly beside her on Knightshill's many acres.

When evening came that day, and they followed the usual routine of dining together then retiring to the parlour where Kitty played the piano while he sipped port, Vere resolved to advance the situation. The dinners *à deux*, and the intimacy that followed, aroused desire he was finding more and more difficult to deny. Such evenings with Floria had led to passion. Kitty was no courtesan, but he was certain she also found their present relationship a strain. They were parting at a later hour every night and, while he gazed for a long while from his window at the moon-washed railway track, he often heard her moving restlessly about the room.

Desire for her was heightened tonight by his decision to speak his mind. She looked particularly lovely in a gown of black and silver figured satin, enlivened by an unusual silver necklet bearing a spray of diamonds on the right side. These tiny jewels lay against her skin in a fashion Vere found surprisingly erotic – a touch of temptation from a woman of dignity. Had William Munroe given her the necklet? Strong resentment rose in him of a man who had possessed then deserted her, but she claimed to have no more loved her husband than he had her. The piece of jewellery was so individual it must surely have been presented by someone who cared for her deeply. Her stepfather, who had honoured his promise to provide a wonderful new life in South Africa? A secret admirer?

When Kitty closed the lid over the keys and rose to pour herself a glass of water from the carafe, Vere said, 'I've seldom seen so intriguing a necklet. The designer must be a man of great imagination.'

Her face was in a shadow as she came across to a nearby chair and sat down. 'During the boom years men from all over the world came to Kimberley. In tiny premises along the muddy street, diamonds were polished and set in all manner of articles in the bid to become rich. Travellers brought in tortoiseshell combs and brushes, trinket boxes, picture frames, screens, purses and silk shoes. All these were adorned with the smaller stones then sent down on trains to merchants who shipped them out. It was possible to have the diamonds from your own claim fashioned into anything you fancied by young aspiring jewellers, silver or goldsmiths. You should have seen Kimberely in those days.'

'Do you regret their parting?' he asked.

'How could I when for every success there was a tragedy? Kimberley was becoming civilized when I left and must have grown more so in the intervening years. My brother's letters describe great changes.'

'You have never considered going back?'

'No.'

Her negative sounded surprisingly final. Vere realized that she had avoided further discussion of her necklet and was slightly piqued. 'Let's hope the siege will be lifted before shelling destroys much of what has been achieved.'

'I have not heard from Gerald since the investment started so I have no news of his situation. I imagine only vital communications are now allowed to be sent from the city.'

He took up that point swiftly. 'I wrote to you from Frere. As you have never thanked me for my letter, I suppose it is still on its way. When it arrives you will find my news out of date, but there is a sketch for Simon of the regimental goat in full regalia. I was then unaware of how very much it would please him.'

'You know exactly how to do that, Vere.' Her eyes darkened with feeling. 'I must thank you for what you attempted to tell him this morning. I'm sure he was impressed by the parallel with Kimber. You are very good with children.'

'I like them, and Simon reminds me so much of my nephew Tim.'

'They have been reared in vastly different circumstances.'

Vere disagreed. 'Not so different. Tim had few friends because his zealous father discouraged them, and he was denied the advantage of going to school where he would have mixed with other boys. He had a sister and a large loving family, of course, but I believe he suffered the same feeling of isolation Simon knows because *his* father became obsessed with a cause and metaphorically deserted him. Luckily, his step-father loves him and understands his needs. He's now attending a splendid school in South America. After that, it will be Oxford and a commission in the family regiment.' He smiled in recollection. 'He always claimed to be an Ashleigh in all but name.'

When there was no response from her he realized she had grown still and tense. 'Is something wrong?' he asked quietly.

'You told Simon this morning of a grandfather who is a famous general, and brothers who are surely no ordinary men. Now you speak of a nephew following a tradition which suggests that the Ashleighs are a family of some consequence. Don't you think it's time you told me who you really are?'

It was a setback. He had intended to enlighten her when he believed the moment to be right, but she had overheard too much this morning. He had no option but to answer frankly. 'I am merely the man you have come to know during these wonderful, peaceful days.'

'Go on!' she demanded stonily.

'I am the second grandson of General Sir Gilliard Ashleigh, owner of Knightshill which stands on a large estate in Wiltshire. The family has a record of distinguished military service dating back to the formation of the West Wiltshire Regiment in the sixteenth century. I am the first male Ashleigh to break with tradition, and my grandfather has vowed that he will never forgive me for becoming what he terms "an effeminate wielder of brushes".'

There was passion now in Kitty's voice. 'Is *that* why you once tried to become the perfect warrior, why you rashly risked your life to help to bring in an ammunition waggon at Colenso?'

He sighed. 'Possibly.'

'Does his approval mean so much to you?'

'It did . . . until I met you and realized nothing else in the world mattered.'

She rose abruptly then, her eyes blazing. 'You must be in the grip of some madness if you believe that. I am a diamond-fields woman who is scarcely accepted by the simple burghers of this settlement. Your fellow-travellers were far more perceptive than you. They saw no cameo, but a supplier of food and beds. *That is all I am, Vere.* You should never have come back. Why, in God's name, did you?'

Vere got to his feet all control lost. 'You know damn well why! You've known it since our first meeting but won't acknowledge it.'

He kissed her with force, subduing her initial resistance until she was responding in a manner that overwhelmed him. Beneath her dignity, Kitty Munroe was a true woman of this country – exciting, challenging and wild. As their passion mounted, something which might not have happened elsewhere became inevitable in a small inn lost in the heart of a vast untamed land. He picked her up and mounted the stairs. Moonlight flooded her bedroom, making the gradual baring of her supple body even more sensual. His fingers shook with emotion as they pulled the pins from her hair to set it cascading in a mass of dark red curls over her shoulders.

For a woman who claimed never to have loved her husband, Kitty was remarkably familiar with sexual desire in its most erotic form. She was graceful and feminine, yet there was an element of boldness in all she did which made her more pleasurably sensual even than Floria Pallini. Perhaps the unconventionality of her background allowed her more freedom of expression. Vere was totally captivated by it.

Moonshine was blending with dawning daylight when they finally lay spent. After a while Kitty led Vere to an adjoining bathroom where a large tub of water stood beside a contraption which substituted for a shower. They stood with bodies touching while Vere worked the handle to pump water to a perforated tin above their heads. He found the whole business erotic rather than cooling, so it took longer than it should have done.

They eventually sat by her window to watch the sun come up from behind a flat-topped hill and gild the blooms on the shrubs so that their colours became intensely vivid. This natural spectacle, the stillness, and the pure immensity of what he saw moved Vere to describe the depth of his present joy.

'As a child I was constantly ailing. I believe I cheated death on several occasions, and was not expected to survive to manhood. Until I was twenty-five I lived with the belief that each succeeding year might be my last. It took a desert to prove everybody wrong.' He touched her swollen lips with his fingertips and looked deep into her glowing eyes. 'If I should die tomorrow, I still would have had more than any man deserves.'

She seized his fingers and kissed them fiercely. 'You deserve far more. I've come across all kinds of men, witnessed their every mood, but if *I* should die tomorrow your face would be the only one I saw as my eyes closed.'

Vere brushed her bare shoulder with his lips. 'Neither of us will do anything tomorrow, my darling, other than to arrange to become man and wife.'

She drew away from him, her expression sobering. 'That's not possible, Vere. Marriages are conducted by a regional minister who comes to Vrymanskop every three months. He is due here again in six weeks, perhaps not even then because of the war.'

'Then we'll go to Durban. I know a delightful hotel where you and Simon can stay while I sort out the formalities.'

She put her hand on his bare arm and shook her head. 'One has to have a permit from the army in order to get a seat on a train. Even Daniel Farren from Millbrook's has been unsuccessful in obtaining authorization to go down the line on urgent business. Trade has come to a standstill since you were last here.'

He sighed with frustration. 'I shall have to leave on the next available train, in that case. Neither of us will be content now this has happened and I can't allow it to continue until I have arranged to make you my wife. One of the army chaplains would agree to officiate at a marriage in the midst of so many funerals. It would then be easy for me to get permits for you and Simon to travel up to join me.'

She stood, pushing back her heavy hair with the hand wearing Munroe's thin wedding band. 'I think you should wait.'

'*Wait?* Why wait?' he demanded, also getting to his feet.

'Because this country has bewitched you, my dear. You have mentioned the fact several times. When you stumbled in here two weeks ago, it was surely in response to an impulse resulting from that enchantment. No, allow me to finish,' she begged, as he made to take her in his arms. 'You are a man of culture and intellect from a country that has been civilized for centuries. South Africa, for you, is wild, spectacular and haunting. Those who live here see it as a challenge; an opportunity for wealth and power, or a last hope of survival. *I* see it as a trap.'

Sitting on the side of the bed she looked up at him frankly. 'My stepfather tied me to a man I could never love, then died beneath tons of earth in a major landslide. Bill Munroe tied me to Vrymanskop by his desertion, then died by means unknown. I was fortunate to be left with this hotel, but it is in the lonely heart of a country *you* see as romantic, and Simon deserves the opportunities a city can offer a strong, healthy, intelligent boy.'

'He also deserves a father,' said Vere sitting beside her again.

She placed her fingers against his mouth to silence him. 'The best I hoped to do for my son was to save enough to move down to Durban. I have put aside some money, but there is little profit to be made in a hotel like this and the war has now almost put an end to business.' After a significant pause, she added, 'Marriage to you while you are bemused enough to imagine it is what you dearly want, would open the door of my trap. *That* is why you should wait.'

Vere studied the face he had likened to a cameo and

knew his first assessment had been right. It mirrored emotions without artifice. He put up a hand to stroke a fall of red curls made vivid by early sunlight, asking gently, 'Are you asking me to believe that you set out to seduce me into offering you an escape, that what you did last night was prompted by no more than a wish to resolve your difficult situation?'

'Perhaps it was,' she whispered. 'I have been alone too long, and you are so very different from the men who come here. On that first evening I sensed danger when you treated me as you doubtless treat the women of your own social class.'

He rose to that swiftly. 'You are the granddaughter of Sir Ralph Brinley.'

'A Brinley only by the blood in my veins. Kitty Munroe is a diamond-fields woman.'

He took her shoulders in an angry gesture. 'Please stop using that expression! I will not accept what you are trying to say, and I've yet to hear a valid reason for asking me to wait.'

'Because you don't *wish* to understand,' she cried with matching anger. 'You're bewitched by me only because I am part of this land you see through the eyes of an artist. I'm drawn to you because I see the possible provider of all my grandparents denied me. You have lured me into looking through your rosy glass.'

Suddenly fearful, he held her close, saying against her temple, 'If I am bewitched, it's because I believed I would never find a woman who could succeed where a military uniform and a reputation for painting humanity failed. You've given me the answer to everything. You've shown me who I really am and what I want for my future.' He kissed her fiercely. 'I love you so deeply and I don't believe for one moment that all you feel for me is a desire to escape your trap.' He drew back, still holding her by the shoulders. 'Now listen to me! I have to fulfil my contract with *The Illustrated Magazine*, so I'll go

173

back up the line on the next train. When Buller relieves Ladysmith I'll arrange transport for you and Simon. One of our generals is a friend of my grandfather so there will be no difficulty. We'll be married in Ladysmith. I'll hire a house there for us which I'll use as my base until the war ends. Then we'll sail for England and look at life through a rosy glass until the end of our days. Is that clear?'

There was a hint of tears in her eyes as she said in smiling protest, 'I fell in love with a peaceful man of gentle nature, not a domineering firebrand.'

His kiss was more tender this time. 'Say you'll marry me in Ladysmith and I'll become anything you want me to be.'

The fat burgher told Vere that a train was due to pass through heading for Frere at eleven the following morning. As they were invariably heavily laden, and there was a long curve in the track leading from the Vrymanskop halt, trains travelled slowly enough to enable an unauthorized passenger to jump aboard. The time passed too quickly for Vere, who was loath to leave his love in the trap she felt she was in. They spent the night in each other's arms again, but he carefully avoided speaking of Knightshill and his plans for their future. During breakfast Vere told Simon that he planned to marry Kitty as soon as Ladysmith was relieved, and would be sending for them both very soon. The boy flushed with undeniable delight but said only that he could not leave without Kimber.

'I took that for granted,' Vere told him with a smile. 'He's special, isn't he?'

Just before eleven they all walked across to the track, the lion-coloured dog at their heels. Sudden constraint descended and Simon squatted to fondle his pet's ears as if seeking something to do during the waiting. Vere smiled down at Kitty as he assured her that it would not be long before they were together again.

Her golden-brown eyes regarded him with a hint of teasing mixed with the frankness he so admired. 'I still say I am the wrong woman for you. Your bride should be a spinster from your own world; a beautiful young creature of impeccable breeding.'

'You're quite wrong, dearest. I was once engaged to someone fitting that description.' The sound of a whistle in the distance caused him to look back along the track, where a shimmering dark shape was now visible.

'Why didn't you marry her, Vere?'

He turned back, his thoughts on the days ahead. 'She fell in love with my older brother.'

She said with swift sympathy, 'How *very* painful for you ... and for him, whether or not he returned her affection.'

The rails had begun to sing the advent of the train and he knew minutes were precious. 'Vorne was killed in eighty-six. Annabel was entranced by nothing more than a heroic legend.' He smiled to show how little this fact now affected him. 'Perhaps she'll find a living hero to adore as a result of this war.'

Kitty's expression was now such that he longed to be able to hold her once more, demonstrate his love for her, but all he could do in this public place was to say, 'We'll be apart only for a short time. The war will be over in a matter of weeks. Then I'll take you home.'

She appeared not to have heard his last words, for she asked almost in accusation. '*You* are your grand-father's heir?'

'To his great disappointment.' As the train trundled inexorably nearer, conversation had to be surrendered for farewells. Vere called to the squatting boy, 'Goodbye, Simon. Take care of Kimber until we meet up again soon.' Gripping Kitty's hands, he said with emotion, 'You have made me into a giant taller than any other man in my family. I'll explain that remark when you join me in Ladysmith, darling.'

He began to trot alongside the train watching for a handle to seize, then hauled himself on to the step of a truck laden with sacks of flour. When he looked back at Vrymanskop, Simon was waving madly but Kitty stood like a statue. Then she began to run towards him beside the train, her face pale and curiously tense. Her words reached him above the rattle of the wheels.

'Don't try to be a perfect warrior again. Not ever!'

He waved acknowledgement a split second before the jutting hillside took away all sight of her. He felt instantly bereft, but consoled himself with the thought of making her his wife very shortly. He could not guess that it would take three months and the loss of seven thousand men before Ladysmith was freed.

Val lay on his stomach beneath the meagre protection of a clump of thorn and studied the ridge through field-glasses. It was half a mile distant and higher by several hundred feet than the one he was on, almost bare of vegetation and greatly serrated. It was tremendously hot on that rocky ledge beneath midday sun. He had constantly to wipe from his eyes perspiration that dripped from beneath his pith helmet. He had been watching for more than fifteen minutes without spotting a giveaway glint of sun on a rifle or one brief glimpse of movement. Yet he knew the enemy must be there in force. It was the type of position favoured by the Boers who had used them to devastating effect over the past two months.

After several horrendous battles, the Kimberley relief column was no nearer to the besieged city. The same fate had befallen those who were attempting to reach Ladysmith. Everyone had stopped referring to 'the farmer army' for, although the enemy counted among its ranks many professional soldiers and officers from European armies who had been former foes of the British, no one any longer doubted the fighting skills of the Boers themselves.

In a curious way, this helped to banish Val's sportsman's reluctance to use his own skills against men he had believed were an unequal foe, but he had had no opportunity to do so yet. The 57th had been engaged in fruitless patrols and outlying picquet duties while their comrades-in-arms had been courageously obeying the orders of incompetent leaders in a vain attempt to reach Kimberley. The martial fire burning within Val almost consumed him; his yearning for a chance to earn a commission in the field was now scarcely containable.

Wiping his eyes once more with the back of his dust-covered hand, Val told himself Audley Pickering would pay for this present discomfort, along with every other score to be settled, when the opportunity arose. The patrol was out to look for small bands of Boers on the move and engage them in arms, if possible. They had seen none, so the foppish lieutenant had ordered his prime adversary to scale a precipitous shale-covered hillside to discover whether or not the distant ridge was manned, while he and the other troopers took a welcome rest within the shade of a large overhang. Val gave Pickering credit for enough sense to realize the Boers were unlikely to betray their presence by picking off a single man clearly visible from their position, but this hazardous and unnecessary reconnaisance was yet another thorn driven under his skin by an officer determined to break a sergeant who constantly cast him in the shade.

Enmity between Val and the subaltern with royal connections had been instant and mutual. Pickering had disliked the new member of the regiment because Trooper Havelock's natural military flair far outshone his own. Val had resented his officer's inadequacy to fill a rank he, himself, had been denied by Julia Grieves. With that envied rank to protect him, Pickering had embarked on a campaign of persecution until his victim had been unable to resist hitting back. That brief rebellion last year had robbed Val of the thrill of representing the 57th in a riding display and earned him instead twenty-eight days in detention. When released, Val's determination on revenge had governed his refusal of the offer to transfer to another squadron away from Pickering. But the incident had increased the troopers' championship of Martin Havelock and deepened their united hatred of Pickering – a dangerous juxtaposition in time of war.

The monocled subaltern now had less opportunity openly to punish a sergeant, so he used more subtle means such as this today. Little did the man realize that his constant efforts to expose Val to danger were actually enhancing his chances of putting himself on the list of the regiment's officers – a goal so tantalizingly out of reach due to lack of participation in all-out combat. When Val was on equal footing with Pickering he would be in a position to deal the fop a blow from which he would never recover. That desire was almost as strong as the one to make Sir Gilliard accept his true worth as a member of the family.

After final fruitless study of the ridge, Val wriggled backwards from beneath the thornbush to start his descent. His neck prickled with apprehension as he snaked across an exposed stretch, sending stones rattling down the sheer north face. His brain told him he was safe; his body tensed in readiness for the pain of bullets entering his flesh. When he reached the gentler slope up which he had climbed he breathed more easily, confidant of seeing Christmas Day dawn tomorrow. Fresh doubts of that arose during his downward progress, however. He lost his footing and slid some yards before seizing a handhold that steadied him until his boots found purchase on some rocks. When it happened several times more his jaw locked in determination. He *would* not give Pickering the pleasure of seeing him break his neck. Going more carefully he frequently set lizards darting from their sunny spots on minute ledges, while the eternal *aasvogels* circled in the cloudless indigo above. A lone man spreadeagled on a baking, barren hillside suggested a future meal to these scavengers of the veld. A harsh, relentless country this!

The troopers made no secret of their relief when their sergeant appeared around the curve of the hill, dishevelled and covered in a fine film of dust. Pickering merely got to his feet and drawled, 'Well, what have you to report?'

Val studied the man's thin features adorned by a drooping, greasy brown moustache and hoped dislike showed in his expression while saying in confident tones, 'Not a sign of them . . . but they're there.'

The familiar sneer curled thin lips. 'You can see through rocks, can you?' Conscious of a ring of sun-burned faces watching this confrontation between himself and a man universally hated by the rank and file, Val used his best tactic on these occasions. He *smiled*. 'In a manner of speaking . . . sir.' Pickering rose to the bait. 'I do not require "a manner of speaking", man. I want facts.'

Although it was cooler beneath the shade of the overhang, Val longed for a drink. Dust clung to his damp face and lined his throat, so he reluctantly decided to cut the business short.

'The facts are that the ridge is a facsimile of those used by the enemy in every engagement so far. It provides perfect cover while commanding the approaches to the *nek* in both directions. This is the route we must use to regain Kimberley, so my instinct tells me the Boers *have* to be there in force.'

'Yet you saw no evidence of them?'

'They made sure of that.'

The subaltern's pale eyes showed momentary satisfaction. 'Your comment suggests that you knew they were aware of your presence. My orders were to make a *secret* reconnaisance.'

Val smiled again. 'That was impossible, I'm afraid. If you had come up there, sir, you would have seen the lack of cover. From that ridge they would easily have witnessed our approach this morning and, once we move out from beneath this overhang, it will equally be possible for them to watch our departure.' He walked to his horse where the water bottle hung over the pommel. 'I'm sure you share my view that we'll be safe enough. They'll not risk confirming our suspicions of their presence until an army of us is about to march through the *nek*. It's the way they fight.'

He unscrewed the stopper and drank thirstily, before pouring water into the palm of one hand to dash over his face. It felt so good he yearned for the shower he would enjoy on reaching camp. The sergeants had erected an ingenious mechanical douche which was immensely popular, particularly with those returning from patrols such as this.

Pickering's insubstantial voice was soon lost in the vastness of the approaches to the *nek* as he gave the order to mount and return to camp. The troopers glanced questioningly at Val, but he smiled and nodded to reassure them that they were safe enough as he swung into the saddle. Although the subaltern was visibly apprehensive as he quitted the protection of the jutting rock, the men trusted their sergeant's judgement and rode in column behind him with every confidence. Val reflected fleetingly that he could have murdered Pickering a moment ago, and every man of them would have supported a tale of their officer being shot by an enemy sniper. Killing was too kind a fate, however. Val would not be happy with anything less than the total public humiliation of his enemy at his own hands – something completely foreign to his nature. But twenty-eight days behind bars had scarred him deeply.

They left the area unmolested, only the ring of hooves on stony ground and the occasional cry of circling vultures breaking the somnolent silence of that sweltering afternoon. It would take them three hours to reach the Modder River camp, where a huge force sat demoralized after two disastrous battles that had decimated their ranks. At Christmastime men were melancholy enough away from home and loved ones, but at this last holy festival of the nineteenth century they were further saddened by the loss of comrades whose graves stood as a constant reminder in row upon row of crosses against the bright horizon. There had been no real victory yet in this war against the Boers. It seemed inconceivable that what was regarded as one of the finest armies in the world should have been outwitted and out-manoeuvred so frequently. The British public was apparently up in arms; the Government desperate to avert a defeat leading to the possible loss of South Africa from the empire. Other great nations were watching in the manner of *aasvogels*, ready to swoop in at the kill and seize this rich land.

Any army fighting abroad must be at a certain disadvantage against those men of the country, and much had been made of the awesome terrain, the heat and the scarcity of water, the lack of maps, the poor Intelligence and the unacclimatized horses. However, every soldier who had seen battle here knew the British troops had faced these obstacles and triumphed in spite of them. Around camp fires, in tents, in hospital beds and everywhere several men were grouped together, it was muttered that those in command had caused the costly defeats through their incompetence. Some went so far as to condemn officers of *all* ranks. There had been tales of several ordering their men forward to certain death in a bid to gain laurels for themselves, but there were as many stories of their immense personal courage under fire to rescue their troops. There were good and bad officers in every regiment, as A Troop were well aware. Val dreaded the moment when Audley Pickering was faced with a life or death decision. Fortunately, the other troop officers were efficient, responsible men he would back to the hilt in any fray.

They had not yet actually faced the enemy head on. The 57th had been kicking their heels at Brookman's Bridge throughout November to prevent it being blown. Then they had been patrolling the area for sight of any large gatherings of commandos along that front. These had, instead, been marching further west to Modder River station. Called in to join the main column after its attempt to cross the river had resulted in a furious battle during which British troops were pinned down beneath a killing sun for an entire day – almost a carbon copy of the disaster at Colenso – the 57th were held as reserves during the subsequent débâcle at Magersfontein.

Val had been detailed as a galloper during that desperate encounter – almost certainly at Pickering's nomination, but with the full approval of Captain Wheeler. This duty undertaken by those known to be skilled horsemen was not an enviable one, in Val's opinion. Carrying messages from one part of the battlefield to another at full gallop could be extremely hazardous. There was no opportunity to return fire as one rode flat out with a written order often issued too late or ignored by the recipient. Two gallopers had been shot before reaching their destination and the orders were never delivered.

On that unforgettable day Val had chosen Colonel Beecham's stallion Riptide as his mount. Vivienne had been true to her promise to persuade her father to give the animal to A Troop, but Val had been spared the obligation of thanking her. It seemed that she and her mother had been unable after all to persuade Max Beecham to grant their wish to follow behind the army, which was as well since it had not advanced anywhere. The pair had instead gone to stay with friends in Kimberley, little guessing the fate about to befall the Diamond City. The 57th therefore had an additional incentive to lift the siege and free the wife and daughter of their popular colonel.

Taking Riptide from the lines to ride to Magersfontein, Val had fleetingly worried about the red-haired girl's ordeal in Kimberley. When he had been in hospital recovering from burns after the stable fire last year, she had written him the most entertaining letters to keep up his spirits. If she would only stop trying to trap him into giving away his true identity he might more readily accept her friendship, for she could be reasonably pleasant when she chose and maybe she really led a lonely life as the colonel's daughter. Yet instinct told him her interest in him was a danger. Not only was she determined to solve a mystery that could jeopardize his career, her penchant for using her status to tease him into uncomfortable, personal situations smacked too much of her cousin Julia.

Thinking now of his housemaster's perverted wife as he rode along the desolate, undulating track, Val wondered how he could ever have been so great a fool. He had matured to manhood in the 57th and vowed never again to be degraded by the lure of a female body. Vivienne Beecham was unattractively thin and freckled, unlike Julia with her curves, huge eyes and shining nut-brown hair, but the girl nevertheless made no secret of her fascination with his strength and physique in the way her cousin had. In consequence, his every sense resisted her advances, verbal and physical. The pleasure to be had with a woman was far outweighed by loss of pride, he had discovered. While he hoped Vivienne was not suffering in Kimberley, he would be more than happy if her experience led to her departure for England when the siege was lifted.

Back at the camp, Val doused himself with water that had been used by four others before hitching a towel around his waist to walk across to the tent he shared with Toby, who watched from a folding chair as he dressed in fresh shirt and breeches.

'You have some impressive bruises,' Toby commented. 'Don't tell me the Boers have run out of bullets and have taken to slings and stones.'

Val told him how the bruises had been inflicted during his descent of the hill, and expressed his reluctance to advance with the column through the *nek* he had studied from the ridge. 'We haven't a hope of getting to Kimberley by that route unless the Boers are driven from there,' he said with a heavy sigh.

'How would you suggest we do that?'

Val sank into their other chair and took up a mug of ale. 'Pound the ridge with artillery for several days, then send a well-armed force through the *nek* under cover of darkness ready for an attack from both sides at dawn.'

Toby pursed his lips. 'Might work.'

'That's the crux of all our problems out here. There's no certainty of any tactic being successful.' Val drank thirstily, then wiped froth from his moustache with the back of his hand. 'Here's one certainty. It's damn good ale.'

'Enjoy it while you can,' Toby advised. 'I heard from the R.S.M. that extra supplies have been sent up for Christmas, but there'll be no more for a while now. A mistake at Tilbury resulted in crates of bullets being loaded aboard in place of comforts for we gallant lads.'

Val tilted his head back and closed eyes weary from the glare of sunlight on barren stony ground. 'How careless! Whatever would we gallant lads want with bullets?' After a moment, he added casually, 'I could have easily put one through Pickering's skull out there today.'

'Why didn't you?' asked his friend, with great interest.

'We would all have been obliged to say a Boer was responsible, then he'd have been hailed as a hero who gave his life for Queen and country.'

'Ah, of course. Don't want that, do we?' There was a pause before Toby added, 'There are enemies enough without having them in our own ranks. Why don't you transfer to another troop, Martin?'

'He'd see it as moral victory,' Val murmured, still resting his eyes. 'I can take whatever he deals, until my moment comes. Whenever he attempts to humiliate me, I *smile*. He can't cope with that and the situation rebounds on him, because the men back me to the hilt quite openly.'

'Well, they would. You were one of them until a few months ago. I don't understand this business with Pickering, though. You're the easiest fellow to get on with; enormously popular throughout the regiment and more intelligent than most of us. Why are you so obsessed by hatred of the poor fool? Not because he put you behind bars for a month, surely. The punishment was justified, or Captain Wheeler would never have ordered it.'

Lost in recollection of that evening when he and Pickering had unreservedly expressed their contempt for each other before four junior officers, Val spoke without thinking.

'He has what should be mine by right, and he abuses it. I'll break him, as he'll never succeed in breaking me, but I hope to God I manage it before half the troops are killed through his inadequacy.'

He was still away on the wings of vengeance, when Toby's voice brought him back to earth. 'I've always known, of course, that you're *not* an orphaned stable-boy generously educated alongside his son by the owner of a large estate. That tale's all right by me. You're a damn good friend, especially in these times, and that's all I care about. But when you were galloping back and forth through shot and shell at Magersfontein, it struck me that there must be someone somewhere who you'd like to have your things if you are killed.' As Val sat up and looked across warily, Toby hastened to say, 'Strictly between you and me. I don't need to be told anything except an address.'

Val was caught unawares. He had no ready answer for a situation that had arisen from his oblique comment that he had every right to be an officer of this regiment. He gazed at the beefy, dark-haired young man who had given undemanding and loyal friendship from the day he had become a sergeant, and knew he owed Toby some explanation.

'You receive letters,' his friend continued almost apologetically, 'so there *are* people at home who would . . . well, perhaps they'd appreciate some words from me if you go.'

'I'm not going to *go*,' Val murmured with an absent smile, casting around for the right words. Things had changed since he enlisted and claimed to have no next of kin. After Max Beecham had discovered his real identity and promised him a commission in the field if it became possible, Val had felt sufficiently confident to write to Margaret, little knowing that she had left Knightshill with Nicolardi. The letter had brought a reply from Vere instead, and they had been in correspondence ever since.

Margaret had written to him as soon as she was able, so he was in regular contact with his favourite sister. Now Charlotte had taken it into her head to write a friendly letter. The cloud of disgrace appeared no longer to hang over him; he was doing well as a sergeant. The only thing preventing open reconciliation with his family was his own signature on an enlistment paper swearing that everything on it was the truth. If he ever revealed that he was, in fact, Valentine Martin Havelock Ashleigh, he would be court martialled and kicked out of the regiment to earn further, more public, disgrace. Toby had just touched on the single blight to his sense of achievement and he had no idea how to respond to his friend's offer.

It was impossible to nominate his grandfather as the person to be notified of his death in battle, yet Val felt it should be Sir Gilliard who first learned that he had, at least, *died* with honour. He had not replied to Charlotte's letter, although he supposed he should. It was difficult to know what to write to a disapproving sister who had unexpectedly sent warm good wishes, and he had never been a keen correspondent. There was always so much else he would prefer to be engaged in rather than sucking the end of a pen while trying to think of words to fill an empty page. Vere was good with words. Val supposed his brother was the best person to be told if he became a casualty. Although he was attached to the Ladysmith relief column as a civilian, Vere would probably ride over to collect personal effects. At that dark thought Val realized he had nothing of any worth for Vere to collect. He had lived on his meagre wage since joining the 57th, so his possessions were few and basic. The several sporting trophies he had won were held by the regiment, with his two middle names engraved on their plinths in praise of a man who did not exist. His family would have to cherish those things he had left at Knightshill if he did not survive this war.

Toby was patiently waiting and Val knew a rush of friendship such as he had felt for no contemporary since Clive's death at Chartfield. 'You're a good sort, Toby,' he said quietly. 'There is someone who would appreciate a note from you, if the worst happens. His name is Vere Ashleigh.'

'Isn't that the artist fellow you told me about . . . the one who went to the Sudan when a girl turned him down?'

'Good Lord, I thought you were half asleep when I told you that,' Val said in surprise.

'Fooled you, then,' Toby joked in an attempt to lighten the atmosphere. 'I remember thinking he was yet another of us taken in by a glowing, innocent face hiding a heartless personality.'

Val thought of Julia and veered from the subject of

female complexity. 'He's with Buller's column. Don't bother to send a package of my nondescript things; just give him the details of how it happened.'

Silence descended on them for a while, then Val said briskly, 'For God's sake stop looking so damned gloomy, you're not going to bury me at sundown today . . . and before I "go", I have to deal with Pickering.' He forced a grin. 'If he and I should happen to be mown down by the same Maxim, promise you'll ensure that my grave is as far from his as possible.'

The subject of dying was not raised between them again, but it had stirred in Val memories that remained with him during that emotive Christmas Eve. Midnight services were conducted for those of all beliefs during a mutual ceasefire. The bands of every regiment massed to play familiar hymns and carols for the troops, who found comfort in singing lustily to beloved tunes from their homeland. As Val stood bareheaded beneath brilliant stars on a chilly plain near the river where men had agonized and perished in vain, his martial spirit gloried in the sight and sound of this army around him. Yet, when the padre began speaking of the country they were representing, his thoughts crossed the sea to the parish church of Dunstan St Mary where he had sat in the family pew with the others on every earlier Christmas Eve he could remember.

Ned always had carriages or sleighs waiting to take them up to Knightshill after the service. Sometimes there were stars overhead – never as bright as veld stars – but more often it rained or snowed, and they sat close together for warmth. On reaching home they enjoyed hot punch and spicy cakes around a log fire in the great hall, where Vere always erected one of the tall firs from the estate and decorated it with candles and sweetmeats. Earlier in the evening carolers from the village had traditionally come up on a cart to sing for family and staff before returning with gifts of produce from the home farm.

Christmas Day had always been happy and noisy in those early days before Philip Daulton became obsessed with teaching the heathen, and Vere had gone away to the Sudan thinking never to return. Timothy and Kate had wanted games. Val, whom they regarded more as a brother than their uncle, had chased them around in hunt the slipper, helped them with their puppet show and played spillikins with as much enjoyment as they. There had been other games in which his brothers and sisters had joined – oranges and lemons, blind man's buff, bagatelle, musical chairs and Brother John.

After the children went to bed, they all dined on roast goose and rich plum pudding. Then Charlotte played the piano while they gathered around to sing popular carols and ballads. Vere had quite a decent tenor voice, and Margaret sang very well. They blended perfectly in duets. Val's own voice, in the process of breaking, made him shy of singing alone until it became a respectable sound to inflict on those dearest to him. Sir Gilliard, who smoked a cigar in solitary confinement away from this musical amusement, then joined them around the fire to relate anecdotes from his distinguished life. Val had loved that time best of all. On a stool beside his grandfather, he had listened to tales of daring and fortitude that had brought a prickle of chill excitement to his skin, and he vowed to live within those exemplary standards to compensate the old warrior for Vorne's heroic sacrifice.

Visions of Knightshill faded to return Val to the cold starlight of a camp near the Modder River, as he sadly acknowledged that his standards so far had been less than exemplary. He had committed adultery with his housemaster's wife, been thrown out of Chartfield School, sworn false testimony on enlisting, and was the only Ashleigh ever to serve sentence behind bars in military detention.

The wave of reminiscences revived his unbearable yearning to earn forgiveness from the grandfather who had provided stability, and a pattern of behaviour to follow. Vorne had done it with great glory. Vere had defied his limitations to find his own brand of glory in the Sudan. Val knew he could never erase what he had done, but war gave him the chance to earn laurels so bright they would dim his past forever. Each day of inactivity here could bring news of Sir Gilliard's death; each day denied Val the opportunity to prove himself a true Ashleigh. Every fruitless patrol left him open to the risk of death from the bullet of a hidden sniper. His stomach knotted at the thought of dying unsung before he had participated in real battle. When they were eventually ordered to advance through the *nek* on the way to Kimberley, he *must* seize any means to achieve distinction before he fell among the carnage that was sure to result.

Val and Toby turned in at one a.m. in reflective mood, their thoughts their own. In the morning they were both engaged in issuing Christmas luxuries to men who had lived rough, fought hard and gone without for three months. Tins containing chocolate and a greeting card from Queen Victoria were given to the rank and file, and there were cigarettes, tobacco, biscuits, cakes, socks, soap and ointment, much of which had been provided by titled women who had badgered their wealthy friends to subscribe to a fund handed over to a group of manufacturers for shipping goods to South Africa. Best of all were letters brought up the track which the Boers had not blown in deference to the holy festival.

Val was kept busy, with his fellow sergeants, serving Christmas dinner to men seated at trestle tables beneath a makeshift awning. There was a great deal of chaffing and ribaldry permissable on this day of the year between troopers and those who usually commanded respect, and Val gave as good as he got from those he knew and liked as former comrades. At such times, he was always aware that when he eventually gained the coveted commission, he would have more understanding of the men he commanded than did officers who had never suffered what they ordered others to do. Carrying plates and tankards back and forth in the blazing sun, he felt happy and confident again. Midnight's regrets had fled with daylight. This life fulfilled him whichever insignia he wore on his tunic. He was principally a cavalryman on active service and would play his designated role as any Ashleigh would.

With his horse to tend it was not until late afternoon that Val had time to line up for the privilege of a tepid shower, then relaxing with a tankard of ale prior to dressing for the Sergeants' Mess special dinner. Toby had collected their mail from the mess tent and was engrossed in reading a batch of letters from his family. Pleased to see that there was one for him from Margaret in South America, and another from Vere, Val first took up a third envelope bearing an official stamp like the one on his brother's. Who else would write to him from the war zones? Slitting it open he took out several large sheets of coarse paper covered in closely spaced lines of handwriting he did not instantly recognize. When he began to read, a sense of mild shock touched him.

Dearest Havelock,

We are each allowed to send one Christmas letter out with a civilian galloper, who has been granted safe passage through to your camp. Mama has written to Father, which leaves me free to do as I please. We were told of the serious reverses you have suffered, but no casualty lists are available to us. I pray each day for your safety and I refuse to believe my words have gone unheeded. I know you are certain to do something very brave, because you are that kind of person, but please promise to be still with the 57th when they march into Kimberley.

Shells come over almost every day. Many of them fail to explode, or they land harmlessly in open areas. It's the noise they make as they pass

191

overhead which is unnerving those who have little faith in survival. Our troops here are splendid. They make constant sorties beyond the perimeter barricades to harry the enemy, even though they have little sleep and their food is strictly rationed. Poor Colonel Kekewich is trying to command his men despite gross interference from Mr Rhodes. It really is a ludicrous situation – or it would be if it were not so dangerous.

Vivienne went on to describe how Cecil Rhodes, who considered Kimberley to be under his personal supervision, overrode the military commander's orders and sent his own signals to the relieving troops giving contrary information to that supplied by Colonel Kekewich. There appeared to be a war within a war inside the city. Val understood very well the feelings the military man must hold for he likened it to his own reactions to Audley Pickering. The ineffective lieutenant had influential connections, as had Rhodes, and as little understanding of military tactics as that great empire builder.

He read the rest of the letter with great interest, finding Vivienne's words unexpectedly affecting. Although she wrote of life within the besieged city in plain terms, the lack of her normal flippant attitude told him more of the strain she and other residents were under than did the words on her page. Their hopes of relief had been dashed several times, and they waited daily for the news that would give the signal to their own troops to set up a counterattack from within. The guns of the relieving force had sounded so close during the disastrous battles, it had been easy to believe that they were almost at the city gates. Vivienne then mentioned plans to kill horses for food, and the storm of protest they had raised.

I know what feelings this desperate measure will arouse in you, so please, dear Havelock, tell them to battle through to us very, *very* soon.

After outlining to him Cecil Rhodes' contingency plans to lower women and children into the diamond mines if the Boers launched a bombardment prior to rushing the city before it was relieved, Vivienne ended her long letter with the fact that the galloper would be given safe passage back to Kimberley on New Year's Eve.

> A new year; a new century! What do you think it will bring us? One thing I have learned here is that there are many ways of looking at life, and it is a person's character rather than their circumstances one should consider important. I hope you agree, and I look forward to the return of the galloper with replies to the letters we have sent out.
>
> Your very special friend, Vivienne

The letter affected Val strongly. He was appalled at the prospect of horses being slaughtered and eaten all because this huge force around him had failed to win its way through after two months of fighting. He took on the guilt of an entire army as he re-read the girl's words, and guessed at the condemnation from suffering civilians and troops who could not know of the wholesale sacrifices being made in the attempt to reach them. He longed to vindicate the profession he loved, defend his own regiment, erase the disparagement of those within the beleaguered city. For once, he was quiet and unresponsive around the dinner table, and no amount of camaraderie put him in the mood to enjoy the excellent Christmas dinner served up that evening. When he finally treated several of his irrepressible fellow sergeants to an uncharacteristic outburst of temper, they wisely left him alone.

He slept badly, dreaming of dead horses being torn apart by starving women and children. Morning found him irritable and impatient of those set on continuing their festivities between the monotonous round of duties. During the pressing heat of early afternoon Val was unable to rest on his camp bed and finally rolled from it to find paper, pen and ink. After writing 'Dear Miss Beecham', he sucked the end of his pen for some while wondering how to continue. Then he wrote swiftly and impulsively.

> Activity is building here daily, so you can be certain your situation will be eased very soon. Although our ranks have been greatly decimated, we are full of pluck and determination. I'm sure you are confident of that and know we are doing everything possible to reach Kimberley. Although the regiment has only so far been engaged in patrol duties, we're all standing ready for the big push in a day or two. Yes, a new century sounds very grand, and we'll celebrate it by marching in triumph through the streets of Kimberley. Don't let anyone kill the chestnut gelding for meat. He's too fine a beast.
>
> Martin Havelock

A few hours after the galloper had departed for Kimberley with the bag of letters, news arrived from Headquarters. Due to the costly failure of both relief columns to lift the sieges of Ladysmith and Kimberley, two new generals had been appointed to take over command. Lords Kitchener and Roberts were highly experienced, thorough and revered by the troops for their military achievements. Kitchener had, of course, recently reclaimed the Sudan and Khartoum in triumphant manner. Roberts, whose dashing young son had been killed in a heroic attempt to rescue the guns at Colenso, had earned acclaim with his astonishing march from Kabul to Kandahar against the Afghans. The greatest of their virtues was that they were brilliantly successful leaders.

Along with this fresh initiative at the highest level would come massive reinforcements. Unfortunately, generals and troops had to travel to South Africa before a big push could be made. The weary, demoralized men already encamped there saw the delay as a welcome chance to recoup their strength. One did not. Val found it tremendously hard to accept that no advance would be made for several weeks yet. Urgency consumed him. An old general's life was ticking away as he waited for that moment in battle which would put Valentine Martin Havelock back up there with other Ashleighs. Each passing day was one nearer to the introduction of horsemeat in Kimberley. *Did no one but himself consider that?*

8

THE KIMBERLEY RELIEF force sat tight for the whole of the first month of the twentieth century, and on into the second week of February. Lord Roberts would have no repeat of the slaughter prior to Christmas. He was determined to be prepared fully before he made the great push through to the Diamond City. This involved very thoroughly resting those who had already suffered the horrors of battle, and acclimatizing reinforcements straight from a cold, grey England. Even those from Australia, New Zealand and India needed a period of adjustment. It also involved gaining the reliable intelligence reports imperative for success. A great air balloon was brought to Modder River camp and this was launched almost every day, a pair of Royal Engineers armed with field glasses in the basket dangling below. In addition, an armoured train made frequent journeys down the track to the river. The men packed inside fired through the rifle slits at suspected Boer positions, but their rate of success was never apparent. The enemy were past masters at concealment.

The most consistent attempt to gain information on numbers and the positions of those defending the route through to Kimberley was through reconnaisance by cavalry patrols. They were given instructions to cover a wider area than before, flush out Boers, and chase them with the object of taking a prisoner or two who might be persuaded to give away valuable information. Day after day, the troopers left their infantry comrades

196

resting in the shade whilst they rode in ever increasing temperatures across terrain on which grass was withering and shrubs wilting beneath the scorching sun. The Boers mostly played their famous trick of lying low, so that the weary, sweating cavalryman had the humiliating suspicion of being watched from just a short distance away by knowing men waiting for their perfect moment to kill. Sometimes, small groups of enemy horsemen were spotted in the distance and chase was given. They were always too fast and seemed to melt into the landscape before their pursuers' aching eyes.

Patrols occasionally fell foul of a trap and lost men in a sudden hail of fire from a concealed *donga*, or from a low hill which gave no hint of being occupied. As January gave way to February, the cavalry regiments felt they were being used merely as human decoys to tempt the Boers into betraying their positions. They hated this brand of warfare and longed for the full-blooded charge which had gained them so many battle honours in other wars. In truth, the troopers and their officers sensed that these forays were making them look ineffectual and impotent in the eyes of their countrymen.

Throughout this period Val's desire for action ruled him, making him edgy and intolerant to the point of inviting a warning from Felix Wheeler, his squadron captain. The officer fell in beside him as he rode through the lines one evening after another tiring patrol along the river bank earlier in the day, which had led to a confrontation between himself and Audley Pickering that had grown dangerously close to a military offence. Captain Wheeler was a good and popular officer, but he was also tired and dispirited which made him less amenable than usual.

'I want a word with you, Sergeant Havelock,' he said somewhat grimly, as his black gelding closed in on Val's grey.

Val saluted. 'If it's about today's patrol, sir, I sent Phipps to your tent with my report over an hour ago.'

'It's about a little matter I'm sure you've not mentioned in your report. Mr Pickering included it in his, however.'

Val's mouth tightened. Trust that weak bastard to bleat about something between just the two of them – something they both knew would be settled only when one had removed the other from the scene for good. Val was damned if he would bleat about it, too, so he said nothing as they rode on between rows of tents where men were gathering up their tins ready to collect supper from the cookhouse.

'I know you are an honest man, Havelock,' Wheeler said heavily, 'so I'd like to know if you have some personal problem. We have all noticed your shortness of temper and an unusual tendency to prefer your own company of late. The men need all the support and encouragement they can get right now, and you are unexpectedly letting them down. If you have a problem with your health, see the Surgeon. If you have worries of a different nature go to the Chaplain, or confide in me. I know you have no family, but there might be someone about whose safety you are concerned – someone in Kimberley, perhaps?'

To his fury Val felt his colour rise. Damn Wheeler! Damn Vivienne Beecham for making her friendship for him so obvious! But his captain was mistaken. It was not that girl's fate but the condemnation of an entire besieged city which bothered him. And the slaughter of horses for human consumption. By the time they reached Kimberley there would not be a beast left alive, and marching through streets filled with starving, contemptuous people would be an empty triumph.

'No, sir,' he muttered.

'Drop that mutinous expression, man. I'm not speaking as your senior officer, but as someone older and more experienced offering advice . . . if you want it.' After riding in silence for a few yards, Wheeler added, 'I continually ask the gods why they chose *me* to be your commander. You've been a thorn in my side since the day you joined the regiment and that damned pride of yours doesn't make my job any easier.' He sighed. 'If you choose not to confide in me, for God's sake get it off your chest to Sergeant Robbins. You share a tent and seem friendly enough.'

'Yes, sir.'

Wheeler sighed again. 'You made it clear as a trooper that you'd not be happy until you gained command of this entire regiment. Colonel Beecham saw fit to give you swift promotion to sergeant, but you've a long way to go yet and must take on only the responsibility your rank demands. When Mr Pickering decides there is little point in pursuing the enemy during a patrol, your place is to accept his judgement. If you feel you *must* put forward an opinion, it should be done out of earshot of the men and in a calm, reasonable manner. Is that clear?'

Val continued to gaze ahead. 'Yes, sir.'

'I sincerely hope it is, Sergeant, because you stand in danger of losing those stripes you were proud to earn unless you listen to sense.' Wheeler reined in to give Val serious scrutiny. 'I allowed you to remain with A Troop after that affair last year because you assured me that you would do your utmost to treat Mr Pickering with the respect you show other officers of this regiment. If I receive just one more complaint from him I'll have you transferred, if not reduced in rank.'

Val had also reined in, and he fought pent-up anger and frustration while listening to this warning. Wheeler was making a rare gesture. Many would have transferred him as far from Pickering as possible after his detention last year, in spite of the fact that the little pipsqueak with royal connections had few friends among the commissioned ranks. Wheeler only ever heard one side of the story. He knew nothing of the vindictiveness Pickering used, or of the man's faint-hearted approach to the patrols. This morning they had flushed out a small group of Boers who had been unwilling to stand and fight. Pickering had let them go, despite Val's heated suggestion that they could be turned and trapped if the patrol split up and rode flat out. Such was his frustration, Val had very nearly overruled the subaltern and set off after the enemy. The men would have followed him, he knew. Had he done so not only would he now be in very serious trouble, Pickering would have scored again. Even Felix Wheeler's tolerance would be exhausted, and Colonel Beecham would reconsider his promise to commission him as soon as possible. Val was growing dangerously impatient for that moment, but it would never come unless he kept in sight the two things he most wanted: the rank of second-lieutenant and the complete downfall of Audley Pickering.

He looked across at Felix Wheeler now and said, 'I'm sorry if you feel I'm letting the men down, sir. I think very highly of them.'

'As they do of you . . . but it doesn't help their present situation to have you questioning orders on which their lives might depend.'

'It won't happen again. Thank you, sir, you've been very decent about it.'

Wheeler gave a rueful smile. 'I said you are a thorn in my side, but you're such a likeable fellow I only feel the pain occasionally. How old are you, Havelock?'

'Twenty-one next week, sir.'

'Ah, well, you'll grow wiser with age, I trust.' He began to turn his horse in the direction of the officers' lines. 'Tell them to give you a party in the Mess if we're still here then . . . and if you're still a sergeant. Don't be a fool and throw it all away. Life's too short and uncertain in this game we're playing.'

What was meant as sound advice only highlighted Val's urgency to achieve his aims before he fell in the carnage certain to come.

Lord Roberts put into operation on Sunday February 11th his plan to relieve Kimberley with speed and guile. The cavalry regiments were formed into a 'flying column' with orders to fight their way through to the stricken city no later than Friday. False messages were sent out to suggest that the British force had decided to abandon Kimberley and instead march on Bloemfontein. To support these, orders were issued to all troops to move out and head south-east. Many truly believed the besieged city was to be left to its fate, but others with more military sense and confidence in 'Bobs', as Roberts was affectionately known, guessed he was playing a crafty hand.

Val was elated by positive action at last. He and Toby packed their gear telling each other they would be inside Kimberley when it was next used, for they had orders to proceed without transport carrying just essentials on their horses.

'My word, I've never known anyone so keen to fight as you are, Martin,' said Toby as he hooked the strap of his pith helmet beneath his chin and joined Val at the entrance to their tent. 'That moody, truculent fellow I've shared quarters with for the past two months has been replaced by a firebrand.' His eyes beneath the jutting khaki peak grew speculating. 'I suppose your eagerness has nothing to do with our colonel's daughter.'

Val treated him to a phrase from a trooper named Deadman, which he found particularly effective to counter awkward remarks. 'Shut yer bloody gob!'

'Ha! Touched on a raw spot have I?' crowed his friend. 'She wrote to you at Christmas – I couldn't help seeing the signature at the bottom of the letter. Did you reply?'

As Val walked away, Toby fell in beside him totally unabashed. 'You look for trouble, you do. First Pickering, who could have you shot for insubordination at time of war, and Miss Beecham who could make you emulate that artist you know just to prove how brave you are. Don't be a fool and throw everything away because of them.'

That echo of Wheeler's words prompted Val to say, 'Whatever I do during the next few days will be for the sake of an old man who expects more from me than anyone else.'

'Your grandfather?'

After hesitation, Val said, 'Yes.'

'In his bad books, are you?'

Walking between tents where men were preparing to depart on a journey many of them would never complete, where the sights and sounds stirred him as no others did, Val felt closer than he had ever been to this young man who respected his deception and had been a true and loyal friend. Because of that, he now confided in Toby.

'I made an idiot of myself over a woman. He can't forgive me. That's why I have to destroy Pickering and take his place.'

'He's asking a hell of a lot of you.'

They were nearing the horse lines now. The smell of hay and warm hides filled Val's nostrils, adding to his sense of anticipation. 'No, he isn't. He's never asked of any of us more than he has achieved himself. If he dies before I've shown him I'm worth his regard . . .'

The sentence was never finished because a groom accosted him to say that several troop horses were showing symptoms of 'flu and should not be ridden. Some minutes elapsed before the two sergeants were mounted and ready to fall in with their men. Riding slowly side by side each of them took from their pockets envelopes, which they exchanged and put away. It was a ritual they followed each time one or the other took out a patrol. Toby's envelope contained a letter to his parents and one or two small personal items; Val's held short messages to Vere and Margaret. The friends would return their respective packets if they met up in Kimberley.

Once on the plain where the flying column was assembling, Val and Toby parted to ride towards their own troops.

'Good luck,' Toby murmured.

'And you,' said Val as they both veered.

'Martin,' the other called over his shoulder, 'you only have to prove your worth to yourself, you know.'

Val ignored that. 'See you in Kimberley . . . and Toby, stop reading the signatures on my letters. It could end a friendship.'

It was a splendid sight as around eight thousand men and horses, together with batteries of artillery, set off in full view and headed south away from Kimberley. Hooves beat the dry ground in a thunderous tattoo, the guns bounced over grassy hummocks with squeaks and rattles, and dust arose in an enormous cloud to coat everything moving beneath it.

Val looked at his companions and reflected that the regiment, nicknamed The Ghost Lancers, was presently living up to that description. It originated from an incident during the Peninsular war when the 57th, in their all-grey uniforms, emerged from the fog to take by surprise the encamped French who believed they must be apparitions. Right now they certainly resembled creatures from beyond the grave, their faces so thickly coated they were much the same shade as their khaki tunics, riding well-rested horses and with lance pennants fluttering in the breeze. He hoped the sight of them would demoralize the Boers as it had the French, but he hoped even more fervently that he would finally come face to face with them in combat.

That hope was not realized until three days later when,

the deceptive manoeuvre completed, they had doubled back to the river, crossed it at a *drift* and shocked a large enemy force into hasty retreat leaving behind all but their guns. The food and forage was welcome after a very long march of twenty-seven miles, and so was the general order of a day's rest prior to the final dash to Kimberley. Piquets nevertheless had to be posted, and patrols sent out to scour the surrounding terrain. At two p.m. Val went on one of these under the command of Giles Manning, a subaltern who could easily become a friend if rank could be forgotten, for they had a great deal in common. Perhaps Felix Wheeler had been diplomatic when arranging the patrols. Val preferred working with this efficient, sport-loving man only two years older than himself than with the vindictive Pickering, especially in a tense situation.

There had been constant firing since dawn, the Boers targeting them with a gun from distant hills. It proved more of a nuisance than a serious threat. More dangerous was the rifle fire from snipers who moved around before they could be flushed out by British cavalry. The prime objective of the patrols was to put these roving groups out of action before the next day's march. One patrol had succeeded in capturing some enemy waggons, but the Boers themselves had fled. The rest reported failure, as usual.

Val commented on the fact as he trotted beside Giles Manning, screwing up his eyes against the blinding light. 'Small wonder they sit laughing at us. They always take up a position in the path of the sun so that we have to ride in its glare. They're off and away before we draw near enough to see them, much less charge.'

Giles nodded. 'You can't charge at the devils, however. The only way to get them with the lance is to encircle them then close in. Guns are more useful, but *we've* not been trained to fire from the saddle so they have the advantage every time.'

'What I'd give to trap a group of them and show what we can do with a lance,' said Val bitterly.

They trotted in silence for a moment or two, then the officer said casually, 'It'll be rather different running it through a human body instead of a practice target, I expect. Can't say I'd like to be on the receiving end.'

Without thinking, Val said, 'My grandfather says you don't consider anything but preventing the enemy from killing you first. It's afterwards that the human element catches up to bother your sleep.'

His companion turned in surprise. 'I thought you had no family.'

'He . . . said that a long time ago. I was very young,' Val said, hoping to cover up his mistake.

'Aren't you from farming stock?'

Val tried to laugh off the question. 'He used to read about Napoleon and Waterloo, and then spoke as though he had been there himself. You know how old men are.'

'I know how *my* grandfather is,' Giles said with a grin. 'One would imagine he personally set up the legal system in England. Oh . . . *hallo*, what's that ahead?'

Their attention suddenly concentrated on a dark blob that became visible as they breasted a slight rise. Still dazzled by the sun, they halted and signalled the men to do the same. Giles took out his field glasses and studied the distance.

'Seems to be a farmhouse – quite a modest affair. Take a look, Sergeant.'

Val focused the lenses on the far-off construction. It was certainly typical of the isolated farms in the area, but there were no grazing animals, no laundry hanging to dry, no sign of occupancy.

He handed the field glasses back. 'They must have moved over the Transvaal border for safety, like many others.'

'That makes it an ideal place for mobile riflemen,'

murmured Giles studying the farm again. 'I'll wager the Dutch owners left food enough for their military brethren.'

'If they're there they will have spotted us by now.'

'Umm. It might well be empty.'

Val said nothing. He knew they could not return without searching the place, but the ground before it would leave them completely exposed as they approached.

'Bit of a poser, eh?' said Giles in a low tone the men would not hear.

Val nodded. 'They'll be expecting us to split and come up on each flank, yet if we made a head-on dash for it their sense of surprise wouldn't last long enough. Either way we shall lose men.' He looked the other in the eye. 'Mr Pickering would suggest a strategic retreat.'

'*Would* he!' The subaltern was lost in thought for a moment or two. 'Pity we couldn't make a surprise approach from out of the sun – as our predecessors burst from the fog. They might be dazzled long enough for us to get amongst them.'

Val thought about that. 'If we go back below this rise it might be possible to ride on beyond the farm, remaining out of sight. *Then* we could turn and rush them with the sun at our backs.'

'It's a long chance, man.'

'It's our best one, don't you think? They might even be duped into thinking we *had* made a strategic retreat.'

'Umm! That still might be the best course of action.'

Val replied heatedly. 'If we find the rise peters out too soon, so that we'd be exposed before we pass the farm, we can think again. Let's at least *try* it!'

Giles gave him a deliberate look. 'I said retreat might be the best course of action; I did *not* advocate following it. Tell the men what we plan to do. Once we get below the rise we'll take a rest. The sun's going down. A delay will give us even greater advantage because it will be fully in their eyes by then.'

The troopers were eager finally to have a crack at the enemy and expressed their hope that the farmouse was full of them.

'The buggers 'as larfed at us too frequent,' declared Jim Mudd, a likeable but somewhat slow member of the troop.

'I'll give 'em larf!' growled the giant Deadman, whose life Val had saved during last year's stable fire. 'When I gets 'old of 'em there'll be nuffink left ter bury.'

'The Colonel wants prisoners, not crumbling remains,' Val pointed out as he sat on the ground beside men with whom he had once shared a barrack room.

'Orl right, Sarge, I'll put a pair of 'em in me pocket and keep 'em reel nice so's you kin dust 'em down and present 'em ter the Colonel when we gets back.'

Val grinned. 'That's very good of you, but you have Mr Manning's permission to do what you wish with the rest. Isn't that right, sir?'

Giles looked tense. He was unable to sit and join the banter which helped men to relax before action, and Val once more realized the penalty of entering a regiment as an officer without personal experience of life in the ranks. This pleasant, intelligent young man was forced to make a decision which could cost lives. His status kept him aloof from camaraderie which eased anxiety, and the lack of rapport made him uncomfortable.

'I think we should move, Sergeant,' he said in clipped tones. 'If we wait much longer we'll be riding back to camp in the dark.'

Val jumped to his feet. 'Right, into the saddle, lads. You know the plan, but if Mr Manning thinks it won't work we'll try something else. No talking from now on. We want to surprise them if we can.'

They went at a gentle trot. Their plan initially rebounded because the lowering sun now so blinded them it was difficult to see ahead. Val cursed the fact. He was keyed up and eager. The gods had smiled on him today by sending him with Giles Manning, for Pickering would never have agreed to this. He was confident they would continue to smile. As if to echo that the higher ground curved away in the direction of the farm, making their advance easy. Giles cast Val a look and nodded his satisfaction. Val grinned back. Everything was going their way.

With the sun then on their right they were better able to see what lay ahead. The ground began to level about three hundred yards off, and they could only guess at how close they were to the farm. Giles halted them, dismounted, and snaked his way up the slope to peer cautiously over the rim of it. He slid down to say quietly to Val, 'We're presently more or less level with the building. Beyond it the ground is covered with tall rotting stubble impossible to ride through at speed. There's still no sign of life.'

'It *must* be deserted, sir. There'd be horses in evidence if anyone were there. How disappointing!'

Giles frowned. 'Yes, indeed. We'll still approach with the sun behind us to make certain. There might be provisions worth commandeering.'

After a swift discussion on tactics they then rode at a fast pace to where the rise petered out, wheeled sharply until their backs were turned to the reddening glare of the sun, and galloped for the farmhouse whose windows seemed almost to be on fire with the reflection of it. Val rode close at the subaltern's heels, his gaze sweeping from side to side and they neared the area of stubble. The total peace of the place told him there was nothing to fear, yet instinct insisted that the tall rotting stalks could hide patient marksmen. His heartbeat accelerated, his nerves grew taut. Samson's hoofbeats on the dry ground combined with the rest to create a thunder that must betray their approach to anyone unable to see more than a dark horde against the burning disc behind them. An awesome sight, he hoped.

They reached the stubble unhindered. The farm looked as it had throughout. Speed had to be sacrificed as the horses picked their way through tough stalks reaching to the top of the men's boots. Although they weaved from side to side so as not to present too easy a target, such progress was unnerving. Val's throat grew dry; his eyes ached from intense scrutiny of the scene. Doors and windows were all shut. No poultry roamed the yard between the house and a large barn. Where he would expect to see wood stacked there was none. The atmosphere was one of desertion.

The patrol rode into the yard and dismounted, carbines at the ready. There was no sound save that of their boots on the beaten earth. The men from a cool, green island home were now used to the wild majesty of this land they were in, but there was something particularly spine chilling in that silent isolation beneath a blood red sky. Val was immobilized by it.

Giles turned to him, his face running with perspiration, a muscle jumping at the corner of his mouth. 'Well, no one here. Take some men and search the barn and outhouses. I'll look inside the house. If there's anything worth confiscating we'll load it up and get going.'

Before anyone could move, a hinged door in the upper half of the barn crashed open and a hail of bullets rained on them. Those still on their feet dived for whatever shelter they could find and prepared to return fire, but the moment they ventured to take aim they were exposed to the enemy and paid the penalty. Val raced for the house and now flattened himself against a side wall, fighting for breath. Dear God, they had walked straight into a trap. How could they possibly survive to escape it?

From where he stood Val could see Deadman and two others crouching behind a crude forge. They dared not raise their heads above the stonework. Other members of the patrol must have found some kind of shelter, but they were outside Val's range of vision and, presumably, equally impotent. As he tried to come to terms with the situation, Val heard moaning from the yard. Whoever was still alive out there would not be for much longer if the marksmen heard those moans. He risked a look around the corner. Bullets whistled past his face to bury themselves in the wall, making him hastily dodge back, but not before he had seen Giles Manning lying ten yards away, his face twisted in pain. An attempt to bring in the officer must be made, and it was his duty to do it. But how?

While Val tried to think, he called softly, 'Keep quiet! If they think you're dead they'll leave you alone.' His message must have been heard because the moans ceased. Although Val knew the troopers were pinned down, the Boers had to be kept occupied while he ran out to attempt a rescue. Looking again at Deadman and those others behind the forge, he waved to attract their attention. Then he went through an elaborate series of gestures indicating that he wanted concerted covering fire while he ran out to the yard. Deadman nodded understanding, then repeated the gestures to others concealed out of Val's vision. After a few minutes, Deadman signalled that all was ready, and the trio raised their carbines. Leaving his own on the ground, Val braced himself.

A nod at Deadman, a deep breath, and he shot out from a crouching start as if taking part in a race. The late afternoon quiet was shattered by rifle fire as the British troopers aimed at the opening in the loft, keeping the enemy from it long enough for Val to check other bodies before picking up Giles to carry him over his shoulders to the relative safety of the house. Yet again he was glad of the physique he had deliberately built up, for the subaltern was also a sturdy six-footer. With chest heaving, Val raised his hand to stop the firing, then set his burden on the ground. There was a hole in the man's chest, and another in his abdomen. Both wounds were bleeding profusely. Much of it now stained Val's tunic. Giles needed attention fast.

Taking the officer's pistol from its holster, Val walked

the length of the side wall and around to the rear of the house where he found a narrow door. He flung it open with a jerk, gun at the ready. The dim room was empty, but there was evidence on the table of a recent meal. Smouldering ash lay in the stove which was hot to his touch. A pitcher still contained water. Cautiously, he penetrated further: the house was deserted. It was mystifying. If the Boers had only split their number between the house and the barn, the patrol would now have been dead to a man. It suggested that they had been at least partially surprised.

It took Val little time to carry Giles inside, strip off his own bloodied tunic to stuff inside the other man's then bind it tightly with his Sam Brown in an attempt to staunch the bleeding. The officer had passed out with the agony of being shifted, but he had to be left in the greater urgency of the situation. Val moved to look from a front window, then gave a cry as the glass was smashed by a bullet that entered his upper arm. All he had heard of the enemy's brilliant marksmanship was being borne out here. Grunting with pain as he lay back against the wall, and too well aware of blood oozing from his wound, Val told himself their only hope was to wait for darkness. Yet night would also cover the enemy's movements and they could get clean away. Next minute, a fresh burst of firing followed by an English oath uttered in panic sent determination flooding back. His brother Vorne had defied danger in the Sudan to take the slenderest chance. Where was his own Ashleigh pluck?

Wincing from the shooting fire in his left arm and shoulder, he tried to recall all the stories told by elderly warriors around the table at Knightshill. They could relate reminiscences of every campaign since Waterloo. Wiping his wet face with his sleeve he collected his wandering thoughts. One phrase had been oft repeated. *We had to flush them out before we stood a fighting chance.* Sliding down the wall to a sitting position, he racked his brains for a means of following this move. What chance did he have of making his enemies leave the barn and come into the open?

Into his fevered thoughts floated the scene as they had come through the rubble. These windows had reflected the sunset as if the house were afire within. Hope sprang. If Boers were regularly using this farm there should be fodder in the barn. Giles Manning carried matches in his pocket. All he must endeavour to do was cross to the barn unscathed. Struggling to his knees he risked a swift glance over the sill. Sinking back he faced facts. There was only one way to go from this building to the other, every foot within sight of the men in the loft. The idea had taken root, however, and he could not abandon it. With fire raging below, the Boers would have to jump out or descend the ladder he would cover until the others joined him with additional fire power.

Noticing with dismay how much blood he was losing Val considered his chances. If he failed to try, the troopers might all die at this remote farmhouse. If he made the attempt *he* might die. This in no way compared with Vorne's sacrifice, but it was there waiting to be done and he was Ashleigh enough to risk doing it.

Deadman spotted him as soon as he emerged around the corner of the house. One of the troopers with him was now lying flat with an arm flung out as if to reach for the rifle blown from his hand. Any lingering doubts flew and Val again gestured for covering fire while he made a dash for the barn. Deadman signalled his wish to go for it, too, but Val made motions to suggest striking a match before indicating his hope to send the enemy leaping from the loft. The huge trooper's rather ugly grin appeared as he nodded understanding, then passed on the information to those of his colleagues left alive around that yard.

Clutching Giles' revolver, Val fixed his eyes on the lower door of the barn and raised his hand to show that he would now go. With the tattoo of shots filling his ears,

Val left the comparative safety of the house. It was far removed from a rugby pitch, but his favourite sport at Chartfield had taught him speed and evasive tactics, so he used both now. Leaping bodies, he zig-zagged across that yard in Natal knowing his life, not a silver cup, was at stake this time. Something thudded against his pith helmet; something else rushed past his leg with an acute burning sensation. But he was almost there. He *was* there.

Bursting into the barn he pulled up short. This lower level was full of horses saddled and packed ready to leave. He then knew that the Boers were about to ride off when they were surprised by the patrol approaching out of the sun. It was why they had failed to take advantage of also manning the house. Gasping with pain and shortage of breath Val tried to count the beasts. It was difficult, but he guessed there must be around twenty-five men upstairs. A difficult decision then had to be made. His love of horses urged him to fling wide the door and drive them out before starting the fire; his military instincts told him their resultant panic at the sight of flames would dissuade the Boers to attempt escape down the loft ladder. He chose to compromise.

With pain dogging every step, he fought his way through the tightly packed beasts to reach piled straw beside the ladder, watching for any sign of a man at the top of it. Once there he had to steady himself before holding the box in his teeth to strike a match with an arm fast turning numb. Tossing it and several more amongst the straw he propped himself against the timber wall of the barn and pointed the revolver at the ladder.

The blaze grew quickly – too quickly. The ponies took fright and Val feared that he would be crushed by their shifting bodies. There was thumping overhead and shouts of alarm as smoke billowed upward. Gunfire continued outside, as Val tried desperately to cross back to the door when the foot of the ladder began to burn. No one would use it now. Coughing and choking he found his own escape blocked by the press of animals. Their squeals smote him, so he put fresh energy into fighting his way through by shouting instructions to calm them. He forgot they would be used to a language other than English.

Very soon the timbers above were ablaze and flames were creeping along the wall towards him. He remembered that other fire last year and how it had felt to burn. The memory overrode other pain to give him almost impossible strength. Retching, his eyes watering, his heart pumping, Val clawed at the warm hides surrounding him. He was not ready to die. There was so much still to be done.

Then, miraculously, cool air swept in when the doors opened ten feet away. The animals bolted to freedom knocking him against wood not yet eaten away by the flames. His path clear, Val stumbled towards his own freedom in a daze. A giant stood just outside watching him.

'You daft sod!' Deadman cried heatedly. 'Yer should've let me come wiv yer. We did it tergevver before, din' we?'

'Thanks,' rasped Val

'You *like* bein' burned?' the other challenged.

'Shut yer bloody gob!' Val returned in the man's lingo.

Deadman grinned, then indicated two bearded men lashed together beside a rotting ox-waggon. 'Saved two for yer, like I promised.'

The yard was littered with bodies, but Val was not yet able to take command. He barely had command of himself. Stumbling to the support of the farmhouse wall he uncorked his water bottle and drank thirstily. Then he gazed out across the stubble standing tall against the last few rays of the sun.

'It's a start, Grandfather,' he said silently.

They arrived back in the dead of night, a sombre cavalcade of exhausted men led by a sergeant keeping upright in the saddle only because of a man called Vorne Ashleigh. Some troopers led horses with bodies draped across them, others had veld ponies in tow. Several of the captured animals were dragging a crude stretcher bearing wounded whose condition had worsened through rough travelling.

The outlying piquets challenged men looming from the darkness, then exclaimed in excitement when they saw evidence of some kind of engagement. Val hardly heard their comments. Loss of blood made him feel sick and giddy. His head appeared to be spinning. His left arm was now useless; his right thigh throbbed from the flesh wound inflicted during his dash to the barn. Every yard seemed a mile, but he was determined to bring in the patrol as its leader.

After handing over the dead and wounded Val prepared to report to Felix Wheeler, but the medical officer detained him.

'You're staying here, man. I'll get word to Captain Wheeler. Sit yourself on one of those chairs until I've examined Mr Manning and these others.' He signalled a young orderly. 'Fetch Sergeant Havelock some tea, then cut off his shirt and breeches.'

Sometime during the next hour Val lost consciousness. When he came to he was in bed with bulky bandages swathing his shoulder, and more around his thigh. He still felt sick and giddy, thankful to lie quietly beneath the canvas roof. First light was dawning; an orderly dozed in a nearby chair. Val was too weary to think, yet there was a curious contentment within him as he lay between waking and sleeping.

The tent flap opened to admit Felix Wheeler dressed for riding. 'I hoped you would be awake,' he greeted quietly. 'How are you feeling, Sergeant?'

'Splendid, sir,' he croaked.

Wheeler's mouth curved. 'As if *you* would say otherwise! Your report will have to wait a while. Deadman gave me basic details of what occurred. He's a good, loyal fellow.'

'The best, sir. How are Mr Manning, Hodges, Greer and Parks?'

'The last three are holding their own.' He sighed. 'I'm afraid Mr Manning's chances are very slim.'

Val was upset. 'He was first rate, sir. Led us in great style.'

'I'm sure he did. First rule of warfare is to pick off the officers. That doubtful honour goes with the privilege of rank.' He put on his pith helmet ready to go. 'We're off in a few minutes with every confidence of reaching Kimberley by nightfall. I'm sorry you'll not witness that triumphant moment, but you handled yesterday's engagement with very commendable qualities of leadership. I'm sure your action won't go unrecognized by Colonel Beecham and the regiment.' At the entrance he turned with a smile. 'I might soon be rid of a thorn in my side. Good luck, young Havelock.'

9

VERE RODE INTO Ladysmith with the bulk of the relief
column at the beginning of March 1900 and was
deeply moved by evidence of the privations of a long
siege. Constant shelling had reduced much of the town
to ruins; the roads were broken by deep craters. The
people who lined the streets as the troops rode in were
not wildly rejoicing at the prospect of freedom. It had
been too long in coming and too dearly bought. In the
main they were pale, emaciated and withdrawn. Vere had
seen the destitute in London but they had not touched
him as deeply as these women and children now did.

The first three months of the twentieth century had
been the longest he had ever known. During them his
two selves had often conflicted, although there had
been no repetition of his folly at Colenso. The martial
instinct had enabled him to understand those around him
and to sympathize with their anguish, frustrations and
uncertainties during demoralizing days and nights so near
and yet so far from Ladysmith. The soldier in him had
shared those long, wearying marches across inhospitable
terrain when muscles ached, throats grew parched and
eyes burned from the glare of the sun; had shared freezing
nights in bivouac beneath glittering stars knowing the
hills ahead concealed an enemy who would bring about
yet another setback. His warrior blood had raced through
his veins when bugles sounded the advance; he had felt
as one with exhausted, filthy, victorious men who finally
gained command of a *kopje* at the end of a day. Over

the tragedy of Spion Kop, bought with thousands of lives then surrendered again through mistaken orders, this artist had grieved as bitterly as anyone. The spirit of General Sir Gilliard Ashleigh's heir had fought as hard as the next man to reach Ladysmith.

The artist in Vere had recorded those three months with insight and sensitivity. Not for him the usual patriotic representation of well-built, immaculate heroes winning the day on battlefields arranged to suit the balance of the subject matter. He showed the life of the soldier in stark reality. Vere Ashleigh's paintings would never be hung on the walls of military messes, or on those of mansions of governors in far-flung outposts of the Empire. Sir Gilliard would never countenance them at Knightshill, but anyone who had ever taken part in the harsh unravelling of war would recognize and be mesmerized by pictures produced by a man with the pain of it in his soul, and honesty in his vision.

An Australian special correspondent had obtained from his newspaper in Sydney a contract for a series of Vere's sketches featuring Commonwealth regiments within the relief force, and this prompted another from Delhi concerning Indian troops. The men in khaki had come to regard with friendship the civilian who had helped to drag in an ammunition waggon at Colenso, and they frequently sought to obtain one of his sketches to send home. Aside from his commissioned work, Vere painted a series of watercolours for himself – the record of an unforgettable period of his life which he hoped to pass on to his children.

This would be his last war. The Sudan had been terrible enough, but he had then been pursuing an identity by laying the ghost of a supposed hero. It had overridden the greater aspects of what he had done during those eight months. Here in South Africa he had witnessed the profound agony and endeavour of conflict, and this had swamped personal introspection. The long, desperate struggle to free Ladysmith had completed the change in him begun on African soil almost two years earlier. The soldier and the artist now lived in peace with each other so that Vere Ashleigh, gentleman of property and heir to Knightshill, could happily seek out his intended bride and take her home. He had told Sir Gilliard that he was already a man – without the assistance of the West Wiltshire Regiment – but that had been only partially true, he now realized. *En route* to Ladysmith he had acquired deeper understanding of his fellow man, greater appreciation of the span of human life against the enormity of creation, and his wisdom had gained additional dimensions. With Kitty beside him he could possibly become the giant Annabel had claimed he would never be.

The relief force camped on the plain beside the damaged garrison known as Tin Town because of its spread of tin-roofed huts. The troops were mostly gladdened by the prospect of a few weeks' rest in a place where there were shops, entertainments and women. The residents quickly recovered their spirits and energy, delighted with the influx of khaki-clad heroes who had given them back their freedom. A few officers regretted General Buller's long delay in Ladysmith, however. One of these was Edward Pickering, badly wounded on Spion Kop. He expressed his doubts when Vere called at the hospital several days after the town was freed.

'This is no time to sit back on our heels, man. Roberts no sooner took Kimberley than he marched on towards Pretoria. He won't stop there. We should also be chasing the enemy until he surrenders. While we relax indulging in morning calls and soirées, Johnny Boer is gleefully regrouping and occupying fresh hills which command the route to Johannesburg. Can't Buller see that? Does he want a repeat of Colenso or Spion Kop?'

Vere accepted the chair offered by a smiling nurse and sat beside his friend. 'Fretting is no aid to recovery,

Edward. You'd do better to concentrate on the delightful young woman who has just walked off with a twinkle in her eye. Didn't you once give the opinion that they must be ladies of great compassion and generosity to do such work?'

'I also gave my opinion of forming an attachment to any female encountered on foreign soil,' he growled in response. 'Can you sit there and say you approve of Buller's tactics?'

'The men do need a rest.'

'They need a new leader.'

Vere studied the man lying swathed in bandages who would be shipped home before long, his military career in doubt and long months as an invalid ahead. Edward Pickering's fate, as much as anything, aided his own decision to go home. He made a blunt change of subject.

'I am going to be married, as soon as I can arrange it.'

His friend's lean face now gaunt from pain registered astonishment. 'Good God, in three days! Don't be a fool, you can't possibly form an alliance with someone you have only just met. Ten to one she presently looks upon you as a hero, and adoration is a potent force, but don't lose your wits like a schoolboy. Remember who you are; the position your wife will have to uphold. You must not surrender to an impulse like this! My dear fellow, do assure me that you have not yet made an offer to this young woman.'

Vere smiled. 'I have, and she has done me the honour of accepting. No, don't look so perturbed. The lady is not resident here. I have known her for some while, but my commitment to *The Illustrated Magazine* has delayed our marriage. It was my intention to send for her when we reached Ladysmith, never dreaming it would take three months. My work is completed; the war is more or less over. I shall now escort her to Durban then sail for England after the wedding.'

'My word, you kept very quiet about all this,' said Edward wearily. 'You should have left me some kind of missive for your fiancée in the event of your death. A fine friend I should have been, unaware that a young creature's heart was breaking and in need of comfort.'

'As I said, I hadn't reckoned on such a struggle to get here. I'm sorry you can't be at my side for the marriage, but you must visit Knightshill as soon as you are able. You will then meet the exception to your belief that attachments made abroad will never survive at home. Kitty is a widow with a eight-year-old son of intelligence and charm. She by no means regards me as a hero, believe me, and I had to fight for her consent to become the future mistress of my family home.' He smiled again at his memories of Vrymanskop. 'Put away your visions of an adoring miss barely out of the schoolroom who has besieged me with her hero worship, Edward. My chosen bride is a lady of great determination and character. She will make previous Ashleigh wives appear pale by comparison. I cannot wait to see the effect she will have upon my irascible grandparent.'

Edward offered his hand with some difficulty. 'Well, I wish you every happiness with your determined bride. Am I to believe from what you have told me that you have finally decided who you are?'

'I have decided that I am an impossible mixture of soldier, painter and philosopher,' he replied with a grin. 'Acceptance of that truth enables me to take up my inheritance in contented fashion, knowing that I can indulge all three inclinations in limited manner while following the destiny laid upon me by the death of my brother.' After a pause he asked, 'What will you do Edward?'

'I shall write my account of this damned mismanaged war and bombard newspapers with letters demanding a critical review of those who presently command the best soldiers in the world.'

Vere regarded him sadly. 'Don't grow into a man like my grandfather at your age. Your impassioned words will be ignored, you know. Human memory is short. We are now lauded at home as the conquering heroes, our humiliating reverses put aside. Will it be long before the Boers are again dubbed "the farmer army" and ridiculed for their effrontery in taking on Queen Victoria's mighty legions?'

Edward's eyes grew moist. 'Someone needs to speak the truth, Vere. My men deserve that from me as the most I can do for them now. I shall miss them – miss the life I've wanted from the day I received my first toy soldier.'

'I know.' Vere leaned back in his chair. 'I was an invalid from birth and, therefore, excused the passion for military status all true Ashleighs have. I was supremely contented running the estate and painting until a beautiful young woman I put upon a pedestal told me I was a pygmy among giants. I ran away to the Sudan in an endeavour to at least *die* in the right clothes. Instead, I discovered life. Coming here has deepened that discovery and made me realize that being regarded a pygmy by any number of people is unimportant if a man is a giant to himself.' He slowly got to his feet and smiled down at the broken man. 'Don't cling to the belief that Edward Pickering cannot exist without a scarlet jacket. It may take a while, but you'll discover life is full of glorious colour no matter what one is wearing.'

'My God, it's clear you're a man in love,' Edward said in mock disgust. 'Heaven save me from the state.'

Vere chuckled. 'I'll remind you of that when you bring to Knightshill your radiant fiancée. I advise you to concentrate on the delightful art of dalliance and leave military tomfoolery to Cousin Audley.'

'Ha! You have it right there. I received another of his infernal communiqués yesterday. To read it one would think he alone freed Kimberley. His assurance that he remained sound in wind and limb did not surprise me. He would have seen to it that danger and Audley Pickering remained well apart. To think that a fop like that will represent the family in wars to come!'

'But you will have done more during your years of active service than he will achieve in a long career. He sees himself as a pygmy. Why else would he write you such pompous nonsense exaggerating his role in any engagement?'

Edward shook his head on the pillow in affection-ate exasperation. 'Go away, fellow! Methinks your philosophizing wearies me.'

Vere gripped his friend's hand. 'Contact me as soon as you reach England. I'll bring my wife to meet you.'

'You say you had to fight for her consent to become the future mistress of Knightshill. Knowing your way with words, I'll wager it was a short fight,' Edward replied with a smile. 'Good luck, and every happiness.'

Vere halted at the foot of the bed. 'One last piece of philosophy. Find yourself a bride and produce a few sons to represent the family in wars to come. A pleasanter pastime than writing your blistering account of this one – and you're certain to excel the Awful Audley in that direction, also.'

Back in the dusty street, Vere paused to grow accus-tomed to the glare of the sun, his heart heavy. It did seem a tragedy maybe to rob one man of the active side of a profession he loved and did superbly well, while another remained untouched and incompetent within it. There was no news of Val. Communications between the two contingents had been difficult, but the communiqué from Audley indicated that letters were beginning to get through. Vere had thought most carefully about his next course of action. Although he had written frequently to Kitty, there had been no reply from her. If she had not received the packets he sent down on the train; if, as suspected, they had never been dropped off at

Vrymanskop and now lay neglected in some mail office in Durban, she would surely be aware of the protracted campaign to reach Ladysmith and understand his long absence. His priority was to get down the line to her. Having done that it seemed more practical to continue to Durban, where he could book passages home.

His wish to meet up with his young brother was strong and he prayed Val was alive and whole. He would not leave South Africa until he was assured of that, but he was eager for Kitty, eager to place on her finger the ring that would legalize passion between them. He could not take time chasing the 57th around the Kimberley area before going to Vrymanskop. When they reached Durban he would do his utmost to make contact with Sergeant Havelock and persuade him to obtain leave for the marriage. At present, it was vital to secure his own affairs.

By now used to 'jumping' trains, Vere thought nothing of climbing aboard one leaving Ladysmith on the following evening prepared to throw his baggage off at Vrymanskop before leaping from it as it slowed around the bend circling the hamlet. He had obtained permits for Kitty and Simon to travel with him to Durban and he had sold his two horses along with the camp equipment rarely used on the march. Most nights had been spent in bivouac beneath the dark, looming hills. All he now carried with him were toilet articles, a spare set of drab clothes, a heavy cloak, a set of watercolours, some perfume miraculously displayed in a Ladysmith store, a kaleidoscope for Simon and a leather collar for Kimber. He would purchase everything they would all need when they reached Durban.

The carriage contained officers going to Durban on leave. This time Vere was welcome in their midst, and he enjoyed their company. They had all seen action since that initial journey which they had broken at Vrymanskop; battle was a great leveller. Soon after eleven, however, Val took his bag out to the platform where one of his companions was smoking a cigar.

'Your destination near here, is it?' he asked between puffs.

'Should be,' Vere responded, trying to make out the dark scene after the brightness of the carriage. 'Difficult to recognize anything at night.'

'Unless it shoots at you.'

'No chance of that now,' Vere countered with a smile. 'Surrender must come within weeks, if not days. But I guess the country will never be the same. Bitterness lingers long after the treaties are signed.'

'Pity,' said the other man, exhaling smoke. 'Stirring terrain. Once it has been fully developed it'll not fall far short of paradise. If I were a Boer, I'd continue to fight for it.' He tossed the cigar butt from the train and turned away. 'Adieu, Ashleigh, and good luck.'

Nights were still cold. Vere shivered, uncertain whether it was due to the chill or anticipation of the meeting so long delayed. Kitty would have retired for the night, and he would be unable to resist the passion that must follow when she greeted him in her nightgown. At that thought the hardships, pain and tragedy of the past three months swamped him to increase his longing for physical release in its sweetest form.

Vrymanskop was still lit by a row of lamps in readiness for the last train to go through that day. A small bag containing mail was tossed from the luggage van as it slid past, after slowing around the long curve. The burgher was astonished when Vere first threw his own bag out, then jumped to the ground after it. In the act of retrieving the mail bag, the stout stationmaster stared wordlessly as Vere then snatched up his belongings and made off towards the hotel at a run.

The building was unlit. The main door was locked. Leaving his bag on the ground Vere ran around to the rear and began throwing earth at Kitty's window. No lamp

225

suddenly glowed within the room. He tried to waken her by this method for several minutes longer, but was unsuccessful. With impatience ruling him he ran back to the main door and began hammering on it in the hope of breaking through her sleep, or even alerting Simon. There was no light, no sound to suggest that anyone heard his tattoo. He paused wondering what to try, then became aware of another presence. The burgher clutching the mailbag was standing in the shadows, watching him.

'It is closed,' he told Vere in guttural English, staring in hostile manner.

'I can see that,' Vere said heatedly. 'I'm attempting to awaken the proprieter to let me in.'

'No one is staying there.'

'Quite possibly, but *I* shall if I can only attract Mrs Munroe's attention.' He resumed his hammering on the door to no avail, then turned back to the man watching with continued hostility. 'Have you a ladder anywhere?'

The burgher shook his head and began walking off to his tiny province beside the track. He doused the lights and closed up his little hut before setting off along the road with the mailbag under his arm. Feeling curiously uneasy Vere ran after him.

'What did you mean about no one staying at the hotel?'

'No one is there.' He walked on in determined fashion leaving Vere standing in the dark street.

'Mrs Munroe and her son?' Vere called out in sharp tones.

'Gone.'

He ran after the retreating figure once more. '*Gone? Gone where?*'

The burgher shrugged and continued plodding.

'When? When did they go?' Vere demanded through a throat grown dry with inexplicable apprehension. 'Were they escorted, did they get a train, has something happened to the boy?'

The questions went unanswered as the man opened a gate leading to a small shack half-way along the road and approached its door. Angry and alarmed, Vere dashed forward to vault the low fence and put himself between the door and his quarry, whose face was no more than a pale blur in the darkness.

'I *have* to know Mrs Munroe's whereabouts,' he insisted with as much authority as he could muster. 'It's a matter of extreme urgency. You'll be well rewarded if you tell me all you know.'

'How much?'

'That depends on how much you tell me. Come on, out with it.'

'What has she done?'

'*Out with it!*' cried Vere, seizing the man's lapels.

'Five weeks, six weeks, perhaps longer, she sold out to Millbrook's for a waggon and two horses. They left early one morning; her, the boy and that hound. Took old Amos Drurie's rifle, and a small chest besides blankets and a mattress. This is all I know. Now pay me!'

'Where was she heading?'

'Through the *nek*.'

'Where does it lead?'

'Anywhere. It is the only road out of Vrymanskop.'

Vere could not believe what he had heard, yet this man was not the kind to invent such a story. He was too dour and unimaginative. He had also stated that they had gone *before* receiving his offer of a reward. Vere asked if anyone in Vrymanskop would know the family's destination.

'No . . . nor would they care,' was the response. 'She was a stranger, a diamond-fields woman. Her kind is not welcome in a decent district.'

Vere clutched the man's coat tighter in anger. 'Was she driven out of Vrymanskop?'

'Not her! Bold she was, and determined. But we all knew what went on inside that place. Hardly a woman there, but she had as many as eight men staying at one time. No respectable widow would do that, and it was only her word that the man she had come here with *was* her husband. She quickly moved in with old Amos when she was deserted. Why would a pious bachelor leave all he had to a woman like that unless she coaxed him to do it? He was only one day buried when she . . .'

Vere's anger ruled him totally as he listened to these words about Kitty. Pushing the man away so roughly he almost fell, he cut the insinuations short. 'A decent district, you say? May God forgive you all your lack of charity and your poisonous tongues. I'll pay you nothing. I hope you rest uneasy in your bed tonight.'

Back at the hotel, Vere picked up his bag and walked around to the *stoep* where he had spent so many wonderful hours with Kitty and Simon. Wrapping himself in a cloak he settled in a corner, deeply distressed and worried, to stare at the surrounding hills whose flat tops were just visible as darker lines against the sky. What could have happened to make her leave in such a manner? How could a woman and a small boy survive on the veld alone? Where *was* she? She had left six weeks ago, possibly longer. She could be anywhere in this vast land by now.

For hour after hour he stared at the distance seeing only those days he had spent with her. She loved him, he had no doubts on that score. Had she tired of waiting and set out for Ladysmith in the hope of meeting him along the way? Had she or Simon, been taken ill *en route* and forced to stay in some outlying place? What should he do now? He was unlikely to learn from the stationmaster when another train was due through in the direction of Ladysmith. Traffic on the line had greatly increased now the siege was over so there was certain to be one tomorrow, yet what was the point in returning to the town he had just left? He could not simply wait there in the hope that Kitty would arrive in her waggon expecting to find him. But where else should he go? He cursed the community which had never accepted a diamond-fields woman, then his fist thumped in angry despair against the wall. *He* was now using that derogatory term!

He sat like a man in a fever until dawn began to put silver fingers across the sky. Only then did he see the obvious. Kitty knew this country well enough to be aware of its vast isolated distances. She could have had no knowledge of how long the battle for Ladysmith would last; so, if some person or event in Vrymanskop had forced her to leave, she would have left a message for him here in case they missed each other in the miles between. She knew he meant to come for her as soon as he could, so she would not risk losing all contact.

Jumping to his feet he began to search. The *stoep* would be an obvious place, or the front porch. Or even the stables. When he had exhausted all the likely spots he guessed Kitty must have given the letter to someone at the merchandizing warehouse which had taken possession of the hotel in exchange for a waggon and horses. Only when he was told by a cheerful manager that the widow Munroe had driven off before Christmas without even leaving a forwarding address, did Vere accept that he had been blind all along. Sitting on a wooden bench outside Millbrook's he faced the fact that Kitty had run away from him.

Time passed unnoticed as he struggled against acceptance of her decision. She was the only woman with whom he wanted to share his future; the perfect soul mate. Yet she had gone because she believed Edward Pickering's maxim that a relationship which bloomed in a foreign country would wither and die at home; she believed herself unfit to be his wife. Vere recalled their parting and her reaction to his news of Vorne's death: 'You are your grandfather's heir?' What a fool he had been to let that fact slip out. At the time he had not noted the significance of her words. Now they provided the answer to his present pain.

Not for a moment while he sat watching the sun climb into the sky did he face defeat. She loved him deeply, but mistakenly. His dilemma and despair were due to the difficulty of tracking her down. He tried to recall all she had said to him during their days together, searching for clues to aid his pursuit. Durban had been her hopeful destination when she had saved enough money. She had frequently spoken of the advantages Simon would have in a major town. His tiny leap of hope was smothered as instinct told him that she had made too much mention of the plan to follow it in these circumstances. He would too easily find her.

As minutes passed, an idea began to grow in his mind. Her brother was in Kimberley – or he had been when it had been besieged. Where else would she go but to her sole relative and the only real home she had ever known? A city under siege would suggest an unlikely destination for an unaccompanied woman and her son during a time of war, but Kitty was resourceful and used to holding her own in a country she had never viewed through a rosy glass. She knew enough of the Dutch language to get along with the farmimg people of the district, and had probably stopped in a safe place nearby until Kimberley was relieved. British troops had broken the siege almost three weeks ago. Vere guessed it would be easy enough for him to trace a young mining engineer named Gerald Jakes. The greater problem was how to get from Vrymanskop to a city half-way across South Africa in as fast a time as he wished.

Kimberley, a city existing purely because of the wealth of diamonds in its blue earth, stood like a rich oasis in the heart of a great arid plain. There was little evidence of the place Kitty had described. In the years since her departure with William Munroe, the Diamond City had acquired elegance and respectability which was impressive, despite damage by shelling amd the trappings of war. Here was a much grander settlement than Ladysmith, which could only boast of being an important rail junction. Here lived the diamond millionaires, the giants who remained after the legion of dead and defeated prospectors had departed the scene. Here lived Cecil Rhodes, whose dreams for Africa had no limits.

Streets were lined with mansions of style and striking architecture. There was a racecourse busily being repaired for a coming meeting, a public library of some consequence, a large theatre, extensive botanical gardens, and stately centres of commerce. Most surprising of all, to Vere, was the Kimberley Club, an establishment along the lines of the most revered of London's refuges for gentlemen of means and status. Viewing it all through a military eye on the day of his arrival, Vere was astonished by the Boers' failure to swoop from the encircling hills and capture this prestigious jewel. The siege had been humiliating enough for the British; to have let such a city fall into enemy hands would have been total disaster. However worthy a foe in other respects, the Boers had made a mammoth tactical error here.

Vere's artistic eye saw something quite different. The streets were lined with vivid blossoms; trees stood brightly green against a cloudless deeper blue sky. White columns of banks and diamond centres contrasted strongly with the red dust streets. A picturesque wrought iron market hall contained colourful fruits and vegetables, rolls of cloth in rainbow colours, beadwork, ostrich feathers and all manner of bric-à-brac precious to citizens who lived in the middle of nowhere. Electric trams rattled through the main street – an incongruous echo of foggy London or drab Liverpool in the heart of a wild, sun-baked area. Even the rearing headgear and mounds of displaced earth which marked the mines had a certain alien beauty. Despite his eagerness to find Kitty, the painter in Vere knew he must stay long enough to record for himself and *The Illustrated Magazine* the heart of this city of diamonds.

The old coaching inn, where a room was reserved for him, was a good place to begin his enquiries for Gerald Jakes. He was advised to ride along to the De Beers offices, where any question concerning mining or those involved in the diamond industry was certain to be answered. Stopping only long enough to wash and change his clothes, Vere followed this advice. It had taken him eight days to reach Kimberley, yet he was now too impatient to waste even a minute. After hiring a horse from the stable, he set off for De Beers telling himself that, even if Kitty were not here, her brother would surely know her whereabouts.

An elderly, pale faced clerk wearing a pince-nez kept clearing his throat in nervous fashion, while searching through a thick ledger until he reached the correct page.

'Ah, yes. Yes, indeed,' he declared, peering up at Vere as he held a finger on the book. 'Mr Gerald Jakes. You are quite right, sir.'

'Where may I *find* him?' asked Vere irritably.

'Well, now. That's a different ledger, sir. If you will kindly wait until I exchange this one for the relevant volume, I believe I shall be able to give you the information you require.'

Vere wondered if the clerk had ever been young, had ever been in love, and even if he was aware that he had been under siege for three months. Possibly, he had been so busy with his ledgers it had escaped his notice. There was further delay after Vere was told which mine Kitty's brother was concerned with, because he then asked for the address of Mr Jakes's lodging. Twenty minutes after entering the office, he left it armed with directions to a quiet street not far from where he stood. The time was just before noon. Should he go first to the mine, or take a chance that Jakes would return home for his lunch? He took a chance.

The house was being painted white after what appeared to be extensive repairs. The ground to the left of it was marred by a crater in the process of being filled in by a team of black men with large shovels. The results of shelling, no doubt. Had Gerald Jakes been a victim of it? Vere then recalled Kitty saying that her brother had joined the Diamond Fields Horse on the outbreak of war. What if the only link with Kitty had been killed?

He dismounted, tethered his horse, then walked swiftly up the steps to the front door reached from the verandah. Before he could knock, however, he was set upon by a lion-coloured tornado on four legs, which was closely followed by another on two.

'*You came! You came!*' shouted Simon, laughing and crying simultaneously while Kimber barked and leapt in joy.

Vere caught up the boy in his arms. 'Of course I came! I told you I would,' he declared in a voice rough with emotion. 'I always try to keep my word, Simon, even when people do the unexpected.'

'Mother said you had been sent to England, so we must come and live with Uncle Gerald,' Simon told him, clutching Vere around the neck as if never to let him go. 'Are you going to be my father and take me to England after all?'

'That's why I'm here.'

'And Kimber, too?'

'If he will stop attempting to knock me over.'

The front door opened. Kitty looked pale and shaken as her gaze met Vere's over the child's shoulder. He let Simon slide to his feet and pushed the dog aside, saying quietly, 'Keep Kimber happy while I talk to your mother.'

As he stepped forward Kitty said in a near whisper, 'How very foolish! What will it take to make you see sense?'

'May I come in?'

'No, Vere. There is no point in further discussion. I left because it was the wisest thing to do. Please respect my decision, and go.'

He put out his hand to grip the doorframe while he looked down at her. 'We made a joint decision to marry, as I recall. I have waited three weary, soul-destroying months for this meeting, and you have put me to a deal of trouble to find you. I've no wish to force an entry, but I will if I have to.'

Kitty spun on her heels and led the way to a lace-curtained parlour, the stiffness of her back and distant manner telling him that aggression rather than tenderness would be needed to win her over. Her determination and strength of character he so admired would have to be countered by his own. Any attempt to take her in his arms would be a mistake. That would have to wait until after the certain clash of wills. When he closed the door she turned to face him, a dignified figure in a high-necked blouse of figured lawn and a long claret-coloured skirt which he could visualize standing in any room at Knightshill and enhancing it.

'How did you trace us?' she asked with a hint of anger.

'Because I remembered every word you ever said to me, even before you promised to become my wife.'

'You coerced me. I was against it all along.'

He shook his head. 'Coercion suggests force or undue threat. The pact was made in the most delightful of circumstances. If force there was, it took the form of very masculine persuasion to which you were more than happy to succumb.'

Although she grew paler still at his words, she remained resolute. 'You were not honest with me. The man I agreed to marry could not decide whether to be a soldier or an artist; he was a man who claimed to be the misfit in a noble family. That last revealed only under pressure, you must own.'

'I thought it unimportant compared with our love for each other.'

'*Unimportant!*' she cried, aloofness flaring into passion. 'I know the penalties of unequal marriages. My mother suffered deeply as a result of her love for Monkford Kellaway, but she was a daughter easily relinquished by her influential family. A *son* is altogether different. He cannot be banished from society when he bears a noble name which will be passed on to his children and their descendants. *He* must continue to be accepted by his equals while they snub his unsuitable wife and malign him for a fool behind his back.'

Vere sighed. 'I thought I had convinced you at Vrymanskop that I don't give a damn about what is said behind my back, and that you are the most suitable wife that I could have. All this was discussed under the most intimate circumstances possible. If you have forgotten, I shall take the greatest pleasure in repeating them to aid your memory.'

She backed away from him, her passion increasing. 'I have *not* forgotten. How could I? It would never have happened had I known the truth about you.'

He knew what she meant. 'I am a man you loved enough to surrender to. It makes no difference whether I'm a younger itinerant grandson or the unexpected heir to an estate and fortune.'

'It makes *all* the difference. An heir has obligations to family and heritage. He cannot pursue an obsession with someone he sees as the answer to his search for artistic fulfilment. An heir must choose a bride with care when the future of a great family is at stake.'

'Exactly,' he said, advancing on her. 'We shall ensure that our children and grandchildren possess all the virtues and graces. You made me a promise which kept me going throughout the terrible months that followed. I demand that you honour it.'

'I did not know all the facts when I made it,' she cried. 'You charmed me into agreeing to something that made no sense after you left. I came here because I knew you'd return for me and that you would live to regret a marriage based on a brief encounter on the veld. You saw it through a rosy glass, Vere. I warned you of it.'

'And followed that warning with several uninhibited nights in my arms to make the glass even rosier,' he retorted with some force. 'For heaven's sake, let's put aside all this nonsense. My patience is wearing thin.'

'Then just hear this! I've scrubbed floors, darned clothes and cooked for my family. I've put men to bed when they came home drunk, and I've cleared up the mess they made. I'm no sheltered creature unused to anything unpleasant or ugly. I've heard oaths enough to last me a lifetime and I've mixed with people of every kind. I've none of the genteel graces that make a female a lady. I'm known as a diamond-fields woman whether I like it or not,' she ended defiantly.

'Then *you* hear *this*,' Vere countered swiftly, advancing on her once more. 'I was once so besotted with the kind of creature you say you are not, that I ran away to die in the steps of her hero when she rejected me. That was when I began to live. I have been rough and have committed the usual sins of military men. I have been put to bed drunk; I have uttered countless oaths. I'm no gilded hero or dutiful heir. My grandfather considers me a total failure as his successor.' He had manoevered her into a corner so that she was neatly trapped. 'My greatest folly so far, however, was to seduce a respectable widow then give her the opportunity to slip away from me. But there's no further escape. I'm determined to marry her and take her home.'

Pressed against the wall with his outstretched arms penning her in, she gazed at him with anguish in her eyes.

'Simon is not William Munroe's son.'

It was a moment or two before he took in the import of that sentence. When he did, it was the shock she had meant it to be. His arms dropped to his sides and aggressive excitement swiftly ebbed. Kitty's face was now quite ashen, but the anguished gaze had changed to one of compassion as she said, '*That* was why I ran from you.'

'And here to *him*?' Vere heard himself ask.

She shook her head. 'He died in the same landslide that claimed my stepfather.'

'I see. Did he know he had a son?'

'Simon was born after the accident.'

'Munroe knew?'

'We had not been man and wife for several years. I had become little more than a housekeeper in his eyes. He was possessed by the drive to find the stone that would dwarf all others. Nothing else mattered to him.'

Vere moved away trying to put his thoughts in order. Was she telling him she remained loyal to her lover, and that the days he had spent with her in Vrymanskop *had* been merely a brief interlude on the veld? His plans, his hopes now seemed out of reach. He felt curiously betrayed . . . and yet he *could* not believe those nights together had been prompted by anything save mutual deep love.

'The diamond necklet with flowers at the side – he gave it to you?'

Kitty crossed the few feet to a window and gazed from it as if seeing the past. 'It now seems unreal. So much has touched my life since that tragic accident.'

'He *did* give you the necklet?'

'He arrived in Kimberley with money enough for a good claim and a modest two-roomed house,' she began in faraway tones. 'He struck lucky immediately, which prompted William to make his acquaintance and persuade my stepfather to invite him to dinner. He had been crossed in love, and we were both lonely. It was easy to offer each other friendship. We had not expected it to get out of hand, of course. He was cultured and gentle – so unlike the man I had married – and I became deeply drawn to him without considering the danger. We tried several times to end our relationship, knowing it could not bring happiness.' She turned to face Vere looking stricken. 'He had the necklet made as a birthday gift. Two days later he was buried beneath tons of earth.'

'You still love him?' Vere asked her.

'I loved him then. He has gone, along with the life I knew. I am a different woman now.'

'You continue to wear the necklet.'

'It's the only token of love I've ever received,' she explained gently. 'When his son marries, I shall give it to his bride. It's Simon's heritage from his father.'

Still shaken and uncertain, Vere said, 'He wants *me* to be his father?'

She came up to him. 'You see now why it's out of the question.'

He looked down into the face he had thought of so often during the advance on Ladysmith and knew he would never be happy again without her. 'Nothing is out of the question when you look through a rosy glass. I offer you mine to share, Kitty Kellaway. If you refuse I shall never see clearly again.'

The convalescent home stood in a long avenue bordered by colourful shrubs in the district where the élite of Kimberley chose to live. The large house was owned by the Honourable Mrs Gort, widow of a wealthy diamond broker, whose son had been killed during a sortie outside the city with the Diamond Fields Horse. Mrs Gort and her two daughters had offered this home to the military medical authorities as a place where wounded or sick officers could recoup their strength and spirits before returning to duty.

Blasedon was just one of many similar grand homes which had been used in like manner from the start of the siege. Val cursed fate for sending him to the very one in which Mrs Beecham and Vivienne had been doing voluntary, unskilled nursing work during their incarceration. In truth, it was not fate but a particular request from Mrs Beecham that was responsible for officers of the 57th Lancers being sent there, if space was available. The arrangement was normally welcomed by the patients, for their colonel's wife was well liked, but the newest subaltern of the 57th found the proximity of her inquisitive, persistent daughter more than irksome.

On the death of Giles Manning, Colonel Beecham had honoured his promise to put Sir Gilliard's grandson where he had every right to be, but Second-Lieutenant Martin Havelock was the first Ashleigh to have fully earned his rank before acquiring it. Max Beecham's report had not only gained Val the coveted commission, it had brought him a D.C.M. for gallantry in rescuing his wounded commander under fire, and for then leading his men in a successful action against the enemy. His own wounds had healed well and he was keen to rejoin the regiment, but the medical officer insisted on a period of convalescence. Hence, what Val regarded as his imprisonment in Blasedon.

In the main, the officers had accepted the promotion of a sergeant very evidently from their own class. One or two took exception to *anyone* being brought into the Mess from the ranks. Audley Pickering was completely enraged. He knew, like Val, that equal rank would make their enmity more subtle. It would also throw them together in social as well as military situations. If Pickering was furious, Val was overjoyed. His arch enemy's days were numbered, on that he was determined. Vivienne Beecham was a different problem. His new rank made friendship of even the closest kind perfectly permissible between them. He would be unable to avoid her, unable to fend off her advances. She was the type of girl to take the fullest advantage of her position and enjoy his reaction to it. She was also now in a better position to probe into his past and to discover his true identity.

She was already making it very obvious that she had what his dead schoolfriend, Clive, had called 'her eye on him'. Comments had been passed by others within his hearing concerning someone who had only just come in by the back door having his sights set on swift advancement. The jocular remarks had contained a bite, and Val cursed the girl for her lack of subtlety. But for that, he might have quite enjoyed her company. They shared a number of interests and she could be entertaining when she abandoned her habit of making *him* the butt of her amusement. He had, in fact, felt very sorry for her on meeting up in Kimberley for the first time. Always thin, she had looked almost skeletal, and her narrow face had reflected the rigours suffered while the relief force had been endeavouring to break through. His sympathy had been swiftly banished by her effusive greeting of her 'mystery man' whom she now saw as the complete hero – a wounded one, to boot. The sooner he could rejoin the 57th the better.

He was strolling around the garden one afternoon in March when Vivienne made a beeline for him across the lawn. Escape was impossible. The path had no turnings and he was in full view of other patients with visitors. She had gained weight, and there was colour in her cheeks today making her look almost attractive in the long white cotton dress with a starched lace collar. There was something different about her hair, but he could not tell what. It was still a harsh carroty red in the sunshine.

'What are you doing prowling around down here?' she demanded in tut-tut fashion.

'I'm not *prowling*.'

'Yes, you are. That leg wound needs rest. Come and sit down.'

'If I sit it'll be on a horse, not on one of those fancy garden seats,' he said impatiently. 'There's no reason whatever for me to be kept here.'

'The medical officer says there is.'

'He's a fool.'

She linked her arm through his. '*Dear* Havelock, he knows very well, as I do, that you're longing to ride off and do something else terribly brave. You've already done more than enough to earn a rest.'

He unlinked their arms and walked on putting greater distance between them. 'Until a peace agreement is signed it's my duty to fight. What's the point in giving me a commission then locking me up in here?'

'What nonsense! Blasedon is not in the least like a prison. You should know that after spending twenty-eight days in one last year.'

Val felt his colour rise at her reminder of something he was ashamed of, and he was furious. 'If you've come after me just to be unpleasant, two can play that game. You're still my colonel's daughter, but my rank now allows me to give you a piece of my mind.'

She laughed. 'You've always done that, even when you were a trooper. That's why I like you so much. The others are scared of putting a foot wrong where I'm concerned, but you don't care a jot whether you upset me. We can be perfectly honest with each other. That makes us special friends.'

Warning bells rang. 'No, it doesn't.' He had no intention whatever of being perfectly honest with her. If she ever discovered his true identity all would be lost.

She swung round to step in front of him forcing him to a halt, and there was a disturbing gleam in her eyes as she looked up at him appealingly. 'Why are you always so prickly when I try to be friendly? Ah, don't say what

you usually say!' she added swiftly before he could speak.
'You're not a sergeant any longer so your stuffy notions
about rank don't apply. Father thinks very highly of you,
and Mother has no objections to our friendship, so why
won't you unbend?'

The bells were ringing louder now. The humiliation
of surrender to Julia Grieves' offer of friendship would
take a long time to forget, and this girl had a hint of
the same desire to get the upper hand. He suffered the
usual inability to counter Vivienne's overtures, save by
withdrawing smartly.

'Aren't you supposed to be on duty? Don't let me
keep you.'

She put both hands on his arms and sighed, 'Oh,
Havelock, you really are infuriating! You wrote such
a marvellous letter in reply to mine at Christmas. All
the time I was looking after our wounded here I was
worrying about what might be happening to you outside.
You seemed pleased to see me when I first visited you
in the hospital, so I thought getting your commission
made all the difference. Now you're up to your old
tricks again.'

He was desperate to get away, but they were in full
view of everyone in the gardens so he could hardly
disentangle himself and march off. '*You're* the one who
plays tricks,' he accused. 'And I always seem to be on
the receiving end of them.'

'That's only when you start getting huffy and arrogant.
You can be awfully nice when you make an effort. Please
do it now.'

Resigned to defeat, Val said, 'Not if you're going to
start asking questions.'

'I won't . . . at least, not about the pack of lies you've
told us concerning your past as a stableboy.'

He turned away and set off in the opposite direction.
'There you are. You're off already!'

'No, I'm not,' she cried, going after him. 'That wasn't

a question, it was a statement of fact. *Everyone* knows you made all that up. You've never acted in the least like a stable-boy.' She fell in beside him. 'I told you once before that whatever it was that made you enlist as a trooper could not have been bad enough to merit such punishment. I *know* you could never do anything dishonourable.'

'Yes, I can. You've just enjoyed reminding me of my month behind bars.'

'There *you* are!' she cried, striding along beside him. 'I did not *enjoy* reminding you of it. I used it to show you how foolish you were to call this place a prison. In any case, that affair last year was caused by Audley's vindictiveness . . . and your own silly pride. You gave Felix Wheeler no option but to lock you up. *Havelock!* Stand still while I explain.'

He strode on. 'I'm not a sergeant any longer. You can't order me about in that haughty fashion.'

Unabashed she ran past and halted in his path. '*Please*, Havelock dear, will you kindly stand still?' Her wide smile disconcerted him enough to do as she asked. Then she added further persuasion in tones that made his heart sink. 'It's because you're no longer a sergeant that you must stop this silly nonsense of fobbing me off. It's perfectly acceptable for us to be seen together now, and you're going to need me in the months ahead.'

'Why?' he demanded bluntly. As she put up a hand to tuck in a whisp of her bright hair with fingers that had bandaged some horrifying wounds, Val thought yet again that she would be all right if she would only stop teasing. To soften his response a little, he added, 'I'll be going up the line to rejoin the regiment soon. The war's not over yet.'

'It will be before long. Then we'll be back to normal peacetime. Most of the officers are quite nice – particularly the married ones – but one or two are pompous asses who can make your life uncomfortable in the Mess.

Audley's livid about your promotion. He'll be out to rob you of it in any way possible.'

'Let him try,' said Val through his teeth.

'*That's* why you'll need my friendship.' Vivienne told him warningly. 'Although he has influential connections, Father still commands the regiment. If Audley oversteps the mark he'll be reprimanded, but he's less likely to persecute you if he sees us together a lot.'

'Good God, do you think I'd hide behind your skirt because of a nincompoop like Pickering?' cried Val indignantly.

'Don't get on your high horse,' she flashed back. 'That temper of yours will be pushed to the limits by him. He may be a military disaster, but he's socially very sly and smooth. You most certainly are not! I'm determined to stop you from walking straight into his trap.'

'But into yours instead,' he said before he knew it.

It silenced her for a moment or two. Then her green eyes softened with enlightment. 'A *girl* was behind it all! That explains everything. You've been deeply hurt and won't trust any female now. Poor Havelock, how you must have suffered!'

Knowing escape was imperative before she began exposing something he had foolishly betrayed, he looked around for some excuse to rid himself of her company. Help came in the most astonishing form as he spotted one of the other volunteer helpers pointing him out to a man who stood on the steps leading to this lower part of the garden. Setting off across the grass, Val was met half-way by the brother from whom he had parted under distressing circumstances three years ago.

'What the blazes are you doing in Kimberley?' he demanded as he gripped Vere's hand. 'I thought you'd be in Ladysmith for some while yet. How well you look! Alderton was wrong all the time then? You've changed. Filled out. You look so happy! Your pictures are splendid. I've seen every edition of the *Illustrated*.

I'm proud to be your brother. I just wish I could tell everyone.'

'Hey, hey, take a pause for breath,' laughed Vere. 'Stand back and let me look at you. I said goodbye to a schoolboy in cricketing togs. My word, you've changed too, lad. You've grown taller, even more muscular, and that fine moustache completes your emergence to manhood. I hardly recognize you. Congratulations on your commission, by the way. I only heard about it when I made enquiries about my "cousin" Martin Havelock. You've done very well. I'm proud to be *your* brother, Val.'

This unexpected meeting with someone who represented the house and family he had lost caused Val suddenly to become choked with emotion. 'Are you? Someone hiding behind a false identity because he let the family down?'

Vere gripped his shoulder and coaxed him to move away from the proximity of a rowdy group to the relative seclusion of a walk bordered by oleanders. 'Look, old son, let's clear the air before we go any further. You merely did at Chartfield what we all do initially – lose our head over a female. I went off to die in the desert for one, and should have had more sense at twenty-six. I don't know the ins and outs of your affair, and have no wish to know, but you were only eighteen and fighting a very superior foe. I hold Grandfather entirely to blame for what happened, and I'm filled with admiration for the way you have overcome all obstacles to gain what should have been yours with his blessing.' He stopped to face Val. 'I'm deeply sorry you've been obliged to lose the family connection, but you're not really using a false identity. Martin and Havelock are both on your birth certificate, so it's just a case of using your two middle names rather than the ones we're used to.' He smiled warmly. 'You've not let the family down. Quite the reverse. I was told you've been recommended for a

Distinguished Conduct Medal for the action in which you were wounded.'

Val nodded, cheered by his brother's words. 'It'll eventually be gazetted, so Grandfather's bound to see it. Will he be pleased do you think?'

'He won't show it . . . but he can't fail to be.' Vere sighed. 'Age is slowly conquering him, you know. When I left a year ago he was fighting the inevitable by dwelling deeper and deeper on the past. I'm afraid we've all been bitter disappointments to him by not following the narrow paths he set us upon. What he has never realized is that, being his grandchildren, we have all inherited his qualities. We have the same determination to live our own lives as *we* desire. I told him that, and suggested that he would have resisted any attempt to turn *him* from his chosen course when he was young. He reacted in typical fashion, of course. I'm afraid we parted on bad terms. I had turned down a commission in the West Wilts in favour of a tour of the Mediterranean with my brushes.'

Val saw the disastrous aspect of this statement. 'Good God, what courage! Poor Grandfather. *Two* of us spurning the family regiment!'

They sat on a seat placed in a sunny recess in the bordering shrubs, while they talked of things they had both done and seen since their last meeting. Then they spoke of their sisters.

'Margaret is so secure with Nicolardi, Val. She looks radiant. I suppose none of us noticed how unhappy she had become with Philip.'

'I did,' Val said, at once. 'The children were also affected. Trouble is, I put it down to your decision to go off to the Sudan.' He leaned back and gazed across the garden. 'It seems so long ago now – like a different existence.'

'It was, old lad. You and I are different people now. We've lived, in the fullest possible terms. Margaret has, to a certain extent. With Nicolardi she'll become the woman she was destined to be.'

'That leaves poor Lottie,' mused Val. 'She wrote to me out of the blue just before Christmas. I naturally thought it was the worst possible news, but it was only a long informative letter in surprisingly friendly tones. I'm afraid I haven't replied yet. I've been busy, and I was never much of a hand at letters.' He made a rueful face. 'I've kept in touch with Margaret, for all that.'

'You two were always close. She practically brought you up after Mother left. Lottie . . .' Vere hesitated. 'She was terribly lonely after we all went off under our separate clouds. I can understand what it must have been like for her with only an old man who cursed us all up hill and down dale whenever he emerged from his nostalgic solitude.'

Val nodded. 'She must have been knocked for six when you left again after being at home for such a short time. She's devoted to you.'

Vere looked slightly uncomfortable. 'Devotion can be unwise in certain circumstances. Poor Lottie misguidely fashioned her life around the family, forgetting that we would fly from the nest. I had the devil's own job not to wallow in guilt over my decision. Then I reminded myself that my life was my own. The old man wanted me to sail to China with the West Wilts; Lottie wanted me to run the estate and grow gardenias. I had to get away and live free . . . until duty called.' He frowned. 'You know, Val, I often wondered if I was partly responsible for your trouble at Chartfield by going off to Egypt as I did, placing the burden of inheritance on your young shoulders. It must have increased your problems no end.'

'By God, no!' Val said in surprise. 'I've never wanted to be Grandfather's heir, because *this* is what I want to do with my life, but I was more concerned with what I thought of as the bloody idiocy of your decision.'

He chuckled. 'You asked me to take care of the girls, and I remember thinking what a fat chance I'd have of doing that. Margaret mothered me, and Lottie thought I was beyond the pale. Neither would have heeded a word I said.'

'So you don't resent having the heirdom wrenched back?'

'Wrench away! I'm bloody thankful to be rid of the responsibility.'

'And Martin Havelock lives on?'

Some of Val's gaiety faded. 'The consequences of being found out are even worse now I've been commissioned, and I'm more likely to be recognized by someone I know. I'm banking on the fact that I haven't been at Knightshill for two years and my moustache is a partial disguise.'

'If you walked past in the street I might think you looked familiar. If I was told you were Second-Lieutenant Havelock I'd not take a second look.'

'Good. Vere, I might not be known as an Ashleigh but I'm still very much one inside.'

'I know that, idiot . . . and I know you'll be the greatest of us all one day.'

Such words were music in Val's ears but he shrugged them off to pursue another topic. 'I can't wait to get back to the regiment. My long-standing vow to destroy that fool Pickering can now be realized.'

His brother looked unhappy. 'I wish you'd drop that notion. If he's a fool he's certainly not worth risking your career for.'

'You don't understand the situation. The little bugger's out to get me. But I'm going to get him first.'

'Be careful. You're skating on thin ice as it is, Val.'

'I know what I'm doing,' he said forcefully. 'There's a bloody long list of insults I'm going to blast away with one massive salvo. When I've finished with him there'll be nothing left but a stinking little pile of manure.'

After a moment's silence, Vere said, 'You not only look

different, you've also become tougher, more aggressive. And you've picked up some very colourful language.'

Val gave him a frank look. 'Life in the ranks is hard, Vere. Boys at Chartfield could be cruel to those who didn't fit in for some reason, but even their worse punishments were nothing to the things a man can suffer at the hands of troopers. My first weeks in a barrack room were indescribable, because a massive character named Deadman with a certain criminal past found that everything about me offended him. His campaign of punishment culminated in the torture of being held face down in a bucket of horse piss until I was on the verge of drowning, then being revived in order to repeat the process. I damn nearly died.'

Vere looked horrified. 'I know enough about being a military misfit to understand that you could do nothing to stop him, but how on earth did you survive?'

'Pickering returned from leave. The moment he began *his* campaign, Deadman and his mates became my fervent champions. They all hate him more than they hated me. Even so, I knew I would have to earn their championship. It was a slow business until there was a fire in the troop stable. Deadman and I brought out most of the horses against the odds. He would do anything for me now, and so would the rest. I was much happier as a sergeant, but I then knew enough to fit in well with the rest.' He gave a short sigh. 'I suppose I've become Martin Havelock to a certain extent ... but I'm sure I'll be a better officer for the experience. My men won't be just a collection of familiar faces to me, they'll be people I truly understand because I've been one of them.'

'Yes, you're right, Val. I've lived amongst young officers. They're mostly suicidally courageous, but many are still senior schoolboys in outlook.' Vere gave a rueful smile. 'When I believed I was going off to a mock hero's death in the desert, I regretted not having been a better brother to you. The wide gap between our ages was mostly responsible – you were away at school much of the time – and our interests were incompatible. I can't tell you how much I'm enjoying getting to know you.'

Val was also enjoying this reunion. They had never before talked on equal terms, never before found such common ground. It was a unique experience to discover a brother after twenty-one years. Vere shortly afterwards referred to those years.

'You came of age last month. I know you could have no greater gifts than a commission and a medal for gallantry, but as soon as I heard the news I decided that I should like to make you a present of your sword. Under other circumstances Grandfather would do the honours. Please allow me to represent him.'

Val flushed with pleasure and found it difficult to reply immediately. Vere saw this and spoke again quickly. 'I'd like to present it to you on Friday evening. I've already been told that you are perfectly at liberty to accept any weekend invitations.' He smiled. 'I want you to meet the lady I'm to marry on Saturday.'

Val was dumbfounded. 'You damned sly old fox! Who is she? Why wait all this time to tell me? Well, I'll be . . . congratulations.' He offered his hand. 'All the very best in the world. You deserve it. Now tell me all the details.'

Val's visions of a second Annabel Bourneville were quickly dismissed as he heard that his new sister-in-law was a widow with a small son. He was further surprised to hear that she was not one of the well-born women who had come out from England to roll bandages and raise money to buy comforts for the troops, but had spent most of her life in the diamond community. Although Val was certain his brother knew exactly what he was doing, he could not help wondering what would happen when the bride arrived at Knightshill. Vere seemed destined to break every Ashleigh tradition ever established.

As Val listened to his brother's plans, a sudden shadow

fell across his knees. He looked up to see Vivienne Beecham regarding them with a smug smile.

'Hallo,' she said pertly to Vere. 'You two have been talking so earnestly you haven't noticed tea has been set out on the terrace.'

Vere got to his feet with a charming smile. 'Thank you for coming to tell us.'

'Not at all,' she responded, her smile widening wickedly as Val stood up glowering at her. 'Havelock is usually hungry by now. You must have had some extraordinary things to say for him to almost miss tea.'

'Well, we haven't met for . . .'

'Miss Beecham is the daughter of my colonel,' Val put in with heavy emphasis, before his brother could continue. 'She was under siege here, unfortunately.'

'I sympathize, Miss Beecham,' Vere said smoothly enough. 'I was with the column that relieved Ladysmith. The tales of hardship and fear I heard there were very moving.'

Vivienne linked her arm through Val's in proprietary manner, completely in command of the situation. 'Which regiment do you serve, sir?'

Vere shot Val a swift glance before saying, 'I'm not a military man.'

'Ah, a columnist for a newspaper?'

'Something like that. You work here as a volunteer, Miss Beecham?'

She was not to be deterred by Vere's attempt to put the emphasis on her. 'Like many others. How do you come to be in Kimberley, sir, when you helped to relieve Ladysmith?'

'The fortunes of war. I suppose you will return to England now the siege has been lifted.'

Val envied Vere his aplomb. He was, of course, well used to social intercourse with females of all ages through his many visits to the London home of stage designer Gilbert Dessinger. Even so, Val knew this was a potentially

251

dangerous situation. Vivienne was not going to abandon the hunt now the fox was in her sight. He cast around for a way to put her off the scent and came to a reluctant conclusion. There was only one way to disconcert her.

Seizing Vere's hand he shook it heartily. 'Well, thank you very much. I'll expect further news on Friday. You must excuse me while I escort Miss Beecham to the terrace for tea.' Squeezing her arm hard against his side to prevent her from freeing herself, and clasping her hand tightly, he marched her with great determination across lawns well populated by patients and their visitors. He received several knowing winks or leers at their close proximity, but he walked on with the girl virtually imprisoned by his hold.

'I wouldn't have missed tea for anything,' he said breezily as he practically dragged her up the steps to the terrace. 'Good-oh, there are ham sandwiches today. Ah, there's Miss Potter with Bramley Sparsholt. Let's join them.'

Only when they reached another young volunteer helper sitting at an ornate table with a subaltern of the Horse Artillery did he release the arm Vivienne had slid beneath his own. Sitting her on a chair beside Amelia Potter with a firmness which brooked no opposition, he said he would bring her tea and crossed to the table covered by a starched cloth. As he filled two plates with sandwiches and cakes he congratulated himself on his initiative in averting danger. When he returned to Vivienne he saw his mistake. Her cheeks were flushed, her eyes starry, and she wore an expression akin to excited hunger as she looked him over from head to foot. He had seen that same expression too often on the face of her cousin Julia Grieves. Life as an officer of the 57th Lancers was going to be tricky. This girl could hold his entire future to ransom.

10

KNIGHTSHILL WAS ALWAYS surrounded by a blaze of colour in April. Azaleas and rhododendrons bordered the walks of formal gardens where forget-me-nots formed carpets around narcissi and wallflowers. In the orchard, fruit trees were smothered in pink and white blossoms, and tall magnolias bearing huge ivory-coloured candles made the park both fragrant and beautiful.

Charlotte surveyed it all with a sense of warm contentment as she strolled with Kate on a sunny morning half-way through the month. Things were looking up. The news from South Africa had put Sir Gilliard in a happier frame of mind. Throughout the sieges he had been outraged, damning then despairing in turn as he read of the disastrous battles endured by the relief columns. He had ranted and raved, vilified the commanders, written countless letters to *The Times* and various military publications, and spent hours locked away with his maps and memories. The three invested towns were now free: the war was virtually over. Regiments shipped out as reinforcements would soon be coming home. Spring in England was celebrating with nature's bunting.

Charlotte's light-heartedness sprang from knowing that her two brothers were no longer in danger. Vere's spasmodic letters had indicated that he was in the thick of the campaign. Val had not replied to her friendly note, but he was also certain to have been in the heart of the conflict around the besieged settlements. They were both now safe. With Grandfather emerging from

253

his black mood, with sunshine and flowers all around her as she walked with Kate holding her hand, it seemed to Charlotte that happiness was on the threshold. Vere would surely come home soon.

As they turned into the water garden where sunshine sparkled the fountains and highlighted shimmering gold and silver carp, Charlotte wondered if the sight of her beloved uncle would disperse the fear which had kept Kate silent for so long. The child had regained her health and appetite and appeared contented in her childhood home, but she still did not speak. After his stern ultimatum that Charlotte could have Kate at Knightshill providing she was kept out of his way and her upbringing was resolved without reference to him, Sir Gilliard acted as if she was not there.

To compensate for this cruel treatment on the part of her great-grandfather, the little girl was cosseted by John Morgan who, as a bachelor, had established a surprising rapport with her. Yet the bailiff's evident fondness and Charlotte's devotion were not enough to break through the trauma that had brought about Kate's silence. Charlotte had initially taken her niece to see Sir Peter Heywood once a month, but the visits had been discontinued when he ruled that Kate had discovered she could get all she wanted with nods or gestures and had grown lazy. His instructions not to respond to her silent messages, and to withhold what she wanted until she repeated words quoted by Charlotte, had been abandoned after just one distressing day.

Letters to Margaret and Laurence in South America took some time to reach them and produce replies. On this issue it appeared they could not agree, so Charlotte was given leave to do as she thought best. Although she did not object to taking such responsibility, she found herself more and more frequently seeking John's opinion and advice. They formed a curious trio – a spinster, a bachelor and a child who looked upon them as substitute parents. Kate clung to Charlotte despite the fact that Nanny, the woman who had looked after the Daulton children from birth, had been re-engaged. Burgeoning loneliness no longer dogged Charlotte's life, but she still dreamed of the day when the Ashleighs would again all gather at Knightshill.

The morning walk invariably ended with hot chocolate in the conservatory, or on the terrace if the weather was good. The sunshine allowed them to sit outside, and they had settled on chairs on the warm flagstones when John came from the direction of the greenhouse and stopped with a smile on the path below them.

'I was hoping for a word with you, Miss Charlotte.' He doffed his cap and swept a deep bow. 'Good morrow, Mistress Kate. Have you visited the rabbits this morning?'

The girl smiled and shook her head, then offered her plate on which was a slice of spice cake.

'Well, now, is that for me or for the rabbits?' When Kate pointed at him he laughed. 'I should get the length of Cook's tongue if she saw me eating that after I've just turned down one of her apple dumplings. You wouldn't want that, would you?'

Kate shook her head and began on the cake with gusto. Charlotte asked why John had been looking for her, and they fell into a discussion on the gardenias in Knightshill's hothouses.

'I'd be glad if you'd take a look at them,' John admitted. 'Benson says the blight that hit so many last year shows signs of bobbing up again. It might be worth taking out the doubtful ones and bringing in new growth.'

'You're probably right,' she agreed. 'There's no sense in risking the loss of them all. Perhaps we should consider something altogether different for next year. Branch out. If Vere *had* gone to China with the West Wilts he could have brought back fresh orchids. I have to say I prefer them to gardenias.'

'Each flower has it's own beauty,' retorted the lover of all growing things.

Charlotte smiled. 'How like Vere you sound. Maybe he'll introduce some rare South African plants to Wiltshire when he comes.'

'You've heard from him?'

'Not yet. Doubtless there's a great quantity of mail delayed by lack of means to transport it. We must be patient.'

John gave her a keen look. 'You're so certain he'll return soon?'

'Of course. He's been away eighteen months. Now the war is won there will be nothing there for him to paint.'

Perching on the low pillar at the foot of the steps, he said, 'I hope you're right. There are a number of things I'd like him to consider and decide on before I go ahead with them.'

'What nonsense, John!' Charlotte told him warmly. 'He gave you a free hand when he left because he has every faith in your judgement. We all have. When Vere gets here, I'm sure he'll be happy to let you continue what you do wonderfully well. He's certain to be much occupied with art commissions. His name is now greatly respected, and his work so generally admired, I imagine he will have little time for estate matters.'

John looked pensive. 'Life plays some funny tricks, one way and another. Mr Ashleigh's been renowned for his war pictures in the *Illustrated*, yet those paintings he did before going off to war are far better, in my opinion.'

'How I agree with you,' she cried with feeling. 'He referred to them as "rustic daubings", but they're more beautiful than pictures of soldiers cleaning guns or lining up to receive letters. I sincerely hope he'll return to his early love of the countryside in his future work.'

He shook his head. 'I shouldn't bank on it. He's not the same man after experiencing all he has over the past three years. *We* think this old house with its surroundings the best place on earth, but I daresay that's because we've spent our lives here. Mr Ashleigh's seen half the world now. He won't look on this tiny corner of it the way he did before. No more will Mrs Nicolardi and young Mr Valentine after their travels.' He smiled. 'You and I are regular country bumpkins, I reckon.'

Charlotte smiled back. 'And perfectly happy to be so.'

'Aye, that's true enough. I've all I want right here.'

On the point of impulsively concurring Charlotte hesitated. The past nine months had been enjoyable ones. John had become a close companion; it had been his opinion she had sought on many things ranging from the progress of the war to Kate's continuing silence. There was no one else to ask. He had revealed surprising general knowledge, and reassuring common sense on the subject of the child left in her charge. The three had spent the greater part of most days together on estate business or in entertaining Kate. They could have been mistaken for a happy little family, except that the girl was not Charlotte's and John was an employee – facts she sometimes overlooked in her contentment. However, complete happiness remained elusive.

'I shall have everything I want only when Vere, Margaret and Val come home,' she said wistfully.

The warmth in John's glance began to fade as he got to his feet again. 'Might as well wait for the moon to fall from the sky as to wait for that to happen. Mr Ashleigh will certainly have to return when Sir Gilliard passes on, but your sister and young Mr Valentine have shaken the dust of this place from their boots for good.' His brow furrowed as he added in gentler tone. 'Don't lose sight of the fact that the little lass will one day return to her parents. Better to make the most of what you have than long for things unlikely to happen.'

Chilled by the reminder of something she did not want

to face, Charlotte rose and walked to him, 'Don't mention that in front of her,' she commanded in a semi-whisper. 'Fear of returning to that life could keep her silent permanently.'

'Aye, and so could your refusal to do as Sir Peter Heywood advised.'

'You set yourself up as expert on children, do you?'

'I'd not be so arrogant, no, nor so foolish, being a bachelor,' he said calmly in the face of her challenging tone. 'But Sir Peter *is*, and what he told you makes a lot of sense to me. She's naught but a scared little creature who will remain that way unless encouraged to come out of her safe corner. A nervous foal will stay in the dimness of its stable all the time food is placed in there. You have to stand the dish a little further away each time to encourage it to venture outside. In some cases the beast will go hungry rather than face what it fears, but deprivation soon drives it to get what it wants by the only means. Once in the open it sees there is nothing to be afraid of.'

'You can't compare a child with a *foal*,' she declared, trying to keep her voice low.

'They're both young, uncertain and easily scared.'

Angered by his level reasoning, Charlotte said with muted passion. 'You didn't witness her distress when I withheld the things she wanted. It was heartbreaking!'

'Aye, there's the problem. You're too caring. Always have been when the family is concerned.'

'*You've* made no attempt to do Sir Peter's bidding. Kate gets all she wants from you.'

John's ruddy country complexion darkened slightly as he said, 'The lass has not been put in my charge. I'm paid to do as I'm bid by members of the family.'

Thrown into confusion by evidence that the situation had somehow become awkward in its frankness, Charlotte mumbled, 'Don't be silly. This is not an estate matter.'

John was clearly still uncomfortable as he settled the cap on brown hair silvering at the temples. 'I spoke out of turn. It's not my place to take you to task.'

'But many times I've asked your advice on what to do, John. You must give your true opinion or I shall not trust anything you say.'

His colour darkened further. 'There's no man you can trust more. I've told you that before. With your brothers away, and Sir Gilliard feeling his age, you need someone to turn to. You know best what to do with your own kin, however.' He began to move away. 'I'd be pleased if you would see Benson about the blight on the gardenias some time this morning. It'd be a shame to lose them all.'

Charlotte watched him stride off and sighed. It was so easy to forget that he was in the family's employ and regard him as the friend he had been since the day she had brought Kate to Knightshill. His words this morning had touched on a source of her own fear: that of the child rejoining her family. Was he right in believing the Ashleighs would never be here together again? Staring out over the gardens in which she had revelled a short while ago, Charlotte knew there was truth in what John had said. Val had always had his sights set on a career which would take him from Knightshill; his regiment would travel the world in pursuit of service to Queen and country. Laurence Nicolardi would travel it in pursuit of distinction, and Margaret would go with him taking Timothy, and baby Jonathan born last month.

Vere would surely have to return, whatever his plans, when their grandfather died. He had returned after war in the Sudan, but their relationship had not been the former warm closeness they had both enjoyed. Vere had been irritated by her attempts to revive it; she had been angered by his careless approach to all he had once deeply valued. Nothing would bring back those early days before Philip Daulton caught mission fever, before Vere met Annabel Bourneville and Val lost his head over the wife of his housemaster. John was right. Might as well expect the moon to fall from the sky. If Kate emerged from her silent state, if her parents sent for her to join them . . . Charlotte turned quickly to the child as apprehension stabbed at her heart. If Kate were ever taken from her she would return to a life of empty loneliness. This little silent child was her only means of escape from it. She fervently hoped the Nicolardis would remain content with their two boys.

After almost an hour in the glasshouses inspecting the gardenias with Benson, and concluding that the infected plants should be removed but not replaced until she had given some thought to the scheme of trying something new the following year, Charlotte took Kate to the nursery before tidying herself in readiness for luncheon. The black mood induced by her earlier thoughts remained as she entered the room where Sir Gilliard was already enjoying sherry.

'Thought you had taken it into your head to forego food today,' he commented glancing at the clock. 'Like punctuality, you know. A man who is punctual makes a good soldier. Disciplined, in command of himself. Never knew a fellow who could not keep to time make anything of his career.'

Tempted to comment that it was fortunate she was a woman, Charlotte merely said, 'I've been inspecting the gardenias. Blight has claimed rather a lot of them, I'm afraid. We shall suffer a loss this year.' Accepting a full glass from him, she added, 'I think we should consider new varieties for the future.'

Sir Gilliard's white eyebrows closed together as he frowned. 'Waste of valuable time! Always used those glass houses for flowers to put around these rooms. Never approved of growing them for moon-faced imbeciles-about-town to present to creatures who prance and warble on stages of theatres. Namby-pamby fellahs with no backbone. Never see a regimental officer make a fool of himself like that.'

Charlotte could not let that pass. 'They certainly do, Grandfather, although I cannot agree that presenting flowers to a lady makes anyone appear foolish – it's a very pretty custom – but I saw several officers waiting with bouquets outside London theatres when I was there with Margaret last summer.'

His frown became a glower. 'I believe I have specifically forbidden you to speak of someone who disregarded all notion of propriety and duty to this family.'

'That happened two years ago . . . and Margaret is still your son's daughter.'

'She forfeited any claim to kinship by running off to live in sin with that man – a damned foreigner, to boot. The subject is closed, Miss. More to the point is when are you going to get yourself a husband?'

Swallowing her anger, Charlotte said, 'I have no wish for a husband, being perfectly content with my life.'

'Poppycock!' he said explosively. 'Never known any woman to be content without a man to guide her through life. I will not live forever – more's the pity – and my place will be taken by a *painter*. Like it or not he will have to produce an heir before too long, and whoever he chooses for the purpose will not take kindly to having you moping around the place under her feet.'

Charlotte rose to that instantly. 'I do not *mope*, Grandfather. I spend the greater part of most days around the estate with John Morgan.'

'The man is perfectly able to manage it himself. Dogging a bailiff's footsteps will not get you a husband.'

'I have Kate to care for and educate.'

Sir Gilliard put down his glass with such force the stem shattered. 'That child was brought here against my express orders. The moment she is cured of her affectation, she is to be packed off to her mother, d'you hear?'

'Yes, I hear. You tell me so every time the subject is raised.' Knowing his mood was liable to continue

261

throughout luncheon unless she redirected his train of thought, Charlotte adopted a conciliatory tone. 'Benson told me that his nephew has returned from South Africa full of praise for Lord Roberts, who ordered the heroic dash for Kimberley. The poor man lost a leg – Benson's nephew, that is – but says he would not have missed the experience of fighting under one of the greatest generals in the army.'

'Hmmm, should have sent Roberts at the outset. The whole affair would have been over within a week. Expressed that opinion in a letter to *The Times*. Prompted a missive from Lord Garnier. His grandson, Edward Pickering, has been kicking up a lot of dust on the same subject and getting himself disliked at Horse Guards. Great mistake! Subalterns should never presume to air their opinions, in print or in words. Damn his chances of advancement, it will, although his wounds make his military future somewhat doubtful, by all accounts. Pity. Good family, except for one weakling. In the *cavalry*, of course,' he added with derogative satisfaction. 'Thinks to get by on connections with minor royalty on his maternal side. Won't, you know. Only thing that matters is a *father's* pedigree. That shows the strength or otherwise of a line, nothing else.'

Riding his hobby horse he led the way to the smaller dining-room, yet Charlotte could not shake off the chill his earlier words had produced. Coming so soon after John's reminder that Kate would have to return to her parents eventually, they again raised an unwelcome suspicion that haunted her quiet moments. Was she ignoring Sir Peter Heywood's stricture only because Kate had been so distressed by having things withheld? Was there not also an inner fear of losing someone who made her life worthwhile, if the harsh treatment brought the child out of herself – imposed silence? Margaret and Laurence had indicated that they were reluctantly leaving Kate in England until she was cured. Their frequent letters expressed concern that no progress was being made. It was clear they missed the girl despite the joyous advent of a new son. Charlotte could not imagine Knightshill without Kate, could not think about sending her away to South America and returning to her own former state. If John was right and the family would never again assemble at Knightshill, then Kate was all she had to make life bearable.

The subject of generals and upstart subalterns occupied Sir Gilliard throughout the light meal, until Winters entered with letters on a tray. Charlotte was then treated to the usual speech concerning the advantages of horse-drawn mail coaches over trains which could not keep to a timetable. She did not listen because the handwriting was Val's on the letter which topped those Winters placed beside her. The envelope was bulky. It was unlike Val to write a long letter, but she supposed he had a great deal to tell her about his exploits during the war. It was certain to be an enthusiastic account of things in which she had no interest, written with the same eager unselfconsciousness he used when relating things close to his heart. It was curious how her feelings for her brother had mellowed, how she now recognized his youth. Sudden yearning to see him after three years' absence took her by surprise. They had never been close – not the way she had been with Vere – yet the sight of his boyish handwriting affected her deeply. This morning had produced too many truths. The threat of a lonely future once more hovered over her.

Keen to go through his pile of mail Sir Gilliard elected to be served coffee in the library, where he spent most of his time. Charlotte declined the drink and took her letters to her room where she sat to read them by the window, warmed by sunshine. She first opened Val's and took out several sheets of paper folded around a photograph. It was a studio portrait of a very handsome young officer in elaborate and highly flattering uniform, with an impressive sword at his side. Charlotte studied the face sporting a moustache as blond as the crisp hair, and at the clear eyes gazing frankly at her. The man must be Val's commander, yet he looked somehow familiar. Putting the picture aside she began to read the letter.

> Dear Lottie,
> I've been commissioned after a small engagement at an isolated farm outside Kimberley. I'm sending the photograph to you because I'm not sure Grandfather would open and read a letter from me, but I want you to show it to him as proof that I'm keeping my pledge to redeem myself. I was given a medal, too. My commission and the award will be gazetted, so he's bound to see the entry. But please tell him yourself just in case he misses it. Of course, I'm still Martin Havelock, which takes the gift off the gingerbread, but I hope he'll be pleased with the news, anyway.

Charlotte reached for the photograph. Was this assured young man the schoolboy brother who had been dishonourably dismissed from Chartfield and joined the ranks rather than face his disgrace at home? He looked so splendid and . . . yes, *of course*, he very much resembled the portrait of Vorne, hero of Khartoum, which hung in the main dining-room. The longer Charlotte studied the photograph, the greater the resemblance to their older brother appeared. How would Sir Gilliard react to this evidence that Val had made good? When was the best moment to produce it? His refusal to discuss Margaret, much less consider forgiveness, suggested that he was unlikely to relent towards Val, yet his obsession with the army might allow a softening of attitude on seeing this photograph. Val looked every inch an Ashleigh whatever he might now be called. Surely the old warrior would feel pride when he looked at his fine grandson in officer's uniform.

The letter continued with a description of a grand

house in Kimberley where he had convalesced after being wounded, and an enthusiastic account of the final dash to the Diamond City by the cavalry.

> You'll know how disappointed I was not to take part in it, Lottie, but the 57th distinguished itself and I'm very proud to be a member of such a regiment *even* as Second-Lieutenant Havelock. Vere presented me with my sword – on behalf of Grandfather. Isn't it a splendid one?
>
> It was wonderful to see him again after so long. We've both changed, so we talked with greater mutual understanding than we had before. He's certainly made his mark as an artist and in a way Grandfather surely can't dismiss. Vere's outshone us all by combining the army with the profession he's so good at. By now you'll have received his account of the wedding, which is certain to be more descriptive and enthusiastic than any I could write, so I'll just say that I like Kitty enormously. She's not as pretty as Annabel Bourneville but much more interesting. I'm sure you'll get on well with her, and Simon will be company for Kate. How is she, by the way?

The remainder of the letter went unread as Charlotte stared at the last few sentences and tried to take in their import. Her first impression that Val had married a girl called Kitty soon faded. He was only twenty-one. His colonel would never have given permission for such a match. *By now you'll have received his account of the wedding.* She quickly sifted through her other letters but there was not one from Vere. *She's not as pretty as Annabel Bourneville but much more interesting.* Charlotte's heart began to race. *Vere* had married someone called Kitty. Why had he not become engaged and brought her home for the wedding? Why such haste? He had not mentioned this girl in any of his letters, so the whole affair must have been unconventionally swift.

Scanning those lines again she knew it was impossible

to interpret them any other way. Vere had chosen the next mistress of Knightshill and made her his bride without consulting his family. Who was this girl? Had Vere lost his head again as he once had over Annabel? Was she a scheming ambitious nobody? Was that the reason for a rushed alliance in a foreign country? Dear heaven, what had he been thinking of to behave so irresponsibly? Yet Val claimed that she and this Kitty would get on well, so the girl could not be too dreadful. However, Val had been mixing with rough characters for the past three years so his judgement could not be relied upon. *Simon will be company for Kate.* Who was Simon? Kitty's young brother? Had Vere married an entire family?

Agitation set Charlotte on her feet with the page in her hand. Going to the window she read that fatal paragraph through again before gazing out across Knightshill's acres. As Vere's wife, Kitty Ashleigh would be mistress of all this. She, herself, had held that position from the day Margaret had married Philip Daulton. A good many years spent as lady of this fine old house, although she had always known her reign was temporary. Vere would never turn her out of her old home, she knew, but his wife might resent the presence of a lone spinster sister once Sir Gilliard surrendered Knightshill to his heir. Even if Kitty did not, her own status might become uneviable. Would she grow afraid to walk freely about the house in case she intruded upon their privacy? Would she detect in them pity for someone ousted from a place she could never again occupy? Would their laughter and private happiness emphasize her lonely future? Would she become merely an unofficial governess for Kate and Simon? Could she stay here under such conditions?

A tap at her door heralded Sarah Clarke, who apologized for intruding during the period in which her mistress normally took a short rest. 'Mr Winters sent me to ask if you'd be so good as to step down to the library at the request of Sir Gilliard. I told him you'd be resting, Miss Charlotte, but he went all haughty as he sometimes sees fit to do and says, kind of sniffy, "The master does not require your comments, my good woman, he requires obedience to his instructions". Well, it's a good thing you're not in your wrapper lying on the sofa, in my opinion, or Mr Winters would be obliged to wait for his "obedience". My duty is to see to your best welfare, not to dance to *his* tune,' she rambled on in aggrieved tones.

Charlotte was in no mood for her maid's ruffled sensibilities. She guessed why her grandfather had summoned her at this hour, when he habitually read his mail in peace and privacy. Hardly knowing what she said to Sarah, she hurried from the room and made her way out at a very fast pace along corridors and down the broad staircase. Only when she neared the library did she feel sudden reluctance to enter and hear something which would irrevocably change her life.

Sir Gilliard was not at his desk. Standing with a letter in his hand by the framed and illuminated chart of the Ashleigh family tree, he appeared a remote and stricken figure as he gazed at the names of his distinguished ancestors. Charlotte waited silently until she grew convinced her grandfather was not aware of her entry.

'You asked to see me?' she prompted quietly, her heart still thumping.

He turned as if in a trance to stare at her. 'I have received some disturbing news.'

'Concerning Vere?'

'Concerning my heir,' came the harsh variation. 'He writes that he has married a foreign widow of mature years, who has a son aged eight. They will arrive in England next month, when he proposes to take up residence here and resume life as a gentleman of property.'

Aghast at this news, Charlotte asked in unsteady tones if she could be allowed to read her brother's letter. It was offered with a lethargic gesture. She scanned the lines written in Vere's elegant script, taking in only the vital phrases . . . *done me the honour to become my wife . . . charming, gifted, highly intelligent . . . late husband a wealthy diamond prospector . . . Simon is a bright but sensitive boy in need of security . . . grand-daughter of Sir Ralph and Lady Brinley.*

Charlotte glanced up from the letter. 'You said a *foreign* widow. She's connected to the Brinleys. I met them when I stayed in London with Margaret. Laurence knew the family slightly. Sir Ralph is very deaf which makes conversation difficult, but his wife is known as an accomplished hostess.'

Sir Gilliard glared. 'The woman has lived from childhood among some of the greatest scoundrels and rogues in the colonies. Any female reared with prospectors in a settlement containing establishments offering the vilest temptations of humanity, and in a country so primitive it is relatively uncharted, cannot be considered a lady and is certainly *foreign*.'

Charlotte unwisely continued in an attempt to lessen her own sense of shock. 'Vere would not marry anyone *unsuitable*, Grandfather. He writes in great praise of her. Charming, gifted, highly intelligent,' she quoted. 'She *cannot* be the type of female you describe.'

The old general came from his initial trance with a vengeance. 'I do not require the opinion of someone totally uninformed on anything other than the running of this household, Miss. You will see to it that appropriate accommodation is prepared for this creature and her offspring until the affair can be brought to a satisfactory conclusion. There are two small rooms at the rear of the east wing, well clear of the main area of the house. Have them cleaned and furnished with the bare essentials. They will be accustomed to far worse.' He turned away and then seemed to forget her presence once more as he muttered aloud his thoughts. 'Buy her off, that's the thing to do. Easy to annul a ceremony performed in some hell-begotten corner of an uncivilized continent. I'll get Parkington-Price on it. Weak! Always knew he was. *Paintings*. It's the end of the line. Can't consider the other one. That boy is beyond the pale and answering to another name.' He put a finger up to touch a name on the chart. 'The pride of the family dead at twenty-four. Bleached bones in the sand outside Khartoum. A giant of a man! A *giant*.'

To Charlotte's additional distress, she watched Sir Gilliard's white head bow as his shoulders began to shake. This sign of weakness in the man who had ruled the family with pride and great moral strength so disturbed her she turned and fled. Ten yards from the library she collided with someone who then held her steady. John looked down at her with concern.

'You'd best come to the office,' he said gently. 'If you need help I'm here to give it to you, you know that.'

Once settled on the chair he pulled forward, Charlotte waited while he perched on the corner of his desk before revealing in quick agitated sentences what he would have to be told. 'Vere's married. No engagement. Married a widow with a boy of eight. In Kimberley. They're arriving here next month. He says he'll resume his old life.' She gazed at him in appeal. 'The acclaim he has earned with his pictures. All put aside as if unimportant! He sounds so ... so *settled*. How could he give it up so instantly? Has he lost his senses? He need not have left Knightshill; spent all those months roaming the Mediterranean gaining experience.' Her distress caused her tongue to run away with her. 'Knightshill was no longer for him. If I had ever seen the desert I would understand, he told me. The world beckoned. He had to broaden his experience, meet people who could influence his career. Now he's thrown it all away in a moment's madness over this woman. How *could* he?'

John stilled her agitated hands by catching and holding them in his. 'I've known Mr Ashleigh since he was a little sickly lad and he's always taken pleasure in a brush and paints. He has a God-given gift. Taking a wife won't rob him of it,' he reasoned calmly. 'Just this morning you hoped he'd return to painting flowers and wild creatures when he came home. That's more'n likely what he'll do.' After some moments of silence during which John studied her with furrowed brow while she withdrew her hands, he said. 'It's not that that's bothering you, is it?'

Still deeply shaken by what had occurred, Charlotte hedged. 'I don't understand.'

'Your brother's not the kind of man to bring to this grand old home of yours a lady who will make you feel uncomfortable.'

He had brought her fears into the open, yet still she avoided them. 'Uncomfortable? Whatever do you mean?'

He continued to confront her, a solid, dependable man who had become a valued friend. 'The new Mrs Ashleigh will be a stranger arriving at an unfamiliar place to meet people from a family which has owned this corner of Wiltshire for thirteen generations. Rather a frightening prospect, eh? She'll look to you to help her settle in, show her over her new home. Without you to advise her, offer her a warm welcome, become her sister, her first weeks at Knightshill could be very unhappy.'

His words conjured up an entirely fresh picture. Kitty Ashleigh could be a sweet, gentle person overawed by her new affluent circumstances. She could be dreading her introduction to Vere's family and friends. Grandfather would possibly terrify her. She would need the friendship and support of her husband's sister.

'She has lived since childhood in South Africa, although her mother's family still resides in Berkshire,' Charlotte told John thoughtfully. 'She will be quite unfamiliar with England and how we go on here.'

'Then she will badly need your friendship and guidance. Mr Ashleigh will be aware of that and knows he can rely on you to give it.'

'Naturally. It's my duty to do all I can for his bride — I think no one could accuse me of failing in that duty when Miss Bourneville was introduced — for, after all, she will be the new mistress of Knightshill.'

'Aye, she will. Another frightening prospect for a lady from another country who knows little about how we go on here, as you already remarked. She'll need you to guide her, take her beneath your wing, so to speak.' He gave a sad shake of his head. 'You'll have little time in the months ahead for Miss Kate. She'll be all right with another child in the family — young 'uns soon warm to each other — but I . . . well, I'll miss escorting you both on rambles and picnics.'

Charlotte smiled. 'Nonsense, John! Summer is now on the threshold. You'll have *two* children to amuse with such things. That's if *you* have time. Vere will probably be full of new ideas and eager to implement them.' She was suddenly struck by the thought that John was about to have *his* position at Knightshill usurped. After running the estate for three or more years on his own initiative, as if it were his own, he would next month revert to consulting and executing the decisions of his employer. Sympathy welled up causing her to stand and put a hand on his arm. 'I suppose we must accept changes here once more, but the important thing is that this time an Ashleigh is coming home instead of leaving. I truly believe the others will follow.'

He stood. 'Maybe. The only constant ones are you and me. We love this place and must pass that love on to the young 'uns.' He glanced at the wall clock. 'I'd best get moving. Mr Ashleigh'll want to see everything in order when he arrives.'

'He's not coming until next month,' Charlotte reminded him teasingly.

'It'll come round before we know it,' he warned.

As she returned slowly through the silent house to her rooms, Charlotte reflected with slight sadness that a pleasant and enjoyable routine would be brought to an end with Vere's arrival. She had certainly been longing for his return, although not under these circumstances, yet the past months had been very fulfilling. She had told John he would have two children to amuse, but it was unlikely. Vere would occupy much of his bailiff's working day, then spend the rest of his time with Kitty and the members of his family. As their stepfather and uncle he would be the principal man in the lives of the children – and in her own, Charlotte conceded. Yes, everything was about to change once more.

Still musing on this, Sir Gilliard forgotten, she entered her sitting-room. Val's letter and the photograph lay where she had left it. Taking it up she re-read the pertinent sentences that proclaimed Kitty more interesting than Annabel. The concept of a sweet, gentle person overawed by her new surroundings vanished. Val would never write this of such a person. He *liked* her. That was surely a compliment from a someone who normally paid little attention to females. Yet he had become disgustingly enamoured of his housemaster's wife. Charlotte began to worry. Kitty was apparently a mature widow. Did Val like her *too* much, find her *too* interesting?'

'Oh, stop, *stop!*' she told herself softly. 'All this speculation is ridiculous. I must wait until she arrives, then form my own opinion.'

At that point Nanny knocked before entering with Kate, who had taken her afternoon nap. 'Do you wish me to accompany you to the village this afternoon? Sarah says you have to collect new shoes from the cobbler and deliver to the rectory a parcel of garments for the poor.'

'No, Nanny, you need not come. I dare say we shall be offered tea at the rectory. Mrs Blunt hopes to solicit my help for the Spring Sale in aid of the destitute, and will soften my resolution with refreshment. She firmly believes such temptations as lemon cakes and sherbet will persuade Kate to speak in spite of consistent failure.'

Nanny's mouth tightened. 'Miss Kate is best left alone. If Sir Peter Heywood cannot succeed, it cannot be done. Prayer might do a power more good than lemon cakes for the poor little soul.'

To distract the woman from the subject on which she was prone to labour, Charlotte told her about Vere's marriage. While Nanny oh my-ed and tut-tutted, Charlotte repeated the facts to Kate in tones of encouragement, adding the exciting news that she would soon have a companion in the nursery. The girl's reaction was difficult to analyze. She merely clasped her aunt's hand tightly as if afraid of losing her.

Once Nanny had departed in delight at the prospect of a second child to rear, Charlotte took up the photograph and held it out. 'Look at this, Kate. He's a person you know, although he looks rather different in this picture from when you last saw him. Do you recognize him?'

The girl gazed for a long time at the photograph of someone she had always regarded as a beloved older brother rather than a young uncle. An expression of joy slowly crossed her face, and she cried, 'It's *Val*.' Reaching for the picture she hugged it against her smocked bodice. 'I'm going to marry him when I grow up, Aunt Lottie.'

Vere's letter arrived on the day following receipt of the news sent to Sir Gilliard. Her brother's rapturous description of his bride created an altogether different picture of Kitty Ashleigh and confused Charlotte further. The new mistress of Knightshill clearly was no submissive creature overawed by her good fortune, neither was she the kind of woman Sir Gilliard had dubbed her. Intelligent, talented, courageous, warm hearted, generous and extremely vivacious was how Vere saw the lady of his choice. Charlotte read with astonishment the news that

Kitty had owned and managed for some years an *inn* in the wild heart of South Africa, and before that had kept house with the help of a *single servant* for her father and husband, both diamond prospectors. However would she settle within the vast spread of her new home? She was a gifted pianist, according to Vere, who played Liszt for him without excessive persuasion. How had she learned this skill in the course of such a life? Most disconcerting of all was the information that Kitty was the daughter of Monkford Kellaway, an *actor*, who died tragically early in a brilliant stage career. Charlotte could in no way imagine the sort of person she must soon welcome as her successor.

The boy, Simon, would surely also be very much a fish out of water. Vere's description of the boy's life at a place called Vrymanskop suggested that he was shy, insecure and lonely. Used to amusing himself and roaming unescorted over unihabited countryside, he seemed unlikely easily to adapt to the daily routine of Knightshill. A vision arose of an unkempt, surly child with little notion of good manners. Nanny would be horrified!

To counteract the apprehension created by Vere's two letters was the joy of Kate's emergence from silence. It had been instantaneous and complete. The child was now talking almost non-stop. Nothing would persuade her to relinquish the photograph of Val, which had created her release from self-imposed dumbness. She had always been intensely fond of him, and Charlotte began fully to realize the effect on Kate of Margaret's secret departure from Knightshill. Tim was a typical Ashleigh with the desire to roam, but his little sister shared Charlotte's love of home and security. Val's photograph remained with Kate. Sir Gilliard was in no mood to see and appreciate what it signified.

The days prior to Vere and Kitty's arrival were hectic. Charlotte immediately wrote to Margaret and Laurence relaying the good news about their daughter. She then arranged a visit to Sir Peter Heywood, believing it to be important to let him hear the child speak and proclaim her complete recovery. The consultation was not without its sting, Sir Peter declaring that the symptoms would have vanished a great deal earlier if his advice had been adhered to.

Charlotte booked a room in London for two nights in the hotel where she had stayed with Margaret and Laurence so that she could do some essential shopping. Vere would certainly wish to introduce his wife to the entire family as well as to local landowners. Visitors would again flock to Knightshill. Charlotte felt she should replenish stocks of linen, napiary and glassware. Kitty would not want that onerous responsibility the moment she arrived, Charlotte told herself, refusing to own that her real reason was to ensure Ashleigh standards were maintained for her beloved brother.

After a morning selecting the best several stores could provide for her home, Charlotte took Kate to the exclusive *modiste* Margaret had patronized. She chose several dresses for the girl, then surrendered to impulse and bought a whole wardrobe of elegant day and evening gowns for herself. The ultimate madness was her purchase of a white velvet evening cloak lined with silk, and two coats, one of raspberry-red fine wool trimmed with satin, and the other a beguiling powder-blue broadcloth with cream-coloured frogging in military style. Several fetching hats were added to this selection, the whole to be sent to Dunstan St Mary by rail within several days.

Back at Knightshill Charlotte set about the next task. Sir Gilliard still occupied the master suite, and Vere's rooms were suitable only for a bachelor, so she had chosen for the couple those once used by Margaret and Philip Daulton. They were situated near the nursery, so Simon would not be far from his mother. Charlotte was still disturbed by the fact of Vere's bride having a son of eight. It was so contrary to what she had always imagined when considering a union which inevitably would end her reign here, and the close bond she had shared with her brother. Yet the break in those wonderful days of happy companionship had already been made, and she had no true justification to resent the woman who had somehow persuaded Vere to give her his name and the right to rule in a lovely old house the like of which an innkeeper with a chequered past never before would have seen.

The set of rooms took on many guises during the length of a week. Furniture was moved in, then out again so frequently that the servants despaired of their mistress ever being satisfied. The two sets of new curtains arrived from London and were first hung then taken down on each alternate day. Carpets were beaten and cleaned, laid, then taken up to be replaced by others. Bedcovers, pictures and ornaments all graced the rooms for a short while without satisfying the woman who was performing her last major task as mistress of the house.

Sir Gilliard made no mention of Vere or his marriage. His avoidance of the subject in any form added to Charlotte's apprehension, which had mounted through being denied the chance of expression. She could not discuss Kitty Ashleigh with the servants, or with casual callers. If only Margaret were still at Knightshill! Although Charlotte had re-engaged Louise, the maid who had served Margaret until her abrupt departure, all she could tell the woman of her new mistress was that she was a former widow with a son, who would be taking over the running of Knightshill.

On the afternoon before that of the ship's early morning arrival, Charlotte was discussing with Benson which flowers she needed to grace the house when John joined them. He looked a happy man. The expected advent of the heir and his bride had injected him with zestful anticipation. Not for him a sense of being usurped from his position. He welcomed the return of the man who owned all he had been lovingly managing for the past three years. John was more than content to work in harness with Vere once more. He had been saying so from the day Charlotte had broken the news to him; had spent the weeks since then making ready to present to the returning heir and his bride, in perfect order, Knightshill and its many productive acres. But John had worked his way up from estate-hand to bailiff. He had not grown up in this house and presided over it by right of birth until now. Therein lay the difference, Charlotte told herself as she nodded straight-faced in response to his smiling greeting.

'You look very pleased with yourself,' Charlotte accused.

'With good cause,' he replied vigorously. 'Belinda foaled half an hour ago. Couldn't have timed it better, could she? Two little beauties, both strong and perfectly formed. What a bonus for Mr Ashleigh! And the little lad will be so charmed with them he'll maybe not feel so strange in his new home.' He gave her a shrewd look. 'I came over to suggest you bring Miss Kate to see them when you finally reach a decision about the flowers.'

'I *have* reached a decision.' she retorted briskly, still wondering if those blooms she had selected would look right against the furnishings presently decking Margaret's former suite.

'Shall I ask Winters to send a message to the nursery?' John asked. 'Or is the child at her lessons?'

Charlotte glanced at the watch pinned to her bodice. 'Mr Maddox will depart at three. I'll bring Kate to the stables then.'

'That's only fifteen minutes away. Winters could ask Nanny to bring Miss Kate down when she's ready ... and if you're finished here, there are several things I'd like to discuss with you in the meantime.'

'Very well.' Charlotte took another look at the flowers, telling herself there would be time tomorrow to change her mind. Vere and Kitty could not possibly arrive before late afternoon. She strolled beside John's sturdy figure lost in these domestic thoughts until he brought her from them with a gentle question.

'What's worrying you now?'

She looked up at him. 'Whatever do you mean?'

'Well, it's clear you've taken no notice of all I said to you two or three weeks ago. It was sensible advice but you've not heeded it.'

'Oh?'

He stopped on the flagstones from which slight haze rose as sunshine dried them after a noon downpour. 'You've been working in the house as if the world is about to end.'

Charlotte felt her colour rising as she turned to face him. 'What nonsense!'

'The servants are confused and anxious. They've never seen you so upset and they are dreading the arrival of the new Mrs Ashleigh.'

Charlotte could not believe what she was hearing. 'They have spoken to *you* about their feelings?'

'To Winters. He confided in me because there have been several serious quarrels below stairs. In all his years at Knightshill there has only been one other instance of discord among the domestic staff. He was starting his first year in his present position when Mrs Ashleigh left you all to go with her new husband to America. The problem then was understandable because they all admired your mother and couldn't understand why she went away. This time, their behaviour is prompted by loyalty to you.' He sighed. 'Your agitation suggests that Mr Ashleigh's wife is not welcome here. They resent their new mistress before she has arrived.'

'They are employed to look after this house and do as they are bid,' she cried heatedly, shaken by John's statement. 'How dare they presume to *resent* the wife of a member of the family!'

John remained calm. 'They sense that you do and

loyalty to you does the rest. And I have to add that I would share their feelings if I was not sure Mr Ashleigh could never choose a lady who would not be welcome at Knightshill. My loyalty would lead me to defend you against any person who hurt you or made you unhappy, believe me, but I think I must have greater faith than you in your brother.'

Unable to respond to this challenge, and strangely moved by his declaration of championship, Charlotte turned and walked on, her limp intensified by inner turmoil. John came up beside her to continue his theme.

'You'll always be an Ashleigh. Knightshill will be your home for as long as you wish it to be. Nothing and no one can ever take that away from you.' When she made no answer he put a hand on her arm to halt her again. 'Things are going to change, that's certain. But you can make it change for better or for worse. It's in your hands. If you start off seeing Mrs Ashleigh as an enemy, someone out to take everything away from you, chances are you'll make her into one. If you take my advice and offer her help and friendship you'll like as not have yourself a new sister in no time. Which is it you want?'

Charlotte drew away and walked on, but he called after her. '*Think*, lass, if you turn your back to her you'll turn it to your brother, too. Don't be foolish enough to do that.'

She swung round in a passion inspired by his soft tone and the familiar term 'lass', which undermined her stance. 'You're employed by my brother to manage the estate, that's all. It is not part of your job to tittle-tattle with the household servants on the subject of the Ashleigh family. I am surprised that you could do so, or that you could ever imagine you have the right to speak to me as you just have.'

His ruddy face paled somewhat and he stiffened. 'I spoke to you as the friend I thought you had been since Mr Ashleigh went away. I must beg your pardon, Miss Charlotte. I see that I was wrong.'

Charlotte watched in dismay as he strode away along the path shimmering with growing heat after rain. He *had* been a friend, a pleasant companion, a stalwart helper. He had made the past two years bearable; no, more, he had made them very enjoyable. At a time of change and uncertainty she had alienated the man who had done so much for her. However, Vere was coming tomorrow. The family would again occupy her time. John would revert to his correct role as bailiff to the Ashleighs.

11

Ned took the large carriage down to Dunstan St Mary to meet the train from Southampton. Winters chivvied his staff to perform their last-minute tasks before lining up in the lofty hall to greet the voyagers and be presented to their new mistress. Knightshill looked magnificent on a day of gentle sunshine and skittish breezes. Floors and wall panelling had been polished to a rich shine, chandeliers had all been washed so that they sparkled in shafts of sunlight. The great canvases of past wars, which hung in the long galleries, seemed brighter and more dramatic after careful cleaning. Porcelain glowed with delicate pastels and gold, mirrors gave out a dazzle of reflections. Huge arrangements of flowers filled the house with colour and perfume. The renowned Great Window let in the late afternoon brilliance to wash over the curving staircase and gleaming banisters.

Charlotte saw all this with a lump in her throat, as she made her way down from her rooms. Had her home ever looked more beautiful and welcoming? How could Margaret have abandoned all this for love of a man she had known for only a few weeks? How could Val bear to follow a profession which would send him anywhere in the world but here? How could Vere ever have believed all this was not enough? Charlotte loved her home passionately. The lump in her throat thickened as she prepared to hand Knightshill over to a stranger whose former way of life would surely never allow her to appreciate her good fortune.

Kate, of course, noticed nothing different as she walked beside her aunt. She was more intent on the prospect of having three more people to talk to. Having broken the speech hiatus she now chattered almost non-stop, as she always had before being uprooted to travel the world with Laurence Nicolardi. The girl looked excited, her normally solemn face screwing up into a succession of vital expressions as she asked yet again about Simon.

'Will he be afraid of the foals, Aunt Lottie? Has he ever seen horses before? Do you think I'll understand what he says? Will he be black like the heathens Father went to Africa to save – the ones who killed him? Simon won't try to hurt *us*, will he?'

'Do be quiet, Kate,' Charlotte told her wearily. 'We have discussed all this several times over and you know quite well that he will be very much like Tim. You must not flood him with questions the moment he arrives, or expect him to be your friend instantly. He will feel very nervous, I expect. And shy. Try to recall how you felt on first arriving in all those new countries with Mama and your stepfather. Simon is certain to feel the same.

As they neared the foot of the stairs, Kate asked, 'Will he stop speaking like I did?'

'I wish you would stop now,' Charlotte told her. 'They will be here at any moment and I need to go over in my mind all the arrangements I have made in case I have overlooked something.'

'You haven't,' Kate pronounced sagely. 'We've been over all *that* several times, too, and you ticked off everything on the list as it was done. It's too late to try to change any of it now, Aunt Lottie. Nanny said to Louise thank heaven, because she was sick and tired of people being unable to make up their minds.'

Charlotte heard this piece of servants' gossip repeated in Kate's conversational tones and remained silent. It *was* too late. She had done her very best for Vere. If his homecoming was not all he hoped for, the fault would not be hers. Whatever Kitty might be used to, Charlotte was certain Vere would want to present his home to her in its very best guise. Cook was preparing a superb dinner comprising all Vere's favourite dishes, which would be served in the main dining-room. Charlotte had decided on this plan to ensure Sir Gilliard joined them.

Clunes had informed her that her grandfather would not be formally greeting Mr and Mrs Ashleigh on their arrival, so she had resorted to luring the bear from his den by making dinner a very formal affair. Sir Gilliard would never refuse to preside over a meal set in the room hung with portraits of ancestors he revered. Having brought together the owner of Knightshill and the new mistress of it, Charlotte would bow out. Kitty Ashleigh must confront her father-in-law with the help of her devoted husband.

Charlotte and Kate waited in the hall beside a window giving a clear view of the driveway as it crossed what used to be a moat, before sweeping round to the front door. Kate looked neat and demure in a new dress of pale-blue moiré with beige piping and sash. Her light-brown hair had been twisted into ringlets by Nanny and kept in place by a blue band. She carried in her hand a small posy of fragrant cream roses to present to her new aunt with a speech of welcome. In the other hand was the photograph of Val. Neither Nanny nor Charlotte had been able to persuade Kate to leave the showing of the picture until a later moment.

Charlotte wore an afternoon gown in rich amber, with a necklet of gold and topaz, which had looked very becoming when she bought it. Paler than usual today, she was slightly disappointed with her appearance, although no one could deny she looked very stylish. She carried no posy, but had rehearsed polite words of welcome for her brother's mature new wife. She prayed they would not stick in her throat when she and Kitty came face to face.

The carriage swung into view and Winters opened the main doors with precise, unhurried movements. The footmen waiting outside sprang to attention. Charlotte took Kate's hand and led her forward, but when she reached the broad step outside the door, she saw with astonishment that the carriage had halted beyond the moat. Vere was standing beside it with a woman and a small boy to show them with gestures the extent of their new home. A large tawny dog ran around them with excited barks until the boy clapped his hands to silence it. Charlotte was nonplussed, then even more so when the three began walking towards the house in animated conversation, forsaking the carriage.

Winters betrayed no emotion as he stood like a dignified statue at the head of a row of similar statues waiting to be presented to the new lady of the house. Charlotte felt anger well up. The greeting ceremony had been planned to the minutest detail. How *dared* they ruin it? Before she could stop Kate, the girl suddenly ran forward to meet the arrivals. Half-way across the moat she reached them and was swung high in the air by Vere before being enveloped in a bear-like hug. From her uncle's arms Kate thrust her posy at the tall woman beside him, before wriggling free to concentrate all her attention on the dog which had recommenced its exciting barking.

The group moved forward again, laughing and chattering as Kate held out the photograph of Val for each one to see. Then Vere looked up, saw Charlotte rooted to her spot by the entrance to her home, and waved energetically. She found she could raise neither of her arms to wave back to the brother who had been as close as a twin throughout their childhood. The carriage moved at a slow pace to follow the four now walking across the broad driveway to the door. Charlotte could see the smile on Vere's face, and the lively expression on Kate's as she ran around with the dog. Simon walked close beside his

mother, but his head swivelled constantly to watch Kate
and the animal. Charlotte could see little of Kitty's face
beneath a large blue hat smothered with gauze roses
of the same deep cream shade as the travelling coat
she wore, but the extreme elegance of her appearance
made nonsense of the notion that Vere had married an
unsophisticated dowd. The woman beside him did not
look in the least out of place here.

As they neared the house, Vere hurried forward to
take Charlotte in a robust embrace. 'Lottie, it's *so* good
to see you.' He appeared not to notice her restraint as
he held her at arm's length. 'You look younger. Kate has
done that. And she's speaking again! How has that come
about? Oh, we have so much to tell each other and all the
time in the world to do so. It's splendid to come home.
I left on a bitter winter day which blunted memories of
how beautiful Knightshill is.' He smiled with happiness
as he drew his wife forward. 'Perhaps Kitty is responsible
for making me see it through a rosy glass.'

Brown eyes regarded Charlotte with shrewdness as
Kitty smiled and offered her hand. 'I feel I already
know you from Vere's description of the happy years
he spent here before going off to war. We thought you
might have come to the station to meet us, but it was
very understanding and perceptive of you to allow Vere
the pleasure of showing us Knightshill as we approached.
Such an impressive sight, but daunting for a woman used
to living in a small hotel in the heart of nowhere. I am
so glad you are here to befriend me.' She indicated her
son, a sturdy red-haired boy with large apprehensive
eyes. 'The past few weeks have been very overwhelming
for Simon. Please excuse his initial shyness.' When the
child bowed and said 'How do you do' in mechanical
tones, Kitty laughed. 'He rehearsed that phrase so often
on the voyage it sounds dreadfully formal. I hope he
will soon call you Aunt Lottie, as Kate does. She's
a delightful girl. You have performed a miracle with

her speech, I suspect. How fortunate the family is to have you.'

Charlotte felt numbed by the astonishing vivacity of her brother, and by this assured woman whose expressive face, shining titian hair and cultured tones removed the last trace of suspicion that she would be unfit to take over as mistress of Knightshill. Her own rehearsed speech was all her suspended thoughts could now produce.

'I am delighted to welcome you to your new home and hope you will be happy here. If anything is not entirely to your liking it can be changed immediately.'

Kate glanced up from stroking the dog and pulled a face at Kitty. 'Aunt Lottie has been practising *that* for a long time, too. She sounds as funny as Simon did.'

Vere laughed as he ruffled Kate's hair. 'Now you have your voice back you use it too often'. He glanced from Charlotte to Kitty. 'Let's go inside and face the formalities, shall we.'

Before Charlotte's bemused eyes, Vere swept the unsuspecting Kitty up in his arms and walked through to the hall with her followed by two children and a frisky dog. Charlotte brought up the rear in a daze, hardly able to believe what her brother was doing.

'*Vere*, put me down!' cried the laughing Kitty, her voice echoing in the vaulted hall.

He did so, steadying her as he gazed down with eyes of a man deeply in love. 'Welcome to Knightshill, my darling,' he said softly. 'We'll fill this house with laughter and happiness.' He took her hand to his lips while she returned his ardent look, oblivious of the row of servants watching with fascination this extraordinary scene in a mansion renowned for its strict military atmosphere.

When Vere led his bride across to Winters, the statue became animated. Contrary to Charlotte's expectations, the ageing manservant made a fulsome speech in reply to Kitty's hope that he was pleased with the addition to the household of a small family.

'Indeed I am, madam. In the old days the house was a most lively place, and now it will be again. You may be assured of my loyalty and devoted service.' His eyes swivelled to look at Vere. 'It's a great pleasure to have you at Knightshill once more, sir. The domestic staff wish to join me in offering felicitations on your marriage.'

The servants were presented to Kitty one by one. Kate followed the small entourage, dragging Simon by the hand to announce in airy tones to her silent, over-awed companion the names of each footman and maid. Charlotte could only stand at a distance watching her sister-in-law assume her new role as if born to it. Vere and Kitty had somehow turned a formality into a relaxed joyous affair. Instead of subdued hostility from domestics who had been bickering for the past two weeks, there was smiling response to friendly words from the Ashleigh heir and his wife. Vere had always been well liked by the servants. His impulsive, unconventional act of carrying Kitty over the threshold had clearly delighted them, and their future mistress was welcomed unreservedly because of it.

The advent of a male Ashleigh with an attractive, friendly wife, a small boy and a dog the size of a newborn calf had suddenly breathed life and light-heartedness into a mansion sombre for too long. The initial resentment Charlotte had known faded as she watched the transformation and slowly became caught up in the happy mood. The first Ashleigh had come home. The rest would surely follow.

Vere and Kitty joined Charlotte at the foot of the stairs. 'I've put you in Margaret's suite,' she told her brother. 'You must go wherever you wish, of course, but I thought the rooms most suitable until you have had time to settle in. They are near the nursery which you will find convenient,' she added to Kitty, as she turned to mount the stairs. 'I'll arrange for some tea to be brought to you. You'll be glad of it after your journey.'

'We shall,' Vere agreed, glancing from left to right as if seeing familiar things for the first time. 'It will set us up in readiness for the summons to Grandfather's rooms.'

Charlotte's heartbeat increased. 'I think . . . I believe he plans to meet you at dinner. It'll be in the main dining-room tonight.'

Vere stopped, Kitty beside him. 'Good God, *four* at that immense table! Whatever is he thinking of?'

'It was my decision, Vere.'

'Whatever are *you* thinking of?'

He sounded angry. Charlotte defended herself. 'It's the only way to handle the situation.' She turned to Kitty. 'He's an old man with a great deal of pride. He has led a distinguished career, and we all benefited from his admirable qualities as we grew up. He has been our pillar of strength, the head of our parentless family. We all owe him a great deal.' She hesitated. 'But he set standards none of us has managed to reach. You met Val in Kimberley so must know what *that* situation has done to Grandfather's hopes.'

'And Kitty knows what a terrible disappointment I have always been to him,' put in Vere, still angry. 'She is also aware of what Margaret did. *You* are the only Ashleigh who meets with his approval.'

'Hardly . . . but that's why I've ordered Winters to serve dinner formally. Grandfather insists on presiding at table there. He's liable to forever avoid a meeting with you, otherwise.'

'Oh, *will* he?' Vere said forcefully. 'I'll not let him get away with this. I hadn't expected him to be waiting in the hall for us, but I have no intention of introducing my wife to him over a glass of sherry with servants standing by . . . and I also have no intention of eating dinner at a mammoth table beneath the painted eyes of ancestors whose disapproval of me matches his.' He moved on briskly towards the rooms Charlotte had prepared. 'Tell Winters to serve dinner in the family dining-room where we can be comfortable and relaxed. Time enough for that military picture gallery when the aunts and cousins descend *en masse*, and scarlet jackets abound! Reaching the suite he flung open the door to allow inside Kitty, two children and a dog, saying to Charlotte standing on the opposite side of the threshold, 'He had best face the inevitable and come to terms with it. As soon as we've had tea and changed from our travelling clothes I'll take Kitty along to confront him.' He gave a sudden smile, saying in softer tones, 'Bless you, Lottie, but my days of military service taught me a few lessons in tactics. Attack when the enemy is least expecting it.'

Charlotte felt obliged to say quietly, 'He's not the *enemy*, Vere. You've been very high handed over this, in his eyes. Give him time to get used to the notion.'

'Delay would be fatal. He would never come round. For once the old warhorse has to see things my way.'

She moved nearer to avoid any chance of being overheard by those already inside the room. 'Go to him alone. I'm afraid he has the very worse conception of . . . of a female reared in a diamond settlement. He will not mince words.'

Vere shook his head. 'No matter what his opinion might be on any subject, he is a gentleman and behaves like one in the presence of ladies. He would speak his mind to me and I to him, making the situation far worse. Whereas Kitty will have him eating from her hand in no time.' He paused to look at her quizzically. 'You doubt it?'

'You know your wife. I do not,' she said.

'You soon will. I am determined to make a good life for her and for Simon here, Lottie, and I'm relying on you to help me.'

Remembering his departure for the Mediterranean with its suggestion that he could not wait to be rid of her clinging affection, Charlotte said somewhat dryly, 'I think you are very well able to manage all you require without any help from me.'

Vere remained angry and determined while Kitty went with Charlotte, the children and Kimber to the nursery where Kate and Simon would have tea. Kitty returned alone, her colour heightened. Vere chuckled. 'You've encountered Nanny, I see.'

She made a rueful face. 'The honours are hers for the moment. I am too new to change her rigid views, but give me time.'

Vere took her in his arms. 'My darling, she feels threatened by you. She has reigned in the nursery for many years. Philip Daulton overruled Margaret and encouraged Nanny to lessen their mother's influence over Kate and Tim. I imagine Lottie has not interfered with Nanny's régime because she is not Kate's mother.'

'But I am Simon's,' Kitty said firmly. 'He will not easily settle here and being submitted to nursery regimentation will add to his distress.'

'Then I'll speak to Nanny.'

'No, Vere, *I* will speak to her. Domestic matters are to be my responsibility. We agreed on that. But I shall not be too hasty.' She moved from his embrace. 'I believe Charlotte also feels threatened by me.'

Vere was uncomprehending. 'Whyever should she be?'

'Because, my dear, I am your wife with every right to give orders to Winters and all those servants I have just met. Once I choose to do so it will deprive your sister of her position here. In her place I would feel resentful of any woman you married. She covered her feelings well, but I'm certain she's far from delighted over our marriage.'

'No, you're wrong,' he asserted as Louise entered with a maid carrying a tray containing tea and small cakes. 'We have been too close for her not to share in my happiness.'

Kitty sat in a blue velvet chair to smile her thanks at the servants. When they departed she began to pour tea, saying, 'It's because you have been close that she is afraid. Much as I love you, I have to say that you are as unfamiliar as other men with the complexities of a woman's life and needs. Charlotte has been the home-maker for you all as well as sharing with you a very special bond. Naturally, she sees me as a thief set to rob her of both those roles. Without them she will have nothing.'

Vere gazed in astonishment as he took from her a cup of tea. 'What nonsense! She will always be my sister.'

'Not if I alienate her. You clearly still don't understand, so I must act alone. Once I become her friend everything will be ready for the final move.'

'My dearest girl, you're speaking in riddles,' Vere protested. 'The final move?'

'To find her a husband. No, don't look at me that way. I know something of loneliness and my heart goes out to her. She is extremely attractive and eligible. It's quite ridiculous to wilt into spinsterish old age because of a slight limp. Why you have all allowed her this foolish pose I cannot understand.'

'It was none of our doing,' cried Vere in protest. 'There were beaux galore at one time. Lottie discouraged every one.'

Kitty smiled across at him. 'Then we must find some more. Knowing that I shall inevitably take over her role as home-maker, and that I have already come between her and the brother who substituted for a husband – oh, yes, Vere, from what you have told me about her I'm certain that is so – she will be seeking a purpose in life and therefore be more susceptible to the prospect of marriage.'

'You continue to surprise me,' he said with a wag of his head. 'I fell in love with a living cameo; a woman of elegance, wit, culture and compassion. I fell in love with a beautiful creature who came eagerly into my arms and gave me such delight I will never surrender it. It now appears that this wonderful person is also a diplomat of the first order.'

Kitty laughed. 'I hope continually to surprise you, darling. That is the spice of life. As for being a diplomat, I suspect that I shall need all such skills during this meeting with Sir Gilliard.'

Vere's light-heartedness vanished. 'I mean to stand no nonsense from him, you know. He is still owner of Knightshill and the head of the Ashleigh family, but he must concede that his time is running out. He has never wanted me as his heir, and I used not to welcome the responsibility, but fate played her hand and we must both accept it. You are the perfect wife for me and, together, we'll serve the family and Knightshill with loving dedication. No man should ask more of his successor. I shall tell him so.'

'But he'll have no proof of that assertion, Vere. It is all in the future. You must see this from his point of view, if you can. You are an unsatisfactory heir and have chosen a wife from a different background – a widow with another man's child, to boot. A double blow for a man yearning for a heroic successor in a scarlet jacket with a blue-blooded wife ready to give him son after son.'

'Ha! His Khartoum "hero" would have been a far greater disappointment as an heir,' Vere said explosively.

'So only you and I know. He does not.'

'Val could truly be the hero in a scarlet jacket, but he cannot do it as an Ashleigh.'

Kitty smiled. 'The poor lad is terrified of females at the moment, so no blue-blooded wife either. Sir Gilliard will have to make do with you ... and with me. He knows that, Vere, but a man with enormous pride will not easily surrender. We must move very carefully with your grandfather as well as with your sister.'

'Dammit, this is *my* home as much as theirs,' Vere declared getting to his feet angrily.

'No, dearest, one is shortly to relinquish it and everything he has held dear, the other is about to be relegated to a small aspect of it. Knightshill is indisputably all yours. That's why you must be generous now.'

After a moment or two's consideration of the face which had become so dear to him, Vere relaxed and smiled. 'They little realize how fortunate it is for them that I became indisputably all *yours* rather than Annabel Bourneville's. That's what I want to make known to them.'

Kitty rose. 'They're both intelligent enough to deduce that for themselves, if they are not set against me by heavy-handedness.' She came up to him in concern. 'Vere, I ran away from you to my brother because of this situation. I am a perfect wife for a military artist roaming South Africa, but not for the heir of a large estate of a noble family. They are entitled to feel as they do.'

'They are *not*, Kitty. Grandfather produced just one son before his wife ran off with her lover, and he spent the greater part of the succeeding forty years following the drum. Knightshill means little to him save as a pictorial mausoleum for scarlet-coated ancestors. As for Charlotte, if she had married any one of her hopeful suitors she would now be happily settled in her husband's home surrounded by her children. Knightshill is all she has. That's why she values it. Of the three *I* am the one who has loved and tended these acres over a period of years. I shall be the first Ashleigh for generations to permanently live in and manage Knightshill. When I choose the woman to be at my side throughout, there is *nobody* entitled to question my action.' His fierce kiss prevented further words on the subject and they went to their dressing-rooms to change their clothes for the task ahead.

A few minutes before setting out to cross to the opposite wing, Vere rang for his valet, Stoner, and sent him to advise Clunes to ensure that Sir Gilliard was prepared for their visit. He would have finished tea and be resting before dressing for dinner in the uniform he wore on every possible occasion. Vere was still angry at the thought of taking Kitty down to eat in the formidable atmosphere of the main dining-room, which would have been a daunting experience designed to show disdain. It seemed a decision uncharacteristic for Charlotte, yet he supposed she had not known how else to deal with Sir Gilliard's attitude. Kitty said he must tread softly, yet for a man of peaceful nature Vere grew swiftly heated on any subject concerning his wife. He doubted his ability to do as she suggested.

Kitty emerged from her dressing-room to surprise Vere once more. Instead of one of the very stylish gowns bought in Durban, she had chosen the dark-green high-necked dress she had been wearing when he had first seen her, framed like a cameo. She looked elegant, of course, but not a woman of wealth and position; she was Kitty Munroe, innkeeper of Vrymanskop. He fell in love with her anew as he saw how clever she was. If, as Charlotte had whispered, Grandfather imagined that a woman reared in a diamond settlement would tastelessly flaunt her new wealth, he would be confounded when introduced to a demure, cultured daughter-in-law whose radiance denied any suggestion of cunning or avarice.

Vere went to her. 'Have I ever said how much I adore you?'

'Frequently,' she teased, loving him with her eyes. 'Will you continue to do so when you are disowned, and thrown out with the advice never to darken these doors again?'

'*You* did that on two occasions,' he reminded her. 'I'm as determined now as I was then. I offer you my arm, Mrs Ashleigh. Together we shall face the onslaught.'

Clunes was agitated, for once robbed of tactful words, as he stood at the door to the inner sanctum of the man he had served for almost fifty years. 'Welcome home, Mr Ashleigh; Madam. Sir, it's not a good time,' he mumbled trying not to meet Vere's eyes. 'The General's resting. Not been himself, he hasn't. It would be as well not to disturb him.'

'Quite possibly,' Vere agreed, 'but I wouldn't dream of being discourteous enough to return after more than a year's absence without seeing my grandfather at the first opportunity. If he has been unwell, there is all the more reason for me to do so to express my concern.'

Taking Kitty's arm once more, he reached for the handle and ushered her through the open door into a room filled with heavy antique furniture set upon a rich red and blue carpet. Sir Gilliard was in a chair beside the fire, dressed in dark trousers and a mulberry velvet smoking-jacket. A book lay open on his lap. He was not reading it, but was instead gazing at the late afternoon sky through a window on the far side of the room. Vere was taken aback. The old man looked frailer than he had expected. Perhaps he really had been unwell. Inborn respect for this man who had been the figurehead of the Ashleigh family over so many years softened Vere's approach.

'Hallo, sir. Clunes says you are feeling tired, so I'll make my visit brief.' Sir Gilliard continued to stare at the window. 'It's good to see you again.' Still no response. 'Our arrival was rather later than we expected, but I could not delay my greetings until we met at the dinner table.'

'I have nothing to say to you, sir.' It was cold, disdainful and remote.

Vere's initial compassion vanished. 'Then I trust you will at least consent to speak to my wife now that I have brought her to meet you.'

A frown furrowed the brow above bushy white eyebrows as Sir Gilliard's head turned slowly. When he saw that Vere had indeed brought a woman to his sanctum, he eased himself from the chair with some difficulty but remained before the flames with his inimitable forbidding stance.

'Has that infernal savage country deprived you of good manners along with your sense of duty?'

'South Africa took away any *pretensions* I may have possessed,' Vere said in clipped tones. 'You frequently reminded me of my duty to marry. You cannot accuse me of neglecting that duty now that I have had the good manners to present my wife to you at the first opportunity after our arrival. I do so with great pride, sir.'

Kitty moved forward to be met with the barest semblence of a bow from a man whose breeding dictated acknowledgement only of the coolest nature. Vere's anger rose, but Kitty took the situation into her hands before he could speak.

'You make it abundantly clear that you don't approve of me, sir. I have some appreciation of that. You had hopes of a daughter-in-law with impeccable credentials and have instead a woman disowned by her grandparents, who has led a somewhat chequered life in the colonies. I assure you I tried every means I knew to prevent this marriage but,' she smiled up at Vere, 'your grandson has inherited your single-minded determination. Only when every avenue of escape had been blocked did I agree to accept his offer of lifelong happiness.' She paused to allow Sir Gilliard a response. When one was not given, she said, 'You remain sceptical? Running a hotel requires a great deal of diplomacy and teaches one to recognize true worth in a man. Vere has it in abundance. He also possesses physical courage, compassion, artistic talent . . .'

'And a very large fortune,' put in the old man bitterly.

'You cast me as a fortune-hunter?' Kitty countered swiftly. 'If I were I would long ago have secured my future with one of many men who dug enormous wealth from the ground in Kimberley. Diamond millionaires are reckless and forever seeking the means of increasing their riches by travelling the world. What an exciting and profitable life I *could* have led rather than bury myself here for the rest of my days.'

Sir Gilliard's lip curled. 'So we understand each other! I have already spoken to Parkington-Price about an annulment. He sees little difficulty. Name your terms, madam.'

Vere moved forward in a fury as he recognized what his grandfather was suggesting, but Kitty caught his arm, saying coolly, 'An annulment, sir? I have a son to consider.'

'He can never inherit,' snapped Sir Gilliard.

'I agree,' said Kitty, still mistress of herself. 'But if the child I am presently carrying is a boy, *he* will. You surely do not wish your heir's son to become a bastard.'

The news was a shock to the old man, and hardly less so to Vere, being alternately angered and amazed by this interchange. While both men stood lost for words, Kitty said to Vere, 'I think we should allow Sir Gilliard to rest for a while. If we are to eat in the grand dining-room he will wish to feel robust enough to recount to me the histories of your noble ancestors whose portraits line the walls.'

Once in the corridor, Vere drew Kitty close to discover that she was shaking. 'I should not subjected you to that, but I didn't believe Lottie's pessimism. Forgive me, darling.' He stroked her hair tenderly while joy replaced anger. 'Is it true about the child? Say that it is.'

She glanced up, nodding. 'I planned to tell you in more romantic circumstances during our first night here.'

'You may tell me all over again in circumstances as romantic as you please,' he breathed and kissed her. 'I thought I could not possibly be happier than on the day you took my name, but I am. You are *magnificent*!'

'No, Vere, I misjudged your grandfather badly. I withdraw my plea for you to be generous and understanding towards him. I'm so sorry, my dear. He's quite, quite ruthless. Small wonder he drove you all away.'

The Waterloo Ball, the first of the new century, was reminiscent of the old days when Charlotte had made all the arrangements together with her sister Margaret. Vere was eager for the affair to be a glittering one and invited a number of his acquaintances from the art and drama world in London. Every member of the Ashleigh family, including doddering aunts and uncles, ageing cousins with their military offspring, travelled to Wiltshire with the intention of remaining there for a short midsummer break, and retired officers of the West Wiltshires turned out to represent the regiment stationed in China. Neighbouring landowners, for whom the traditional ball was the highlight of the summer season, all accepted invitations very promptly, agog to meet Vere Ashleigh's unconventional bride. A diamond prospector's widow with a young son! Whatever had the man been thinking of? He had always been the odd one out in that family.

Charlotte was in her element when Kitty confessed that she could not possibly take on such a mammoth task. 'You will know exactly what to do, whom to invite and which rooms in this great mansion each of your relatives prefers to occupy during the visit. I will do all I can to help you, but I beg you to organize the ball as you always have, Lottie. Vere says you are peerless at ensuring nothing can go wrong, however difficult some guests might be.' She smiled. 'He gave me a most amusing account of several elderly relatives who are always practically impossible to please, but says although your diplomacy is stretched to the limit it is never confounded.'

'I know them so well I anticipate their demands,

that's all,' Charlotte responded, pleased by Vere's compliment.

'My tolerance has been tested on only a small scale. An inn on the veld houses some enigmatic people overnight, and I have to pit my wits against them. But it's easier to be forceful when guests are *paying* for what you provide.' She sighed. 'My way of life did little to prepare me for the kind of social elegance you have at Knightshill. I dare not think what I would do without you to guide me.'

They worked in complete accord to plan an evening which would measure up to Vere's hopes and also be adjudged by the guests as the best Waterloo Ball ever held by the Ashleighs. They achieved their aim. Charlotte had not enjoyed the event for the past three years. Being unable to dance because of her withered leg, she had usually concentrated on ensuring that all ran smoothly during the ball while Margaret acted as hostess on the dance floor. It had been difficult without her sister. Kitty replaced her this year. In a gown of shimmering silver brocade, with the Ashleigh rubies on her finger and the matching necklet glowing against her pale throat, she successfully silenced the sneering conjecture of many guests. The military men were inevitably drawn to the woman from a country in which their comrades had recently fought with such losses. They wanted to question her on its complexities and hazards. Vere's artistic friends without exception generously greeted Monkford Kellaway's daughter and plied her with invitations to visit them. The Ashleigh relatives on the whole declared Vere's wife to be somewhat better than they feared and decided to accept the *fait accompli*.

The only dissenters were ladies either jealous of someone who had succeeded with the Knightshill heir where they had failed, who resented the attention paid by male guests to a woman reared among colonial adventurers, or whose principles would not allow them to believe she was anything but a social climber. Yet it appeared that

Sir Gilliard had accepted Kitty Ashleigh as the future mistress of Knightshill. Nothing had yet been announced, but whispers in Dunstan St Mary had it that the heir had swiftly done his duty and the happy event would be in December. The old general would accept *any* woman who produced a son to ensure continuation of the bloodline, they told themselves.

As summer passed, Charlotte's initial relief over Kitty's undemanding attitude within the house mellowed into an easy friendship with her. It was a friendship with limitations, nevertheless. Roughly the same age, Kitty was more experienced, assured and sexually mature, and her approach to the servants was natural, friendly but firm. They responded happily. A new liveliness sprang up in the corridors and salons. Men and women who had moved about the silent mansion with slow tread and straight faces now smiled and bustled about their tasks. Numerous social events meant that carriages rolled up to the door with a frequency that delighted Ned and the stable-lads, who had had little to do for months.

Vere's guests also breathed life into Knightshill. Cosmopolitan, intellectual, scholarly, artistic, young officers vastly different from Sir Gilliard's aged acquaintances prone to tell the same old exaggerated stories, they found greater rapport with their host's unconventional wife than with his sister. Although Charlotte found these visitors entertaining to observe she had no desire to be like them. Domestic arrangements for these visits gave her greater satisfaction than intercourse with the guests. Yet it was good to have company other than a grandfather who had used her merely as a listener for his views and theories.

Sir Gilliard made infrequent appearances at the dining-table and then retired early. Age was finally overtaking him, and Charlotte sometimes wondered if he was simply waiting for Kitty's child to be born before dying, his private world secured. Certainly he showed no interest in the estate and, when Vere insisted on producing Val's photograph, adding a verbal account of their meeting in Kimberley, Sir Gilliard gave an impression of total disinterest in his younger grandson so eager to earn approval and forgiveness from him.

Charlotte's life fell into a new pattern as summer ran into autumn. It was a curious pattern. Kate was no longer in her sole charge. The child was again part of a family with a beloved uncle, a new aunt and a youthful companion in addition to someone who had petted and spoiled her during a period of confusion. It was inevitable that both children, together for lessons given by a tutor employed by Vere, should become almost inseparable and go jointly to Kitty with their problems. So Charlotte was slowly relieved of responsibility for her sister's daughter. She felt no resentment. Kitty was a mother who understood children far better than she, and Vere provided a father figure for a child shattered by the change in her own family group. There was no doubt of Kate's new vitality and happiness, which must be the prime consideration. Charlotte nevertheless missed the little girl's dependence upon her which had made her feel needed.

No one could reasonably claim that Vere had committed utter folly in marrying as he had. He and Kitty were evidently deeply in love, and Charlotte had never seen her brother so full of pride for the manner in which his wife accepted the rôle so many had believed she could not handle. Kitty did not necessarily do things the way the daughters of the house for years had done them, but her less formal approach brought changes to Knightshill that were not altogether unwelcome.

Vere threw himself into estate matters with fresh enthusiasm. When he rode his acres with John, he invariably invited Charlotte to accompany them. It was less a brotherly gesture as of old, than recognition of her deputization during his long absence and, although he included her in discussions on future plans, Charlotte knew he was merely being considerate. Her days as a decision-maker were almost over. Kitty frequently made a foursome on fine days. They were happy times, all at ease with each other. John readily responded to Kitty's easy manner, and the suggestion of two natural couples crept in without Charlotte being aware of it until a day in October when leaves were being blown from trees in russet flurries.

Vere and Kitty had taken the children to Salisbury and would not be back until late afternoon. Overcast skies made the house dark; the empty corridors were reminiscent of former lonely months with only a bitter, introspective grandfather for company. Charlotte stood at her window watching the wild weather outside, finding curious identification with it. Autumnal bluster would give way to winter bleakness. Vere was a fond, but more detached, brother. Kitty was a friend whose future was assured as wife, mother and mistress of Knightshill. Kate would one day return to her own family. Sir Gilliard would die. At present she, herself, was caught up in the life of each member of her family, and was part of their urgent activities, yet winter would overtake her as time passed. She could not forever live through the lives of those around her. Where was *her* future?

Minutes ticked past as she grew increasingly heavy-hearted. What she had feared since receiving news of Vere's marriage had actually happened, although in the kindest manner. It had been inevitable, of course, and she was fortunate to have Kitty rather than Annabel Bourneville for a sister-in-law. The latter would have ejected an unwanted spinster by making life at Knightshill impossible for her. Kitty would never do that. Charlotte had herself made it impossible from the day that she had devoted herself to her brothers and sister, turning her back on youthful suitors. It was too late now. She was thirty years old and established as an old maid.

Into her mind then came recollection of a conversation she had had with Margaret in London, when her sister had explained why she had run off with Laurence Nicolardi. 'I knew I could not face bleak years with Philip. I *could* not. I thought of Vere running from a life without Annabel, and Val taking *any* risk to avoid a career in the West Wilts, and I decided that a female Ashleigh had every right to follow their lead. It takes enormous courage, Lottie, but it *is* possible to change something unendurable. Vere discovered health and artistic fame, Val has found fulfilment in the cavalry. You have evidence of my own great happiness. Think how miserable we three would now be if we had not challenged fate.' Charlotte sighed. Margaret had run to Laurence's arms, Vere to war in the Sudan, Val to his beloved horse regiment. There was no obvious escape for an untalented spinster with a deformed leg.

On the point of turning from the window she saw John approaching from his cottage, and felt a sense of relief. Here was someone to talk to, someone whose friendship had never wavered throughout the last few difficult years. She had no real purpose in going to his office, but the prospect of long hours stretching ahead until Vere's return was so daunting she hurried from her room.

John was studying some files as she entered. He glanced up and his smile was like a glow of warmth on a bleak day. Charlotte felt that warmth flowing right through her as he greeted her with obvious pleasure.

'So Knightshill is not altogether deserted! The others may come and go but you're always here to brighten even a dull day. 'Tis a raw one. We'll have an early winter, if I'm not mistaken.'

'You're probably right, John,' she replied heavily, knowing that he had the true countryman's knack of reading nature's signs.

303

He put down the files and came round the desk to her. 'The prospect doesn't please you?'

'It's been a good summer. Why does it have to end?' she heard herself ask.

His frank blue gaze studied her face with soft concern. 'Every summer comes to an end, lass.'

His use of that term brought memories of the time she had been thrown from her mare after the Waterloo Ball last year. John had held her so tenderly, spoken in those same tones as he had begged her to stop frightening him and open her lovely eyes. All at once, Charlotte saw in a startlingly different light a man she had known all her life. A face so familiar was suddenly very dear; a voice softened by regional accent was sweet music to her mood of desolation. Only now did she realize how subtly their relationship had changed since Vere had returned. No longer the person to whom he must refer, if only as a formality, for decisions concerning the estate, Charlotte had been accepted as John's natural companion by everyone at Knightshill. They were the stalwarts, the ones with their roots in this corner of Wiltshire. They belonged here. They loved every inch of the land around them. Why had she not before recognized John as the one person in her life who would never disappoint her, hurt her or leave Knightshill? Why had she not admitted to herself how contented she felt in his company, how essential he was to her sense of confidence and wellbeing?

Studying him now Charlotte finally accepted something she had for years chosen not to recognize. John's devotion to her was a great deal deeper than that of a bailiff to a member of the family he served. The knowledge warmed her further as she faced the fact of her own deep devotion to him, which she had also ignored. Because of their social differences, or because she had deliberately shunned the possibility of that brand of love? Or because she had held Vere as a loving shield for too long. The shield had been removed to leave her exposed and vulnerable. If she ran from the truth now, summer might have ended forever.

'Do you never feel lonely, John?' she asked softly.

He showed his surprise at her question, but said, 'Aye, sometimes. Why do you ask?'

'When? *When* do you feel lonely?' she persisted.

'Winter evenings, when I can't get out about the estate as I do in the summer.'

'Is that why you work here in the office until late?'

'Possibly,' he agreed, regarding her with curiosity.

Taking her courage in both hands she said, 'I feel lonely on winter evenings, too. We ... we should keep each other company.'

'You have your brother and his wife.'

'No, John. They have each other, and Kitty likes to retire early now. Once their child is born they'll be a complete small family and I shall be lonelier than ever.' John remained silent as she went further. 'Being a spinster in a large family is an unenviable position. Vere's wife is destined to be the mistress of Knightshill. When Val marries, his wife will be second in line for that position. When Grandfather dies and Margaret can come home again, she will have greater claim than I to Knightshill by dint of being older.'

Although it was clear John had to struggle to remain silent, he succeeded. Charlotte then realized he would never seize the initiative on this particular subject, so she took a breath and asked, 'Are you going to leave me to face long, lonely years because of convention?'

He studied her face for a long while with heightened colour, and it was all she could do not to turn and run from this situation she had instigated. Yet she felt it was now or never.

'I'm not certain what you're asking, lass,' he said eventually. 'You're an Ashleigh.'

'So is Vere, but he's married a woman from the middle

of nowhere and made her mistress of all this. Perhaps I am also destined to flout convention.'

John fought to put the situation into perspective. 'You know I'd do anything for you. I've made that plain enough over the years, but I've too much respect for you to do what I think you're suggesting. I can see that it would solve your problem for a while . . . until you began to regret it. Better to choose someone from your own class.'

She stiffened as his meaning grew clear, and she said with force, 'I believed you had a higher opinion of me. I'm not grasping at straws, out to snare any husband I can get. I'd sooner be lonely all my life, indeed I would.'

As she turned away he gripped her arm to hold her there. His eyes were alive with feeling as he said, 'I'm a simple man, as you know. Will you put into simple fashion what you have been saying?'

The strength of his grip and the force of his verbal demand gave birth to passion of a sweeter nature. Words tumbled from her. 'I would have put myself on the marriage mart years ago if all I wanted was to shelter behind *any* man who would give me his name and ease my loneliness. It's taken me a long time to see the obvious, but how foolish it would be for you to spend long winter evenings working in this office, and I sitting alone in my room. What I have been saying, dear John, is that we should spend them together in happy harmony . . . for the rest of our lives.'

'Your grandfather would never agree,' he said, still resistant to something he dared not contemplate.

'The rest of my family have done what they wish *without* his agreement.'

'But I've nothing to offer you.'

'You can offer your devotion and the freedom of Knightshill's acres. That's more than enough for me.'

He touched her hair with a gentle hand. 'Do you truly mean that, lass?'

Charlotte smiled. 'What a fool I've been to delay it for so long. As soon as Vere gets back from Salisbury we'll recruit his help to face Grandfather.'

John drew her into his arms with a shake of his head. 'No, my dear, I'll do that on my own. I may not be an Ashleigh, but I've got their fighting spirit when it comes to getting what I want.'

Flooded by happiness, Charlotte asked, 'It *is* what you want, isn't it?'

'Ever since you grew into the loveliest young woman I'd set eyes on, which is half my lifetime.'

Accepting his gentle kiss, she said, 'I'll do my utmost to make the rest of it so good it will be worth all that waiting.'

12

SIR GILLIARD FLATLY refused to consider marriage between an Ashleigh and an employee. John Morgan was told he was insolent, presumptuous and no longer Knightshill's estate manager. Charlotte had no need to beg Vere to intervene. He was so angry he confronted their grandfather less than an hour after John had broken the news to them all. The poor man was shaken and prepared to bow out of their lives until Vere, backed by Kitty, told him not to abandon his hopes and to carry on as usual while a few facts were put to the old general.

'It won't do any good, Mr Ashleigh,' John warned.

Vere gave a tight smile. 'If you're going to be my brother-in-law you'll have to forget formality, John. And you'll have to grow used to clashes of this nature with Sir Gilliard.'

Vere was used to them to the extent of knowing his grandfather no longer dominated him into impotency. Fiery and implacable the old man might still be, but Vere now knew how to counter those traits. The Sudan had strengthened him, and Kitty's love made him the giant Annabel had said he would never be.

Clunes was disapproving when Vere arrived at the master suite shortly before noon. The former military batman seemed almost prepared to defend the door leading to the room of a distinguished soldier he had served for many years.

'The General is upset, sir,' he declared, barring entry by planting himself squarely in Vere's path. 'You'd be

308

risking his health by disturbing him, I'm afraid.'

'You're a good man, Clunes,' Vere told him warmly, 'but if my grandfather is stout enough to ruin Miss Charlotte's future, and dismiss a bailiff who has served him faithfully for most of his life, I think I shall present little risk to his health. Stand aside, there's a good fellow.'

Sir Gilliard certainly looked flushed and angry, but he was indulging in a glass of sherry whilst standing by the window which gave a splendid view of his land; standing erect and as formidable as many young officers had seen him during humiliating interviews. He did not look in the least danger of succumbing to ill health, and soon made it clear he was in fine fettle.

'I daresay this infamous business is your doing, sir,' he growled as Vere approached. 'Lost all sense of propriety. Warned you of the dangers of abandoning duty to mix with namby-pamby fellahs with paint brushes. Never should have frequented those countries along the Mediterranean. Raffish ideas. No concept of morals or hygiene. Half of them are peasants with no learning, the other half damned smooth and acquisitive.'

'I never found them so,' put in Vere calmly. 'They were extremely cultured, with beautiful manners and great appreciation of the social and philanthropic problems in their own country as well as other parts of the world. If one of them were to say military men are all aggressive, unyielding, pompous and narrow-minded, you would be outraged and challenge their words, claiming they knew very little about soldiers, wouldn't you?'

Sir Gilliard turned away, saying coldly, 'What are you doing here? I do not recall summoning you.'

'I'm not one of your subalterns. I'm your grandson and heir, who should be free to discuss family matters with you at any time.'

Sir Gilliard swung back at him. '*Family* matters, you say? My bailiff is not a member of this distinguished line, sir!'

'Neither is he attempting to be. His name will forever be Morgan, and he has his own lineage.'

'Damned lowly lineage! How dared he come to me with such a proposition?'

'Because he is devoted to my sister, and she to him.'

White eyebrows met in disgust. 'Pah! Has *she* now lost all sense of honour and duty? I'll not hear any more from you. Get out!'

'No, Grandfather,' said Vere standing his ground. 'If you refuse to allow Lottie happiness after the years she has spent entertaining your guests, planning the Khartoum Dinner, the Waterloo Ball and numerous other social events, and bearing your irascibility without complaint as the only one of us to remain at Knightshill, I shall act in your place to see that she marries the man that she loves.'

'Love. *Love?*' the well-known voice roared. 'You are all the same. The whole pack of you.' Sir Gilliard advanced full of ire, glass in hand, to thrust his face close to Vere's. 'Your mother abandoned you all to cross the Atlantic with a damned foreigner who dressed in clothes more suited to a clown, all in the name of *love*. Your sister brought shame on us all by running off to live in sin with one of those smooth Mediterranean fellahs, and the boy tore the clothes off a respectable woman to assault her while he was *still at school*. You, sir, chose as your wife a creature brought up amidst gamblers, swindlers and frequenters of whorehouses, and now I am told that the last of your mother's changeling brood has a mind to ally herself with someone of peasant stock. *No, sir, no!* I am still head of this family, and I say *no!*'

Recollection of a previous quarrel along the same lines made Vere pause before repeating words designed to hurt as much as he had been hurt. He did not want too many regrets when this splendid old warhorse lost his final battle, and there was much truth in his words. They *had* all initially let him down in their search for happiness, yet each was entitled to personal freedom outside his rigid code . . . and all were now compensating for those things of which this proud man accused them.

Picking his words carefully, Vere said, 'You refer to us as our mother's changeling brood, but we are as much your son's children as hers. You have always condemned my artistic bent as having been inherited from her, and you are possibly right, but you cannot claim that *six* children have none of their father's qualities. I remember little of my father, but Mama always spoke of him with great fondness so it seems probable that he loved her. Have you ever condemned *him*? There's nothing shameful about strong passion, sir, especially when it brings happiness. Mother found it with her American; Margaret with a man of great distinction who saved her from misery and, as we later discovered, from a hideous death at the hands of African tribesmen. Val simply lost his head over an older, calculating woman, but you refuse to listen to my account of how he is living up to all you demand of your grandchildren. Love of honour and glory rules him and he is alive with happiness.'

He took a deep breath to control his temper. 'You speak of my wife in derisory terms, but she is from aristocratic stock. Setting that aside, she is admirably fulfilling her rôle at Knightshill and will shortly give birth to the child you have for several years been urging me to father. Would you be better pleased if I did not *love* her? Were you so hurt as a young man that you still resent those who love and find joy in it?'

Sir Gilliard stood for long moments gazing at Vere in a manner that suggested he saw an entirely different face. Then he visibly returned to the present. His upright stance loosened as if he were crumbling. 'Your ultimate weapon, as I recall. You have used it ruthlessly whenever on unsafe ground. The thrust beneath the guard no real gentleman would use.'

'You think so? My reference to your unfaithful young

wife is no less gallant than your treatment of Kitty, who is completely undeserving of it.' He continued in the same forceful manner. 'John Morgan is also undeserving of your contempt for wishing to marry my sister. He is a good, loyal man who has cared for the estate as if it were his own. He is deeply devoted to Lottie, but would never have spoken of his feelings if she had not encouraged him to do so.'

His grandfather turned away to sink into a chair with evident weariness. Staring at the floor, he said heavily, 'When my only son died of his wounds in this house I gave him my word that I would protect and guide his children in the Ashleigh tradition. I have failed with all but one.'

This oblique reference to Vorne robbed Vere of any sympathy for a man who truly believed what he had just said. 'We are not failures simply because we used the Ashleigh qualities you so much admire in ways you choose not to recognize. Lottie will marry John with my blessing. If you refuse her the dowry to which she is entitled, I'll give it to her instead. As I have been managing the estate for you since I came of age, and paying Morgan's wage, you have no power to dismiss him.' He took a breath and chose his words carefully. 'Is it really your wish to turn your back on a granddaughter who has cared about your comfort and wellbeing over many years; how you mean to honour your promise to our father?'

A pale, strained face turned upward to him. 'Is it your intention to bury me before I am dead?'

'No, Grandfather,' Vere said more gently. 'I'm simply demonstrating my ability to head this family so that you may leave it in my hands, with confidence, now that you are growing tired.' Squatting before Sir Gilliard on a sudden compassionate impulse, he added, 'There comes a time when even the most distinguished general accepts that he is no longer able to lead his army, and makes way for a younger man with new ideas. He nevertheless remains an inspiration to those who follow in his illustrious steps.'

A suggestion of sudden moisture in eyes still vividly blue surprised Vere, but the bark was back in Sir Gilliard's voice. 'Get up, man! You are all determined to go to the devil behind my back. I wonder you even have the courtesy of informing me of the fact. I will not *dine* with a bailiff, mark you. I am still master of my own table, sir, and will choose with whom I share it. Distinguished generals are accorded *that* privilege when they hand over an army, damn you!'

As autumn passed into winter Charlotte's fondness for John deepened further. Her marriage would not be rapturous like Vere's, nor as exciting as Margaret's to Laurence Niclardi, but security and contentment would be hers and she would still have Knightshill. Vere had risen to the occasion in astonishing fashion after his interview with Sir Gilliard. During several stormy meetings, he had emerged as victor over John's stubborn pride which maintained that he must provide for his wife by his own efforts. Sir Gilliard made no attempt to deprive Charlotte of her rightful marriage dowry, and Vere swiftly quashed John's determination not to accept a penny of it. After the third heated discussion, the two men came to the room where Charlotte and Kitty were sitting discussing the family wedding and christening gowns. Vere looked determined, John resigned.

'Shall I ring for tea?' Kitty asked diplomatically.

'In a moment. We'd like to tell you both what we have decided,' Vere shot a swift glance at John, 'after studying every aspect of the subject. On one matter we're both in total accord. Charlotte must be given every consideration. Do sit down, John,' he urged, as the man stood awkwardly just inside the doorway. Settling next to Kitty on the settee, Vere smiled at Charlotte who was more concerned with her fiancé. She knew he was not finding things easy.

'You cannot imagine what it was like when Margaret insisted on marrying Philip Daulton,' she told him as she indicated the chair next to hers. 'A handsome young curate instead of a handsome young officer. Grandfather was *furious*. He never approves of the partners we choose. The only one who met with his criteria was Annabel Bourneville, and she was *completely* unsuitable, wasn't she, Vere?'

'Completely.'

'Val is certain to displease when he finds his match.'

'Ho, that handsome, merry lad is presently terrified of female attention,' chuckled Kitty. 'By the time some determined young woman has snared *him*, Sir Gilliard will no longer be with us.'

'He has the consoling thought that Vorne undoubtedly would have selected a bride of unsurpassable perfection,' said Vere in such cutting fashion Charlotte was taken aback.

He resumed the subject in question. 'John will no longer be employed as bailiff, although he will do all he has always done and receive a percentage of the estate profits, as I do. We shall work together as brothers-in-law, but he understands that I shall devote long periods to painting whenever I wish which will leave the brunt of responsibility still in his capable hands.' He smiled at Charlotte. 'You cannot live with him in his cottage, and he now agrees that his plan to find something suitable in the village would not work.'

'It's a question of access, especially in winter,' John explained. 'You know how bad the snowfall is some years.'

'So what have you decided on?' she asked him.

'Mr Ash ... *Vere*,' he corrected clumsily, 'has offered us those rooms at the back of the house.'

'The guest rooms next to Val's, near the staircase?' She turned to her brother. 'What a splendid idea! We can make them into a complete suite like yours.' She had dreaded the thought of leaving her home for a rented cottage in Dunstan St Mary and was grateful to Vere for solving the problem with diplomacy. 'It will be so convenient for your office, John. That staircase runs right to it.'

'It won't be my office,' he told her somewhat stiffly.

Vere swiftly intervened. 'John and I will both use it to store the paperwork and for serious discussions on estate matters.' He smiled. 'We do not wish to bore you ladies with business when we all gather elsewhere in the house.'

'How very commendable,' teased Kitty.

'We'd like you to continue handling the growing and selling of our hothouse flowers, Charlotte. John says you would prefer to try other varieties next year. Go ahead. You and John have been successful with orchids and gardenias. I'm sure you'll do as well with whatever you choose to grow. The flowers are a good source of revenue, despite the fact that they're only seasonal.'

'I enjoy it,' Charlotte confessed. 'Flowers are a beautiful alternative to cows and pigs.'

'You leave *them* to me, lass,' John said starting to relax.

'And me,' added Vere smoothly. 'The men of this family will deal with the livestock.' Getting to his feet he walked to the bell-rope and pulled it. 'Time for tea, I think. We'll toast our amicable arrangement with something stronger at dinner. You'll join us, John? Good,' he pronounced before the man could say no.

The wedding was to be a quiet pre-Christmas affair conducted in the tiny chapel of Knightshill, rather than in the church of Dunstan St Mary. Sir Gilliard had declined

315

to attend the ceremony, so his absence would have added to village gossip about the unequal alliance, and Kitty could not appear in public so near to the birth of her child. Ashleigh relatives made the excuse of distance to stay away, and John had no family to come and wish them well. Messages and gifts from Margaret and Val were all Charlotte needed to make the day a happy one, however.

The Nicolardis arranged with a leading London store to present the couple with a handsome linen chest filled with a selection of the finest items available. They wrote of their complete happiness with each other and their two boys. Their baby was flourishing and Tim had advanced at school with leaps and bounds after his repressed education at the hands of the Reverend Daulton. They all hoped Kate was continuing to enjoy her life with the family at Knightshill and felt she should remain there for the present.

Val sent a typically hearty letter of congratulations together with a pair of wood carvings that were all he could afford on his subaltern's salary. The greater part of his letter concerned the love of his life. He gave his opinion of the war that was over yet had not been won, because half the enemy were continuing to fight despite the call to surrender by their own commanders. His regiment was presently quartered near Pretoria during this stalemate. He deplored the lack of action but was using surplus energy in his favourite sporting pursuits. He was at last what he had long wanted to be – a cavalry officer. If only he could again be an Ashleigh.

Gifts arrived from Charlotte's many Howard and Carlton-Jay relations, the modesty of which betrayed the senders' opinions of the match. Charlotte did not care. She would not be obliged to deal with their demands and complaints during the January visit for the Khartoum Dinner. Once she had recovered from the birth of her child, Kitty would become sole mistress of Knightshill with Charlotte's blessing.

The marriage ceremony was attended by Kitty, Simon, Charlotte's maid Sarah, Stoner who still valetted for Vere, Ned who represented the stable staff, Nanny and Cook. Vere deputized for Sir Gilliard and Winters acted as John's best man. Kate was a very self-important flower girl in a long silk dress embroidered with Michaelmas daisies. Charlotte had decided against wearing the Ashleigh wedding-gown with its eight-foot train and elaborate appliqué work. Margaret had last donned it for her marriage to Philip. It had not brought her happiness. The heir's bride had married abroad, so the gown's importance had waned. If Val ever married, perhaps . . .

Standing before her mirror on her wedding morning Charlotte was satisfied with her choice of ivory satin in a simple style. The lavishness of her sister's wedding was a far cry from her own, but John was a dear man who would make her life bright with hope when it had been for so long dull with dread. Margaret had always craved excitement. She, Charlotte, was tied to her roots with a bond of deep commitment. All she desired of today was to be joined as one to a man who shared that bond.

Vere arrived several minutes early to escort her downstairs, kissing her warmly. 'Are you nervous?'

'Not in the least, my dear. It's not as if I'm about to parade through some vast cathedral.'

'You should, Lottie. I've seldom seen a more beautiful bride.'

She smiled, 'Flatterer!'

Turning her back to face her reflection, he said over her shoulder, 'It's not flattery. You've consistently underestimated yourself, and I feel more than partially responsible.'

'What nonsense, Vere! Whyever should you feel that?'

His hands dropped from her shoulders as he sighed. 'I accepted your willingness to become my constant companion in the sick-room. I *was* an invalid, but you were coerced into believing yourself one, also. You deserve more than you have received from life. Your devotion to me robbed you of it.'

He had touched on something she had frequently considered. She was now quite honest in her reply. 'My devotion to you had a possessive quality for which only *I* am responsible.' She turned to smile apologetically. 'I mistakenly believed we would never change. Thank heaven we did.' She took his hand. 'Life has given me a great deal, Vere. As the one Ashleigh who prefers not to roam I have all I could possibly want right here at Knightshill.'

'I'm so very glad,' he said with sincerity. Then he brought from his pocket a long velvet box to offer to her. 'The pair of horses was our wedding gift to you both. This is quite apart from that, Lottie.'

She opened the box and gazed in astonishment at the rope of large lustrous pearls coiled inside it. She looked up swiftly. 'They're *beautiful*. I . . .'

'Let me tell you a story before you say any more,' he intervened, taking the rope from the box and letting it hang from his hand to gleam in the sunlight. 'I've spoken of this to no one, including Kitty.'

Charlotte could not take her gaze from the creamy pearls. 'How very mysterious you sound.'

'Not mysterious. Reminiscent,' he said quietly. 'Lottie, whilst I was in Cairo two years ago I was contacted by a certain Contessa Pallini, who asked me to go to her villa. She was . . . *is* . . . a most cultured, vivacious creature whose elderly husband had vanished in the desert some years before, during an expedition.' His expression was inexplicable to Charlotte who had no notion what was to come. 'An almost certain widow, Floria had met and grown to love Lieutenant V.E.R. Ashleigh.'

'*Vorne!*' exclaimed Charlotte. 'She knew Vorne during that terrible campaign?'

Vere nodded. 'When she heard, as people in the East

so mysteriously do, that Vorne's brother was in Cairo, she sent for me. I think she had no idea then of making the gesture but, after we talked for some time during which she learned that I intended to follow in our brother's footsteps to Khartoum, she took off these pearls and gave them to me.'

'I don't understand,' she said. 'They look very costly.'

'I've no doubt they were. Vorne presented them to Floria as he left for Khartoum. She never saw him again.'

'If she loved Vorne, why give his parting gift to you?'

'Because she saw a family likeness in me, and because she believed, as we all did, that I was also going to my death in the desert.'

'But . . . why give her pearls to someone who might lose them along with his life outside Khartoum?'

'She told me to send them to the girl who had driven me to make such a gesture for love of her.' A wry smile touched his lips. 'By then I had almost forgotten Annabel, so left the pearls in the bank with instructions to return them to Contessa Pallini on my death.' He laid the rope in the box again. 'After Atbara I returned to Cairo. Floria introduced me to Armand Lisère and obtained my first commission with *The Illustrated Magazine*.' He moved away to stand by the fire. 'I fell a little in love with her . . . but I was not Vorne. When I left for the final push to Khartoum I gave her *my* pearls. I've remained uncertain what to do with these until you told me of your intention to marry John. I knew then that you should have them.'

'Surely, Kitty . . .'

'No,' he interjected swiftly, 'two Ashleighs have been connected with this necklace given with love. The woman to wear them should be an Ashleigh, also. I give them again with love, Lottie, and as a tribute to your courage in breaking with tradition to find happiness, as we all have.' When she still hesitated, he said, 'Would you rather they

319

went to Annabel Bourneville with my thanks for sending me to the war? Or, more appropriately, as a momento of the man whose memory she revered above all else?'

This confession of why her brother's engagement had been broken came as something as a shock, but she responded warmly. 'Of course not! Forgive me, Vere.' Reaching up to kiss his cheek, she said, 'I shall treasure and keep them in the family.'

His smile was one of pure happiness. 'Let's no longer keep poor John waiting anxiously for his beautiful bride.'

Charlotte thought no more about the curious story surrounding the rope of pearls, her concentration centred on the import of the following hour. Kate sailed through her rôle in style, but John was uncharacteristically nervous throughout the ceremony. He only began to relax when he emerged with Charlotte to find the domestic staff assembled in the hall, to offer good wishes, and an embroidered counterpane for their linen chest. The bride promised them some wedding cake, and her husband thanked them for their kindness and generosity.

Cook had provided an excellent wedding breakfast. Kitty entertained them with tales of her days in Kimberley, which reduced the formality of Knightshill's aura and eased John's nervousness. Charlotte was grateful to her sister-in-law, and to Vere who had championed their cause. She knew her future would be filled with contentment, yet one thing spoiled what should be the most momentous day of her life. What had started as a small dark blob on the horizon grew until it overshadowed the happy gathering and drove her to her feet.

'You must all excuse me for a short while,' she said to a ring of surprised faces. 'There is something I must do.'

Clunes registered even greater astonishment when Charlotte arrived at Sir Gilliard's door. Aside from stammering his good wishes, the former batman seemed incapable of thought or action as the satin-clad bride declared her wish to visit her grandfather.

'He ... he is eating luncheon, Miss ... madam ... er ...'

'Mrs Morgan, Clunes,' she informed him calmly. 'I'll announce myself.'

The sitting-room was yellow with lamplight. The sun had not shone for her wedding so the house was dark within. After the conviviality she had left, the sole figure at a small table beside the fire struck a note of bleakness. She hesitated momentarily then realized that she had achieved something extremely rare. Sir Gilliard was rendered speechless by her appearance. It did not instantly occur to her that a female figure in a shimmering pale dress, appearing without warning before eyes dulled by the years, might cause an ageing heart to quicken with fright. Yet it was a stronger emotion than that. Frozen into stillness, the man who had put the fear of God into many others stared at her and croaked, '*Caroline!*'

For several seconds Charlotte was as shocked as he. Her impulsive act had cruelly, but unwittingly, suggested a ghostly vision of her grandmother – the young wife who had run off with a lover leaving her husband the butt of humiliating scandal. Full of remorse Charlotte walked further in to the room, yet still those vivid eyes gazed at her in chilling fashion.

'Grandfather, it's I, Charlotte,' she ventured. 'I did not mean to alarm you.' Frankly afraid then, because his expression was so tortured, Charlotte halted and hastened to explain why she was there. 'I know you were disappointed by my decision and I'm deeply sorry that you should be, but this is my wedding day ... and I have come to ask for your blessing.' Fear made her rush on. 'You have cared for us all since Father died, and Knightshill has always been home to me. After Mother left you were our only guide and teacher. We all spent wonderfully happy childhood days here. When the others went away, we two continued the familiar routine. I know you have always wished Margaret and

I had been boys, and took little interest in our feminine occupations, but we are both fond of you and grateful for all you have given us. I especially, as the one Ashleigh who stayed at home.' She took a breath. 'John is an honest, loyal man who will make me a good husband ... but my happiness will only be complete if you take my hand and wish me well.'

It was as if the entire room held its breath, until Sir Gilliard said in strangled tones, 'You look so like her. Why have I never seen it before?'

'Like Grandmama?'

'A bright little creature. All smiles and laughter,' the old man mused, away again in another world. 'They told me I would rue the day, but youth never heeds wisdom until it's too late. Her laughter died when I sailed to India without her. Didn't understand that infants rarely survived the rigours of the country.'

Charlotte crossed to him in concern. He appeared to have already forgotten who she was. The filet of chicken with macédoine of vegetables lay half eaten on his plate. A full glass of wine stood beside it. The past had overtaken him and would not retreat.

'That was too long ago,' she suggested gently. 'It does not matter now.'

'Both parents approved,' he continued, as if she had not spoken. 'Why should they not? She was but eighteen, in full health and in possession of a handsome dowry. In return, she would gain entry to a distinguished family and live in luxury on a fine old estate. Ah, yes! It was a grand affair in true military style. The abbey was filled to overflowing with some of the greatest names in the country. Her father was determined on making it one of the events of the year.' He sat for a moment, his face working. 'Great mistake. Scandal was all the bigger because of it.'

Kneeling beside him, Charlotte laid her hand on his arm. 'It's all forgotten now. You're known for your gallant deeds in the field; the way you led men to victory. You've had a splendid life. We all respect and admire you for that.'

Blue eyes seemed to bore into hers, yet she felt they saw nothing but introspective images. 'Had to put in double the effort. Had to achieve more than most. When a man's revealed as a fool he has to overcome that humiliation before he can ever *begin* to advance. Hard on him. Can never let up. *Never!*'

Distressed over the way she had resurrected something so painful, Charlotte sat back on her heels. The story of her grandmother's infidelity had never before touched her as it now did, because the brand of love between a man and a woman had been unknown to her. Relating her grandfather's experience to her own life, she began to understand and feel compassion. What if John should later abandon her for a fascinating woman passing through the district? What pain he would cause her. If she were part of a large group – a regiment, for instance – how much worse the shame and sense of failure. This stern old man suddenly became a very dear person in the winter of a loveless life. If only she had realized the fact sooner.

'You can let up now, Grandfather,' she told him with eyes growing moist. 'Vere is happily settled at Knightshill and about to welcome his firstborn. He'll live up to your high standards, never fear. Margaret has found her perfect partner and become a very successful diplomatic hostess. Val has redeemd his reputation with a commission and a decoration for gallantry, and I . . . I have formed an honourable alliance which allows me to relinquish with grace the position I have held here for so long. Your family have also had to overcome humiliations, and have done it with your example to follow,' she added fondly.

Sir Gilliard frowned. He studied Charlotte for long moments as he returned to his surroundings. 'You think so? Only one lived up to expectation. Died a hero.'

'Val's a *living* hero. So is Vere, I suspect. Don't neglect them. They so much want your approval. And so do I. Please give me your blessing.'

For a while she believed he had retreated once more. Then he patted her hand resting on his arm. 'Come and see me sometimes. I am a trifle lonely now the days have grown dark.'

'Of course I'll come,' she assured him warmly. Then she obeyed impulse and kissed his cheek, something she had not done for many years. 'Thank you, Grandfather.'

When she reached the door, he called after her in stronger tones, 'When this boy is born, be sure to give me the news without delay.'

Charlotte returned to the parlour uncertain whether he had, in fact, known who she was.

Kitty went into labour two days before Christmas. Having had Simon she knew what to expect, but Vere was appalled by the extent of her suffering. Experience of battlefields did nothing to prepare him for the sight of a woman in anguish, particularly one he loved. After twenty-eight hours, Kitty knew something must be wrong. Simon had not taken so long, nor had his birth caused so much pain. She confided her fears to Vere who immediately overrode Dr Alderton's protests and sent for a physician from Salisbury who was experienced in difficult cases. He blamed himself for not engaging the man from the outset, but Kitty had been happy and confident whilst George Alderton declared all to be normal.

When Charlotte came to his rooms early on Christmas Eve, Vere expressed his sense of anxiety. 'Lottie, unlike Grandfather, I have no fanatical desire for a son – for any child – if it means I shall lose the dearest person on earth.'

'Shhh, you must not think of that,' she told him.

'Dr Barker will know what to do. John has gone to the station with Ned to meet his train. They should be back before long.' She took his arm in the affectionate gesture that two years ago had irritated him. He now found it comforting. 'Have you eaten anything since breakfast? Starving yourself will be of no help to Kitty. Let me call Stoner to bring you some dinner.'

'I couldn't eat anything at the moment. Perhaps when Barker has conferred with Alderton and set my mind at rest.' He sighed. 'Alderton is old. I know he's been the family physician for years, but that very fact should have told me Kitty should be placed in the care of a younger man. I will never forgive myself if . . .'

'Please, Vere, you *must* have faith,' Charlotte insisted. 'Kitty is strong and healthy. She has had a child before. There is no reason why she should not have this one safely. She will undoubtedly be tired and possibly have to keep to her bed a little longer than usual, but I have no doubt that you will have a happy wife *and* a child when the church bells ring in Christmas Day. I suppose he will be named Noel or Crispin . . . perhaps Nicholas.'

Vere began to relax. She sounded so confident. Since her marriage his sister had bloomed. She had become a new, assured woman. It was strange to think that she and John had been living side by side for so long without recognizing an obvious attraction. Only when left at Knightshill alone had Charlotte been free to get to know John well, he supposed. Perhaps she would one day have a child. Poor Charlotte – poor *women* to have to suffer as Kitty was in order to bring others into the world. He thought then of his mother who had had eight children – two of whom had been stillborn. To have endured so much pain to produce a dead child; to have reared six only to abandon them for a chance of personal happiness when forced to choose between them and a man she loved! He must believe that a widowed life at Knightshill under Sir Gilliard's rigid régime had been so unbearable she had had no choice but to escape.

He was jerked from his thought by the sound of voices in the corridor. 'That will be Barker.' He strode to the door and flung it open in relief. 'Thank God!' he said as he shook the hand of a tall, bespectacled man in his early forties. 'Thank you for coming at short notice. I think Alderton needs your opinion on my wife's condition. She has been suffering for almost two days.'

Dr Barker merely nodded, unsmiling, and pointed in questioning fashion at the door across the room.

'Yes, I'll take you to her.' Vere moved forward hastily.

'No, I will examine your wife and discuss her condition with Dr Alderton, then give you my assessment. Please wait here, Mr Ashleigh,' the new arrival said briskly, before vanishing into Kitty's dressing-room which led to the bedroom.

'He knows best, Vere,' Charlotte said.

He ran a hand over his hair. 'I hope to God he knows what to do to put an end to her ordeal.'

John, who had brought Dr Barker up from the station, came to stand beside Charlotte. 'I don't mean to be disrespectful in any way, but I've sat up all night enough to know that young 'uns take their time coming into the world. It's the same process for livestock as it is for people, you know, and sometimes a little help is needed. Dr Barker will best be able to give it, never fear.'

The minutes dragged for Vere as he stared at the door through which Barker would reappear with encouraging or bad news. A diversion was caused when Clunes came yet again at Sir Gilliard's instigation to ask if there was anything to relay. Vere lost his temper.

'We have a critical situation here, man. My grandfather must not send you again to compound it. When there is anything to tell him, he will be told. If he cannot accept that, put it into words he *will* understand. A *communiqué will be issued when lines of communication are reopened.'* He said the last sentence with such force Clunes' mouth tightened.

'Very well, Mr Ashleigh. I'll tell the General he'll be the first to know and you will tell him straight away. I'll not intrude on your privacy again, sir.' He went out with such military erectness and precision he could well have been on guard duty.

'He lives in a world of his own – one you surely understand, Vere,' Charlotte said with a hint of sympathy. 'He and Grandfather have never left the army.'

'I understand it well enough,' he replied rather savagely, 'but one can't apply military procedure to childbirth.' His heartbeat quickened as Dr Barker beckoned him from the dressing-room, and he hurried forward with nerves tense. 'Is my wife . . .?' A frown silenced him until the other man closed the door to speak to him more privately on the subject.

'Mrs Ashleigh is having a prolonged labour because there are *two* babies in her womb. They are both in incorrect positions for birth, at present. I shall endeavour to move them to allow this to take place. I must warn you, however, that your wife's strength is diminishing hourly.'

Vere grew cold. 'What are you trying to tell me?'

'Exactly that. She is growing weak from her lengthy ordeal. If birth is long delayed the second child has little chance of survival.'

'And my wife?'

'We shall do all we can.' He frowned again. 'I suggest you take some rest. It will be some while before I have any news for you.'

After waiting for several minutes in the dressing-room that bore the fragrance of Kitty's lotions, Vere returned to Charlotte and John with the details he had been told.

'*Twins!*' cried Charlotte. 'How is it Dr Alderton did not know?'

For the first time Vere took in the truth of what had been said, yet he felt no pleasure. Kitty was his sole concern. If the babies died he supposed she would be deeply upset, but he cared only that she should survive. If she did he would never want her to go through this again, heir or no heir. Val would have to do *his* duty in that direction instead.

'Alderton is too old,' he repeated heavily. 'I shall engage a younger man to attend us.'

'You'll also require a nursemaid for your children. Nanny cannot look after two babies in addition to Kate and Simon.'

Vere sank into a chair. 'We don't have two babies yet, Lottie.'

His sister glanced up at her husband. 'I think we should go to the nursery for a while. It *is* Christmas Eve and the children must not be neglected completely. The carol singers will also be up from the village soon and there are the gifts to be distributed. Will you help me?'

'Of course.' John looked across to Vere. 'Is there anything I can do for you?'

'Deputize for me, if you will.'

'I can hardly do that,' John protested.

Vere wearily tilted his head against the wing of the chair and closed his eyes. 'Your wife has done so for the past few years. Do it for *her*, man!'

The door clicked shut as they left, and Vere felt a sense of relief. He needed to be alone. Kitty had been his for a mere twelve months, yet he knew life would be empty and meaningless without her. He had expected to die young. It would be too cruel if she were to do so instead. He would have to leave Knightshill once more and wander in search of something this time he would not find. Surely that was not his destiny.

The lamps burned low. In a state of half-awareness he heard young voices singing carols. Memories of youth stirred momentarily then drifted away. His mind was burdened by numbing fear. It could not hold any thought for long. The coals in the grate shifted noisily bringing him fully to his senses. A glance at the clock showed him it was nearing midnight. He had grown too cold and moved stiffly to add fuel to the dying fire. As he did so he heard faint cries from the bedroom. They continued without a pause, adding to his fear until he could take no more. Dropping the coal tongs with a clatter in the hearth, he headed for the bedroom like a man possessed.

The sound of wailing chilled his blood as he flung open the door. The scene represented purgatory at first glance. Bloodsoaked sheets, two men with gory arms, the smell of sickness, lamplight yellowing pale faces, the midwife with a bloody apron holding a child's corpse by the feet and beating it, steam hovering over bowls of reddened water. In the bed Kitty lay still and ashen. Brought to a halt by a sense of horror, Vere was accosted by one of the doctors who handed him a rolled sheet.

'Take this, man. We still have work to do.'

The sheet was warm and moving. Vere held it in a continuation of the nightmare, until he saw a small red face amidst the folds. The tiny mouth was open to let forth surprisingly strident shrieks. Awareness dawned. It was over and this baby was very much alive. Next moment, the shrieks doubled and another rolled sheet was handed to him, warm and moving. The midwife's damp, shiny face beamed at him in the yellow glare.

'Two little girls born each side of midnight, Mr Ashleigh. What a wonderful Christmas gift.'

For a moment Vere's attention was centred on the double miracle that was the outcome of love expressed in the most intimate way. Then he was distracted by activity around the bed, and fear returned.

'My wife!' he cried moving forward, his gaze on the still figure lying with a mass of damp red hair spread across the pillow.

The man with spectacles barred his way, then took his

elbow to lead him from the room. 'We have saved her and both infants. God must have been with us, Mr Ashleigh. Your wife is exhausted. Alderton and the midwife will clean up and make her comfortable. Then you may go and sit with her. She will sleep for a long while, but you should be there when she awakens to tell her the situation.'

Bemused and still clutching his twin daughters, who had fallen asleep, Vere halted. 'The situation?'

Dr Barker removed his spectacles to rub his eyes with his knuckles. 'It has been a long day. Mrs Ashleigh was hardly aware of the arrival of her infants. She will wish to hear the good news from you. Then you must tell her something else.'

'Something else?' echoed Vere once more, his brain dulled by anxiety and the lateness of the hour.

Putting the spectacles back on, the man said heavily, 'Bearing these twins so damaged your wife she will be unable to have more children. I'm extremely sorry, Mr Ashleigh.'

A sense of relief invaded Vere. 'You must not be. I had no intention of risking my wife's life in this manner a second time. I thank God she is safe. Here are two healthy infants in my arms. I could not ask for more.'

Dark eyes regarded him shrewdly. 'A son, perhaps?'

As Vere studied the red puckered faces of his daughters he saw a vision of a beautiful, blue-eyed half-Egyptian lad, who, but for the lack of a marriage certificate, was heir to Knightshill as Vorne's child. Then he thought of his own artistic personality, and of a boy determined to join the cavalry instead of the West Wiltshire Regiment. He shook his head slowly.

'A man can think so little of a son he can abandon him in a foreign country and never return, or he can be so disappointed in one who does not live up to expectations, he drives the boy away. These girls will grow to be as lovely, talented and courageous as their mother. They will be surrounded by love, valued as the people they choose to be, and never be made to feel they have failed.'

Although news of the birth was immediately relayed by Stoner to Clunes, as promised, no message of congratulation arrived that night or on the following morning. In fact, two weeks passed without any word from Sir Gilliard. Vere was too concerend with Kitty's slow recovery and delight in his two daughters to care about this snub from his grandfather. He spent almost all his time with his wife, leaving John to run the estate and Charlotte to deal with callers and the many gifts which arrived from all parts of the country. His sister and her husband were sympathetic over the circumstance that made Val indisputable heir to Knightshill on Vere's death. Kitty was initially distressed by the news that she could never give her husband the son he should have, but Vere quickly dispelled her mood by convincing her that he asked no more of her than her continuing love and their twin daughters.

Once able to leave her bed, Kitty determined on confronting Sir Gilliard and resolving the ridiculous situation that had arisen. 'We cannot leave things as they are,' she reasoned, despite Vere's stubborn inclination to let the old man sulk, if he wished. 'Holly and Victoria are his great-granddaughters. He *must* recognize them. I'll not allow him to do otherwise.'

Vere stood beside the two cradles looking at the tiny babes with Kitty. 'How do you propose to get your way?'

She glanced across at him and he was struck by the new fragility of her face and body. Yet her inner strength remained. 'I shall request him to wait on me so that I may tell him something of immense importance to the perpetuation of the Ashleigh line. He will be unable to resist such a message, Vere.'

He took her in his arms with great gentleness. 'You will deal him a bad blow.'

'No worse a blow than he has dealt you in his time,' she replied firmly. 'We all of us have some dreams cruelly broken and have to recover from bitter disappointment. He must do the same. There is Val to pin his hopes on. Somehow, we must change his unreasonable attitude towards a young man bursting to become an impossible hero, who is being treated with unjustifiable scorn.'

'Let me go to him,' he urged. 'You're still weak, in no condition to withstand his relentless tongue.'

'No, Vere, it is because of *me* that you're denied a son. I want him to be quite clear on that point.'

'I am responsible for causing you to be damaged by the birth of our girls,' he insisted. 'I would prefer you not to do this.'

'I know you would, but my mind is made up. Will you send Stoner with the note, or must I tell Louise to deliver it?'

Knowing her well enough by now, Vere scribbled the request for his valet to deliver then waited, half expecting a written refusal. However, at four o'clock Sir Gilliard arrived dressed in his tweeds. Vere walked across to greet him with a smile, as if the two-week silence had never occurred.

'It's good of you to come, sir. Will you have tea, or a glass of something more warming?'

'I shall enjoy *that* at dinner-time, and Clunes is preparing my tea, as usual.' Sir Gilliard bowed stiffly in Kitty's direction. 'You have something important to convey to me, I understand, ma'am.'

'I have,' she agreed in tones that were pleasant, despite the lack of a smile. 'I should first of all like you to go with me to the nursery to see your great-grandchildren, Holly and Victoria Ashleigh.'

Kitty rose from her sewing-chair and began walking

towards him, but he soon halted her. 'I shall go with you when there is a boy child, not before.'

Kitty stopped before him, a very slender woman in an afternoon gown of bronze silk, whose appearance belied the strength of her character. 'Then you will be obliged to wait until young Val marries and fathers one, for the doctors have informed me that my child-bearing days are at an end. I cannot provide my husband with an heir. That is the information I wished to tell you, sir.'

Disbelief was chased from that proud face by an expression of deep contempt as Sir Gilliard turned to Vere. 'You have consistently failed to live up to my expectations, and have failed yet again. The blame for this lies with *you*. Your wife produced a boy sired by another man of evident greater physical and moral fibre, yet all you can beget are creatures as weak and sensitive as yourself. If you imagine I am about to retire from life and hand you Knightshill to treat with the disregard I have seen you use towards all I value, you are mistaken. I shall remain as master here until I have found a worthy heir to succeed me when you abandon this and go off again with your confounded *paint brushes*.'

He almost spat the last two words, and had turned to go when Kitty intervened with plain words. 'Those paint brushes have made the name Vere Ashleigh highly respected in both military and art circles. Your expectations must be unique, sir, for my husband has exceeded those of everyone else who has been fortunate enough to know him. The time has come to put an end to your unforgivable persecution of an heir many men would be proud to own.' She stepped round to confront him head on. 'Not so you. He ran away to almost certain death because your condemnation, added to that of a very shallow young woman, persuaded him he was worthless. Fate took a kinder view.'

As Sir Gilliard made to pass her, Kitty stepped into his

Emma Drummond

path. 'I have not finished. Have you sufficient courage and good manners to hear me out?'

Vere went to her to signify that she was wasting her efforts on someone so steeped in his inflexible attitudes, but his grandfather stood his ground unable to force a way past a woman set on detaining him.

'Vere fought bravely at Atbara and Omdurman, earning the respect of his fellows. He also exceeded *average* Ashleigh distinction by additionally recording the campaign with brushes and colour so that the rest of the world would appreciate the suffering and endeavour of those who had taken part. In South Africa he exhibited great courage in helping to bring in, under heavy fire, a waggon laden with ammunition. This, mark you, when he was no longer in uniform and under orders. Are your expectations of *any* man you know greater than that?'

Well into her stride, Kitty continued with passion in her voice. 'I vainly hoped you would give your congratulations on the birth of twin children; the first occasion in the history of the Ashleigh family, I believe. But you see nothing commendable in the fact. If they had been twin *boys* the news would have been shouted from the rooftops. If two girls had been fathered by *Vorne* Ashleigh, possessor of every virtue, *he* would have been lauded for such a feat, but the proud father is someone who has consistently failed, according to you. He's once more vilified; his accomplishments ridiculed.

'As for my husband treating with disregard all you value, I must point out that he is the first heir to this great estate who has not abandoned it for a life in the army. He has already done more for Knightshill than you have in ninety years. The manner in which you have valued it, sir, is to spend forty or more years away from it and the rest sunk in your military manuals and memories while John Morgan did the job for you.'

Vere put his hands on her shoulders to persuade her to stop, but she caught at one of them and held it lovingly while she added what she could not hold back.

'That none of your grandchildren has said this to you is not due to lack of courage, but because they owe you some gratitude and have a kind of respectful affection for you, although how any of them can still feel the latter I cannot imagine. You have forbidden Margaret her home because she copied your wife in running away to find happiness rather than face a lonely, loveless life. You banished Val and robbed him of a name he's immensely proud of merely because he longed to be an officer in another regiment quite as distinguished as the one you served. Charlotte has been treated as no more than a housekeeper and you now refuse to acknowledge her husband. Vere has been shamefully insulted whatever he has done. He cannot please you whether he is on a battlefield, receiving public acclaim for his artistic gift, or wholeheartedly tending the acres you claim to value so highly. Would you approve of your family if they all wore the uniform of the West Wilts and saluted you each time they passed? I doubt it. You are a man without a drop of warmth in your blood. The only reason *Vorne* Ashleigh is revered by you is because you can make of him what you wish; endow him with impossible virtues no living heir could sustain.'

Kitty's voice began to break and Vere would not allow the interview to go on any longer. Ignoring his grandfather, he coaxed Kitty across to their dressing-room leading to the bedroom where she could recover in private. Even so, she looked over her shoulder to add final impassioned words.

'I pity you. You have barricaded yourself inside your stronghold and rejected four people who could have given you the love you have denied yourself for over half a century. Make amends before it's too late.'

Vere kicked the bedroom door shut then took Kitty to the bed and settled her on it with care. She sank back upon the pillow to gaze at him intently as he covered her with the counterpane.

'Why the tears?' she asked softly.

He sat on the edge of the bed and took her hand, deeply moved. 'I love you beyond life. Nothing else matters to me. Nothing else in the world. Please believe that.'

'I do, my dearest. I am now looking through your rosy glass and everything I see is warmed by your love.'

13

V AL HAD BEEN in South Africa long enough to appreciate the freshness of a glorious blue and gold mid-winter day. The sky was clear and vivid, the land burnt ochre by sunshine which had now lost its blazing ferocity. As he rode his grey stallion, Nimbus, bought with the generous allowance Vere gave him, Val was filled with the usual longings. Youth bubbled within his strong, healthy body, but it was beset by frustrations of various kinds.

July 1901. Queen Victoria was dead and the war not yet won. The sieges of Ladysmith, Kimberley and Mafeking had been lifted last year, Pretoria had fallen into British hands banishing Paul Kruger's Boer government, and General Roberts had returned to England as the heroic victor of an unpopular clash of arms. Although called upon to accept defeat, thousands of Boers determindly continued the fight. The character of the war had changed significantly. Battles between hundreds of thousands on open plains were horrors of the past. New tactics comprised sudden swoops on British camps by small parties of the enemy who seized guns, horses and cattle before riding off with their plunder to be swallowed up by the vastness of the land. Although casualties no longer numbered thousands, many men died or were wounded in raids which were invariably successful due to total surprise.

Smaller outposts were often completely overrun, the Boers then taking everything they wanted almost without opposition. Prisoners were an unwanted encumbrance for roaming commandos, so any British troops not killed in the initial attack were stripped and chased on to the veld to fend for themselves. Thick khaki uniforms were welcome replacements for clothes wearing thin, but the more fanatical burghers soon saw the greatest advantage of this booty. Wearing the stolen tunics and breeches complete with badges and insignia of rank, they could approach outposts or patrols quite openly in daylight then fire at almost point-blank range. This practice was considered by the British, and many Boers, to be against the rules of warfare and attitudes hardened further.

In a bid to bring to an end this demoralizing harassment by the Boers, Kitchener had ordered blockhouses to be built across the veld with barbed wire stretched between them to snare an enemy which mostly travelled at night. Each blockhouse was manned by six or seven men whose duty it was to fire on those attempting to break through the wire. The tactic was no more than moderately successful, since the distance between blockhouses was too great for the few guardians to control. All too often they, instead, became the victims.

An additional measure taken to hamper the roaming Boers was to deprive them of food and shelter by burning the farms of sympathizers and confiscating livestock. This practice was abhorred by some British troops; others relished it. It led to a further debatable move. The women and children made homeless were taken to hastily prepared camps which served a dual purpose. Besides preventing the women from further assisting their menfolk, the wire-enclosed camps were intended to protect them from falling victim to vengeful black servants and ensuring that they did not starve. Unfortunately, the makeshift camps housed many more than anticipated and scarcity of sanitary arrangements bred disease on a large scale. The deaths of a great many from epidemics inflamed the Boers, who felt *any* means

of retaliation was acceptable. Chivalry became a virtue of
the past in this war the Boers could never win, but which
the British seemed incapable of rapidly concluding.

Val's sense of impotency was as great as that of his
fellows. It was humiliating for crack troops to be unable
to pin down the elusive enemy and claim victory. His
pride in his regiment was deeply bruised by its many
failures on endless patrols. This was not as they knew it,
it was deadly hide and seek in a country which favoured
the men who roamed and understood it.

In addition to the professional frustration, Val suffered
personal disappointment. Although he had sent Charlotte
a photograph of himself in the impressive uniform of an
officer of the 57th, and had reasonably modestly, he
hoped, mentioned the award for his part in the encounter
on the farm, his sister's reply had mentioned only that the
arrival of the picture had released Kate from her months
of silence. Val was naturally pleased at that news, but
remained hollow hearted over the absence of signs that
Sir Gilliard had been told of his commission granted on
the strength of his bold action against the enemy. Vere
made no direct mention of their grandfather showing
interest in the career of Martin Havelock, but frequently
referred to Sir Gilliard's continuing inflexible attitudes
and his grudging acceptance of Kitty's condition which
made Val the next in line to inherit Knightshill.

To an ardent young man yearning for the chance to
win honours so close to Vorne's that *no one* could fail
to acknowledge them, letters filled with domestic trivia
were of no interest. He had last seen Knightshill over
three years ago and life since then had been vastly
different from that of the schoolboy dreaming of a
golden future, who had been seduced by an experienced
woman's promise of obtaining it. News of marriages and
babies – Charlotte was expecting one in October, and
Margaret in November – spoke of a life so far removed
from his that Val found it all unreal. His sister could be

excused for being excited about a baby, but Vere had
known war, had been here and lived with the army. How
could he dismiss it all and fill page after page with details
of cattle sales and crops?

Val paid little heed to the fact of being the next heir.
Vere was apparently in good health now and was not
yet thirty. In any event, how could a man named Martin
Havelock inherit the Ashleigh estate? The question of
succession mattered little against the quest to gain Sir
Gilliard's recognition of his worth.

As Val rode in the hills on that exhilarating day, his
thoughts eventually reached the minor pricks suffered
daily in his life as an officer. Although one or two
of the more hidebound members of the Mess openly
showed their disapproval of those commissioned from
the rank and file, Val had been welcomed by the rest
with varying amounts of warmth according to how they
viewed Colonel Beecham's championship of a former
trooper who had shown himself to be of officer class
from the start.

Although he was now where he should always have
been, Val found life among equals more difficult than
with the more rough and ready rankers. He had constantly to hold himself in check for fear of betraying
his true identity, and the stress of maintaining the lie
he had lived for almost three years was beginning to
tell. For that reason he had made no real friend in his
new environment. He missed Toby and the fellowship
of other sergeants, who had accepted him at face value.
On the few occasions that he sought Toby's company, he
found their relationship irrevocably changed. It was not
possible to meet openly due to protocol of rank. Toby
seemed to watch his tongue to the point of becoming
almost a stranger, and Val's obligation of loyalty to his
fellow officers forbade him to speak as freely as he had
done in the past. After one conversation during which
Val had impulsively reiterated his vow to break Audley

Pickering, only to be countered by Toby's snapped reply that, having got what he had always wanted, he should grow up and drop this ridiculous vendetta, they both knew the friendship had run its course. Whenever Toby saluted as he passed, Val knew a pang of regret for days now gone.

Gaining what he had coveted for so long had its penalties. Always on guard against revealing facts about his background, Val remained aloof from men in whose company he should have felt supremely at ease. Pickering constantly goaded him, sensing that he could not, or would not, defend himself. When Felix Wheeler or some of the more amenable subalterns spoke up for him, Val was further piqued because Pickering sneered at a man who needed others to protect him from a little harmless baiting.

In addition to his arch enemy, there was the problem of someone who was anything but. Vivienne Beecham was embarrassingly open in her determination to show her affection. With no further barriers to their close friendship Val was hard put to repudiate her frank hints that he was hers for the taking. Mrs Beecham smiled fondly on her headstrong daughter and the newly commissioned young man of evident distinction. Val was certain neither the girl nor her mother were aware of who he was – his colonel had sworn never to reveal the truth – but was alarmed at approbation of an obvious link between a girl of just twenty and a subaltern of merely twenty-two. He did not understand Mrs Beecham's leniency, which made it difficult for him to fend off her daughter's advances. It never occurred to him that where she saw a normal healthy friendship between two very young, rather lonely people, he saw Vivienne as a younger version of her cousin, Julia, set on seducing and humiliating him. That experience had burned deeply into his pride and would not easily be cast aside.

In truth, Val was lonelier than he had ever been. At

school, as a trooper, and as a sergeant he had never been short of friendly companions. His personality was such that he was at ease in all masculine company; his enthusiasm for active pursuits and those things dear to men made him popular with his fellows. Not so now. He no longer even enjoyed the respect and fond loyalty of the troopers amongst whom he had started his career. Protocol demanded that he must command those who could not take advantage of his former lowly rank, so Second-Lieutenant Havelock was now with S Troop of Lockheart Squadron. Felix Wheeler had finally lost the thorn in his side, and Val no longer had the courageous giant, Deadman, to call upon in a tight spot.

John Fielding, the man who had once seen Val at Knightshill but failed to put a name to a face when they met up again as trooper and captain, no longer commanded the squadron. He had been killed *en route* to Kimberley, as had many others. The regiment had a number of replacements so new faces abounded. S Troop were a mixed body of hardened old soldiers and green youngsters from home. Val was happy enough with them, and they with him. Captain Marley was another matter. On transfer from another lancer regiment, and fresh out of England, Thorn Marley was experienced in Indian campaigns against tribesmen. He likened the guerilla tactics of the Boers to those he had faced in the vast, savage areas of that other jewel of the Empire. As a soldier he was assured, ruthless and respected. In the man assurance became arrogance, his ruthlessness remained, and respect for him was clouded by personal dislike of his overbearing manner towards anyone weaker or less fortunate than himself. He did not relish having among his subalterns one promoted from the ranks, whom everyone in the Mess agreed had almost certainly committed a crime against society for which his family had disowned him. A family of *minor* landowners, or tradesmen, most probably, or he would never have stayed the course as a trooper. Anyone of true breeding could not have endured such conditions, much less earned the loyal friendship of his fellows, Marley concluded.

Although he could not find fault with Val professionally, the troop captain would barely acknowledge him socially. It was something of a relief for Val. The man was an inveterate name-dropper who apparently was intimate with several families known to the Ashleighs. He had once boasted of meeting Sir Gilliard and the heroic Vorne, adding that the latter's death on the sands outside Khartoum had smitten him deeply. On that occasion Val had longed to challenge him, but was silenced by the eye of Max Beecham. In a strange way, his colonel appeared his sole ally now Val had gained that for which he had sacrificed honour and family name during his ill-judged passion for Julia Grieves.

The sun was lowering in the sky when Val reluctantly turned Nimbus to retrace his path. Little fear of marksmen in these low hills. The regiment was resting from weeks of exhausting pursuit of phantom commandos; phantom because they could vanish before one's tired eyes as if they had never existed. Six weeks in the large tented camp outside Pretoria brought the chance to relax from constant stand by, and to indulge in pleasant social pastimes. For Val there were enjoyable polo and cricket matches during which he could become his true self for a while. He could also ride out alone with Val Ashleigh to escape the strain of being Martin Havelock to everyone around him. Where some took out guns to bag animal trophies, he preferred to leave the creatures in peace. There was enough taking of life among the people roaming this land.

Most men welcomed the opportunity to enjoy female company denied them at outlying camps. Balls and dinner parties were arranged for the officers and their ladies, while the troops pursued servants and shopgirls. Val hoped to avoid all but compulsory events of a social nature. He soon discovered, however, that an officer was duty bound to uphold his regiment's honour in salons and ballrooms as well as on the battlefield. Such evenings were purgatory to someone around whom young women swarmed, shameless in their determination to dance and flirt with him. Perversely, the cooler and more discouraging he grew, the more ardent they became. He thought longingly of his days in the ranks when he was only expected to serve the 57th in a martial capacity. If only he were still a sergeant spending happy, companionable evenings with Toby and a few tankards of ale. That brown brew was also denied him in the Mess, yet he could not find the same quenching satisfaction in fine wines or champagne. The latter gave him curious nausea; the former made him drunk faster than ale ever did. By choice he would forego alchohol, but it would be regarded as a sign of weakness by men whose unofficial motto was: *Ride hard, eat hearty and chase any petticoat that is not on another man's wife.*

Wending his way over the uneven brown grass towards a clump of rocks marking the start of the track leading down to the great spread of white tents now visible, Val prayed the remaining two weeks would fly past. The dangers of being picked off on patrol, or being overrun and killed by Boers in British uniforms, was infinitely preferable to the grimness of social availability in Pretoria . . . and he still had to seize the chance to perform a deed of heroism 'above and beyond the call of duty'. He would not do that by warding off females set on making a fool of him, and themselves. Another year had passed. Sir Gilliard was almost ninety-one. Time was fast running out. If the old man died, or if the war suddenly ended . . . Val could not pursue those painful suppositions.

Rounding the clump of rocks, brief alarm ran through him at the sight of a horse and a solitary seated figure. Instinct made him reach for the revolver he was not wearing, before reality calmed him. This was no enemy but a young woman in a toffee-coloured habit with a wide-brimmed hat lying beside her. She was more shaken than he, for she jumped to her feet and shrank back against the rock, white faced. Val was nonplussed by her evident terror, and by the sight of a cut surrounded by a dark bruise on her cheek. Instinct urged him to ride on, yet inborn chivalry kept him there.

'I'm sorry to have startled you,' he said awkwardly. 'I didn't know you were here.'

She could not recover as swiftly as he and remained gazing up at him with frightened blue eyes as if expecting him to attack her. Val dismounted with inner dismay. He could not leave her without assistance, although the last thing he wanted was to become involved in something which promised to be awkward.

'Did you have a fall?' he asked, studying the livid mark on her cheek.

It was a moment or two before the stammered reply came. 'Ye . . . Yes. A . . . a fall.'

'Are you all right?' He did not know what else to say.

'Oh, yes . . . yes, thank you.'

'You should visit a doctor as soon as possible you know,' he told her, seeing how he could pass on the responsibility. 'Do you live in Pretoria?'

She shook her head, then appeared to relax as she drew away from the rock to step towards him. 'You are Mr Havelock, aren't you?'

He frowned as he tried to recall where they had met. It seemed discourteous to reveal that he did not remember her at all.

She spoke again in the same hesitant, shy manner. 'It's clear you don't recognize me, but why should you when I look so . . . so . . . *unkempt*,' she finished, then burst into tears and collapsed against him as if unable to stand without help any longer.

Well and truly trapped, Val cursed fate for sending

this girl to the hills just as he was returning. The more he attempted to disengage himself the more fiercely she clung to him. Soon, even to his inexperienced mind, it became obvious that she was in a state of severe shock, so he held her with a supporting arm while stroking her hair, murmuring, 'There, there,' as he used to do when comforting Kate after a tumble. When she grew calmer and tilted her face up to his he realized this was not in the least like comforting a five-year-old niece. Tear-drenched lashes framed deep-blue desperate eyes that appealed for help, and the body pressed against his was enticingly soft and curved. As his hands savoured the submissive quality of female pliancy, he was momentarily shaken by an urge he had hitherto ruthlessly subdued with physical activity. For several seconds he fought the instinct to press his mouth hard against her full, parted lips. Thankfully, restraint prevailed.

Thrown by the unexpected sexual challenge, he said, almost roughly, 'You've had a shock. I'll go for a doctor.'

'*No*! Please, don't leave me,' she begged, fresh tears flowing.

Val's heart sank. 'You're in no state to ride back, and you need medical help.'

'I don't want to be left alone,' she insisted with a return to panic. 'If you go back for a doctor, *he'll* come with him.'

'Who?'

The name came out on a rush of fear. 'Thorn.'

A succession of thoughts led to identification of whom he held in his arms. Val released her smartly and stepped back. His troop captain had brought from England a very young bride so pretty everyone likened her to a doll. The round, long-lashed eyes contained terror unknown to a toy. That rosebud mouth had a sensual quality which had tempted him a moment ago; the delicately tinted cheeks were presently ashen and marred by an injury.

'Why are you riding alone, Mrs Marley? Does your husband know where you are?'

Shaking her head, she turned away to seek support from her brown mare by clutching the saddle. 'I wish he would send me back to England as he constantly threatens to do.'

As Val gazed at the slender figure outlined against a sky turned pale greenish-yellow by the fading sun, he had no idea how to deal with the situation. An anonymous resident of Pretoria was one thing; the wife of his troop captain quite another. Into his silence, she continued in a faraway voice as if by not meeting his eyes he became a father confessor.

'The life of a soldier's wife is not easy. She is left alone for weeks while he goes to war which may leave her a widow. So she finds friends to cheer her spirits until he returns. He then demands that she gives them up to be at his beck and call at all times. War makes a gentleman forget how to be kind. He gives orders and expects to be obeyed. If he is not, he punishes.'

Val thought briefly of Sir Gilliard, but she turned to face him before he could respond. 'I am afraid to go back, Mr Havelock. He told me to stay in our tent, but I could not. *I could not*,' she repeated brokenly. 'I thought I was running away, but when I reached this place and saw the miles stretching in the distance I saw how foolish I had been. He will be more angry than before.' Her hands twisted within each other as she pleaded with him. 'What can I do?'

Unusual perception left Val appalled at the inference of her words. '*He* did that to you?'

'He . . . he ordered me to stay out of sight while he put it around that I was indisposed. He will never forgive me for disobeying.' She crossed to grip his arm. 'Please say nothing of meeting me here.'

'But you must have that cut treated,' Val insisted, filled with an unfamiliar brand of anger. 'I'll escort you back to camp.'

'No!'

'You can't stay here all night. A full search would be mounted. That would anger Captain Marley in the extreme.' He glanced down at the spread of tents glowing in the fast approaching dusk. 'It will soon be dark and the alarm will be raised. You *must* come with me.' Sudden gentleness overtook him and he took her icy hands in his. 'I assumed that you had come a cropper while riding, so that is the tale we'll tell. It will be universally accepted without question. I shall say I came upon you soon after the fall.'

'But there will be talk concerning why I was riding in the hills alone,' she said with continuing apprehension.

'Oh Lord, so there will!' He thought for a moment, conscious of night descending fast. 'You had arranged to ride with a friend who cried off at the last minute. I was passing the horse lines and offered to escort you. That's *perfectly* acceptable.'

'But *how* did I fall?'

Inspiration arrived speedily. 'Your mare was startled by a snake while following a narrow path in single file.' A thought occurred. 'At what time did you leave camp?'

'When Thorn went on duty at two o'clock.'

'Whereas I set out much earlier.' He frowned. 'I can claim to have visited Pretoria first. That should suffice.' Growing confident, he said they must move before it became too dark to see the paths. 'I'll help you to mount, ma'am.'

'How kind you are, and how splendid to contrive a means of rescuing me from my predicament. How can I ever thank you?'

Warning signals began to ring as Val saw in her expression the kind of admiration displayed by many young women who gushed and giggled in his company.

Cursing fate for this encounter, he remained silent until they were both in the saddle and ready to leave.

'Let's pray we get there before half the regiment is turned out to search for you,' he muttered in a manner designed to discourage further compliments.

The plan was carried through without a hitch. Cecily Marley was returned to her tent and the ministrations of her maid before her absence had been noticed, and Val related his lie to the Medical Officer who promised to go straight to the patient. Always careful to see that his horse was properly tended, Val spent a while in the lines before making for his tent to prepare for dinner. Pleasantly tired after his long ride, he decided not to dally for long in the Mess and turn in early. After a wash in his canvas tub, Val dressed in the tight two-tone grey mess dress while his batman emptied the bath water then tidied away towels and Val's riding clothes discarded in careless style, as always.

Outside his tent Val stopped for a while gazing upward. On cold winter nights the stars were particularly brilliant. The sight of them somehow accentuated his lonely restlessness tonight. Around him were the sounds that stirred his blood: deep-throated laughter of men relaxing, the snorts and occasional neigh of horses, and a bugle's clear notes ordering a familiar routine. Beneath those glittering stars were sights in which he revelled: rows of pointed tents turned yellow by lamplight, the glow of camp fires illuminating the faces of men telling tall yarns after a day of hard physical labour, distant piquets being posted, horses being led to the farrier, their coats gleaming in light thrown by leaping flames, smart officers strolling in leisurely fashion from tents to their canvas Mess for a meal served on delicate china with wine sparkling in expensive crystal glasses. All this was what he had craved from the age of comprehension, yet the ache inside his breast was almost unbearable.

Cecily Marley's words came back to him. *War makes*

a gentleman forget how to be kind. He gives orders and expects to be obeyed. If he is not, he punishes. Sir Gilliard had given orders to serve the West Wilts or no regiment. He had issued a plain ultimatum. Val had disobeyed. His punishment was to have all he desired in exchange for the loss of his identity. Val Ashleigh would not be standing here reluctant to join his fellows; *he* would not look with envy at men sitting together on the grass around a fire in close companionship. He would not wish to turn back the clock.

Sudden enlightenment touched him as his gaze returned to the stars so far out of reach. As Thorn Marley would never change, would not repent his treatment of someone who had dared to cross him, so Sir Gilliard would never forgive a grandson who had defied him and disgraced the name he so valued. Not even the bravest of deeds would compensate for disobeying an order; a chestful of medals would mean nothing on the jacket of Martin Havelock. Trooper or subaltern, he would make no impression on someone whose punishment was worse than a blow on the cheek, and lasted forever.

Val's heart began to lighten, and he was grateful to that young woman who had shown him the truth. The burden of constant pursuit of courage fell away. The drive to prove his worth no longer applied. Let Val Ashleigh melt into the background so that Martin Havelock could be the man he had now become, and feel free.

In this liberated mood Val entered the Mess to find ladies gracing this masculine stronghold. He then recalled that influential guests were being entertained to dinner tonight. No chance of retiring early, but it meant he could remain on the periphery while all attention was centred on the guests. As the most junior officer he would have to give the loyal toast, but not be called upon to impress anyone. He had forgotten the constant hazard, however. When Colonel and Mrs Beecham entered with their distinguished companions, his heart missed several beats. The grey-haired brigadier standing a foot taller than those around him had been a frequent visitor to Knightshill. Sir Rigby Scott knew the Ashleighs well.

During dinner Val felt conspicuous alone at the far end of the table, although the only pair of eyes to watch him almost constantly were those of Vivienne Beecham looking falsely demure in pale-primrose heavy satin. Even at a distance he detected undisguised accusation in them and knew he was in for a confrontation when the meal ended. Light-heartedness vanished as swiftly as it had come out there beneath the stars, and yet again he wished females to the devil. Why could she not emulate his sisters: marry and concentrate on babies? He gloomily suspected that she had that plan lined up for *him*.

The loyal toast was correctly proposed, and drunk with pride. It was then Val feared the game was up, for he saw Sir Rigby lean towards Max Beecham to nod towards his end of the table and embark on confidential conversation. Curiously, now that the moment he had dreaded was upon him, Val felt calm. Having realized he could never redeem himself in Sir Gilliard's eyes, what was about to happen would not matter so much. He owed these people around him no bond of devotion or gratitude. He had served them well as Martin Havelock and had truly earned the rank he presently held. He had given as much as Val Ashleigh would have given; there was nothing to be ashamed of. Could a man be dubbed a villain because of his name alone?

As ladies were present the drinking of port was put aside, and everyone gathered in the second tent for polite conversation. All too soon Val saw his colonel bringing the main guest across, and something in Max Beecham's eye told him why. He braced himself.

'Sir, may I present Mr Havelock, whom I was delighted to commission in the field after a gallant action in which he took over command from his mortally-wounded officer and routed the Boers.'

Sir Rigby nodded, unsmiling. Not a man of much humour, Val recalled. 'Good thing to give a fellow a commission he has already earned,' he commented in surprisingly meek tones. 'Too many wearing the rank they fail to live up to. Been the trouble out here. Should have been over within a few weeks. Come out to see what can be done about this ridiculous state of affairs. Can't let it go on. Becoming a laughing stock around the world. What do you think about it, Mr Havelock?'

The question was shot at him like a sniper's bullet and Val answered without thinking. 'Chasing the enemy is a waste of time. They have every advantage over us, sir, and disappear into secret hideaways in the hills. They are determined to continue fighting, so I think we should sit tight and let them come to us. Instead of scattering our men in many small units easily overrun, we should concentrate in several very large forces. To attack us they would need greater numbers than they have available. I've been told many members of commandos are weary of war. They long to return to their farms, and only continue their attacks because there is little risk attached. If they were confronted with half an army once more, they would have no stomach for it.'

'Tried that. We would lose thousands, sir.'

'Not if we reversed our tactics and installed ourselves in the hills, as they always do. *They* would then be exposed on the plains.'

'They're too canny for that,' said Sir Rigby flatly.

Conscious of Max Beecham watching him closely, Val pursued the subject, waiting for the moment of betrayal certain to come. He had nothing to lose by arguing with this surly commander. 'Exactly, sir. They would not relish approaching across an open plain, but if we stayed in the hills inviting attack they would have to do that or kick their heels indefinitely. After a time they'd give up the game and go home.'

The grey-haired man almost barked the next comment. 'You mean we'd refuse to fight them?'

'No, sir. We would be using a tactic they proved to

be highly successful. We had no choice but to expose ourselves on the plains because we had to raise three sieges, but they *would* have a choice. Attack us in the hills and be decimated, or call it a day and end hostilities.' Well into his stride by now, Val added warmly, 'My grandfather is a firm believer in holding an advantageous position while the enemy exhausts itself in costly attacks.'

Sir Rigby's eyes narrowed. 'Your grandfather? A military man, is he?'

As Val stood speechless, realizing the gaffe he had made, Max Beecham intervened smoothly. 'A student of Napoleon, by all accounts, sir. Isn't that so, Mr Havelock?'

'Yes, sir,' Val murmured through stiff lips.

'I see. Well, warfare has advanced since then, Beecham. What do you think of this fellow's theory?'

Colonel Beecham shrugged. 'As a theory it would work, but the practical aspects make it impossible. The Boers have ponies well able to move swiftly in the hills, and they live off dried meat each man carries with him. Our animals are not bred for this brand of fighting, and our troops require decent meals from mobile cookhouses. Hard rations for a short period would be acceptable but if, as Mr Havelock suggests, we sat in the hills until the enemy tired of the game, we would very soon have insurmountable problems trying to feed and supply troops scattered over difficult terrain.'

A ghost of a smile touched Sir Rigby's long face. 'Quite so. However, I like a man who can respond to an unexpected question with an intelligent reply. Shows he can think. Some can't. That's been obvious throughout this deplorable business.' He began to move away, the interview over, saying to Max Beecham, 'Amazing resemblance to the Ashleigh boys. Same assured manner, same way of speaking. Spitting image of the hero of the family. Killed by savages outside Khartoum, you'll recall. Another has made his name as a war artist. You must have seen his work in *The Illustrated Magazine*. The youngest must by now be up at Oxford, I suppose. They're not cavalrymen, but I had quite a start when young Havelock proposed the toast. It was like looking at a reincarnation of Vorne Ashleigh.'

As Val began to breathe with relief he found himself looking at a girl with excitement written all over her narrow freckled face. From frying pan to fire!

'*Are* you a reincarnation, Havelock?' she demanded softly. 'A reincarnation of a hero?'

'Shouldn't you be looking after your father's guests?' he asked pointedly.

Her sly smile appeared. 'Am I getting close to solving the mystery? I always know you are on dangerous ground when you start being rude to me.'

He longed to be far ruder than protocol allowed, but instead tried to make her feel foolish. 'All this nonsense about a mystery. I suspect you read too many romantic novels and live in a world of imagination.'

She shook her head. '*You* do that, dearest Havelock, when you repeat that ridiculous fiction concerning your past as a stable-lad.'

The regimental orchestra at the far end of the tent began to play for the entertainment of the guests, so Val took refuge in the sudden burst of sound to avoid further comment. Vivienne never gave up when pursuing a subject, and moved uncomfortably close to him to continue it.

'The spitting image of Vorne Ashleigh, eh? The other made his name as a war artist out here, did he? Rather like the man who visited you at the convalescent home in Kimberley. The one who seemed much more friendly towards you than an interviewing newsman. You rushed me away from him to give me tea. Remember?'

Val grew angry. She always riled him when she began piecing together those inconsistencies her sharp eyes never failed to miss, and making of them something which put him in a vulnerable position. Still shaken over the meeting with a family acquaintance which had only turned out well thanks to this girl's father, and the supposedly unbreakable link between a family and an infantry regiment, Val knew the ground beneath Martin Havelock's feet was growing shaky.

'I can't imagine why I ever wanted to give you tea, Miss Beecham. We've never yet held a conversation without you being spitefully inquisitive.'

'And you being arrogant and secretive,' she retorted.

'There's nothing secretive about not caring to discuss one's private life with someone whom it in no way concerns.'

To his chagrin she laughed. 'Every time you say something like that you make nonsense of that stable-boy story. Everyone knows it's a pack of lies, and Father has made it more than clear he accepts your right to your rank.'

'He also accepts my right to privacy,' Val countered, casting around for an eye to catch as an excuse to leave her. All present were deep in conversation. The volume of voices was competing with the orchestra and it was growing hot within that tent illuminated by a number of lamps.

'So do I, silly,' Vivienne said with warmth. 'You should know me well enough to trust me with your secret.'

'Stop being melodramatic!'

'*Are* you connected to the Ashleighs Sir Rigby mentioned? A cousin, perhaps,' she probed, to his consternation. 'That would explain why you look so much like the family hero. And why you have those same qualities. The visitor at Kimberley, was he the artist Vere Ashleigh?' Her look of excitement deepened. 'He *was*. I can tell by that defensive expression. Now you *have* to confess all.'

With his back to the wall Val hit out. 'You're determined to put two and two together and make it whatever you wish. You're being quite ridiculous!'

His voice carried in the quieter atmosphere created by a break in the music. Those nearby glanced around in surprise then resumed their conversations. Others were more persistent.

'Is this *fellow* annoying you, Miss Beecham?' drawled an affected voice at Val's side.

Vivienne's glance was scathing. 'Not in the least, Mr Pickering. There was no need to interrupt a private conversation to ask about something you should know could not possibly happen.'

Infuriated by her snub, he replied, 'There are those present who might think otherwise on hearing a raised voice during a social occasion. It's very ill-mannered and we have some important guests tonight.'

'As Mother and I have been entertaining them for most of the day, I'm well aware of that ... and Sir Rigby has just listened with the greatest interest to Mr Havelock's ideas on how to bring a swift end to this war.' She turned to Val. 'In fact, he asked for them, didn't he?'

Val would have been amused if Pickering did not arouse such intense dislike in him. As Vivienne had put the focus on him, he voiced it. 'I wonder why he chose not to ask the opinion of someone with royal connections. Perhaps he has heard you have none.'

The thin, pasty features flushed darkly. 'I have manners, which is more than can be said of a fellow whose behaviour is conducive with having being reared in the stables. Even if you learn a few, Havelock, the smell of the barrack-room will still be offensive.'

Val smiled. 'Those months in the barrack-room taught me my trade. You've yet to learn it.'

'What did twenty-eight days behind bars teach you?' Pickering snapped. 'Not enough to make you accept your true place in this regiment. You clearly need a harder lesson. Gentlemen will tolerate an upstart for just so long, then their retribution is total.'

'Then you'll have to take care, Pickering. You've been masquerading as a leader of men for almost four years.'

The other man's eyes narrowed with venom. 'People like you invariably invite their own destruction. When your unwarranted arrogance leads to your downfall *every man* in this regiment will turn his back on you.' He gave Vivienne a stiff half-bow. 'Miss Beecham.'

As he sauntered away, she looked up at Val in concern. 'He's an insufferable, puffed-up fool but he has relatives in Horse Guards. I can be as rude as I like to him, but he can make life difficult for *you*.'

'He already has, on numerous occasions,' Val said grimly. 'Now we have equal rank it's my turn to humiliate him. No one else appears willing to do it.'

'They value their careers. You're constantly jeopardizing yours.'

He gave a confident grin. 'I've risen from trooper to subaltern in two years. Not much wrong with that.'

'But you're now among a breed who are particular about who joins them. Some stubbornly accept the stable-boy story and decline to acknowledge you. Others recognize your true status but believe you're a fugitive from scandal and won't trust you.' Adopting an exaggerated tone, she mimicked, 'Once a bounder always a bounder, what!' She cast him a frank look. 'Some of them are awfully silly men. Those who aren't either respect your privacy and hold back, or they resent a mystery man who constantly puts them in the shade.' She put her hand on his in beseeching manner. 'Why don't you tell me the truth? I'm the only true friend you have now, yet you consistently insult me.'

'I do not!' he contradicted heatedly.

'Well . . . you *hurt* me.'

'That's only because you . . .' He fell silent, unable to put his suspicions into words.

'Because I what?'

As he gazed at her unexceptional face with its determined mouth and frank green eyes, he fleetingly wished he could believe she wanted to be no more than a friend. Not that he could reveal to her his true identity, but she was shrewd, intelligent and lively, and he *was* lonely.

In the face of his silence, she added ammunition to her attack. 'I know you were sometimes in hot water with Felix Wheeler, but he let you off lightly because he likes and admires you. Thorn Marley is vastly different. His arrogance exceeds yours, and he's jealous of his record on the Indian Frontiers. Felix is a nice person and a good, reliable officer, according to Father, but Thorn was twice decorated in Bengal and his reputation for fearlessness is enviable. He's also reputed to bully those under his command.'

'I'm not easily bullied.'

'I know that,' she exclaimed with impatience. 'I also know you're worth ten of him. But he gives orders and will jump on you if you attempt to question them, or even hesitate before obeying. He'll also exploit your weakness if you rile him.'

'Oh, what's that?' asked Val, falling into her trap.

'You tell lies.'

'What?'

'You've done it to everyone since you joined the Fifty – seventh. A man of Thorn Marley's type will see it as weakness to hide behind a pack of obvious lies rather than face up to the consequences of whatever it is you've done. Others see it that way too.' Her eyes began to glow with something Val recognized too well and her voice grew soft. 'Dearest Havelock, *I* know you are really someone very special. When I hear people patronize you, I long to leap to your defence. I can't unless I know the truth. *Are* you related to the famous Ashleighs?'

Val then saw red and reacted accordingly. 'What I need more than anything is a *female* to protect me from my bullying fellows. If she's the colonel's daughter, so much the better. Here's the truth, then. I killed two men in duels, then ran with my sword still dripping blood to claim the beauty I had saved from these villians. Her noble father demanded that I further prove my worth by taking the Queen's Shilling and pretending to be a stable-boy until I became the colonel of the regiment and revealed my true identity as a Prussian prince.'

For several moments Vivienne gazed at him as if in shock. Then, to his surprise, Val saw tears spring in her eyes and an expression of immense distress dawn on her face. The effort of speaking seemed insurmountable, at first, until she mananged to say, 'Audley is right. You'll destroy *yourself*. When you do, don't count on my friendship. I've just withdrawn it.'

Val watched her thin figure in yellow satin push through the convivial groups towards the end of the tent, where her mother was playing gracious hostess. He remained disconcerted as he saw Mrs Beecham beckon to Felix Wheeler, who collected her daughter's cloak before leading her into the night. What had prompted the girl to act so uncharacteristically? They had sparred from his earliest days with the regiment, and she had always given as good as she got, appearing to enjoy their verbal sword – crossing. He had never known her other than bouncy and full of confidence, yet she had just resorted to tears. It was completely unlike her. Surely she had not . . . no, she could not possibly have believed that nonsense about duels. He had merely elaborated his accusation of reading too many romantic novels. It had been no more than a piece of deliberate sarcasm to counter the dangerous conclusion she had formed from Sir Rigby's knowledge of the Ashleighs.

Sudden insight suggested it had been a mistake. Whereas Vivienne could meet him on equal terms, she could not accept ridicule at a time when she had been sharing genuine concern for his loneliness. He told himself he had averted disaster in the most final manner. Although she had always before come back for more, he guessed she *had* withdrawn her friendship. He could not have allowed her to follow her suspicions to the correct conclusion. All would then be lost. She would now discontinue her probing into his past and her personal pursuit which had underlying tones of Julia's. He had finally rid himself of someone who had been a thorn in his side throughout his days with the regiment. Why, then, did he feel curiously heavy-hearted and more than usually restless?

Once the guests left, officers were free to do as they wished. Some settled to dedicated drinking, others sat at tables to win or lose on the fall of cards. Still in depressed mood, Val slipped out into the frosty night shortly after official socializing ended. He walked slowly, gazing at the stars once more as he reversed his earlier vow to become Martin Havelock. He would always be Val Ashleigh in everything he did, and Vivienne had just now revived an ego trapped inside a man who longed to release it.

'A moment, Havelock,' called a voice behind him.

Val halted while Thorn Marley came up with brisk steps. When they were face to face in the pale light of night, the other man spoke in a vigorous undertone without preamble.

'You brought my wife in from the hills and told everyone a cock-and-bull story concerning a fall caused by a snake.'

'I told the surgeon. No one else,' Val said, taking exception to the man's manner. 'Mrs Marley needed attention, so it seemed the best way out of the situation.'

'What *situation*?' Marley challenged. 'You clearly have no notion of how gentlemen behave. I will soon teach you, I promise, unless you concentrate on soldiering and stop chasing other men's wives.'

Val was furious. He had saved the man's reputation by inventing that story. 'I was not *chasing* your wife. I came across her by accident when she was in distress. As a gentleman, I did the only thing I could for her. I thought you would be grateful, in the circumstances.'

'I don't care for your tone,' the other said almost through his teeth as two officers strolled past. 'I've watched you whenever females are present. There's nothing you enjoy more than having every one of them clustered around you in admiring fashion. You monopolized Vivienne Beecham this evening. Don't think your penchant has gone unnoticed. There is a move afoot to curb you of it.'

'My *penchant*!' cried Val. 'That's quite ridiculous. I have little time for young women. I prefer to spend my days playing team games. Look, what is this all about?'

Marley grew ugly. 'Don't take that attitude with me! I'm your superior.'

'Only in military matters,' Val flung back, astonished by what was happening. 'This appears to be extremely personal. And as it is, I'm free to tell you I had no wish to become involved in your marital quarrel, but your wife was unwilling to return to camp until I invented the tale of the snake and assured her it would be generally believed. I assume it was.'

'The tale concerning friends who were to have ridden with her was not. No friends had made such an arrangement.'

'Of course they hadn't,' said Val explosively. 'That was as much a lie as the snake. You and I know how she really came by that cut on her cheek.'

Marley moved nearer in threatening manner. 'She took a toss during an assignation in the hills with you. Chatsworth and Pickering saw her ride off alone in great haste some while after you had left camp, also alone. Don't deny it.'

Feeling that the evening was taking on an air of lunacy, Val said, 'You've had too much to drink.'

As he turned away Marley seized his arm with iron fingers. 'You'll stay and listen to me until I say you can go, or you can be placed under arrest for insubordination and dishonourable conduct. Which do you prefer?'

Val was silenced by the sheer madness of the situation. Either this man was the victim of delusions, or Mrs Marley had told a number of lies this afternoon. Had she fallen during an assignation with someone else, who had not cared to ride in with her, or *was* she a victim of marital violence? Either way, he had walked into a hazard of others' making. Val knew he had a right to defend himself in the circumstances, but if he was being accused of some kind of liaison with this man's wife, it was the devil of a situation. Marley could ruin his career with ease. He dared not let his apprehension show, nevertheless.

'I'll stay and listen to what you say on condition that you release me,' Val said eventually. 'I did what I thought best for your wife this afternoon and will not be held here by force because of my foresight.' He smoothed his sleeve after the man's hand dropped to his side. 'I was led to believe facts I might have misconstrued, but my only intention was to help Mrs Marley. There is not, nor ever has been, any desire on my part to be alone with her. If she did go to the hills for an assignation it would have been with someone else.'

'What are you suggesting?' demanded Marley hotly.

'It's what *you* suggested.' Val replied, knowing he must somehow end this ludicrous confrontation. 'Or perhaps Chatsworth and Pickering put the notion into your head,' he added, spying a subaltern named Atwood heading towards them. 'I wouldn't put it past that pair.' With those words he moved swiftly aside to accost his saviour. 'Ah, Giles, I wanted a word with you about the polo match on Thursday.'

The gambit took Thorn Marley unawares, and Val walked on unhindered with the amiable Atwood who was also a keen sportsman. Keeping the dark-haired subaltern in conversation at the mouth of his tent until Marley stumbled past towards the large one he shared with the woman he may or may not have struck this afternoon, Val then bade Atwood goodnight and went to bed. He could not sleep. For several hours he lay on the narrow camp bed telling himself he had made a complete mess of his life by being a stubborn fool. If he had accepted his grandfather's ultimatum he could be with the West Wilts in China fighting the Boxers. He could have all that was now his, with the added distinction of being an Ashleigh in a regiment founded by his own ancestors. He could be free to speak of his family and of Knightshill. He could greet men like Sir Rigby Scott openly and talk of their earlier meetings. He would not have to pile lie upon lie, would not be subjected to the contempt of the Pickerings and the Marleys of the world, and would not be tormented by the likes of Vivienne Beecham. He would never have fallen victim to Julia Grieves who had robbed him of self-respect and his right to his identity.

In the early hours he rolled from his bed and pushed back the flaps of his tent to stare at the night. Fires had burned low to become no more than crimson glows dotted throughout the sleeping camp. Brands flamed around the perimeter illuminating the figures of piquets, wrapped in their heavy cloaks. No fear of being overrun by Boers here, but Val relived the tension of nights when creeping figures could have come from behind rocks, when he could have awoken with a rifle butt at his throat, when the sound of shots and screaming men could have broken the dark silence. He relived that dusk when they had stormed the farm to be met with a hail of bullets. Fear had possessed him during that dash across an open yard in a desperate bid to escape slaughter, yet he had not hesitated.

For that action he had been decorated for courage and gained the privilege of soldiers' obedience to his orders. They respected and liked him, yet he was treated with scorn by his equals because they did not consider him worthy enough to join them. What more must he do to meet their standards? The Ashleigh name should gain him entry to even the most élite military circles, but discovery of it now would bring the end of his career and any further hopes of military service. With a great sigh, Val yearned to be back with those men who had not given a damn about his background, men who accepted others on evidence of their deeds, not their bloodline. Men who had been his friends; men prepared to risk their lives for him. He had given them up to be where he had every right to be, and he now saw how unequal the exchange was.

He had entered a world where approval depended upon ancestry, former school, influential acquaintances and wealth. Val Ashleigh met all those criteria, but Martin Havelock was an upstart with the 'smell of the barrack-room' about him, and therefore not to be trusted. Although he had grown up in this same world, it had never before struck him in this manner. All the people he had met *had* been of the correct ilk, yet he had judged them by personality and their liking for the things he liked. Rapport had been far more important than status. He had not cared about their relatives or wealth, only whether or not they shared his passion for rugby, cricket and horses, and were easy companions. They had not received his contempt, if not. He had never been treated to theirs.

As Val gazed at the tents housing men who had embraced him without reservations with their comradeship, the sense of loneliness grew so strong he found his cheeks growing wet. For the first time in his life he considered the prospect of sudden death at the hands of the enemy a welcome event. Sir Gilliard would never offer forgiveness. Martin Havelock was generally mistrusted and disliked, more and more he had to curb his tongue whilst living a lie, and he had made a new enemy tonight. What a mess his stubborn pride had led him into!

A horse whinnied in the lines then fell silent, and

Val's Ashleigh spirit gradually revived. This was the life he loved. He was good at it. Max Beecham had known about the masquerade and still promoted him, so that man must believe him capable of holding his own amongst those ready to condemn. His colonel had come to his aid this evening. Martin Havelock owed him total loyalty by living up to the high opinion proved by his recommendation for a commission. Max Beecham was the captain of a team. Val knew from experience how important it was to have the support of each member.

He turned away from the spread of tents and returned to his bed. The business of Cecily Marley would blow over in a week or so. Vivienne would recover from her imagined hurt; if she did not it would not matter. The 57th would be riding out for patrol duty again shortly. Audley Pickering still offered a challenge Val swore to meet at the first opportunity. As for Sir Gilliard . . . well, there was always the chance of heroism even *he* could not ignore once the regiment was back in the fray. And if Martin Havelock should fall, so long as his death was honourable the old man *might* feel a pang of regret.

14

THE SKY GREW purple with storm clouds. The rumble of thunder was reminiscent of distant artillery opening a great battle. Lightning began to sizzle across the darkness overhead and hit the dry earth where solitary trees dotted an immense plain. Early September and the rains looked set to start. If they continued for long the *drifts* would become impassable and tracks would turn to mire. Life in tented camps deteriorated as sodden canvas added chill discomfort to that of damp bedding and clothes, and cooking on field ranges was hampered by the downpour.

Val rode with a contingent of Lancers which was joining the rest of the 57th after six weeks on duty near several blockhouses. They were to have chased Boers trying to break through the cordon, but reports from the guards of the bastions always arrived well after the enemy had gone. It had been demoralizing duty involving long fruitless pursuits of horsemen who were not even dots on the horizon. Each report had to be followed up, however, and anger grew against an enemy unwilling to concede defeat or even play by the rules.

For Val it had been a particulary difficult time. As much frustrated as the rest, he was unfortunate to have as his Mess fellows Audley Pickering and Thorn Marley. Only the addition of a senior subaltern named Greer, and the pleasant young polo player, Miles Atwood, made life bearable. Toby was one of the sergeants in the contingent, which merely emphasized how much Val missed his easy friendship. The troopers were a mixed bunch of old hands and replacements who had arrived after the sieges were lifted. They grumbled and swore, but gave no trouble. Everyone in the detachment was glad to be rejoining the main body of the regiment in a small town housing divisional headquarters, which promised some diversion from the endless veld. Even the approaching storm could not dampen their spirits.

Captain Marley rode at the front with his second-in-command, Stanton Greer, and Pickering. Val brought up the rear with Miles Atwood. They chatted about polo, the approaching cricket season, and the prospect of swimming in the river when they reached their destination. Sport was all they had in common. The Atwoods were mostly female and resided in a small country vicarage with their widowed father. Giles regretted entering the army – his heart was not in his profession. It was, in fact, in Kimberley with a girl barely out of the schoolroom, and all he could think of was the best way of getting back to her before she cast her flirtatious eye elsewhere. He had realized Val grew bored by talk of romance, so kept silent on the subject. This meant his mind was elsewhere a great deal of the time, and Val's words fell on deaf ears.

The storm broke fifteen minutes later. Rain descended in oblique walls of water that blinded them as they rode into it. Marley gave the order to halt and don cloaks. These gave little comfort, for their uniforms were already very wet. As they rode on into the downpour, their horses unhappy and hampered by the beating rain, Val thought they should have stopped until it abated, and said so to Atwood.

'He doesn't believe in sparing anyone,' the other said miserably. 'Always raves on about what they endured in India and how robust his men were despite the heat, dust, monsoons and fevers. I truly believe he's a masochist, only happy when he and his men are suffering.'

'I'll agree with that,' said Val, tilting his face away from the stinging rain as he recalled the cut on Cecily Marley's cheek. 'He believes punishment strengthens character.'

They struggled on for almost an hour travelling only a short distance which, had they halted, they could have covered swiftly to make up time once the rain stopped. When it did, as dramatically as it had begun, they were all sodden and weary, the horses chilled and miserable. The storm rolled on in purple splendour shot with vivid lightning, leaving a clear late-afternoon sky enhanced by fluffy pink streaks created by the dying sun. The order to halt and take off cloaks was greeted with surly relief by men who felt they should not have been made to tire their horses, and themselves, unnecessarily. But there was no rest to be had. As Val was rolling his saturated cloak, a shout went up from one of the troopers. There, about five hundred yards off, was a large group of Boer horsemen riding away from a farm.

A few moments of suspended thought, then everything happened at once. The distant riders took stock of the cavalry detachment, saw that it outnumbered them, and resorted to flight. Thorn Marley's experience told in the swiftness of his action. Leaping into the saddle he gave swift orders. Lieutenant Greer and Miles Atwood were to take their own men, and Pickering's, to give chase with him. The rest were to go with Val and Pickering to burn the farm and destroy the livestock, before continuing on to join up with the regiment. As he raced off in the best chase that had come their way for months, Marley threw a fat envelope at Audley Pickering.

'Sealed orders for Colonel Beecham. Give them to him as soon as you arrive.'

Three quarters of their number galloped off on the heels of a man who had tired them so much they stood less chance of outrunning those fresh and dry from shelter in the farm. Val watched them with resentment as he mounted and prepared to follow his hated enemy, who had a year's seniority over him and was therefore in command. Marley had overlooked Pickering because he was useless, and himself because of that business with Cecily. No honour and glory must be allowed an upstart who paid attention to other men's wives. That would be the rule whenever Marley could enforce it.

The farm was similar to others they had destroyed. Val was always unhappy about putting a torch to the homes and land of the people who had worked hard to establish themselves in this difficult country. The first one he had burned to the ground had been vacated by the owners and housed a number of Boers who had been attacking them, but flagrant destruction of someone's home and valued possessions because it might occasionally succour the enemy was quite different. In this case he had seen them ride away from it, so he supposed it was justified. Pickering had no qualms. He regarded homesteaders as peasants of no consequence, but he had never lived in a barrack-room with troopers and learned that even the simplest folk deserved full consideration.

They approached with caution. There was no way of knowing whether or not the entire group had left after the storm. All appeared innocent enough as they rode into the yard with carbines at the ready, scattering poultry and a few wild-looking cats. Recalling that time when a door above the barn suddenly opened to allow a hail of bullets to rake them, Val's neck prickled with apprehension. All remained quiet, however. He dismounted with the others and crossed to the barn, revolver in hand. Nothing more sinister than a store of fodder, barrels of beets, and basic tools hanging on nails. Two veld ponies stood dozing in rough stalls. Someone must be here. A fusillade of shots sent him running from the barn with quickened heartbeat. There was no enemy. Troopers were gleefully using the poultry and cats for target practice, whilst mounted men rode among cattle with their lances. The yard was covered with blood and feathers, the air was rent by the plaintive lowing of animals being speared in an orgy of revenge.

Val strode towards the man lounging against a wall of the house watching the scene with sadistic indolence.

'Did *you* order this?' he demanded.

Pickering's thin features, made more disdainful by a drooping, greasy brown moustache, looked Val over. 'I thought you were hiding in the barn.'

'Stop them, for God's sake! We can take the cattle with us.'

'You may eat animals fattened on fodder stolen from our camps at the cost of British lives. *I* don't.'

'Then kill them humanely. This is . . . obscene,' cried the young man from Knightshill estate, where cattle were treated with care and respect.

'And rob the men of their hour of revenge?'

'On whom?' he shouted. 'A few chickens and cows?'

Pickering's lip curled. 'I always knew you had the courage of a farmhand. Go inside and torch the house if you've no stomach for this.'

Breathing hard, Val knew there was no way he could stop what this man had instigated, but he could control the next step. 'There are two ponies in the barn. Someone must be in the house.'

'They'll soon appear when they start to roast.'

'You're a bastard, Pickering,' Val said in disgust. 'I'm not setting this place alight until I've checked each room.'

Pickering followed as Val went inside, revolver at the ready. The kitchen was empty, although dishes and plates piled by the sink showed that a number of people had eaten there a short while ago. It was a pretty room, touched by the hand of a woman with skill in her fingers and home-making in her heart. Bright patchwork cushions enlivened chairs lovingly polished. An intricate rag rug lay before the stove where a kettle stood with steam streaming from its spout. Yellow curtains were confined by chintz bands with frilled edges. Lamps were shaded by matching yellow. This was a family home.

Swallowing his reluctance, Val went from room to room, certain he would find the woman who had put her all into this house many miles from any other. The place appeared empty. As he stood uncertainly in a room containing a wooden crib, a small bed and some toys, he detected the acrid smell of smoke. Running back to the kitchen he found Pickering dragging the rag rug from the stove to fling it, alight at one end, on to the settee covered with cushions. They were soon blazing just beneath the hems of curtains.

Pickering looked across at Val. 'I shall report that you refused my direct order to do this.'

'Report what you bloody well like,' Val snapped. 'It won't convince Colonel Beecham that you're of any value to the regiment.'

Pickering turned ugly as he swept the dishes to smash on the floor in a useless gesture of destruction. 'The last time you defied me you spent a month locked up like a common criminal.'

'I was in better company there than I am now,' Val retorted with contempt, as furniture began to blacken. 'You're very brave against china and furniture, aren't you?'

'We'll see how brave you are when I break you, Havelock.'

'I'll break you first, I swear.'

'With what; the help of your fellow stable-lads?'

Across the room fast filling with smoke, Val said, 'Without anyone's help. The pleasure will be mine alone.'

He walked across to the door glad to quit the sight of a room starting to blaze. Soon, flames would engulf that room where toys lay scattered. The slaughter continued outside, but beside the corner of the house Toby stood, pale and retching. Val stepped over to him.

'You, too? Perhaps you now understand my hatred of the man.'

His erstwhile friend glanced up balefully, 'I always have

371

understood. I simply didn't think you should risk your career over the bugger.'

'What's amiss with you, Sergeant?' demanded the man in question as he reached them. 'Why aren't you with your troops?'

'A touch of the sun, sir,' mumbled Toby, and walked away with as much dignity as he could muster.

'One of your ranker chums, as I recall. No stomach either.'

Val had no chance to counter that because, from the corner of his eye, he spotted two figures appearing from the back of the house and ordered them to halt as he raised his revolver instinctively. When he lowered it he heard Pickering cock his ready to fire.

'No!' he cried. 'It's a woman.'

'It's a *Boer*.'

As Pickering's finger tightened, Val brought his clenched fist down hard on the other's hand. The weapon fired into the ground before falling at his own feet. Putting his right boot over it, Val said heavily, 'I've just thrown away the chance I've been waiting for. There's a big enough outcry over Boer women and children dying in our camps. If I'd let you shoot them in cold blood you'd have been *finished*, you bastard. Be thankful I'm not prepared to pay for what I want with their lives.'

Kicking the revolver aside, Val walked towards the woman who stood beside a boy of around eight years. The lad had tears running down his ashen cheeks as he watched the animals he had tended being done to death. The woman, also white-faced, surveyed the scene with stony eyes. She turned as Val approached, shocking him with the vitriolic hatred in her whole demeanour.

'You were sheltering men who continue to be our enemies,' he said curtly. 'We had no choice but this. You and your son will be taken to a camp.'

She continued to damn him with her malignant stare, lips

shut tightly, but the boy began to shout choked, incomprehensible phrases, apparently fearless. The woman cuffed him around the head, and he fell silent as his eyes swivelled again to watch the orgy of killing which was so distressing him.

Val knew many Boers did not understand English or, if they did, pretended ignorance of the language, so it was useless to waste time on further explanation. On the point of indicating that they should wait beside his horse, he spotted a couple of troopers setting fire to the barn. Yelling to the men that there were ponies inside, he ran across the yard thick with bloody feathers and carcasses, slipping and sliding on the results of earlier carnage. As he ran he was conscious of shots coming from outlying areas where, their initial savagery blunted, troopers were ending the suffering of cattle and oxen with their carbines. Val's only thought was to bring the horses from the blazing barn – something he seemed fated to do at regular intervals – and he thrust his gun into its holster to have both hands free in a place he had already checked for hidden enemies.

Although the troopers still wore wild expressions, they were cavalrymen, and horses were beasts they loved and respected. They hesitated only long enough to take in what Val shouted at them, before plunging in to the barn which was starting to disintegrate. Coughing and choking, Val ran through the smoke to reach the heads of the panic-stricken animals. In no time he released the tethers and coaxed them from their stalls until troopers were able to lead them through the hot, stifling air to safety. Regaining the yard himself, Val pulled up to stare at the scene with a heavy heart. Dead animals lay everywhere in pools of thick, dark blood. Behind him the barn was crackling and burning. Ahead, the house was engulfed in flames. The sky was full of dark, drifting smoke; the air was tainted with the stench of burning and slaughter. Where men had ridden through infant crops, green shoots lay broken on earth still wet from the storm rains. No one would use this farm again. He sighed, remembering Knightshill's glorious acres. This was not his idea of military action.

Troopers began coming in to join those standing in and around the yard. Many now looked strained, if not a little sick. Toby and his fellow sergeants were grim faced, knowing they should have tried harder to control something that had run out of hand. Val decided on a swift departure and gave orders to the N.C.O.s to assemble their men, then crossed to where he had tethered his horse. It took his troubled brain a while to accept that Comet was no longer there, and that Pickering's fine stallion, Erasmus, had also freed himself.

He began to run. It would be difficult to catch them if they had bolted in fright. The veld was endless. Beyond the house, he prayed he would see Comet a short way off waiting for reassurance from the rider he trusted. His prayer was not answered. The distance lay empty. The two beasts were not even dots against the horizon. Momentarily thrown, he wondered if Pickering had untied them for some purpose of his own. Where was the man, anyway? He then thought of the woman and boy. Where were *they*?

Hardly had a faint sensation of foreboding touched him than he spotted a white bundle, a short way off on the track along which they had approached. He walked slowly towards it, a sick feeling growing with each step. His throat was dry, his heart thudding as he drew near enough to recognize Pickering in his underwear, bleeding profusely from a chest wound. Val's heartbeat increased further as he guessed the dread truth. The Boer woman had somehow snatched Pickering's revolver, forced him to strip off his uniform, then shot him. She and her son must have ridden away on the two stallions, doubtless to join up with her husband's commando. Only as he squatted to discover whether or not Pickering was still alive did Val recall that sealed envelope Thorn Marley had tossed to the man. Those secret orders were in the pocket of Pickering's tunic. Foreboding now deepened into a sensation akin to the one he had felt when the headmaster of Chartfield had burst in to his room on the evening Julia Grieves had shattered his future.

The court martial of Second-Lieutenant Martin Havelock was held in the small town where he had hoped to swim in the river. Due to the gravity of the charges the trial was accorded top security. A sentry was posted at the door of the local courtroom commandeered for the occasion. Newsmen who, by the mysterious means of their profession, arrived there sensing a story of sensational quality had their suspicions confirmed on being refused access to the courtroom and not even given the smallest facts of the case. The accused officer under house arrest was escorted to and from the white-stone building in a closed waggon.

The case could not have come up at a worse time. World opinion was against the British for waging war against the men who had settled the land with blood and toil over two centuries. Empire builders, they were called in derogatory terms. Their military failures in trying to lift the three sieges had badly damaged the prestige of a famous army, and this would not revive all the time the war dragged on in humiliating fashion. Even the sympathies of the British public had undergone a reversal when hostile newsmen published the death toll from epidemics of women, children and old people in the inadequate camps where they had been confined because their farms had been torched. Of course, these condemnatory people and officials had not been obliged to fight the war, and spoke from the comfort and safety of their armchairs. Even so, the court martial of a British officer on charges which, even singly, could earn him the death sentence was liable to complete growing disenchantment with the integrity of the Empire's army.

Val lived through those days confined in a small house with Miles Atwood as his jailer. All emotion was mercifully suspended by disbelief at what was happening. He was charged with four of the worst crimes in the Army Act: using violence against a superior officer, disobeying a direct order, disgraceful conduct unbecoming an officer and a gentleman, and losing into the hands of the enemy, by neglect, sealed orders for his commanding officer. These charges made at a time of war assumed the utmost severity. Anyone found guilty of them could be taken out and shot.

Day after sweltering day Val sat on a hard wooden chair beside Miles Atwood, and a major of artillery who hailed from a legal family and had initially intended to follow tradition. John Railes undertook to defend the accused officer to the best of his limited ability. A major from divisional headquarters staff acted as prosecutor. Audley Pickering, the principal witness, was brought from the local hospital to give his evidence on the first three charges, but was himself also facing the fourth, that of losing to the enemy secret military documents.

Toby came forward to offer his slight evidence of events at the farm, but all he could say was that he thought Lieutenant Pickering had allowed the men to exceed their duty by running wild, and appeared to enjoy the destruction wreaked as he watched. He had seen both officers emerge from the burning house together because he had been vomitting at the corner of it. Mr Havelock had seemed angry at the unneccessary suffering of the beasts and sympathized with his reaction to what was going on. Mr Pickering had then come up and castigated him for leaving the troops, and that was the last he knew of what was happening at the house itself. No, he had not seen a woman and a child, neither had he seen Mr Havelock knock the revolver from Mr Pickering's hand. Yes, he supposed he had to agree that he knew the two officers did not like each other – it was common knowledge throughout the regiment. Yes, he had been Mr Havelock's close friend when he had been a sergeant. *So you are not exactly an impartial witness?* Toby replied that as he had not witnessed any of the events on which the accused was charged he very clearly *must* be impartial.

One after the other, various troopers were marched in to give insubstantial evidence. Two said Mr Havelock had run towards them when they set the barn alight, shouting a warning that there were horses inside. Yes, they *thought* they had seen a woman and a child, but could not say whether or not Mr Pickering held a revolver. Mr Havelock had put his own away as he ran across the yard. Yes, they knew of the enmity between the officers and would prefer to follow Mr Havelock any day. *You were not asked to give an opinion. Just answer the questions.* Other men, believing they were helping Val, spoke out about the way Pickering had singled out Havelock when he was in the ranks and ordered him to do hazardous or exhausting duties that were often completely unnecessary, but this served only to confirm Pickering's claim that the accused had refused to set fire to the house, saying, 'Report what you bloody well like. I'll break you, I swear.' Havelock clearly had every motive for wishing Pickering out of his hair for good.

Both counsels knew the case hung on the conflicting evidence of two officers known to have detested each other. With no witnesses as to what had happened at the farm, it left them the unenviable task of making the court decide which man to believe. Havelock had pleaded guilty to striking a superior officer by violently knocking the revolver from his hand, but claimed he had done it to save the lives of a woman and child. While this sounded noble enough, and would have mitigated the charge if the Boer woman had not consequently shot Pickering and made away with his clothes containing military orders, it now availed the young commissioned ranker little. A not guilty plea to the remaining charges would only hold if Havelock's version of the affair could be proved. His defender did not see any certain way of doing this, yet a man's very life, as well as his military career, hung in the balance.

Felix Wheeler gave a good account of the accused's character and dedication to duty, but was forced to agree that he, himself, had sentenced Havelock, when a trooper, to twenty-eight days' detention for refusing to obey the direct order of an officer. Yes, that officer had been Audley Pickering. Other officers testified to Havelock's over-eagerness to take command; his intractable desire to make his mark. Yes, they would also concede that he was an outstanding cavalryman who had earned his rank through hard work and loyalty to his regiment rather than by his social standing.

Thorn Marley gave damning evidence which took the defending major by surprise. Havelock was extremely insubordinate and arrogant. Only recently the man had displayed his lower-class origins during a private remonstration on his behaviour, boldly countering advice given with the best of intentions and using threatening language. The young subaltern's reputation with women was well known. Not content with the ladies in each town they passed, he had been rather too free with other men's wives. No one should be surprised that he determined to deal with the Boer female himself. Any woman was fair game to him.

Several other officers testified, somewhat reluctantly, to Havelock's popularity with the female sex, but drew the line at the suggestion that he would consort with the enemy. The flimsy threads were spun, then broken, until there were no more possible witnesses. Colonel Beecham was then called to give witness to both officers' characters. He said little about Pickering other than that he had a pristine record, which told the court there was neither reprimand nor praise upon it. He said even less about Martin Havelock. (He could not reveal Val's real identity, or even say he believed him to be a true gentleman formerly involved in scandal. Both would condemn him further, rather than help.) He cited the action which had earned the accused a decoration for gallantry in saving the lives of many of his men, but agreed that Havelock was headstrong and keen for advancement.

In the end it all came down to Pickering's evidence which, if believed, would lead to the execution of a twenty-two year old who had glittered like a bright star for the short time he had been with an élite Lancer regiment. If Havelock's own story were true, he would be found guilty on the count of knocking the gun from the other's hand and of causing, by dint of running away to rescue the horses, the sealed orders to be lost and a fellow officer to be shot. The first could be mitigated on the grounds that he believed Pickering would shoot an unarmed woman with a child, the second on the grounds that he had no reason to suspect the woman could overcome his fellow officer, force him to strip, then ride away. And the documents had been Pickering's responsibility, in the main.

The court retired to consider their verdict on one of the most distasteful cases they had judged. Havelock was a mystery man. Clearly a gentleman's son who had enlisted as a trooper. Why, unless he had been involved in something unsavoury? And there was his record as a womanizer. Was he the kind of man who told the truth? Yet, he *was* a brilliant soldier, a first-class sportsman and undoubtedly fearless in the face of danger. He had saved men's lives; he had brought horses from a burning stable in Oxford at risk to his own life. He was arrogant and insubordinate. What were they to think? How could they judge this man of many parts?

Pickering, on the other hand, was simplicity itself. From

an impeccable background and related to minor royalty, he was an undoubted gentleman. That was about all one could say. He was an asset to an officer's mess, but a possible burden to the regiment as a whole. He had neither distinguished nor disgraced himself throughout his service. He was clearly disliked by the rank and file, which championed Havelock, but that often happened with officers of very high social rank. They aroused violent resentment in those less fortunate. He had hardly distinguished himself in this affair, however. Whether or not Havelock *had* kicked the revolver to the woman before running away to the barn, leaving *her* to do to Pickering what he had threatened to do inside the house, the blue blood himself had made little effort to save that sealed envelope from falling into her hands. He had tamely stripped, handed her the uniform and allowed her to march him along the track to shoot him. He was to be charged on that count as soon as the doctor declared him fit enough to stand trial, so it should not influence the verdict on Havelock. But it must, because the young subaltern was being indirectly blamed for losing those orders. What a hell of a mess!

While members of the court argued and cursed, Val remained in his small prison overlooking the cool, running river. He was still empty of feeling, despite facing a death sentence. Everything he had lived for was over. Thank God he was Martin Havelock to the world. The Ashleigh name was safe and his family's distress would not be added to by alerting others to this appalling affair. Nothing would lessen Grandfather's sorrow, however. He would carry the secret shame to his grave with a curse on the only Ashleigh to dishonour thirteen generations of noble warriors; the only one to die before a firing squad rather than the enemy.

Miles Atwood appeared to be suffering more than he as they waited all day in vain, and faced another night of suspense. Food was brought by a robust subaltern, who relieved Atwood so that he could have dinner in the Mess and relax until he must return at ten p.m. George Marsh had been friendly enough to Val, but he was voluble in his opinions now. While Val sat ignoring the food, Marsh damned Pickering heartily.

'Only a pipsqueak of his calibre could have allowed a woman to get the better of him in that fashion. I mean, she wouldn't have shot him *before* he stripped off his uniform because it would be of no use to her man with a hole, and blood all over it. When he took off his tunic why didn't he fling it at her and grab the revolver? Why didn't he try any number of ruses to reverse the situation? You would have. So would I, but he appears to have done everything he was told without putting up a fight. Good God, what a laughing stock he's made of the regiment! The Boers'll have even less respect for us after this. Come on, old chap, eat up! They'll never convict you. It's plain as a pikestaff Pickering's lying. They'll not accept his word against yours. Mind you, he's related to some very influential people at Horse Guards. That shouldn't influence the verdict when a man's life is on the line, but you never know. Careers have been ruined before now because some old general takes umbrage over his nephew's treatment.'

Val got to his feet and crossed to stare from the window at a river turned pink by the reflection of the sun below the horizon. Marsh apologized. 'Sorry, didn't think what I was saying. The board comprises some wise old birds. They'll see that justice is done no matter who Pickering's relations are.' He crossed to Val. 'Nearly forgot. There was a letter addressed to you in the Mess. I cleared it with Colonel Beecham before I brought it here. It's marked urgent.' When Val made no attempt to take the envelope, the other said awkwardly, 'I do think you should read it. It might be important, old chap. Last words, and all that.'

A few seconds later Val heard the sound of an envelope being slit, then Marsh read aloud the contents. 'I could never withdraw my friendship, you must know that. You need it more than ever now. I made enquiries about the family mentioned by Sir Rigby. They are extremely well known by repute amongst military men. The youngest is not at Oxford, but in South Africa with the family of a schoolfriend. No one is sure of his exact whereabouts, but I am. I *know* you could not have done what you're accused of – know it more than ever now. Please keep your courage up. It will soon be over and you'll be free. My prayers are *all* for you. There's no signature, Martin,' Marsh finished quietly, as he placed the single page on the windowsill.

Val continued to stare at the river having heard nothing but the echo of Sir Gilliard's demand to live Vorne Ashleigh's curtailed life for him; to walk in the steps of a hero.

Prisoner and escort were called to hear the verdict just before noon the following day. Val stood facing the men who had listened to Audley Pickering claim that Martin Havelock had refused an order to burn the house. Then, when the occupants appeared, had violently disarmed him and kicked the weapon towards the woman to whom he crossed for a short private conversation. He had then run off leaving his superior officer unarmed at the mercy of a Boer woman known to be helping the enemy. The president of the court lost no time in speaking. His deep voice echoed in the vaulted room.

'Second-Lieutenant Martin Havelock, you have been found guilty on the first charge, in that you refused an order to burn the farm given by Captain Marley and repeated by Lieutenant Pickering on arrival at the place. You have been found guilty on the second charge, in that you used violence towards Lieutenant Pickering by knocking his revolver to the ground, thus disarming him.' He paused momentarily to clear his throat. 'On the third charge of disgraceful conduct unbecoming an officer and a gentleman you have also been found guilty, in that you ran off leaving a fellow officer, whom you had deprived of his means of self-defence, to face a hostile woman known to be working with our enemies. He was consequently shot and very seriously wounded.'

The grey-haired colonel cleared his throat once more. 'The fourth charge of causing, by negligence, the loss into the hands of the enemy secret documents addressed to the colonel of your regiment is not proven, awaiting the trial of Lieutenant Pickering on whose person the documents were being carried at the time.' He stared at Val with a piercing gaze. 'The combined sentence for those crimes of which you have been found guilty is death by firing squad.'

The most blessed words he could hear! The struggle, the shame, the burden of living up to a hero, would be over. Dawn would bring an end to Martin Havelock, and Val Ashleigh would silently die with him. The family could say that he had met with a shooting accident and he would trouble them no more. He was about to turn away when the official voice continued.

'The death sentence has been commuted on the rec-ommendation of a small majority. You are instead to be cashiered.'

The numbness of the past days melted in an instant, bringing pain so acute Val almost cried out. The room began to spin and Miles Atwood stepped forward to grip his arm in steadying fashion. Val jerked free, turned, and walked from the room with the help of iron willpower. In the waggon taking him back to his prison he began to shake, but his companion sat silent and unmoving on the facing bench. Val almost stumbled as he climbed down and entered the stone house which grew unbearably hot at the height of the day. His heart hammered so thunderously it created agony in his chest. He had to fight for breath in the stifling atmosphere. Acute nausea swept through him so that he staggered to the spartan closet before retching convulsively for some minutes. For a while he believed merciful oblivion would overtake him, but he remained conscious throughout the physical punishment. Had he not deliberately built a physique that would withstand the utmost effort and pain?

Miles brought him a cup of tepid water but it merely revived his sickness. He could not stop shaking as if in freezing temperatures, yet perspiration dripped from every pore. Reaching for the bar across the small window, Val gripped it until his knuckles grew white. Tears ran unchecked down his cheeks as his whole body shook with sobs. He had hoped to die. What he faced was a living death. He had been tried and sentenced. It was too late to take the honourable way out . . . and he knew what the 57th Lancers did to those who betrayed them. For the first time in his life he doubted his own courage as he thought of what would happen the following morning.

Because of the desire for secrecy over the affair, Colonel Beecham ordered his regiment to parade on the veld two miles north of the town at sunrise. The 57th Lancers was an élite regiment proud of its record of battle honours. It did not tolerate those who dishonoured them and the distinctive grey uniform which had earned them the nickname The Ghost Lancers. An ancient tradition was kept alive by its officers, who saw no reason why it should not be played out at this time of war. Whatever his private feelings on the injustice of the trial, Max Beecham had openly championed the man who now sullied the reputation of the regiment, and had no option but to agree to equally openly condemn him.

For once, his wife and daughter could not move him. For the whole evening they both pleaded with him to dispense with the customary ceremony on the grounds of an existing state of war. Mrs Beecham privately entreated her husband to search his conscience before submitting the young man to an outmoded punishment far exceeding his crimes if, indeed, he had really committed any. To her cry of, 'Isn't it time that barbaric practice ended?' he replied that he would be glad if she would be good enough to stop interfering in regimental matters beyond the range of her understanding. He also reminded her that, but for his own evidence of the man's character and courage when facing danger, they might well have upheld the death sentence.

Vivienne would not be silenced, however. She wept, she begged, she even went very dramatically on to her knees to implore her father to continue his championship of someone he had always liked and encouraged.

'You *know* he did none of those things Audley claimed. It's completely out of character,' she urged emotionally. 'Everyone was aware that they hated each other and that it would come to a head sooner or later, but this is so *unfair*. I'm no fool, Father. I've lived with the regiment all my life and it's blatantly obvious they're afraid of upsetting Audley's influential relatives. Don't shake your head; you know it's true. They're making a supposed nobody from the ranks a scapegoat because they daren't officially rule that a gentleman's word cannot be believed against that of a commissioned trooper.'

Max Beecham grew very angry because she was almost certainly right. 'Get off your knees, child. You are extremely immodest, *and* impertinent. This is no stage melodrama but a very serious regimental matter. Pickering was *shot*. If he had died, Havelock would have paid the full penalty.'

'Do you *truly* believe he kicked the revolver to the woman so that she would kill Audley?' was her impassioned response. 'He was determined to break that pathetic nincompoop personally. He would *never* have done a cowardly thing like that.'

'That's enough! I know you have always befriended young Havelock, but he has contravened the Army Act. If those sealed orders had outlined battle plans, a number of British lives would have been at risk.'

'But they didn't!' she cried. 'They concerned new regulations on replacing worn uniforms. How could any man be shot for losing *that*?'

'He is not going to be shot! That charge is suspended.'

'Then why is he being so harshly treated on the others? All you can say to me is *if* such and such had happened. None of it did. It's so *unfair.*'

Max Beecham called upon his wife. 'For heaven's sake get her off her knees. I *will not* be subjected to this ridiculous behaviour. This is an entirely military matter. It is quite unforgivable to expect me to discuss it with *you* in my drawing-room. I'll say no more on the subject.'

Mrs Beecham was a determined woman. 'I have to say that I do not understand it myself, my dear. Vivienne and I have followed the regiment across Africa and served it to the best of our ability. We both worked to help the wounded during the siege of Kimberley,' she pointed out in firm tones. 'If that was not a military matter I cannot think what else one would call it. As your wife and daughter we have made an effort to get to know the men you command, and we have both written personal letters to relatives of each one killed during this war. We have tried to ease the tension and loneliness of the officers by entertaining them and taking an interest in their families. They all know I would do anything I could to assist them with any personal problem they felt they could not bring to you.'

She moved forward to help Vivienne to her feet, then stood with an arm around her daughter's waist. 'We are part of this regiment, Max. We have tended its wounds and mourned its dead. Now we are deeply upset by something we find difficult to understand. Where else are we to discuss it with you? Do you wish us to parade outside your office to request the Adjutant for an interview?'

Caught in a trap of his own making the colonel tried to bring an end to this difficult marital confrontation. 'I'm fully aware of the parts you both play in the regiment. If I have not expressed my gratitude often enough I am deeply sorry . . . but this affair is not merely a regimental matter. A court martial is a trial conducted on behalf of the Crown by the army which defends it. *I* did not serve on the court, neither did I bear witness to anything more than the characters of the two involved. Which I did with scrupulous fairness, I must add.'

'I am certain you did, Max. You have always been a just man.'

'Then why am I being accosted for something completely out of my hands?' he demanded, growing even more irate.

'We are simply asking you to exercise your scrupulous fairness over something that is entirely *in* your hands. This harrowing ritual was instigated more than a century ago and should be abolished.' She glanced pointedly at Vivienne before adding, 'It has taken place once over the twenty-five years I have known you, and I shall never forget it. The poor man collapsed, which added to his humiliation before the entire town and garrison.'

'*He had seduced a fellow officer's wife,*' Colonel Beecham said with force. 'One of the worst crimes in the book. He was a *blackguard*!'

'But Mr Havelock is *not*. In your heart you must know he has been victimized in favour of someone with too much influence. The war gives you a reason for saving him from further punishment.'

'It's because of the war that the business will take place out on the veld. There's no question of the townspeople witnessing it, as they normally would. He's fortunate.'

Vivienne lunged forward to grip his arms, saying tearfully, 'I know him better than anyone. You might just as well shoot him as put him through this. Haven't you *any* idea what it will do to him?'

'What it is meant to do to men who blacken the reputation of the regiment,' he snapped, freeing himself.

'You wouldn't *dare* do it to Audley because he has the power to say things that could put an end to your hopes of promotion.'

'That's *enough*! Go to your room,' he ordered.

The girl was in too great a state of distress to listen or obey. 'If you knew his real identity you wouldn't dare do it to Havelock, either. This whole affair would have been hushed up if you knew who he is.'

Beecham grew very wary. 'What are you suggesting?'

'Only that he is by no means a nobody, an upstart trooper keen to make his mark. He has as much right as Audley to be an officer of any regiment he chose. That's been the basis of their emnity. Because Havelock had to remain silent, Audley treated him abominably. Every officer in the Mess knows that, but they did nothing in case it reached the ears of those who make or break careers.' She wiped the tears from her cheeks with an angry gesture. '*This* will reach ears they little suspect and I hope they all suffer because of it.'

By now deeply suspicious, father challenged daughter. 'Has Havelock confided to you something of which I am unaware?'

'No, he wouldn't. I discovered it for myself.'

'And?'

Vivienne shook her head. 'I promised to keep the secret.'

'Even from me?'

'Yes, Father. I gave him my word.'

Max Beecham breathed again. 'I see. Very commendable.'

When his daughter took his hands, he was stricken by the anguish in her eyes as she begged, 'Please, *please* don't do this to him.'

Knowing it was too late to reverse his order, he said something unworthy of the just man he truly was. 'He should have considered that before throwing away his career at that farm. He only has himself to blame.'

The closed waggon arrived fifteen minutes before dawn. Miles Atwood, dressed in full ceremonial uniform, looked white faced and haggard as he held the door open for a fellow officer about to be publicly humiliated. Val got to his feet, staring at the dim shape of a vehicle that looked like a tumbril of the French Revolution, except that he would not be beheaded at the end of the vilification. He must live with it for the rest of his days. Confined in tight-fitting tunic and breeches in two tones of grey he forced himself to climb in and sit on the rough bench. He felt icily cold and his facial muscles appeared to have seized up. A sensation of choking forced him to swallow convulsively every minute or so. The tall, square-topped helmet seemed unbearably weighty; the gold strap too tight around his chin. The sword Vere had presented to him hung at his side. Its blade had never penetrated flesh. It now never would.

The waggon lurched and rattled over the rough track leading to a plain where the 57th Lancers would have already formed up. Atwood stared wordlessly at the floor as the morning gradually grew lighter outside. They came to a halt and his head jerked up. 'We're here,' he said unnecessarily. He climbed out first and stood waiting for his companion to join him.

It was a chill, clear morning allowing a view for many miles; the kind of morning Val knew so well. He had ridden out on patrols with the sun creating an apricot sky on the eastern horizon; he had lain with his troopers waiting for an enemy attack out of the dawn; he had cantered with high spirits through a waking camp during his days as Sergeant Havelock; he had tumbled from his bed to indulge in horseplay with Toby in the tent they had shared; he had stood quietly and been humbled by the splendour of this land at war on mornings like this. All these things had been the very air he breathed, the

389

lifegiving force of a man born to be what he was. Take them away and he would die.

An entire regiment on parade was an impressive sight. This one, clad in smart grey with silver embellishments, and with pennants fluttering on tall lances, seemed to stretch forever into the distance as Val stood on the grass twenty feet from the end ranks. The total silence made the sight even more awesome. Colonel Beecham out in front of his men drew his sword, raised it, then lowered it until it pointed to the ground. Atwood glanced at Val, said in a croaky voice, 'Quick march,' and they went side by side towards a spot marked by crossed swords which lay ten feet ahead of the commanding officer. Atwood halted them behind the swords, then gave the order to about turn.

Val then knew the true meaning of loneliness as he faced six squadrons of mounted men and their officers dressed in the uniform each had sworn to die for. The veld had never seemed so vast; he had never felt so exposed. Atwood stepped smartly forward, then turned about face looking even more ashen. In the continuing silence he reached up to remove Val's shining brass helmet with its yellow and white plume, and placed it on the ground. He then unbuckled the sword belt, drew out the weapon, and drove its point into the ground before laying the scabbard beside the helmet. The heavy, encrusted hilt swayed from side to side on the fine blade as Atwood appeared to falter momentarily. Val's choking sensation had increased so that he was forced to swallow every ten seconds or so as he stared beyond Atwood to those ranks which, in the half-light, resembled the phantoms imagined by the French in Portugal during a different war.

Then Atwood was ripping from Val's tunic epaulettes, buttons and all insignia of rank which he had last night loosened in preparation. These joined the items already on the ground along with the yellow ceremonial sash and the cross-straps. Throughout this indignity, the unhappy subaltern's fingers shook and a muscle jumped in his cheek. The final act he must perform was to remove the ornate spurs worn by Lancer officers. When these lay in the pile, he stepped away, turned, and marched back to the waggon.

Val stood out there alone beside the things he had worn with such pride. The wind ruffled his hair and blew open the buttonless tunic as a subaltern left the ranks at the far end and slowly walked his horse across to the spot. When he reached it he leaned down from the saddle to grasp the hilt of the sword. After drawing it from the ground he flung it on to the emblems of rank, then turned to face Colonel Beecham. Saluting the senior man of the regiment, he asked in barrack-square tones for permission to proceed. Beecham's return salute gave it. The subaltern Val knew to be a recent replacement, then commanded, 'Mr Havelock, fall in!'

As the man began to ride away very slowly back to the far end, Val feared he would be unable to move. The strength appeared to have drained from him. Only superhuman effort allowed him to get started on the walk that would complete his humiliation. The silence was terrible. Even the horses condemned him with it. If only a bird would sing. He followed the brown gelding at a dragging pace, staring at its swaying haunches as if in a living nightmare. When a sound finally broke the silence it added to that nightmare. Distant bugles called men to the stables at the start of a busy regimental day; sounds he would not hear again without re-living these moments.

They reached the far end of the massed horsemen at last. There, he was halted and turned to face the long line ranged along the plain. Almost immediately, Max Beecham shouted an order. This was taken up by the first squadron-commander as Val began to walk behind the gelding towards the waggon three hundred yards away. Corunna Squadron executed the precise manoeuvre which turned the ranks ninety degrees. During the time it took Val to walk the gap between squadrons, Waterloo was similarly turned, and Corunna faced front again. The orders were repeated by each successive commander so that the members of the 57th Lancers showed their contempt by turning their backs on a man they now rejected.

By the time he reached the fifth squadron Val thought his breast would burst open from the pain within it. He prayed it did not show in his face as he forced one leg after the other in almost funereal pace behind the walking horse. The slower the pace the longer the ordeal. The subaltern had received his orders.

The fifth squadron was Napier, the one Val had served until receiving his commission. As he approached the first ranks, Felix Wheeler gave the order to turn and guided his stallion round. He and his troop officers found themselves facing ranks of men who had not moved. Wheeler repeated his order in sharp tones, but not one member of the rank and file obeyed. There was nothing he could do with a hundred or more men who refused to insult someone who had lived and fought with them as their friend and champion; someone they would have followed into the thickest battle fray, if necessary. The same thing happened with Lockheart Squadron, the last ranks at the end of that terrible walk. The men he had so recently commanded, and those of the other troops stood their ground to show their loyalty and high regard for a fine, courageous soldier.

The ancient ritual almost over, the mounted lieutenant led Val back to the spot where his sword had been flung to the ground. He stood out there alone in the blinding horizontal rays of the rising sun while the rider rejoined the ranks, and he continued to stand there as the regiment he had sacrificed everything to join rode in procession back to the town. He remained on that stark, barren plain his head echoing with Sir Gilliard's demand that he live Vorne Ashleigh's life for him, and with his own youthful voice saying, 'I swear I'll not let you or the family down, sir, and I'll serve my country with my last breath . . . but I can't live my brother's life for him. I *must* live my own.'

He had no idea how many days he had been on the move. A man lost count of time on the veld. It was easy to skirt towns and hamlets; there was no difficulty in avoiding people. People condemned; people jeered. He had been cast out. The wilderness was the best place for him. Thick blond stubble adorned the chin of a haggard face burned dark brown. A network of fine white lines spread out around blue eyes that stared with the haunted gaze of many who had travelled this land alone. The rough jacket and breeches he wore were stained and filthy; his hands on the reins were streaked by grime. The horse he rode and the other he led were in good condition. His love and respect for these beasts rose above all else. *They* were noble creatures still.

He knew the time had come to release them. From the top of the hills he had seen a small settlement, but distances were deceptive in this clear air and it was still some way off. He would try to get closer to ensure that they were able to smell other horses and the familiar scent of humans when he said goodbye.

Two miles on he fell from the saddle for the fourth time and lay beneath the scorching sun unable to move or think, until a velvety nose nudged his cheek and warm air was blown through nostrils to fan his closed eyelids. They opened lethargically to see a long, long nose and trusting brown eyes watching him. His comatose brain roused enough to tell him his equine friends would not leave him, so he could not die here. It was imperative to go on and tether them near enough to the settlement for them to be found.

He rolled over and slowly found his feet. The effort

made the earth spin. Without strength enough to climb into the saddle, he set off in a stumbling walk knowing the horses would follow. Forcing one leg before the other he imagined he could see the swaying flanks of that gelding; that he could hear those orders clear and sharp in the dawn. Through bleary eyes he saw the grouped houses and choked back a sob of thankfulness. The destruction of Martin Havelock was almost complete.

He tethered the animals to a tree on the outskirts of the settlement, then struck out for the wilderness alone. The farewell was deliberately brief. They had served him more loyally than he had served them. Blindly staggering onward to put as much distance as possible between himself and other people, he eventually encountered a hollow, lost his footing and keeled over. This was as good a place as any. A horseman would one day come across a corpse surrounded by *aasvogels* and ride on fatalistically. There would be nothing on it to give an identity. Just one more traveller of the veld, lost and down on his luck.

Oblivion was broken by voices shouting nearby. The sound penetrated the blessed nothingness and rattled around in his head, gradually taking on some meaning. It was a sound that sent a message to his weary brain; one it could not ignore. His eyes slowly opened and saw nothing but sky. They closed again, but his mind refused to allow him the peace he wanted. The voices were still shouting. The language they used sent a signal of danger to his senses and muscles. His eyes again opened; his right arm moved. He must alert his troopers. His right leg bent as he slowly rolled on to his stomach. The voices came from the west where the lowering sun was about to be obscured by a cloud. He reached out to pull himself forward but advanced only a foot or so. His limbs were reluctant to obey his will, yet it was strong enough to keep him crawling painfully towards the rim of the hollow.

Panting and giddy, he clutched the short spiky grass and hauled himself high enough to peer beyond the slope on which he was spread-eagled. It was some while before his eyes focused well enough to make out what they saw. A group of six men were squatting beside a long, thick, black line. They were laughing and shouting instructions to each other as they fixed two bundles to it. Then they stood, walked to their horses, mounted and rode off laughing.

He lay staring at the bundles until they became identifiable as sticks of dynamite. The long black line then became a railway track. It took some while for him to work out the significance of what he had discovered. No sooner had he done so than he heard something immediately recognizable: the whistle of a train. Instinct set his head turning left and right. The track stretched for no more than a hundred yards in one direction around a jutting rise of ground. In the other, it ran for less than fifty yards before curving out of sight.

He called to his troopers but no sound came from his parched throat. Pulling himself over the rim to level ground, he began the struggle to get up. Once on his knees he pitched forward again with his face on the coarse ground. He turned it to the right and saw a spiral of smoke rise up beyond the high ground. The train was nearer than he thought. Pushing himself up on arms deliberately strengthened by constant training, he willed himself to a kneeling position then to his feet. With his legs buckling at almost every step, and zig-zagging towards the bundles his blurred eyes saw in several different places, he now heard the rails begin to sing the imminent approach of a train.

He was willing himself onwards across the sands outside Khartoum with a vital dispatch. Although each step was agony he must go on. The Mahdi's men were close behind him. He could hear their shrill cries. No, it was an engine's whistle, and those bundles must be removed before they blew it sky high. If only he could see more clearly; if he could just stop his legs from folding up and sending him in the wrong direction. All his troopers had been killed. He must do this for them to show that he had not, after all, let them down. His face was wet with perspiration . . . or was it tears? They had not turned their backs. They knew he would not let them die out here from an unseen enemy.

Lance-Corporal Johns and Sergeant Crookes, one of the best shots in their regiment, were riding as lookouts in the driver's cab. As they lounged against the sides of it they were discussing the prospect of being stationed near Pretoria for a spell.

Sergeant Crookes broke off in the middle of a sentence, saying to the driver, 'Do you *have* to keep making that row?'

'Yes,' snapped the man. 'Although we're going slowly around the bends there won't be time enough to stop if there's anything on the line. The whistle scares off animals if any are crazy enough to graze along the tracks.'

'Ha, I'd run the stupid buggers down,' was the reply.

'Yes, *you* would. It's not your country,' the driver said in disgust. 'Apart from killing buck for food, *we* don't slaughter our wild animals for sport. They are given the freedom of the veld along with any man, woman or child who decides to cross it. All you khaki lads think of is killing. Anything! Why don't you . . . there you are, there *is* an animal on the line,' he finished, reaching for the handle to blow a blast on the whistle once more.

The sergeant had his field glasses trained on a dun-coloured creature on the line, now visible, which stretched out towards the next curve. 'Funny looking animal. *Shut that bloody row up!*' he snarled, as the driver hung on the whistle handle in a continuing attempt to move the creature. Still studying the hunched shape that appeared to be moving very slowly, he was puzzled. The shape then straightened up slightly, and so did he. 'Blimey, it's a bloody Boer!'

'What?' cried Lance-Corpoal Johns, hanging over the side of the cab to see for himself.

'It's a bloody Boer . . . and in his hand he's got bloody *dynamite*,' yelled the other, dropping the field glasses to dangle on their strap as he snatched up his rifle. '*Put on the brakes, man!*'

'It's too late.' The driver prepared to jump from the cab, but Johns grabbed him by the collar and roared at him to brake.

'We've got five 'undred men on this train and you're not leaving it, mate,' he added grimly.

A rifle cracked across the cab, and they all saw the man fall clear of the line as the brake was applied and wheels screamed on tracks. The train came to an eventual halt several yards round the bend, still intact. An officer jumped to the ground and called to Sergeant Crookes for an explanation. The N.C.O. ran back alongside the train where heads were looking inquisitively from open trucks.

'A bloody Boer planting dynamite on the track, sir,' he panted. 'I got him, never fear.'

'Only one?' queried the captain. 'That's unusual. We'd best get moving in case it's an ambush gone wrong and the rest rush us. Detail a party to go back for the dynamite. Don't want to leave it lying around for them to have another go. And tell them to be *quick*,' he called after the retreating man. 'We can't hang about longer than a few minutes.'

The Fuseliers who were given an unenviable task had never moved quicker than they did then. Expecting a volley of rifle fire from the higher ground at any moment one snatched up the dynamite, threw the two bundles into the air so that his fellows could fire at them, then they all hared back to the train with the echo of explosions in their ears. The blood-stained body was left beside the track. The vultures would clear it away. The train was moving even as the Fuseliers clambered back aboard. Within a very short time silence returned to that spot, no more than a spiral of smoke in the distance showing that a troop train containing five hundred soldiers had ever passed by.

Two black men rose cautiously from behind a large aloe. They had hidden there when the six bearded horsemen had appeared. They disliked and feared Boers. It was best to melt into the landscape whenever they were in evidence. After looking around warily, they descended to the figure sprawled face down beside the track. They were mystified by this man who had crawled from a hollow when the Boers rode away. How long had he been there? *Why* had he been there?

From the way he had moved it seemed probable he was hurt, even dying, when he went to take away what the Boers had put there. They knew what it was and the damage it could do, even before the soldiers had thrown it into the air and fired at it. This man could not have known the danger or he surely would never have done what he did.

Reaching the body they turned it over and stared down at it. He was a big man, strong. Even the rigours of the veld could not disguise what his physique had once been. Blood oozed from his chest in the vicinity of his heart. His eyes were closed, his mouth open in final anguish. The black men looked at the golden hair and facial stubble, then one squatted to prise open an eyelid. A cornea of vivid blue gazed sightlessly at the *aasvogels* starting to gather overhead.

The second man then squatted to point out faint movement just below the stranger's right ear. They conferred. This man could not be a Boer; he had disconnected the dynamite only seconds before the train arrived. This man had the looks of English people they knew. Why, then, had his own soldiers shot him and left his body to the mercy of the veld predators? This man possessed great courage. This man still lived. The Lord clearly favoured him, so they must tell Father McBride at the mission.

One rose and ran off effortlessly to fetch help from the settlement ahead. The other sat beside the stranger, shading his face from the sun with his own body, until the mission waggon arrived with bandages and medicines.

15

THOSE AUTUMN DAYS of 1901 were touched by curious events, culminating in the end of an era at Knightshill. No member of the family had a premonition of what was about to happen. Instead, life was happy and peaceful for them all. Charlotte and John had settled into a contented married life and were eagerly awaiting the birth of their child: a gift both thought forever denied them until a year ago. John had been integrated into the family after some difficulty due to his many years as an employee. Now nine months had passed, his reservations had been overcome so that he and Vere ran the estate on easy terms with each other. Charlotte handed over the reins almost imperceptibly and was so occupied with the orchids Vere had now invested in very heavily, as well as impending motherhood, she hardly noticed that she was no longer the first lady of Knightshill.

Kitty fulfilled all her husband's hopes by making their home the lively, cultural retreat he needed. Very, very gradually the martial dominance of that great house was softened by visits from many acquaintances who had not once worn a scarlet jacket. Vere had never wanted to completely banish the military flavour of a house owned by generations of soldiers, but a balance between culture and gallantry was struck. The old mansion came alive with voices and laughter throughout the year. Balls and dinner parties were frequent; extra staff were employed to cope with the new lighter régime in a house which itself seemed to welcome the fresh breeze of change.

Sir Gilliard, unexpectedly docile in his ninety-first year, appeared to take on a new lease of life. Armed neutrality with his daughter-in-law might have contributed to it, or maybe the old warhorse recognized a worthy opponent, for once. The succession still obsessed him, however. Vere and Kitty took every opportunity to impress upon him that he had another grandson who was legally next in line. On one occasion when the time had been right, Vere again produced Val's photograph and the gazette entries of his commission and award of the D.C.M. The initial reaction was all Vere could want.

'A very fine looking fellah! Looks one straight in the eye. Always tell a man's character from that. If he's shifty he'll never make a good officer. This one will. See it in his face. Every inch a replica of our hero, don't you think?'

'He does strongly resemble Vorne, yes,' Vere agreed, knowing Val to be a far finer person. 'A grandson to be proud of, wouldn't you say?'

The old man handed the photograph back as bleakness touched his expression. 'No grandson of mine is called *Havelock*.'

This bothered Vere also. Val was carving out a distinguished career with the 57th Lancers. He was happy and fulfilled. He did not want the responsibility of Knightshill. Yet he *was* the legal heir after Vere himself, and his first-born son would be the indisputable second in line. How Val would ever resolve the identity barrier he could not think. To claim the inheritance he would have to reveal his masquerade, and end his miltary service under a cloud. To marry and produce an heir, he would also have to declare his true name. Yet he surely could not live to the end of his days as Martin Havelock, bachelor. He had put himself in an impossible situation which could only complicate further as year succeeded year. Vere always shrugged off this problem by telling himself he was only just twenty-nine, and set for a long wonderful life with Kitty and their enchanting twin daughters. Martin

Havelock could survive until he became captivated by a woman, too. Then he would have to make an unenviable decision which was his alone.

Sir Gilliard no longer lived reclusively in his suite of rooms. Although he still did not approve of Vere's friends from the world of art and theatre, he frequently joined the family when military or diplomatic guests were present and enjoyed their company. Pointedly ignoring John, he nevertheless showed signs of recovering something of his former verve in company. Part of this was his penchant for dominating conversations with long anecdotes from his distinguished past. As these were, in the main, highly entertaining, Vere allowed his grandfather leeway until he felt it was time to intervene.

Later, Vere realized this pleasant period had been the lull before the storm. At the start of November he received a note from Edward Pickering telling of his engagement to the cousin of an old school friend. *You teasingly invited me to stay at Knightshill with my fiancée when we parted in Ladysmith, oh, so long ago,* he wrote. *May I confound you with that invitation designed to persuade me that I was not the half-man I believed I was then, and come for a few days with Helen? She cannot wait to meet the artist she so admires.*

Vere replied telling his friend to come for as long as he wished the following month, cheered by the evidence of Edward's recovery beyond all expectations of his surgeons. He recalled the man's fervour for a military life which matched Val's, and guessed it had been a case of mind over matter. He looked forward to the meeting.

By the next day's mail came two letters which were to change the pattern of his life in most unexpected fashion. The first was from the family solicitor stating that he had received from a legal firm in the state of Texas notification of the death of Mrs Clarissa Mulhone, formerly widow of Roland Ashleigh of Knightshill. Mrs Mulhone had survived her husband by three years, and their extensive property in the United States had been willed her on his death. A copy of her will sent by its executors showed her fortune and estate to be bequeathed in equal parts to any of her children by Roland Ashleigh who survived her by twenty-eight days, except the youngest, Valentine Martin Havelock, who should receive an additional portion to compensate for her desertion of him whilst a babe of tender years. Mr Simms requested a date when he could wait on the late Clarissa Mulhone's children for a full reading of her will.

Vere was strongly moved for someone who had last seen his mother at the age of eleven. For the sake of happiness with a man who had offered her security, and a life in which he would not be chasing wars all over the world, Clarissa Ashleigh had left her five children to the autocrat who would not allow her to take them from their inheritance, and had abided by his stipulation that she should have no further contact whatever with them. With children of his own now, Vere tried to imagine his mother's anguish over the past eighteen years, particularly for a toddler who would have been the most difficult to surrender. Her life at Knightshill must have been unendurable under Sir Gilliard's rule.

An extensive property in Texas! A cattle ranch of many hundred acres, he had once been told. He would have to go out there to settle the business of selling it. He did not imagine either of his sisters would care to live there, or Val. If it was hugely profitable they might all agree to appoint agents to run it and divide the profits, rather than sell. There were other possibilities, of course. Any number of them. He grew excited at the notion of travelling to the New World. Another experience, fresh opportunities for widening his artistic scope. Maybe he and Kitty could go there with Charlotte and John, the latter of whom might better assess the property than he. Then he smiled as he thought of the impecunious Martin Havelock who would find this bequest a godsend. He penned a note to his solicitor telling him to come on the following Monday. Then he put aside the man's letter feeling very much as he had in the Sudan, when the past had suddenly reached out and changed the direction in which he had been heading.

The second letter he opened immediately divided that direction so that he faced two paths stretching into the future. *The Illustrated Magazine* had been contacted by the representative of an Indian Maharajah who wished Mr Ashleigh to paint a series of pictures of the regiment his father had raised to fight with the British in Afghanistan. The Maharajah understood that Mr Ashleigh's own father had been mortally wounded in the war of 1878. For this reason, and because he was deeply impressed by his work published in the magazine over the past three years, the artist was offered a commission to be executed before November of the following year. Mr Ashleigh would be given an apartment in the palace for as long as he required it, and would be expected to represent the regiment in every aspect of its routine. From these pictures a set of four would be chosen to present to King Edward VII when he visited India at the end of 1902 to be officially proclaimed Viceroy of India. The remaining studies would be given to persons of importance to commemorate the occasion. The editor of *The Illustrated Magazine* offered Vere his own commission to cover preparations for the King's visit.

After reading the letter through several times, the honoured artist was still overwhelmed. Since his return from South Africa he had done very little painting, despite several offers of rich commissions from clients begging him to produce something spectacular for the bare space above a mantlepiece. He had declined, explaining that he did not work that way, but now he knew eagerness to take up his brushes again. An Indian regiment; those proud dark faces and elaborate uniforms. The stirring backdrops to such pictures would be an inspiration in themselves. He had enjoyed carrying out the contract in South Africa to sketch and paint Indian troops serving with the Ladysmith relief column. If the terrain there had thrilled him, that of another wild and beautiful continent would surely do the same.

For the next few hours he and Kitty discussed this offer, and his mother's bequest. Finally, she said with quiet reason, 'I cannot make this decision for you, my dear. It *is* possible to do both if you are prepared to spend half the year away from Knightshill and the twins.'

'Are you?' he asked.

She smiled. 'I will come with you to the Texan ranch, but any wife would be wise to steer clear of a man grappling with artistic genius.'

'Then I'll decline the Maharajah's commission.'

'And regret it forever? You are again facing the conflict of your mixed personalities, Vere. It will crop up throughout your life, I suspect. All other Ashleigh men, including Val, have known exactly what they are. Being far more complex, you no sooner decide that you are, at heart, a landowner and host to the talented and cultured than the artist in you rises up to demand satisfaction. It will be forever so.' She kissed him with lingering tenderness. 'You *must* accept the commission. Although King Edward may hang the Maharajah's gift in a small room at the rear of one of his official homes, you will gain enormous prestige from his royal connection with your work.'

'Maybe,' he said with a touch of doubt, 'but I shall pay a high price for it. Three or four months without you will seem an eternity.'

'Also for me, darling, but you won't be going to war as other Ashleigh husbands have. I'll know you'll return. I suspected when I married you that the artist would not be subdued for long. Only if the warrior in you revived would I grow afraid.'

'That will never happen,' he assured her. 'I'm leaving

warring to Val. He'll gain enough military distinction for us both.'

Although the matter appeared to have been settled, Vere made no definite commitment to go to India. He had been faced with a difficult decision two years ago: China with the West Wilts or a tour of the Mediterranean as an artist. He had wound up in South Africa dragging an ammunition waggon to safety under fire. Two years before that a girl had driven him on a course which, until then, had never been a possibility. Experience had taught him that his life was not entirely his to order. Fate had plans for him regardless of his own decisions. He would not rush into anything.

Charlotte greeted the news of her mother's death in typical manner. 'I cannot accept your theory of life being so unbearable here. We have all lived with Grandfather and survived.'

'He drove three of us away,' Vere reminded her.

'No, Vere, Annabel drove you away. Philip did it to Margaret, and that woman at Chartfield was responsible for Val's abscondence. Mama had every comfort and advantage here. She must have been the envy of many less fortunate army widows.'

'But I remember her as a gentle, artistic creature. She sang beautifully, and did the most exquisite embroidery and lace work. I believe she must have loved Father deeply because she was distraught when he died. Remember how she collapsed at his graveside? Exhausted by grief and the bearing of eight children, I suspect she was not strong enough to withstand Grandfather's domination of the five who survived. When Mulhone offered her affection and a brand of dominance based on *that*, she saw an escape from a life in which she was gradually being stifled.'

'So she selfishly took it, leaving us to fend for ourselves.'

'No, Lottie, we have only had to do that on leaving Knightshill. We had every comfort and advantage you

claim Mama had. Everything would have been fine if
Grandfather had not set us all such an example of strength
and resolution. He did not forsee that we would emulate
it in directions he had not suspected.'

Charlotte would not concur. 'We were *abandoned* by
Mama, however you try to excuse her. Would you go off
and leave your dear twins to be brought up by servants?
Of course not. This bequest of Mama's was made to salve
her conscience. We wanted her caring, not the money she
inherited from the foreigner who took her away from us.
Margaret will agree with me.'

Vere saw that she would never change her opinion, and
sighed. 'Then it's useless to invite you and John to go with
us to view this ranch in Texas next year. It might be wiser
to employ a bailiff than sell. You, Margaret and I will
have children who might one day care to live there and
manage it. We should consider that. Then there's Val. If
he should be forced to give up his army career because
of severe wounds, he could well choose to take it over
on our behalf. Kitty and I were hoping you two would
also make the journey to assess the potential of Wildeast
Ranch.'

'I see. Well, I shall ask John,' she said, mollified by his
persuasive tone. 'What of the children?'

'They'll be safe in Nanny's care. Mathilda will tend the
new baby along with the twins. If you agree, of course,'
he added quickly.

The solicitor's visit revealed the ranch to be amazingly
prosperous. The fortune left to Clarissa's four surviving
children was staggering. It gave Vere further food for
thought, and he had not reached any conclusion when
Edward Pickering and his dark-haired, vivacious fiancée
arrived with several large bags, for an extended visit. The
pair easily integrated with the four younger residents, who
were proud to show Knightshill to the grandson of Sir
Gilliard's old acquaintance, Lord Garnier. Accordingly,
dinner was served in the formal room lined by military

portraits and Sir Gilliard presided at the long table. He was delighted to have a military officer sitting at it, for Edward was back with his regiment on full active service having astonished doctors, and angered men at Horse Guards with his articles and letters in the newspapers deploring the conduct of many commanders in South Africa. His grandfather was presently very cool with him he confessed. But he was unrepentant, as he explained to Vere and Sir Gilliard after the ladies and John had left them with port and cigars.

'You know quite well, Vere, that terrible mistakes were made trying to lift the sieges. You saw the slaughter first hand. It was unforgivable. Buller should be shot for needlessly sacrificing so many lives.'

'Now, look here, sir,' countered Sir Gilliard, climbing aboard a beloved hobbyhorse, 'a general issues orders only after receiving reports and Intelligence from every available source. If those are misleading he is in no way accountable for the outcome, and if his divisional commanders see fit to amend or disregard their orders it is *they* who cause wholesale slaughter. With poor regimental officers no general can succeed.'

Edward was unabashed by this and said slyly, 'But did I not see several letters from *you* damning Buller's performance, sir?'

'You did, indeed. I think it may be conceded that one general is qualified to criticize another. It is when subalterns and captains pronounce on what should or should not have been done that it amounts to effrontery,' was the smart retort. 'In India a fellah called Pontefract – the name alone tells you the kind of man he was – stood up in front of . . .'

Vere sat back with his port knowing his grandfather would produce numerous anecdotes to support his theme. Edward would be amused by them, so he would not stop the flow just yet. Having heard most of them many times, Vere let his thoughts stray to the poser confronting him.

Should he go to India and leave Kitty? If fate was planning to intervene once more, he wished she would do so soon and save him from making a decision which would lead him somewhere altogether different from his planned destination. The port flowed as richly as the conversation until he indicated that they really should join the ladies.

Sir Gilliard took a while to get to his feet these days. While they waited for him to do so, Edward said to Vere, 'You heard about Cousin Audley, of course. Needless to say I did *not* receive a communiqué from him on that disgraceful affair.'

Vere grinned. 'What affair?'

'You don't know?' he asked in surprise. 'Thought your cousin would have told you, hotfoot.'

'He . . . he doesn't write often.'

'Ah! Well, the business was conducted in secret and was supposed to remain that way. Not the sort of thing we wanted splashed all over the front pages of international newspapers. British officers fighting each other instead of the enemy. Undermines morale . . . and the pride of our army. Just what our critics need.'

'You're one of them, aren't you?' Vere teased.

'Certainly, when this kind of nonsense goes on.'

'What kind of nonsense?' demanded Sir Gilliard, flushed from a large intake of port.

The three stood by the head of the table while Edward related a story he had no way of knowing would have such a dramatic outcome.

'I've never made a secret of my opinion of Audley, as you know, Vere, so you'll probably share a popular saying that if a man's no good for anything else he'll end up in the cavalry. It's harsh on the majority of stalwarts in mounted regiments, but nincompoops like Audley who have the right connections and a noble name are often to be found in élite cavalry ranks where they gain advancement through influence rather than skill.'

'Don't believe in that,' ruled Sir Gilliard. 'Fellah must

make his mark through efficiency and devotion to duty, no other way.'

'Exactly,' agreed Edward. 'Colonel Beecham is a good man running his regiment on those principals, and saw fit to commission a sergeant who rose from the barrack-room on pure miltary merit. It seems Audley had given him a rough time in the ranks, so there was no love lost between them and this fact was known by the entire regiment.'

Vere's neck was beginning to prickle with apprehension as he said quietly, 'Go on.'

'Fate decided that they should both be with a detachment of men ordered to burn a farm from which a number of Boers had been seen riding away. The captain gave chase with the main body of troops. Before departing he threw an envelope containing sealed orders to Audley, telling him to deliver them to Max Beecham on arrival at headquarters. No one knows the truth of what happened then except the two officers concerned, but the facts are that when a Boer woman and child appeared from the burning house, the other subaltern knocked Audley's revolver from his hand and kicked it away from his reach. After speaking privately to the woman, he apparently ran off to rescue two horses from the flaming barn. When he returned to the scene he found Audley in his underwear, shot in the chest. The woman and child had escaped on his and Audley's horses, taking with them a uniform with a pocket containing the sealed orders.'

Feeling very sick by now, Vere knew Fate had made her move. 'Your cousin survived?'

'Oh, yes. The Audleys of this world will always survive. He charged the commissioned ranker with disarming him, kicking the weapon to the Boer woman, then running off leaving her to do what he had threatened to do on several occasions. There were no witnesses and Audley threw in additional charges of insubordination and physical assault. They were both court martialled, of course;

410

Audley a month later due to his wound. You may guess whose story was officially believed. My cousin declared that he had been shot *before* being able to conceal the orders for Colonel Beecham, this despite the subsequent inference that the woman stripped him after he fell to the ground. Is it likely that she would delay long enough to struggle to remove a uniform holed and covered in blood, when speed of getaway was the essence? The court failed to prove otherwise and, as the orders were merely routine rulings on stores which were of no use to the enemy the findings were inconclusive. Audley's credibility was severely blackened, however, and Beecham gratefully accepted his resignation on the day after the trial ended.'

'And what of the other fellow?' asked Vere through the tightness in his throat.

'Havelock, the scapegoat? A death sentence was remitted to cashiering. The poor devil was treated to an old tradition whereby the guilty man is marched before the entire regiment, stripped of his rank, then obliged to walk along the parade whereupon squadron after squadron turn their backs in contempt. Typical cavalry!' he concluded in disgust. 'Time they brought themselves out of the dark ages and abandoned such practices. Especially when there's a war waiting to be finished off.'

There was a moment's intense silence before Sir Gilliard spoke. 'Which regiment did you say?'

'The Fifty-seventh Lancers, sir. Good regiment; indifferent officers.'

'And the guilty man's name?'

'Havelock.' Sensing an atmosphere, Edward asked, 'Not a friend of the president of the court, are you, sir?'

Sir Gilliard turned and walked away through the door leading to his library without another word. Edward looked at Vere in concern. 'I say, have I offended the old boy in some way?'

Smitten by the thought of his vital, eager young brother

411

being submitted to total military humiliation, aghast at the implications of Val's scintillating career coming to such an end, Vere knew he must act swiftly. With his eyes still on the closed library door, he murmured, 'Go and join the others, will you? I'll join you later.'

He expected to find Sir Gilliard bowed and broken. He should have known better. The old general was snapping pencils and throwing them in the fire as if each was a knife to the heart of his enemy. He spoke without turning. 'Once a villain always a villain. That boy is lacking in honour, integrity, truthfulness and every other quality which graces gentlemen. I long ago predicted that he would destroy himself, and now he has.'

'You heard Pickering, sir,' Vere countered heatedly. 'His cousin is the villain you've just described, not Val. Whatever the truth of the affair at Chartfield, he has more than proved his worth in the Fifty-seventh.'

'Pah!' was the contemptuous exclamation.

Vere strode round to stand beside him. 'Have you ever lived in a sweltering, smelly barrack-room with the rough mix of men who enlist, and made them all your friends and champions? Has any Ashleigh? He has, and become a better man for it. Have you worn sergeant's stripes and taken orders from a pipsqueak with royal connections who punishes you for his own lack of ability? Has any Ashleigh? Val has, and survived victorious. Did you earn your commission *before* you gained it? Did any Ashleigh? My brother did. How *dare* you say he has no honour or integrity!'

Sir Gilliard swung round, his face working. 'And how dare you adopt that tone with me?

'Because you drive me to.'

'Then I'll drive you further, sir. I'll not have his name mentioned within this house ever again, and he will not enter it. Don't imagine the likes of him will do the decent thing with a pistol against his temple. He'll come slinking home to lick his wounds in safety. The door will be shut in his face, d'you hear? This family will no longer acknowledge him, here or anywhere. His name will be expunged from all records connected with the Ashleighs.' His voice rose to the intimidating roar known to many. 'All monies and property due to him on my death will be willed elsewhere. I shall wipe him from family documents so that he can never inherit a square inch of land, a cowshed or one penny of Knightshill's estate and income.'

'You can't do that,' cried Vere with rising fury. 'He's *my* heir.'

'Oh, is he? You are not yet the owner of all this, and I shall ensure that you get it with the proviso that you cannot pass it on to any other son of Roland Ashleigh.'

'But he's legally next in line.'

'Not after I've seen Simms tomorrow. There is a clause which allows the head of the family to exclude any of his direct line from inheriting.' He poked his face forward to emphasize his next point. 'It has never been used until now.'

Still stunned by what had developed, Vere raged, 'I won't allow you to do that.'

'Ha! You cannot stop me, sir.'

'I can never have a son to succeed me. You know that.'

'That has never been my fault,' Sir Gilliard said in ringing tones. 'You will have to hand over everything to that red-headed child.'

'The son of a diamond prospector! That's out of the question.'

'Then you have no choice but to take a different wife who will give you a boy of your own.'

Vere lost the last remnants of his temper then. 'You have always considered me unfit to head this family, but I would defend each member of it with my last breath. All you have ever done is condemn them.'

'Because they are all weak and selfish, including you.'

'We are all the children of your son. You condemn him too?'

'He was a man of honour.'

'And passed none of that honour to *his* sons?' Vere demanded in wrought up tones. 'Val inherited all Father's qualities, and most of yours, including obstinacy and the inability to suffer those who don't live up to the highest of standards. It has ended in tragedy for him, but that in no way makes him a candidate for your blind injustice.'

Sir Gilliard gave him a withering look. 'Get out before I decide to give Knightshill to one of the stable-lads.' He brought his fist crashing down on to the table, and roared, '*I will not own him*! There was only one of you fit to succeed me and he lies in a hero's grave at Metemma.'

'No, he doesn't!' Vere snapped, knowing the truth must now be told. 'The grave had been desecrated. When I went to Metemma it was impossible to distinguish my brother's bones from the others scattered there.' The effect this had on his grandfather should have silenced him, but the anger of years, the effort of keeping to himself what he knew whenever Vorne Ashleigh's name was revered led Vere to smash a legend with short, savage sentences.

'I followed in my brother's footsteps all the way to Khartoum. I learned what kind of man he really was. I settled his staggering debts in each place we stopped. I bought off the Egyptian who produced a boy who, but for the lack of a marriage certificate, is your true heir. Perhaps you'd like me to fetch him from the brothel he serves and bring *him* to Knightshill.'

As he continued, his tone grew more and more bitter. 'Your "hero" was a licentious, drunken liar. He was also a coward!' His hand shook slightly as he pointed in the direction of the room they had just left. 'That painting showing his last courageous moments is fantasy. In Omdurman's cells I came across a man who was in Khartoum with Gordon. He told me of the British officer who got away just before it was overrun. He had openly declared that he had no intention of staying with a white madman determined to be a martyr, only to be killed by a black madman determined to be a god. That communiqué was a ruse to allow him to save his skin. The real prize he carried was a priceless family scarab entrusted to him by the Egyptian I encountered in Omdurman, who was persuaded by this enterprising officer also to part with a large sum which would be of no further use to him with the Mahdi's fanatics at the gates of Khartoum.'

The pent up anger of years welled up as Vere said, 'Vorne Ashleigh was killed for that jewelled scarab and the money he carried. He knew before he left Khartoum that it was far too late for any communiqué to summon help. The stronghold was already irrevocably doomed when he arrived there, and he was not man enough to stay and help defend it.' Fighting for control, he added, 'That is the man you have held up as an example to us for almost seventeen years. That is the man I was once ready to die to emulate. *That* is the man for whom young Val has ruined his life trying to match. Thank God your "perfect heir" did not live beyond the age of twenty-four. Heartbreak would have sent you to your grave long ago.'

Shaking with a depth of anger he had never before experienced, Vere walked away. At the door he turned back. 'I've kept that shocking secret for three years out of respect for you ... which is something you appear never to have had for any of us. If you rob my brother of his rightful inheritance, I shall take my family to live on the ranch in America which our mother has just willed to us ... and you may do whatever you wish with Knightshill.'

General Sir Gilliard Ashleigh died sometime during that evening. His loyal batman, Clunes, broke down and cried as Winters told Vere how he had found the grand old man in the library when he went in to check on the fire. Having struggled to behave normally before his family and friends after leaving his grandfather, Vere did all he had to do in a state of deep shock. By the time the doctor left it was two a.m. Knowing that only Edward and his fiancée might be able to sleep, Vere went to his sister's rooms and asked her and John to come along to his own because he wished to tell them something he could not keep until morning.

Kitty was sitting in a woollen wrapper waiting for him. She looked up with concern, then rose to pour him a glass of brandy. 'Drink this, my dear. You must need it.' Taking Charlotte's arm, she added, 'I suppose it's useless to suggest that you have a little brandy too. Tea, then?'

'John and I have consumed more than enough in the past two hours,' she replied dully. 'I still find this difficult to believe. He had been so much livelier recently, and was in fine fettle at the dinner-table with Edward to regale with his favourite stories. It's . . .' She grew choked. 'It's the end of an era, much as when the Queen died. Knightshill will never be the same again.'

Somewhat revived by the brandy, Vere asked them all to sit down around the fire then embarked on what he had to say. 'I am afraid I am responsible for what has happened tonight. I killed Grandfather.'

'*What?*' cried Charlotte.

John took her hand in comfort. 'What exactly do you mean, Vere?'

'I caused him to die by dealing him a blow from which I knew in my heart he would never recover.'

Kitty went to him immediately. 'You're overwrought, darling. Of course you didn't cause his death.'

He gazed into her puzzled eyes, and sighed. 'I accept full responsibility for it. When you have heard all I have to say, you'll understand that I had no choice but to do what I did.' He walked with her to the settee and settled her on it. Then he took the place beside her and tugged off his bow tie to loosen the tight collar. After a moment of silence, he said, 'I have two very unpleasant things to tell

416

you. One concerns Val. The other . . .' He sighed again. 'The other is something I have kept to myself for three years. It must now come into the open between us.'

John spoke up swiftly. 'If this is a family affair I should not be here.'

'You are part of the Ashleigh family now, man. All I ask is that what I say will not be repeated to anyone. Margaret and Val will have to know eventually, of course.'

'You sound so very serious,' said Charlotte. 'What has happened to Val?'

'Is he all right?' asked Kitty quietly.

'I . . . I don't know. That's the worst part of this wretched business,' Vere told them. 'He has suffered most from Grandfather's impossible demands. I just could not stand by in silence while he was vilified yet again. He is my only brother, and all he has ever wanted is to make the old man proud of him. We all know the heroic legend celebrated each January with stirring reverence. That boy was steeped in it from his infant years. My own failure to fulfil the military role demanded of me put on Val the mammoth burden of compensating for both his older brothers. Only someone as splendid as he would ever try.'

Kitty put her hand over his at that point. 'Just tell us what happened this evening.'

He glanced round at her and knew that, at this moment, she was the stronger. 'Edward Pickering is the cousin of an officer in Val's regiment who is a totally useless soldier, but related to minor royalty,' he told them all. 'Audley Pickering and Val hated each other on sight, for reasons you'll guess. Pickering used his rank to mount a campaign of persecution against Trooper Havelock which continued until he was commissioned. Knowing Val, you'll not be surprised to learn that the lad was determined on revenge, and said so on several occasions.' He spread his hands in a helpless gesture. 'Edward, not guessing that Martin Havelock was even known to us, tonight related details of an affair at a Boer farm which resulted in a double court martial for his cousin and this fellow Havelock.' He linked his hands between his knees and stared at the floor for a moment or two. 'Val was apparently accused by the other of insubordination, violent assault, and being the cause of his being shot and robbed of sealed military orders. Pickering was believed and cleared, but immediately resigned.' He glanced up at Charlotte. 'Val was found guilty on all counts and given a death sentence, which was commuted to cashiering. He was apparently submitted to public humiliation before the entire regiment.' He swallowed hard. 'God knows what that did to him.'

'How terrible!' Charlotte cried.

'It's the way the army is run. Honour is a hard-won prize in such communities.'

'That *poor* boy!' said Kitty softly. 'It'll break him. Sir Gilliard heard all this, of course.'

Vere related almost word for word his grandfather's reaction to this news, then said, 'I learned something in the Sudan which I had kept to myself because I knew it would break the old man's heart. Tonight, love for my family overrode any other consideration and I broke my silence. May God forgive me, but I could no longer have that false hero revered while Val was cursed and deprived of all he had struggled so hard to honour.' He looked around at their strained faces, then spoke bluntly. 'Vorne Ashleigh travelled from Cairo to Metemma leaving behind a trail of enormous debts, betrayal of trust and friendships, and at least one son: a handsome half-Egyptian with vivid blue eyes which made him especially attractive. His mother showed me my brother's coin purse with the initials V.E.R.A. Remember how he used to say Mama must have wanted a girl, Lottie?'

Charlotte had grown even paler and her large eyes gazed at him in continuing shock. She gave the faintest of nods.

'I paid the boy's villainous grandfather a considerable sum of money for his education, and so on, but I doubt if he used it for that purpose. The Sudan is a corrupt, harsh area. Its people continually fight for survival.' No longer able to sit still, Vere got up and walked to the decanter for some brandy. From the sideboard he added what he found the most difficult to say. 'In Omdurman I met a man who told me a terrible tale. I'm afraid I have every reason to believe it. Vorne persuaded General Gordon to send him with a communiqué only as a means of leaving Khartoum before it was overrun. He knew rescue was impossible and wanted to save his own skin. His two native companions killed him for the jewelled scarab and money entrusted to him by an Egyptian whose last wish was to get it to his son in Cairo; a mission I am certain my brother had no intention of completing. There was no heroic, agonizing crawl across desert sands with the vital communiqué for the relief force. It was three days' journey away, and the Mahdi's horde was already at Khartoum's gates.' He tossed back the brandy, then stared into the empty glass, seeing again that group of haggard, bearded men who had suffered in Omdurman's prison for thirteen years. 'We have each January given a toast to a coward and a libertine.'

Charlotte began to cry and John put his arm around her, saying, 'There, there, lass. Tears are better shed than stored.'

Vere felt totally drained as he continued to stare into the past and recall his long, long ride beside the Nile, while Kitchener and his officers conducted a memorial service for those who had been massacred at Khartoum.

Kitty arrived beside him to take his hands. 'Your rosy glass has turned dark, Vere.'

He looked at her through aching, blurred eyes. 'I shall have to live with the knowledge that I killed a proud, courageous, old man whose only weakness was an inability to allow others the right to follow his

419

example and be masters of themselves.' He gripped her hands tightly. 'You approved of my silence on the subject when I told you about Vorne. Was I right to break it tonight?'

'Of course, my dear,' she agreed softly. 'You have withstood so many contemptuous personal comparisons with someone you know to be worthless, and would have continued to do so, I know. Only because it was Val being vilified in the "hero's" name did you speak out. You had no choice but to defend one brother against another.'

He studied the face that was dearer to him than any other in the world and knew the glass would one day become rosy again. 'I have to go back to South Africa to find him . . . or a headstone bearing his name somewhere on the veld.'

Dunstan St Mary seemed immune to change. Now the war in South Africa was over, and young men who had volunteered to go out there and fight had returned, the farming community resumed its old ways in this year of 1903. The motorcar was growing in popularity in towns, despite mass protests from cab drivers concerning horses frightened by the noise and speed of the machines. They were rarer in villages and one had not yet been seen in Dunstan. Airships were being developed by rival manufacturers in the race to build the fastest, most manoeuvrable, flying balloon. There had been a brief sighting of one over Wiltshire, and Simon had been so excited by it he studied everything he could find concerning the massive, silent, gas-filled skins. He was now at Chartfield after Vere coaxed Dr Keening to take his stepson, even though he was not an Ashleigh. The school still displayed Vorne's name on the roll of honour, together with an account of his heroism which had earned him a posthumous D.S.O. The truth was jealously guarded by a family which had discontinued the annual Khartoum Dinner after Sir Gilliard's death.

The Edwardian era had brought changes in social attitudes and fashion. Victorian values vanished beneath a desire for gaiety and pleasure. Britain's army, apart from small uprisings in various dominions, was not engaged in a major war. King Edward enjoyed reviews and parades, so soldiers on garrison duty at home were much in evidence amid people who wanted their faith in scarlet-coated warriors restored. These military spectacles took place far from the area immediately surrounding Knightshill, and everything continued as before.

Charlotte welcomed the unchanging scene. The villages she had for years visited for shopping knew her as well as she knew them. It was very comforting. Life at Knightshill had settled again into its peaceful pattern, although sadness still touched it. Sir Gilliard's presence often manifested itself in long corridors temporarily deserted, or in rooms entered suddenly on quiet days; his voice echoed through the house when the wind rattled windows and countryside debris was blown against the panes to sound like rain. It was still impossible to be in the main dining-room without feeling that he was looking down in accusation from the new portrait hanging there, painted from a photograph by a friend of Vere's. Sir Gilliard and Knightshill had been inseparable for the whole of Charlotte's life.

Vere had been unable to discover what had happened to Val during the four months he had travelled from region to region, twice being shot at by jumpy soldiers uncertain who he was. All the family knew was that Martin Havelock had ridden out with two horses, and little else, shortly after the ritual rejection parade. Three days after Sir Gilliard's funeral Vere had received a large parcel from South Africa. It contained Val's sword, and notification of the amount received from the auction of his other military equipment which had been donated to

421

the fund for regimental widows and orphans. Slipped in with the sword was a curious letter from the daughter of Max Beecham, which clearly indicated that she had known Val's real identity. Why else would she send Martin Havelock's sword to Knightshill? The letter had been brief, merely stating that Mr Ashleigh should not believe ill of his brother who had been the victim of cruel injustice. *He is a splendid, courageous person*, she wrote at the end of it, and expressed her fervent hope that the owner of the sword would one day wear it with pride.

Vere had attempted to see the girl, but the 57th had been shipped back to England just before he landed in South Africa. He thought it advisable to let the matter stay as it was. Aside from that cloud of uncertainty over Val's fate, it was a contented family group living at Knightshill. Although he had surrendered the commission from a maharajah to paint the man's private regiment, Vere had made a brief visit to Texas to view the ranch. It had impressed him so much they were all planning a visit early next year. The twins were almost three years old and healthily robust despite their dainty build. Charlotte's son, Richard, was taking his first steps confirming his father's firm belief that the child was the most wonderful ever born. John doted to a fault on him and Charlotte hoped the arrival of her second baby next month would not cause ructions in the nursery, which was a lively place once more.

Kate, almost thirteen, missed Simon now he was at school. She continued having lessons from the tutor, but Vere added to her knowledge by taking her when he and Kitty visited London for art exhibitions or theatrical shows. Although she clearly enjoyed the outings, she was glad to return to Knightshill and the children.

Charlotte now glanced at the girl as they walked together through Dunstan St Mary towards the church. Kate's face was still a serious one, but the primness of earlier childhood had gone. She had grown quieter since

Sir Gilliard died, and was often seen gazing into space as if in another world, yet she seemed curiously neutral about her mother and brother. The Nicolardis were still in South America and Kate now had two stepbrothers, but she had no desire to join them and Margaret did not push her to do so. Charlotte supposed her sister would come home eventually.

As she walked slowly through the village returning the greetings of people who had accepted the marriage of an Ashleigh to a bailiff, the baby inside her moved so violently she gasped. From the evidence of its activity it seemed likely to be another boy. Poor Vere! She and Margaret were producing male children with ease, yet he could never have a son to succeed to all he held dear. With Val gone she supposed he must endeavour to appoint Margaret's son, Tim, as his legal heir. Not that the boy would welcome it. At fourteen he was apparently still steadfastly set upon an army career. Grandfather had been quite wrong about *his* ideal heir, and Vere had stepped into the rôle quite magnificently.

Charlotte and Kate reached the church and went through the gate. Only four male Ashleighs were buried here. The rest had graves elsewhere in the world on long forgotten battlefields. There were a number of wives and children, however, so the family had a large corner of the churchyard devoted to it. Rounding the eastern side of the church Charlotte was startled to find someone already beside Sir Gilliard's grave. The man was dressed in rough clothes and was crouching by the flowers Charlotte had come to replace. She approached warily, uncertain what he was doing, and clutched Kate's hand tightly. Their feet made no sound on the grass, so it was not until they reached the foot of the grave that he grew aware of their presence. When he turned to look up at her, Charlotte was shocked to see tears on his cheeks.

'What are you doing here?' she asked sharply.

He stood up, staring at her in most unnerving fashion.

He could have been a foreigner, his skin was so dark a brown, and yet his hair was milk-fair and the eyes burned vividly blue in a face that was curiously familiar despite its haunted expression. For a moment or two she was inclined to run, for he was a big, strong man, then her heart began to race and she took a step forward.

Kate was quicker than she. '*Val!*' she shrieked, and threw herself at him with unrestrained joy.

There were also tears on Charlotte's cheeks as she stretched out her hands in loving welcome. Another Ashleigh had come home to Knightshill.